The Other Euclid

Mick Scott

For Grace

Author's Note
(Do not skip – important stuff!)

The atmospheric happenings in the Prologue and the storyline concerning Edward Talbot/Kelley are based on real events, documented in Dee's diary and reported elsewhere. It's unclear exactly when Dee and Kelley's first meeting took place; it was either 7th or 8th March 1582. For the purposes of this novel I have Kelley turning up the day after the skies turned to blood. Kelley's odd comings and goings while residing at Mortlake have never been explained.

Nicholas Saunder was also a real person. His portrayal in the book is entirely fictional, apart from his supposed involvement with the looting of Dee's library and other possessions. There is a wealth of information about Dee and Kelley online. The following websites are a good place to start:

www.gutenberg.org/files/19553/19553-h/19553-h.htm
www.esotericarchives.com/dee
www.rcplondon.ac.uk/news/lost-library-john-dee
www.britishmuseum.org/collection/term/BIOG24819
www.elizabethan-era.org.uk/john-dee.htm

A brief description and a selection of pop-up images from Henry Billingsley's *The Elements of Geometrie*, published in 1570 with a foreword by Dr. Dee can be found at:
www.amusingplanet.com/2020/06/a-16th-century-math-book-with-pop-up.html

My main source for the section related by Euclid was *"The Queen's Conjuror, the Life and Magic of Dr Dee"*, by Benjamin Woolley (*Harper Collins 2001*).

According to John Aubrey's biography of Doctor John Dee in *"Brief Lives"* (published in 1813, though written over a century earlier), the good doctor had 'a very cleare rosie complexion… a long beard as white as milke. A very handsome man… he was tall and slender. He wore a gowne like an artist's gowne, with hanging sleeves, and a slitt. A mighty good man he was.' That's the complete entry. You can't fault Aubrey for knowing the meaning of the word brief.

Prologue: 1582

The eighth day of March started exactly the same as the previous five; cold, wet and miserable, but by late afternoon heavy rain had given way to fine drizzle. Banks of broken clouds meandered sullenly across from the east towards a hint of redness on the horizon, which finally seemed to promise that tomorrow would be better. A flimsy crescent moon shone through occasionally but by evenfall the clouds increased once more and darkness fell with no particular drama over the house of Doctor John Dee, astronomer, mathematician and adviser to the queen, Elizabeth. At least the rain had finally stopped.

At the time of his birth, Dee's father was employed at the court of Henry the Eighth, making clothing for the royal household as well as buying and supplying fabrics for the King. The young Dee was educated at a school in Chelmsford, then entered St. John's College, Cambridge in November 1542, where he studied Greek, Latin, philosophy, geometry, arithmetic and astronomy.

His house, in the small town of Mortlake, Surrey, was an old rambling mish-mash that had seen better days. His mother had purchased it soon after his father's death and he had gone there to live with her when his income from the Queen, who was notoriously tight with her money, had become strained. Thirty years had passed since then and his financial situation had barely changed. He lacked the status and social graces to persuade patrons to fund him, so he was stuck in Mortlake, like it or not.

A few years before his mother had died in 1580 she had granted her son ownership of the house. Since then he had extended it in various directions, purchasing small adjoining tenements which he turned into libraries, laboratories, an observatory and rooms for a busy hive of workers and servants. The house backed onto the Thames, standing to the north-west of the ancient church of St Mary the Virgin and separated from the High Street by a large herb and vegetable garden. Nearby, Mortlake Manor and Cromwell House were the only other buildings of note.

The sight of grand personages arriving and leaving his house was commonplace and he had been visited on a number of occasions by the Queen, when she had been travelling between Whitehall and Richmond, each occasion costing him money he could ill afford. The locals kept their distance. There was a feeling amongst them that his many pursuits were not natural. It was well known that he was a magician, a necromancer and worse, a caster of horoscopes.

Just after nine o'clock that evening Dee was in his study, writing in his diary, when he was disturbed by shouts from the garden. As he rose from his desk to investigate, his wife, Jane, burst in.

"John, the sky! It's on fire!"

He hurried outside and watched in awe as an orange-red glow, like a new sun above the clouds, roiled and boiled over the town. Slowly, it began to stretch out in all directions, illuminating the surrounding land so much that he could clearly see and recognize two people by the door of St Mary's about thirty yards away, staring up at the spectacle.

Suddenly, dozens of flashes streaked across the sky in all directions, turning the clouds the colour of blood. He imagined two huge armies of gods throwing giant thunderbolts at each other high in the heavens, engaged in a war of epic proportions. Eerily, the firestorm was totally silent except for one large boom, which was all the more chilling to the watchers on the ground, many of whom had fallen to their knees muttering prayers and crossing themselves continuously.

Some of Dee's servants were in tears and shouting and wailing could be heard from other parts of the town. One of his assistants ran in great fright across the road to St. Mary's, where he fell to praying at the altar, along with another dozen souls. The end of the world was nigh, the apocalypse was upon them and they hastened to assure God that they were worthy.

The demonic display lasted just over a quarter of an hour before the skies darkened once more. An awestruck Dee wondered what the spectacle foretold and went back into his study to cast a chart, leaving his wife to calm the distraught servants. The Queen would certainly be demanding an explanation and it wouldn't be in his interests to have nothing prepared. He knew he could expect largesse if he offered a good explanation to Her Majesty.

Later, in his diary, he wrote, *'At about the ninth hour of the night the sky was burning with fire, in different parts of the sky it was seen to be blood red, especially in the north and the west, all bloody and frequently above our heads, over our house and finally then towards the south.'*

Although by far the most frightening event he had ever witnessed, this wasn't Dee's first direct experience of unexplained phenomena. The late 16th century had more than its fair share of heavenly spectacles. Ten years before, on 11th November 1572, a new star, a nova, appeared in the constellation of Cassiopeia, throwing the supposedly fixed state of the universe into confusion. Scientists of the day had just two records of similar events, both taking place in what is now Israel. The first, in 125BC, was supposedly followed by 'great commotions' among the Jews, although opinions differed as to the specifics and nothing is mentioned in the Bible. The second, more auspicious, was the appearance of the Star of Bethlehem. Therefore, it was obvious to anyone who took an interest in the matter, the coming of a new star would herald momentous changes for mankind, the kind of changes that might see kings or queens toppled from their thrones and the natural world order turned upside down. The Danish astronomer Tycho Brahe bravely forecast the end of the Roman Catholic Church's supremacy. Czech astrologer Cyprian Leowitz declared, 'new worlds will follow.' Neither event happened.

During Elizabeth's reign the heavens represented certainty in a world of turmoil. The universe was believed to have remained constant since the Babylonians first noted the fixed positions of stars in the sky and, according to the ancients, unchanged since God created it on the First Day. The accepted wisdom stated that the earth sat at the centre of all things, the sun, the moon and the planets revolved around it, transfixed forever to the peripheries of a series of concentric spheres. Beyond the outermost sphere of fixed stars was heaven itself. Only in the space between the earth and the moon was it thought there could there be change, a space which allowed the presence of phenomena such as comets and meteors. According to the Church, only madmen and heretics believed differently. A change anywhere else in the heavens was a genuine act of God.

The age of the universe was generally held to be about six thousand years and the furthest stars were between twelve and eighteen million miles away, according to the calculations of Ptolemy, a mathematician, geographer, astronomer and astrologer (the last two disciplines were fairly interchangeable) who lived in Alexandria between 100 and 160AD. The problem now was that this new star was in the wrong place, too far away to be inhabiting the immediate sphere, which was where it belonged. A further significant problem was its level of brightness, which was not constant. Stars were supposed to be stuck in space, illuminated by heaven's light. This star had appeared from nowhere, brighter than anything else in the night sky apart from the moon, but it was slowly getting dimmer. It remained visible to the unaided eye until March 1574.

For adherents of classical cosmology this caused great consternation, but for others, such as Dee, it meant new theories could finally be considered. Copernicus had already suggested his heliocentric system some thirty years earlier, but fear of being accused of heresy, as would happen to Galileo over forty years later, had always suppressed any desire on the part of scholars to espouse this view.

Although Dee subscribed to the Copernican theory he had to be guarded in his views as he had already been suspected of sorcery during Queen Mary's time and had even been imprisoned for a short time, accused of 'calculating', or using mathematics and having cast the horoscopes of Queen Mary and her sister Elizabeth. His solution to the problem was revolutionary. He posited that because light from the star was growing fainter, it must be moving away from the earth. If this was true it meant that it must be moving beyond the limits of the outermost celestial sphere and therefore there must be space for it to move into, a space which had previously been the preserve of heaven. It further implied that all the stars and planets that already existed were not fixed either. In which case the universe was much bigger than anyone had so far imagined.

After the nova of 1572 the omens continued. In 1577 a new comet appeared which terrified all who saw it. The court of Elizabeth was in panic and the Queen immediately consulted Dee upon its meaning. Dee's interpretation was that it heralded a great future for the queen and the fulfilment of her destiny. For once, he was paid handsomely for this information.

In April 1580 the Dover Straits earthquake, with a magnitude of 5.5 and lasting two minutes, struck the South-East and parts of Northern France. In London, half a dozen large chimney stacks and a pinnacle on Westminster Abbey came down. In October of 1580 another comet appeared, this one lasting a month. Then, over Mortlake, the battle of the heavens began.

PART 1

The Present. Thursday 21st June. 8:30am.

1.

Cornelius Pye woke with a start to find himself sitting on a concrete floor. He was propped against a wall, his legs doubled beneath him at awkward angles and his left hand tie-wrapped to a metal ring fastened into the wall at about waist height. His eyes watered with pain so, almost immediately, he closed them again, unable in that short time to make sense of his surroundings. His head felt like it had been inflated to bursting point and placed in a tumble-dryer, where it was rotating uncomfortably. Where he wasn't numb the rest of his body ached screamingly, while his mouth felt dry and gritty, as though it had been filled with sand and washed out with sea water.

He tried opening his eyes again, then thought better of it. His eyelids seemed to have become glued together with tears and he worried that forcing them to open again might tear out his eyelashes. Finally, a little at a time, after rubbing them gently with his free hand, he managed to open them wide enough to see where he was. He closed them again, still not being able to comprehend where he was. He gave it a few more moments and tried for a third time.

He couldn't see very much. He was in a small unfurnished room. What little light there was came from a murky, barred window set high in the opposite wall, the sun casting fuzzy shadows against it. To his left a flight of stone steps led up into darkness. The walls were bare red brick, broken occasionally by small alcoves. There was a light fitting in the ceiling but no bulb. He concluded he was in a cellar, cleanish at least and empty but for half a dozen old dining chairs stacked in pairs in one corner, and a bucket by his side. Nothing to indicate where he might be or, more importantly, why.

He closed his eyes and drifted off again, telling himself he must be having a particularly bad dream and if he left it for a few minutes everything would resolve itself into normality. Unfortunately, when he opened his eyes again nothing had changed except that the spinning sensation was starting to calm down.

He tried to move one of his legs but the pain made him stop. He waited awhile for it to ease then tried again, succeeding at last in getting first one, then both legs straight out in front of him then had to wait while the blood rushed painfully back into them. When the numbness eventually subsided he twisted his torso and tried to move his hands, discovering finally that one of them was tied to a metal ring.

Gradually, feeling returned to most parts of his body and he stretched himself. His head felt as though it had come free of its moorings when he turned to his wrist to check the time. His watch was missing. Then he noticed he was in his dressing gown and slippers. Further inspection revealed he was also wearing his pyjamas. An urgent indication from his bladder gave a clue as to the presence of the bucket and with a supreme effort, ignoring the stabs of muscular pain all over his body, he managed to twist himself into a half crouch and after an awkward minute of fumbling was finally able to relieve himself.

There was definitely no party; he thought to himself, I didn't have any alcohol last night. It had just been an ordinary evening, no different to many others. He vaguely remembered getting ready for bed, sometime around eleven. He was dressed as he was now and had been brushing his teeth when the doorbell rang. He had answered it, half expecting it to be his girlfriend, Angela Miller, who would sometimes turn up unannounced at odd times of the day. He suspected she was trying to keep him on his toes. In some respects, she could be a little demanding. That was as much as he could remember. Except, no, hang on. He had the odd feeling something similar seemed to have happened once before. He left that thought in limbo and tried once again to assess his situation.

The question was, why was he here and why was he wearing his dressing gown? No, hang on again, that was two questions. Cornelius tried to get a grip on his thinking processes. Slowly, other questions formed themselves and a number of recent events gradually became a little clearer.

While he was pondering these the door at the top of the stairs opened and a tall, balding man descended. He was dressed in a suit and tie and wore frameless glasses. He gave Cornelius a look of deep disdain. He was bearing what appeared to be a bacon sandwich on a paper plate and a cup of tea in an old, chipped mug. Cornelius suddenly realised how hungry he was and how desperate for a drink.

14

"What am I doing here?" he tried to say, but the words came out thickly, as though he were trying to talk through cotton wool.

"I've brought you some breakfast."

"Thank you, but that's not what I asked." he said after he'd taken a drink from the mug. The sip of tea suddenly made talking easier. He attacked the sandwich.

"Better eat up. You've got a long day ahead of you." The man turned and went back up the stairs.

"Hang on! Does your mother know what you do for a living?" he shouted, realising as soon as he'd spoken that it wasn't much of an insult. "You could at least let me wash my hands." A waste of breath as the man had gone.

With the sandwich and the tea his mind cleared a little and his head seemed to deflate to an approximation of its normal size. He felt certain that the odd feeling he'd had about something happening twice was true. He paused and tried to gather his thoughts. Twice? Yes, it was. Twice he'd answered the door late at night and twice he'd woken up somewhere unexpected.

The first time he'd woken up sitting against the wall in the hallway outside his flat, dressed only in his pyjamas, feeling as though he'd drunk the best part of a bottle of scotch. At least he'd still been home so that wasn't so bad, apart from the splitting headache, aches and pains and the odd look from his neighbour, who'd chosen that moment to leave the flat next door on his way to work. "Bit of a night out, was it?" he'd said. Cornelius could do no more than grunt in reply as he lifted himself painfully and re-entered his flat, to find he had been burgled.

The second time was here and now in this cellar.

Cornelius Pye, twenty-seven years old with an MSc in quantum mechanics from University College London, was tall, spare and slightly awkward, as though his body was never quite able to fit within itself. His life appeared to have veered away from the norm after his Uncle Sedgewick's funeral the previous Friday.

A week before that, he'd been summoned by his Aunt Lucinda to visit his uncle at the hospital in Barnes. He was, as she quaintly put it, on his last legs. His uncle told him that after his death, Cornelius would receive something from him which he described, portentously, as 'a great gift'. He'd returned home after the funeral carrying a large, heavy antique book, a letter and a box containing a journal and assorted papers. Three nights ago he had answered a knock at the door of his flat. Immediately after opening it he remembered nothing, waking the next morning to find the book had been stolen.

Then last night another knock and he'd made the same mistake again, waking this time to find himself here. Nothing made sense. They, whoever they were, already had the book. What more could they want? Try as he might, he could think of no reason why he should now be sitting on the cold floor of a cellar, tied to a radiator.

For the first eleven years of his life he'd lived with his parents, close to the university in Hull, where his father was a science lecturer and his mother was a research chemist. One morning, just before the summer holidays, he'd been called out of class and taken to the headmistress' office where he'd found a policewoman and his rather scary Aunt Lucinda, waiting to tell him his parents had been in an accident and he must be brave.

He discovered then, that in addition to his aunt, his relatives on his father's side were an uncle, Sedgewick, who lived in London, and another aunt, Violet, who lived somewhere near Watford. He had never met them. His mother had been an only child and her parents lived in New Zealand. When he was seven they had visited there once as a family, but he didn't remember much about them. Relations between his mother and his grandparents had been strained as they weren't happy she had run off to England.

As leaving home to live with relatives he barely knew on the other side of the world would have been a bit of a wrench for a traumatised eleven year old, it was decided the best thing would be if he went to live with his aunt, a formidable looking woman in her late forties who had a stern eye and a big voice. Cornelius didn't get a say in the matter, even though his aunt generally made him very nervous. His childhood home was sold off and the proceeds joined the rest of his parents' estate in a trust fund for when he came of age.

So Cornelius went to live in a small village a few miles to the west of Hull, not too far from where he used to live. He stayed at the same school, although he now had to catch a bus to get there instead of the short walk he'd once had.

At first he'd been quite scared of his aunt. Whenever he'd visited her with his parents she would tower over him, lift him up to give him a sloppy kiss, put him back down, ruffle his hair, then ignore him for the rest of the visit. She had always made him feel as though he were about to do or say something wrong, so he normally sat as quiet as he could without moving until it was time to leave. He generally took a book along with him, as a sort of protection.

In his aunt's defence, she didn't have children of her own. Her husband had died almost twenty years earlier and she hadn't remarried, much preferring her own company and full run of the comfortable house she'd moved into when she'd married, working as a librarian at the university and belonging to a raft of clubs, societies and groups, from within whose circles she'd been able to conduct a series of discreet romances over the years.

She had no experience of young children so didn't quite know what to make of Cornelius. She had shocked herself by agreeing to look after him, even though she knew it was the right thing to do. When he first came to her, she'd tried treating him like a young adult, expecting him to know how to respond, but he had stayed acquiescent and quiet, trying to draw as little attention to himself as possible. Then everything changed one night about a week later. He had gone to bed as usual after saying good night as politely as he could. About an hour later his aunt had gone upstairs to get a book from her bedroom when she heard him sobbing. After a little gentle questioning he said he missed his parents and it hurt so much and he didn't know what to do. She'd broken down herself at that point and the subsequent hugs and kisses changed the relationship to something much softer.

He missed his parents almost daily, even now, but his aunt had become his rock in the fifteen years since the event. She had protected him when he'd needed protecting and pushed him when it was necessary. To everyone's surprise except hers he'd grown up to be a capable and well-grounded individual.

However, Cornelius was not outgoing. Even before the accident physical activities held little of interest for him, preferring instead to read books about maths and physics and devoting much of his time to logic problems. Afterwards, he withdrew further into his books, which didn't endear him to his classmates and meant his social circle was not particularly well developed. His only real friend at this time was his classmate Daniel Vaughan, something of a chess prodigy. They called themselves The Two Loners and thought themselves clever, delighting in the oxymoron. They still kept in touch now and again through social media but they hadn't seen each other for over a year.

After school Cornelius attended university in London and five years later, after completing his Masters, he accepted a post with Lightsource, a highly prestigious research company based in Highgate, pursuing the field of battery technology using quantum entanglement. His work was currently centred on the theory that a special array of graphene batteries could provide the necessary power to enable quantum computers to function longer than the few brief seconds which were currently possible. The pay was good, but not great, but it was work he enjoyed doing. He lived alone in a small flat a few minutes walk from Highbury & Islington tube station, which he had been able to purchase with help from his trust fund.

His life revolved mainly around his work, which led him to be a little vague or absent-minded. Angela thought he was slightly eccentric, a view shared by many of her friends. When they'd first met, she'd thought this trait was endearing. Now she wasn't so sure. Exasperation had succeeded endearment. The phrase 'on the spectrum", used these days to describe anyone a little bit different, had been applied to him more than once, but it was without substance, an example of lazy pigeonholing.

He'd met Angela a couple of months earlier at a party thrown by his work colleague, Ruth Seaton. At work, Ruth seemed to be some kind of small whirlwind, forever bustling about in pursuit of answers. She had the dark hair and skin tones which hinted at a Mediterranean background, although she had been born and raised in Brighton. Despite the busyness she was generally quiet, not given to idle chatter, for which he was grateful. She was very intelligent and had the uncanny knack of being able to come at a problem from unexpected angles, something Cornelius admired very much. She had been at university with Angela and while not close friends, they would meet up occasionally at social events and she had no qualms about inviting her to the party. A mistake, as it turned out.

Cornelius had been working with Ruth for just over three months and she'd tried to get him to come out after work a number of times.

Previously, he'd always managed to wriggle out of it, spluttering that he wasn't very good in social situations.

"But it's my twenty-fourth birthday, Cornelius, and I need to celebrate it with all my friends. And you are my friend, aren't you? Please say you'll come?"

There was such a look of pain on her face that in the end he'd changed his mind and given in. He was secretly pleased to be considered one of her friends and if he hadn't been so shy he might have asked her out.

He'd been standing at the party alone, looking lost, when Angela began talking to him. One thing led to another and before he knew it they were back at her place, where, for Cornelius, things rapidly got out of hand. He'd had girlfriends before but he'd never had sex like that. He'd returned home late the next day, tired and with a big smile on his face.

Back at work on the Monday Ruth had been distant. He was sure he hadn't annoyed her, having barely spoken to her at the party, so he was at a loss as to what could be wrong. He had no idea that Ruth had fancied him for ages. Having finally got him to agree to come to her party, her plan had been to get him alone, ply him with a few drinks, back him into a corner and take it from there. As with most well laid plans this had gone awry almost immediately. Soon after Cornelius had arrived she had been called away to supervise a small explosion in the kitchen, the result of someone trying to mix a Bloody Mary in the blender without ensuring the lid was properly secured. When she'd returned from clearing up a mess that looked like a scene from a zombie film, she'd found Angela deep in conversation with Cornelius, who was staring at her intently, oblivious to everything else.

She'd realised then that compared to Angela, her charms were much less obvious and she left them to it, not realising that Cornelius would have given half his kingdom to be extricated and that the look on his face was actually one of panic. However, one thing led to another and by the time the party had ended Cornelius was the latest of Angela's little projects. Ruth knew Angela was not the right person for Cornelius but was resigned to let nature take its inevitable course. She knew from past experience that, for Angela, the novelty would soon wear off.

Angela was almost the polar opposite to Ruth, blond and willowy, with Botticelli features. She always knew what she wanted and generally managed to get it. She worked as a hedge fund manager in the City and was very keen for Cornelius to make something of himself, rather than waste his time doing research.

It annoyed Angela to know she earned at least three times more than Cornelius, but in that one thing he was immovable. He loved his job and had no intention of leaving, no matter what financial or other attractions were on offer. It was a bone of contention between the two of them. Her problem was that she did quite like him but there were areas of his life that needed improvement. She was starting to wonder if it was worth the effort.

One Friday afternoon a few weeks ago, a phone call from his aunt informed Cornelius that his Uncle Sedgewick would like to see him as soon as possible. She had recently come down to London to help his uncle after he had fallen out with the latest in a long line of housekeepers and carers. He'd always been a bit irascible and she was the only person with whom he felt comfortable. Cornelius immediately felt guilty as he knew his uncle hadn't been well for a while. Although he knew he should have visited more often it had been about six months since he'd last done so. He was uncomfortable with illness, especially in someone he knew and liked. On the call his aunt hadn't pulled her punches.

"I'm at the hospital in Barnes. You need to get yourself over here as soon as you can. He might not last the weekend."

"Bloody hell, Aunt Lu! I knew he wasn't well but I didn't realise he was that bad. I've been meaning to come over, honestly."

"Well, you can come over now, quick as you like. They've got him settled and comfortable. He's conscious at the moment but the doctors don't think he's going to last. He keeps asking after you. He's got something he has to tell you before he goes. When can you get here?"

"I'm on my way now. I'll be there as soon as I can."

He explained to his boss, Mr Singh, that he had a family emergency, then dashed outside and ran to Highgate tube station. For a Friday afternoon, he made good time and forty-five minutes later, breathless, he was by his uncle's bed in the hospital, where he found his aunt stoking his uncle's hand.

"How is he?" gasped Cornelius, taking in the breathing apparatus, the life support machines and the various tubes snaking ominously around the bed.

"He's very weak, but he's calm. Come and sit down, let him know you're here."

Cornelius sat and took his uncle's hand.

"Uncle Sedgewick? It's me, Cornelius. How are you doing?"

His uncle's eyes opened at the sound of his voice. "Ah, you're here. Cornelius. Thank you for coming." His uncle could only speak in short, breathy sentences.

"You're going to get better, aren't you? I'm sure they're going to have you up and about again soon. I'm sorry for not visiting you more often. When we get you back home you won't be able to keep me away, you'll see."

"Very kind of you. Not going back home. Not now. But listen. Important. Something to give you. Sort of heirloom."

He paused, and Cornelius thought he'd drifted off. Then, with a sudden intake of breath he continued, "Passed down. Through the family. For hundreds of years. Now it's your turn."

"No, Uncle, you need to get better. Then you can give it to me yourself."

"Too late, Cornelius, too late. Known for a while I wouldn't last much longer. Managed to write it all down. Before it was too late. Your aunt will explain. There's a letter. Things you need to know. It's a book, a very old book. Don't let anyone know. It's priceless if you use it right. Make sure you use it right, Cornelius. Make sure..."

His uncle closed his eyes. For a second Cornelius thought he was gone, but the machine by his bed continued bleeping normally and he saw the gentle rise and fall of his uncle's chest as he breathed, far too shallowly to sustain life, he thought, glumly. He looked round at his aunt.

"What does he mean, a book? What sort of a book?"

"I'll tell you, later."

They sat with him for another hour before he quietly passed away. The book wasn't mentioned again and Cornelius didn't give it another thought.

Afterwards, he told Angela about his uncle's demise and when she heard he had lived in a large, semi-detached Edwardian house, backing onto Barnes Common in south west London, she convinced herself that Cornelius must be in line to inherit.

"Just think what a house that size must be worth," she'd said, "a couple of million, at least. Sell it off and with the money you could start your own business."

Cornelius thought that if he did inherit the house, selling it wasn't an option. He didn't deserve it, although he couldn't tell Angela that. He tried to explain he was never particularly close to his uncle and apart from meeting him only a couple of times since arriving in London a few years previously he'd rarely seen him since he was at school. He told her there was no reason to suppose he would inherit anything at all.

"It'll all probably go to some charity or other," he said. Then as an afterthought, he added, "He liked cats."

2.

Cornelius remembered staying at his uncle's house in London when he was twelve. He'd been taken there by his aunt for a couple of weeks during the summer holidays. After watching him climb into his shell since the death of his parents she thought he needed to see more of the outside world. His days at his uncle's were filled with visits to museums, art galleries and historic buildings, one coming after the other at such a pace they all appeared to roll into one entity, which he would for many years after remember as The Visit.

It seemed to Cornelius that Uncle Sedgewick was extremely old even then, although he would have been only forty-five. He was kind to Cornelius but also a bit scary, like his aunt had been at first. He supposed it must be something that ran in his father's side of the family. In describing his uncle to friends Cornelius usually compared him to a very slim version of Patrick Moore, the astronomer who used to host 'The Sky At Night' on the BBC. His uncle had the same piercing gaze, which seemed to come from two different directions at once, but much wilder hair. He usually wore an ancient and baggy tweed suit which drooped loosely from his skeletal frame, while his ever-present MCC tie was set at a jaunty angle around his scrawny neck. Unidentified marks all over the front of his suit showed that eating was something he did while he concentrated on something else.

When he arrived his uncle had been keen to engage with him, promising him all sorts of adventures and talking about rather dangerous experiments they could do together, a thrill for any boy and he was looking forward to them. However, after a few days his uncle seemed to lose interest in him and disappeared for hours at a time into his study, to do what he gloriously referred to as 'research', although into what was never explained.

Uncle Sedgewick didn't seem to do anything in particular for a living. While Cornelius was there he never left the house. His aunt said he'd once worked for the government as some sort of scientific advisor, hinting there was something 'hush-hush' about it, discouraging further questions. Cornelius liked to think of him as a mad inventor, or something along the lines of "Q" in the James Bond films.

The house itself could only be described as lived-in. Nothing had been changed for many years. The carpets were thin, the furniture was worn-out and the walls were covered with patterned wallpaper dating back to the early fifties. There was no television so the only entertainment in the house came by way of an old radiogram which promised the choice of exotic and long dead radio stations such as Hilversum, Athlone, Österlund and Vienna. There were a few old jazz albums inside the radiogram, but the artists' names meant nothing to Cornelius. The only concession to modernity was a bright red telephone in the hallway. The rest of the house was filled with old books and packing cases full of scientific equipment. He was under strict instructions not to touch anything on the various tables and benches throughout the house in case he changed the outcome of whatever experiment his uncle was doing at the time, although Cornelius couldn't for the life of him work out what was supposed to be going on. All the test-tubes, beakers and chemical jars were empty and covered in layers of dust.

He was also never allowed into his uncle's study at the top of the stairs on the first floor, which, in addition to more books and packing crates, contained a large desk, piled high with papers and weighted down by a large, old book. A huge black cat, Jehosophat, often snoozed on the south facing windowsill in the study, taking in the sun.

One particularly hot day, when Cornelius was trying to find somewhere cool to while away an hour or so before afternoon tea he ended up sitting on the ottoman on the landing just outside the study. The door was slightly ajar and from the other side he heard voices. As there was no telephone in the room and his uncle didn't possess a mobile phone his curiosity was piqued. He poked his head round the door to see who was there and found only his uncle sitting at the desk with the large book in his arms, who looked up crossly and told him to go away and close the door, which he did.

He sat back down for a moment on the ottoman before heaving a bored sigh, then decided to go see what his aunt was baking in the kitchen. He stood and turned to go down the stairs, only to find his uncle coming up them at breakneck speed with the book in his arms, laughing dementedly, pausing only to shout out, "It works, it works!", then rushing into his study and closing the door behind him. When he tried to explain to his aunt what had just happened she told him not to be so silly, people couldn't just jump from one place to another, it was against all the rules.

In the years afterwards Cornelius told himself that as it was so hot and as he was feeling so drowsy he must have nodded off for a few moments, during which time his uncle must have exited the study, gone down the stairs for something and then returned. What it was that worked or why he was rushing up the stairs, when his normal speed was never more than sedate, he had never been able to explain. His uncle always changed the subject when he brought it up.

His visits to his uncle thereafter were few and far between, although he had been to see him a couple of times when he first moved down to London. They didn't have very much in common. His uncle used to question him about his work but he didn't seem to take much notice as he would ask the same questions on subsequent visits. On the last occasion he'd visited, nearly a year earlier, his uncle had become quite morbid; saying he hadn't much longer left on this earth and told him he would be leaving him something to remember him by, but didn't add any further details.

The funeral, held in Mortlake Crematorium, had been a drab affair, a sudden cold spell and lashing rain hadn't helped. His uncle had specified a humanist ceremony and a succession of rather grey people rose to speak a few kind words. His aunt, who had stayed on at his uncle's house, didn't know any of them but assumed they must have been fellow boffins from his time working for the government.

Surprisingly, there were two other family members there, Violet Duncan, his only other aunt, slightly older than Lucinda, with her son Francis, neither of whom he had met until then. According to his aunt, Violet had fallen out with Uncle Sedgewick over twenty years earlier and as far as she knew they had never spoken again until a couple of weeks previously, when she'd visited unannounced. Lucinda hadn't been in the room with them but she'd heard raised voices and then the slamming of the front door as Violet left. Uncle Sedgewick refused to say what had been discussed and she never discovered what the argument had been about. She told Cornelius that Violet was the bad sheep of the family, who had broken their father's heart over something his aunt wouldn't discuss. Apart from the brief moments when she'd let Aunt Violet into his uncle's house this was their first face to face meeting in many years.

Francis was probably somewhere close to Cornelius' age but looked much older, as if he'd missed his teenage years altogether and gone straight from child to grown-up. If Cornelius had to guess he would have said he was probably an accountant. Apart from these two, the only other living relative they had, according to his aunt, was a Great-Aunt Camille, who ran off with an American beat poet in the 1950s, briefly became a nun and now lived in a nursing home in the north of England, regaling anyone who would listen with tales of Kerouac, Cassidy and Ginsberg and what naughty boys they were.

The only high point of the service was the final song, which was, curiously, given how unlike the uncle he knew, Cool for Cats, by Squeeze.

Immediately after the funeral Cornelius and Lucinda walked to a nearby pub where a buffet had been laid on for the mourners. He and his aunt sat at a table in the corner of the room, away from the boffins, who eventually drifted away back to their own world. His new-found relatives finally wandered over and joined them. Violet looked at him with undisguised loathing while her son sat staring into space, biting his nails. Judging from the looks that passed between the two aunts there was no love lost.

Cornelius had assumed there would be a will but Aunt Lucinda told them she had been appointed executor by his uncle and everything was now under probate, awaiting a valuation, after which Cornelius would inherit the house and its contents, while she herself would receive a pair of Sèvres Porcelain Urns with Courting Couples amid Landscapes, which his uncle knew she'd always admired. There was no money; it had all been used paying for carers over the last few years.

Aunt Violet was very annoyed about Cornelius getting the house, which she thought she should at least have had a share in, ignoring the fact that Lucinda had not benefited in any significant way. She was even more annoyed that her son had received nothing.

"You've got a damned cheek to expect anything at all, Violet," his aunt replied, "considering you haven't been near Sedgewick for years until just a couple of weeks ago. And then I bet you only came to see him because he was on his way out and you thought it was about time to sneak in and persuade him to leave you something."

A sharp intake of breath indicated his Aunt Violet had been mortally offended.

"I did not!"

"Anyway," continued Aunt Lucinda, "the house is close to collapse and probably not worth as much as you think. Cornelius will have to sell it as soon as he can to pay off the death duties."

"Well, can you blame me for staying away? The place was a mad house, with chemical stuff everywhere. It wasn't safe for man nor beast. I certainly wouldn't let Francis anywhere near the place. Any sane person would have kept away, but not you, Lucinda. Oh no, you were there, making sure you got your cut!"

"My cut!", shouted Aunt Lucinda, "a pair of sodding vases!"

"Ladies, please!", hissed Cornelius, aware heads were turning in their direction.

"And what's happened to that old book he kept ranting on about?" hissed Violet. "The one that was supposed to make all our fortunes?"

"What *are* you talking about?" countered Lucinda.

"You know very well what I'm talking about. The book that got him buying all that useless stuff that's cluttered up the house for years."

"I don't know anything about any book," said Lucinda, primly. The aunts exchanged hard looks. The bickering might have gone on all afternoon, had not Francis finally piped up to ask his mother when they were going home, as he was bored solid with 'this old stuff'. After a few further acrimonious exchanges Violet and her son departed, leaving Cornelius looking warily at the seething cauldron that was his aunt, seated across the table from him.

"Go and get me another drink, Cornelius, a large one. That woman!"

When he got back his aunt took a large gulp from her glass and fixed him with the eye she had used when he'd done something wrong as a child. This time however, the ire wasn't directed at him.

"That Violet makes me so mad," she whispered, "especially as I've just had to lie to her."

"What do you mean?"

"What I mean is all that stuff about the old book your uncle told you about at the hospital. Do you remember?"

"I do, now you mention it. I'd forgotten all about it, to be honest."

"Your uncle used to go on about it being some great repository of knowledge which would change our lives forever, but I never realised till now he'd ever breathed a word to Violet. I wonder if that was the cause of their falling out all those years ago. He told me about the book before but he swore me to secrecy. I wonder how many other people he told."

"So what is this book?" asked Cornelius.

"It's back at your uncle's house, along with some old papers and a letter. He wanted you to have it, but didn't want to leave it to you in his will as it's supposed to be a secret. When he finally admitted to himself he was getting ill and not likely to recover he started to worry it might go missing or be stolen by one of his carers, so a couple of weeks ago he asked me to look after it and pass it on to you when he died."

"But what's so special about it?"

"I have no idea. He never told me anything about it, apart from the fact it was supposed to be the answer to all our prayers, but for the life of me, I can't see how. He used to get a bee in his bonnet about all kinds of odd things so I didn't take a lot of notice. If you take me back to the house I'll hand it over. You're the brains of the family, Cornelius, perhaps you can work out what he meant."

"But how come I've got the house? Why would he want to leave it to me? I'm sure I don't deserve to have it."

"Well, who else is there? You're his brother's son. I think it's to make amends. You see, he should never have got the book at all, but when your father died the book was given to Sedgewick to look after. You should have received it from him when you turned eighteen, but he conveniently forgot."

"My god, this family!" exclaimed Cornelius.

Back at his uncle's house his aunt handed over an ancient book bound in a plain cover and measuring about thirteen inches by nine, along with a small cardboard box containing the fragile remains of a small and very old notebook and a number of papers covered with various formulae and equations. There was a sealed letter from his uncle, addressed to Cornelius, with instructions on the back that he should show its contents to no-one. He opened the book and discovered it to be an early English edition of Euclid's Elements of Geometry. He had a modern copy on his bookshelf. He started to leaf through the pages, amused by the tiny hand-written notes and drawings in its margins.

"I don't know very much about it," said his aunt. "Your uncle was always a bit secret squirrel about it. Maybe it'll all be explained in his letter. He thought it would make him rich. Ha! You can see how that turned out."

She grasped his hand. "Do me a favour, Cornelius, don't fritter away your time with it like he did. He was never the same after he got that book. I looked through it a couple of times when I knew he wouldn't catch me. There'd have been hell to pay if he had." She smiled at the thought. "I couldn't find anything special in it."

Closing the book, he promised his aunt he'd take care of it and assured her if there was a secret he was sure he'd find it. Then, as time was getting on, they ordered a takeaway. It was well after eight by the time he left. His aunt intended to return home the following day.

He arrived home quite late. He called Angela and told her about inheriting the house. She seemed quite pleased and for a change he felt as though he had done something right, through no fault of his own. He decided not to follow that train of thought to its logical conclusion, the day had already been quite emotional and he was too tired. Following his uncle's wishes he told her nothing of the book, so it, the letter and the cardboard box containing the notebook and papers sat on his bedside table, where they stayed while Cornelius showered before plonking himself in front of the TV with a large glass of wine. He decided his brain had coped with enough for one day so his uncle's inheritance could wait until the morning.

Outside it was still raining.

3.

The next morning, Saturday, Cornelius woke later than usual and had no time to inspect his inheritance. He had a hurried cup of coffee before rushing off to the gym for his usual couple of hours of misery and boredom. He'd joined the gym soon after meeting Angela, with every intention of working out daily, but now his visits were mostly confined to the weekend, with the occasional midweek swimming session when he could be bothered. The fitness regime was Angela's idea. She felt he should be looking after his body. She was keen on Tae-kwan-do and went to the gym most mornings before work and some evenings too. She spent weekends either horse-riding or playing tennis, two more things for which Cornelius couldn't summon any enthusiasm.

On his return from the gym, he was just starting to fix himself a bite to eat when his phone rang. It showed an unknown caller. Suspecting a spam call he answered guardedly.

"Hello?"

"Oh, hello," answered a reedy sort of voice, "is that Cornelius?"

"Yes?"

"It's Francis here. Francis Duncan. We met at Uncle Sedgewick's funeral yesterday."

"Oh, yes. Hello, Francis. Sorry, I didn't recognise your voice at first." He couldn't remember having heard his voice at all but felt he ought to be conciliatory. "To what do I owe the pleasure?"

"I hope I'm not interrupting anything important. I got your number from Aunt Lucinda. To be honest, I don't think she really wanted to tell me. You might have noticed she and my mother don't exactly get on."

"Yes, I did get that impression," said Cornelius, wondering where this was leading.

"I think I managed to persuade her I wasn't like my mother." There was a pause. "Mother is inclined to go off on one now and again. Anyway, she relented and here I am."

"Well, it's good to hear from you, Francis. How can I help?"

"The thing is, there's something I'd like to discuss with you, if you don't mind, concerning Uncle Sedgewick, in a way. I was wondering if

30

it might be convenient to pop round and see you. If you're free, I mean."

"When?"

"Would this afternoon be okay? I promise not to take up too much of your time. I'm sure you're very busy at the weekend. Most people are." Francis said these last few words a little sadly, thought Cornelius, as though he envied them.

"I'm sure I could make room in my heavy schedule." There was silence from the other end of the line. "Only joking! I didn't really have any plans after lunch. What about two o'clock? Would that be okay? Let me give you the address."

Now I wonder what that's all about, thought Cornelius, as he ate. Find out soon enough, I suppose.

When he'd finished eating he retrieved his uncle's letter from the bedroom and read the following:

'Dear Cornelius,

You are now in possession of a very special book. It is a rare first edition of Euclid's Geometry, the first translation from Latin into English, printed in 1570. This particular copy was owned by Elizabeth the First's scientific advisor, Dr John Dee, who also wrote the Preface. This book was one of around five hundred volumes stolen from Dee while he was travelling on the continent, with the collusion of his brother-in-law Nicholas Fromond. Many ended up in the hands of a man called Nicholas Saunder, who was subsequently found to have lots of Dee's personal items in his possession. It is likely that if he himself was not the thief, he was a receiver of stolen property on a large scale.

Some years later, in 1612, one of our ancestors, Maccabeus Pye, was told by a bookseller that he had acquired the Euclid believed to have been part of Dee's lost library. Maccabeus immediately recognised its importance, not only as a fine book in its own right but as a particular one Dee himself had told him about many years earlier, as the book he missed the most following the theft of his library. They had been acquaintances of sorts in the 1590s, when, as a young man, Maccabeus had collaborated briefly with him on an alchemical study. Dee had told him it was the book upon which sat the crystal through which he first began to converse with angels. We may laugh now, but in those days work of this kind was deadly serious and there were no boundaries between what we now call science and other arcane subjects.

Maccabeus was by all accounts a very clever man and he soon realised the true value of the book. He did not think it would let him talk directly to angels or other spirits, as Dee had averred, but, according to his journal it did indeed talk to him in some way he never quite understood. Under its influence he was able to conduct his business affairs in such a way that he greatly enhanced his profits and became a tolerably rich man. In the box accompanying this letter you will find among other things the remains of his journal for 1612, in which he sets out quite clearly his procedure for communicating with the book.

Maccabeus died in 1629. His only son, who inherited it, didn't have the same keen interests as his father and probably never read a book in his life, being more interested in gentlemanly pursuits such as hunting, fighting and drinking. It ended up shelved in his library until he died a few years later in 1633. It has since been passed down through the family and is the only item of Maccabeus' library to survive. Although the whole episode was taken with a grain of salt by his heirs it was always handed down reverently, known by now as the 'magic book'. Even though a few of our ancestors read his journal and tried his methods the book has remained stubbornly silent.

Pye family tradition requires the book to be handed down to the person in the male line who has the oldest male heir. When my father passed away I had no children so naturally my brother, your father, inherited, even though he was younger than me, something I always thought was very unfair. Then, after your parents' accident, I was granted possession of the book in loco parentis, as it were. I'm afraid I've held on to it longer than I should have and for that I am sorry.

Although I had been shown the book in my father's library when I was young and had seen the delightful pop-ups that are such a feature, I was never allowed the chance to study it, as my father said it was an heirloom and must be treated with respect. This meant locking it away in his desk 'for safety's sake'.

I'm sorry to say I cannot tell you what your father made of it. Unlike me, he was a man more interested in plain facts than romance and I get the impression the book was put into a cupboard and forgotten about. At that time I knew nothing of its so-called magic, nor that there was a journal, which I was finally able to read when it came into my possession. It was this which was to turn my world on its head and lead to my interest in the experiments of Dr John Dee and the conclusions of my ancestor, Maccabeus.

It pains me to say that investigating these experiments cost me a great deal of money and came to nothing. After acquiring the book it was as though something was urging me on and I found that once I'd started it was like a drug, almost impossible to give up. It was the same with the Maccabeus journal. Although I followed his instructions to the letter I made no headway communicating with the book for many years.

Then one hot summer's day, while you and your Aunt Lucinda were staying with me, I reached the end of my tether. Completely exhausted, I sat down in my study and shouted, "I give up!" and collapsed with my head in my hands on top of the desk. And then I heard one word. "Why?"

I sat up and looked around but there was no-one in the room. As I sagged back into my chair I heard as clear as day "You've not really been listening"

"What?", I said and back came the reply "You need to listen". And then I twigged. "The book. You're the

33

book!", I said, picking it up and clutching it to me like a long lost friend.

"Now you're listening", it said.

It was exactly then that you poked your head around the door and I'm afraid I was rather rude to you and you closed the door in a hurry. Almost immediately, I wanted to apologise and, thinking you'd probably run back down the stairs I imagined myself at the bottom waiting for you to come down. At which point, there I was, standing with the book in my arms, breathless with shock and clutching it like a comfort blanket. Again, I must have seemed very rude to you, because I raced up the stairs, right past you and back into my study, locking the door behind me.

You must have guessed by now it was the book which enabled me to move from one place to another instantaneously. Quite how this happened I have no idea, despite spending the last twenty-five years trying to find out. That time I moved from my study to the bottom of the stairs remained the only occurrence. I never again quite got to the same state which allowed it to happen the first time. I felt for some reason I wasn't in tune with the book but that if I were I could go almost anywhere.

I can't tell you how many hours I've wasted, trying to get the book to talk to me again, to no avail. It must work in some way but I gave up trying a long time ago. I'm hoping you will have better luck than me. The only advice I can give you is to read Maccabeus' journal and 'Listen.' If you get nowhere please don't sell it. Keep it in the family and pass it on as I have indicated. If not you, let one of our heirs crack the code.

Your loving uncle

Sedgewick'

"A magic book. I've inherited a magic book!" Cornelius couldn't help laughing, then just as suddenly he felt guilty, as he realised his uncle must have been deadly serious. What on earth could make a supposedly sane man believe in magic, especially someone who had been a scientist? At least now Cornelius had an explanation for the packing cases full of equipment and the weird experiments. He felt sorry for him. What a strange life he must have led after reading Maccabeus Pye's journal.

He did an online search for a first edition of the book and was amazed to find a copy had been sold in 2016 by the New York branch of Christies for a staggering fifty thousand dollars. With the provenance of the journal, proving his copy had once been Dee's, with additions in his own hand, Cornelius had no doubt it would be worth considerably more. He was just about to rise and fetch this miraculous book from the bedroom when the doorbell rang. He glanced at his watch. Two o'clock on the dot. He folded his uncle's letter and put it behind the clock on top of the bookcase, then went instead to the door and let his cousin into the flat.

Francis looked exactly as he had at the funeral, like an accountant who, having mislaid a ledger, was now wandering aimlessly around trying to remember where he'd put it. He was wearing, if not the same suit as the day before, one very much like it, with the same sort-of-beige shirt and monochrome dark blue tie. He had a soft, slightly flabby chin and a thin mouth below a small button nose. Two watery grey eyes stared out at Cornelius. There was perspiration on his forehead, which looked like a permanent feature. Thinning, wispy straw-coloured hair made it easy to see that in only a few years time he would adopt the comb-over as his hairstyle of choice. Overall, the only word Cornelius could find to describe him was 'saggy'. Francis held out a hand to Cornelius, who gripped it and shook, then wished he hadn't. It was like holding a warm, damp sponge.

"Hello," said Cornelius, uncertainly, "come on in."

"Thank you for seeing me at such short notice. I appreciate it."

Francis wandered into the flat, looking about nervously, as though he expected someone to jump out at him.

"Please, sit down," offered Cornelius. "Tea? Coffee? A nice cold beer?"

"Ah, no thank you. Just some water, if you wouldn't mind. It's warm, isn't it?"

"Yes, warm," echoed Cornelius, who went into the kitchen to get the water for Francis and a beer for himself.

When he came back into the sitting-room he found his guest perched on the edge of the sofa, a faraway look in his eye.

"Your drink," offered Cornelius. Francis seemed to come to with a slight start and took the glass from him. They both sat.

"I suppose you must be wondering about the nature of my visit," he ventured.

"Yes, I suppose so," countered Cornelius. Francis had only been in the flat a few minutes and already it seemed to Cornelius he'd been there forever. After a short pause, during which Francis took a genteel sip of his water, he began.

"I'm afraid what I'm about to tell you doesn't show your uncle in a very good light. If I'm right, you have received a book, Euclid's Elements of Geometry, the 1570 edition, which was translated into English and contains a foreword by the person to whom it belonged, a Doctor John Dee. Would I be correct?"

"You'd better tell me a little more before I answer your questions," said Cornelius, puzzled. "You obviously know things I don't."

"Very true, Cornelius, very true. The thing is, after mother and I left the pub yesterday afternoon I hung around outside and waited for you. I followed you and Aunt Lucinda back to uncle's house and I saw you leave a few hours later with a large carrier bag. I assume it contained the book. Would I be right?"

"What the hell were you following me for? This is all beginning to feel a bit creepy. I never even knew who you were before yesterday."

"Yes, you're right to be annoyed. I'm sorry, but, you see, I was paid to do so."

"Paid? By whom?"

Francis took another sip of his water before continuing.

"Ah, I'm not really at liberty to tell you. Client confidentiality, you see. The fact is, I'm a private detective and I've been hired by someone to, er, try and purchase your uncle's book."

"You're a private detective!" laughed Cornelius. "You're joking!" Francis looked hurt.

"What's wrong with being a private detective?" huffed Francis.

"Well. I mean, er... You don't look like one," stammered Cornelius. "Isn't that the point?"

Cornelius considered it. As unlikely as it seemed, Francis must be telling the truth. Why else would he be here?

"Right, fine. I'm sorry for doubting you. But I thought this book was supposed to be a great secret. How come your client knows about it?" It was all Cornelius could do not to waggle his fingers in the air to punctuate the word 'client'.

"I'm afraid that's down to Uncle Sedgewick. He may have implied that the book was a secret and maybe Aunt Lucinda still thinks it is, but in spite of that he wasn't very good at keeping secrets. When he first came into possession of the book sixteen years ago he couldn't resist telling both his sisters about it, separately, swearing each of them to secrecy. Not only that but he also took it to a dealer in antique books and manuscripts to get it valued. I don't believe he ever meant to sell it. Just curiosity, I suppose. I'm sure that's how the word got out in the first place. Then, about a month ago my mother went to a book dealer in London to find out how much such a book might be worth. That's where my client first picked up that it might be for sale. These people have contacts all over the place, willing to sell on little titbits of information to the right person. You know how it is."

Cornelius wasn't sure he did. There was another infuriating pause, while Francis picked up his drink and sipped delicately. He replaced the glass gently on the coffee table before continuing.

"Anyway, mother must have left her contact details because a few weeks ago a man came to see her, acting on behalf of my client, to find out what she knew about the book and whether it would be coming onto the open market. I was there when he called, which is how I came to be involved."

"But why would your mother think it would be for sale?"

"Well, she didn't really, but when she found out Uncle Sedgewick had been taken ill she was set on going to see him to try and get him to leave her something in his will. She told me she didn't get much from our grandfather when he died, it mainly went to your father and Uncle Sedgewick, so she thought she deserved something. She was hoping to talk him into leaving her the book, seeing as how Uncle Sedgewick always used to say it would make everyone rich."

"I'm sorry. I didn't know about any of that. I suppose the same must have gone for Aunt Lu."

"I think mother and Aunt Lucinda inherited about the same amount. Aunt Lucinda invested hers wisely, I think, but mother gave hers to father, who put it into some madcap scheme which went bust pretty quickly and left her with nothing. My father was never very good with money, I'm afraid. He was practically penniless when he died so she's had rather a hard time of it."

"And did Aunt Violet get to see Uncle Sedgewick?"

"Yes. That didn't go very well. Uncle wasn't the easiest of men to get on with at the best of times and mother isn't known for her tact. All she came away with was a bad temper."

"So how does this client of yours get into the picture?"

"Well, Dee's own copy of the book is well known in rare book circles as one of the famous lost books and there have been rumours of it for many years. It's supposed by some to contain magical incantations written in Dee's own hand, which makes it highly desirable to certain people. Completely mad, if you ask me. So when this man came to see mother he asked her if she knew anything about it. That was when she suggested I get involved and act as agent to try and secure the book on his behalf. He and I met up a few days later, where he paid me a small retainer up front and laid out the terms for a sizeable commission if I managed to come up with it. A few weeks ago I also went to see Uncle Sedgewick and offered him what I thought was a very reasonable price for it. He sent me away with the proverbial flea in my ear. Soon after, he was dead, but my deal with my client is still intact, so here I am."

Cornelius didn't know what to say, so he stayed silent and waited for Francis to continue, which he finally did.

"So you have the book, I take it?"

"It would seem silly to deny it, especially to a private investigator. I assume you'd have other ways of finding out."

"Well, I'm not Sherlock Holmes," said Francis, with something which could have been a chuckle but sounded like air escaping from a punctured tyre, "but it appears you would be the main suspect."

"I'm not sure if suspect is the word you're looking for," said Cornelius.

"No, sorry, I see what you mean. Anyway, the long and the short of it is my client is willing to offer you a hundred thousand pounds for the book."

"A hundred thousand! That's crazy."

"I could see if he will increase the offer if you think it's too little but I've been assured it is a very fair price."

"No, I wasn't saying… I mean, I'm sure it's very reasonable but I had no idea it could be worth so much."

"So you do admit to having the book?"

"Yes, I have it." He stood and walked over to the window, just to check the world outside was still going on as usual. A small questioning cough came from his cousin.

"No," said Cornelius, finally, "no, I don't think I want to sell it. You see, I've only just discovered it once belonged to my father and Uncle Sedgewick only had it by accident. If my father hadn't died when I was young it would eventually have come to me, anyway. In an odd sort of a way, it's come home. Do you see?"

"Yes, I do. A shame, but nothing to be done, I suppose."

"Sorry. Sorry about your commission. When I get the house sorted I should be in a position to try and make it up to you. Tell your mother I'm sorry, too. If there's anything else I can do for her please ask her to get in touch."

"I will. Thanks." Francis stood and made for the door. "I think I'd best be getting along, let my client know your decision. I'll leave you my card, in case you change your mind. Goodbye."

And then he was gone.

A little later Cornelius sat at his breakfast table in the kitchen with the book before him and opened the battered front cover. On the title page he read the following:

> 'The Elements of Geometrie of the most aunctient Philosopher Euclide of Megara. Faithfully (now first) translated into the English toung, by H. Billingsley, City of London. Wherunto are annexed certaine Scholies, Annotations and Inuentions, of the best Mathematiciens, both of time past, and in this our age.'

He had to look up scholies and discovered it was an old word, the plural of scholium, which meant in this case a note added to a proof as amplification. As he turned the pages he became more and more mesmerised, especially when he came to the small pop-up illustrations which clarified for the reader exactly what the original author had stated. He realised these were the inventions mentioned in the title. Many of the pages had handwritten annotations; sometimes notes, sometimes complex equations using symbols he didn't recognise which, unsurprisingly, he found difficult to follow. He inspected the book closely for about an hour but he could find nothing which might suggest untold riches.

When he researched online he discovered that John Dee was, among other things, a mathematician, who in 1558 became the trusted advisor to Queen Elizabeth on astrological and scientific matters. His high status as a scholar allowed him to play a role in Elizabethan politics and he nurtured uneasy relationships with her ministers Francis Walsingham and William Cecil, who were credited with founding and maintaining England's secret service.

He devoted much of his life to the study of alchemy, divination and Hermetic philosophy (based on writings attributed to Hermes Trismegistus, an Egyptian priest-king who was supposedly a contemporary of Moses) and was a proponent of the British Empire, a term generally attributed to him. He straddled the worlds of magic and modern science just as the latter was emerging and did not draw distinctions between mathematical research and investigations into magic, angel summoning and divination.

Dee built one of the great private libraries of sixteenth century England and claimed to own more than three thousand books and over a thousand manuscripts, which he kept at his home in Mortlake, near London. When he travelled to Europe in 1583, he entrusted the care of his library and laboratories to his brother-in-law, Nicholas Fromond. According to Dee's diary, Fromond *'unduly sold it presently upon my departure, or caused it to be carried away.'* He was devastated by the destruction of his library. He later recovered some items, but many remained lost. A large number of books ended up with the mysterious Nicholas Saunder, under murky circumstances.

It was one of those lost books Cornelius now possessed, a book of almost a thousand pages, with copious notes and references to other mathematicians, considered to be the first and most important translation into English. The pop-up paper cut-outs had been hand-glued into each copy in the section on solid figures and the preface was written by Dee himself.

The more Cornelius read about John Dee, the stranger things got, not least his penchant for conversing with angels. One of the most learned men of his age, Dee had been invited to lecture on the geometry of Euclid at the University of Paris while still in his early twenties. He was an ardent promoter of mathematics and a respected astronomer, as well as a leading expert in navigation, having trained many of those who would conduct England's voyages of discovery.

Dee devoted much time and effort in the last thirty years or so of his life attempting to commune with angels in order to learn the universal language of creation and bring about the pre-apocalyptic unity of mankind. He died in either 1608 or 1609, largely forgotten. Shortly before his death, for reasons unknown, he locked some of his precious notebooks in a chest and buried them in fields near his home. Fortunately, many of his documents were excavated ten to twenty years after his death by an antiquarian, Sir Robert Cotton, only to be lost again soon after.

In 1662, a confectioner named Robert Jones was moving a large old coffer when he heard a rattle. When he investigated he found a secret drawer containing papers, books and a small necklace. By some mischance he left some of the papers on a kitchen table. Blissfully ignorant, his maid used about half of the papers to line her pie tins before anyone noticed what she was doing. Luckily, most of them were salvaged.

In 1672, they were shown to a wealthy lawyer and collector, Elias Ashmole, who immediately recognized their value. These hand-written papers contained, among other things, Dee's Libor Mystoriorum, his book of mysteries, which was reputed to contain all the secrets of the universe. If it had not been for Sir Robert Cotton, Robert Jones and Elias Ashmole, almost all of Dr. John Dee's writings would have been lost to posterity.

Cornelius sat with the book for many hours, reading certain sections and attempting to make sense of Dee's marginalia. What was his uncle talking about? How could this ancient book talk to anyone? While he read he kept noticing a slight tugging in his mind, as though there was something he should know, but he couldn't quite put his finger on. He re-read the letter from his uncle, hoping for a clue, but came to the conclusion his uncle must have been a little unhinged. But then, what explained how his uncle had suddenly rushed up the stairs towards him all those years ago?

He was about to read Maccabeus' journal when he noticed the time. He'd arranged to take Angela to dinner that evening so he rose reluctantly from the table to get ready. He took the book and the journal into the bedroom and slid them under his bed, amusing himself with the thought that maybe he ought to invest in a safe. His earlier valuation of the book had since doubled. He decided not to let Angela know. She would be sure to want him to cash in on his good fortune. He'd told his aunt he would investigate the book's so-called magical properties so he definitely wanted to hang onto it for a good while longer. It might turn out to be fun.

4.

Sunday was a bit of a blur. After dinner with Angela the previous evening they'd gone back to her place in Belsize Park, where he received the full force of her charms, which left him exhausted but with a smile on his face. She was very pleased with him for inheriting the house, as though he'd somehow been the instigator. She referred to him as a 'clever boy' on more than one occasion and insisted on working out how much he'd be left with after death duties if he put the house on the market. She couldn't see how it could be worth less than a couple of million, even in the state it was in. Cornelius was staggered. He then felt guilty about inheriting it when his aunts and his cousin were to receive nothing. He decided he would do right by them, another little thing he didn't mention to Angela.

Early the next morning Angela disappeared to the gym while Cornelius was still sleeping. When she returned they had a late breakfast together then drove out to Henley and went for a long circular walk, taking in the deer park and views of the Chiltern Hills before indulging in a lazy lunch while watching the swans parade up and down the Thames. By the time he finally arrived back home, pleasantly exhausted, it was nearly seven.

He spent the evening on the sofa looking through his ancestor's papers, which he spread out untidily around him. The book sat on the coffee-table. Some of the papers were very difficult to read and were mostly concerned with alchemical experiments. These must have been from the time Maccabeus first met Dee. Sure enough, close inspection of Dee's handwritten notes in the book matched up with a few terse notes in the papers. None of it made any sense to him so reluctantly he skipped over them and tried instead to read through the battered journal. It must at one time have been much more substantial as it was presumably meant to cover an entire year. All that remained was a few pages. The handwriting was a little easier to read than the papers and what remained appeared to be devoted to communicating with the book, where Maccabeus had written:

'January 22nd 1612

When the Booke of Euclide had come unto mee the day before I was grately pleased, knowing it to be of the Library of Dr John Dee by the inscript within, even though it had been part Scrap'd out by anotheres Hand and that I had had the very best bargain of it. It is indeed a marvellous booke but as I sat last evening to read it I was Stopp'd of a sudden by a voyce seemingly by my side. There being no other in the House at that time I was arrested by an Uncommon Fear and went about calling out who was there. Upon resuming my reading I once more heard the Voyce that spake but the one word, "Listen".

Ful knowing that it was Doctor Dees booke I then suspected that some Magick had been work'd and that it must after all be talking directly to mee. Therfore, knowing the good Doctor to have been a Tollerable man I decided to be resolute and give in to that command so that it might say what its Message would bee. Accordingly, I relaxed myself and allowed all Thoughts to fly from my head so that there would be Peace and Tranquillity within. And then again I did hear its Voyce calling unto mee sayinge "Listen, for that I have many things to tell thee." I asked the Booke to speak further and tell me its misteryes.'

There was a little more in the same vein, but despite the book's hints and promises nothing specific was mentioned. After the 22nd January there were no more entries, just a few blank pages before the end. Not much to go on there. Cornelius wondered what had happened to his ancestor after he had heard the book speaking to him. He opened the Euclid again and went through it page by page to see if anything could be cross-referenced with the journal, but found nothing. The secret, whatever it may be, wasn't going to yield easily.

He read his uncle's letter one more time, hoping somehow for enlightenment, but there was nothing new. As he read, he couldn't help feeling he was missing something, as though he'd already seen the answer.

Reluctantly, he closed the book and put his uncle's letter back behind the clock on the mantelpiece. The journal went back into the box of papers, which he stored under his bed. It had been a long day so he made himself a quick supper and got ready for bed. As he was brushing his teeth he heard the doorbell.

Later, he blamed his tiredness for the fact he never checked who it might be. He went to answer it, then couldn't remember anything else until he woke up early the next morning outside the door of his flat. When he had finally roused himself enough to re-enter his flat, a quick inspection revealed the book had gone.

After splashing his face with water and swallowing a revitalising cup of strong tea, he spent nearly an hour on the phone to the police, going through the sequence of events three times for three different people. He was asked for Francis' details and he read them what was on the card he'd been given. They arranged to send someone round that evening.

After a hurried call to Aunt Lucinda, giving her the details and receiving a withering blast in return he called Angela to tell her what had happened, hoping for a little sympathy. Instead, she asked him how he could let such a thing happen, on his own doorstep. Not so much of a clever boy now. Things got worse.

"Now don't forget", she said, "we're going to Barbara's birthday party on Thursday. You can pick me up at seven-thirty." Cornelius groaned. He didn't particularly like Barbara. Whenever they met, she greeted him along the lines of "Hello, Professor, how are the experiments going?"

Cornelius was late into work and spent ten minutes with Mr Singh, his department manager, apologising for his lateness and telling him what had happened. Mr Singh asked him if he needed to go home and recover but Cornelius said he'd rather be working than sitting at home, fretting. Later, Ruth met him in the kitchen as they were getting ready for a meeting. She regarded him with sympathy.

"My God, you look awful!"

"Thanks very much," he said, glumly.

"By the state of your eyes you must have had a bit of a heavy weekend. Were you drowning your sorrows after the funeral?"

"I've hardly touched a drop all weekend," he countered, defensively. "The funeral went off without a hitch and Uncle

Sedgewick had a very nice send off. It was mostly calm and dignified, unless you count the meeting with my Aunt Violet in the pub afterwards. No, the reason I look like this is because last night I was drugged or something and burgled."

"What? You're joking!"

"I wish I was. I was just getting ready to go to bed when the doorbell rang. I honestly can't remember anything after answering the door, except that something was sprayed into my face. I can't even remember seeing anyone there. I spent the entire night crashed out in the hallway. I woke up this morning stiff as a board. I feel as though I've been hit by a train."

"Was there much taken?"

Cornelius stopped for a moment and considered how much to tell her, bearing in mind his uncle's exhortations about the book being kept a secret. He reflected that his uncle hadn't exactly kept his mouth shut and nearly everyone he'd met in the last few days seemed to know about it, so he couldn't see much harm in telling her, as long as he didn't mention the details. If he started talking about magic and alchemy she might think he'd gone loopy. He realised he'd prefer it if she didn't.

"That's the worst of it. The only thing missing is an old book my uncle left me, a family heirloom. I've only had it since Friday. I was given it by my aunt after the funeral, along with a journal written by one of my ancestors and a letter from my uncle."

"Just a book? Are you serious? What's so special about it?"

"It's a first edition of Euclid's Geometry. It was once owned by Doctor John Dee, who used to be an advisor to Elizabeth the First in the fifteenth century. Do you know who I mean?"

"I think so."

"It's worth a fair bit of money."

"A fair bit?"

"One just like it sold for fifty-thousand dollars."

"Wow! That's more than just a fair bit. Who knew you had it?"

"Well, apart from Aunt Lu there was only my cousin, Francis, who knew for certain. His mother, Aunt Violet, must know by now as well. When we met up with them after the funeral, in the pub, Aunt Violet seemed surprised the book hadn't been included in uncle's will. But my Aunt Lu swore blind she knew nothing about it. There's bad blood between them. Then on Saturday, Francis turned up at my flat and made me an offer for it on behalf of a client. It turns out he's a private investigator. I turned him down"

A thought came to him. "You don't think it could have been Francis, do you? He looked like he couldn't harm a fly. He spent most of the time at the pub gazing into space."

Ruth considered it for a moment then said, "It doesn't seem likely your cousin would steal the book. I mean, he'd be straight at the top of the list of suspects, wouldn't he?"

"I wouldn't put it past his mother, though", muttered Cornelius. He paused a moment. "No, that's silly. She might be a bit scary but I don't think she's any kind of criminal mastermind."

"A bit of a dragon then, this mother?", asked Ruth.

"Most of my relations so far have turned out to be pretty scary on first meeting. With my uncle and my Aunt Lu there was a softer side, once you got to know them. I don't think Aunt Violet has a softer side. Aunt Lu called her a nasty piece of work. She said you can choose your friends but you can't choose your relations. Luckily, I can't see our paths crossing too often."

"So why would a thief steal just the book and nothing else? It's a bit specialized. It might be worth a lot of money, but it's not the kind of thing you could easily off-load, except to a collector. Someone else must know you had it. Who was Francis' client? How did he find out about it?"

"That's a good question. I did ask him, but he told me it was confidential. The problem is, even though my uncle told me it was a secret, he seems to have said the same thing to a few other people, but as for who they may be, I'll never know. According to Francis, my uncle once talked to a dealer about its value, so who this dealer talked to is anyone's guess. Apparently, Aunt Violet has also been bothering the book trade about what it might be worth so I imagine half of London knows about it by now."

Cornelius hesitated, then thought, what the hell. If he couldn't trust Ruth, who could he trust? He knew she wasn't the type to repeat anything she'd been told in confidence. "I know this sounds silly, but my uncle believed this book could talk to him".

"No way!"

"And not only that, it could transport him from one place to another."

"Wow! You're uncle really was eccentric, wasn't he?" gasped Ruth.

"But what if other people believed him? Might not that be a reason to steal it?"

"I hope you didn't mention that to the police."

"No. I thought they might not take me seriously if I started babbling about talking books".

They went into their meeting and the subject was dropped. The rest of the day passed in a haze, with Cornelius spending most of the time at his desk, mulling over his uncle's letter. It didn't make sense that a book could speak, let alone transport a body through space. Try as he might, Cornelius couldn't remember that day in his uncle's house with any finer detail. The more he thought about it, the more it slipped away from him.

Around four o'clock, Mr Singh came over and told him to go home as he looked absolutely terrible. Cornelius thanked him, promised to be in bright and early the next day, and headed gratefully for the door.

The police came around later that evening and he went through everything once again, this time with actions. They told him they'd checked out Francis' movements and he had an alibi. He had been at a book club meeting with half a dozen others in Tring, where he lived with his mother. He hadn't left until after eleven. After the police had gone he phoned Francis, from whom he gleaned the fact he'd not mentioned the book to anyone apart from reporting back to his client that negotiations had stalled. The mystery man had thanked Francis and told him he'd be in touch again with fresh instructions. Francis passed on his commiserations, which Cornelius accepted glumly.

The next day passed without incident. During the morning, Cornelius moped around in the lab, mentally kicking himself every few minutes.

"It's a wonder I'm allowed out by myself," he said to Ruth, "I ought to have a full-time carer or something." She did her best to make him feel better but nothing could cheer him up.

In the afternoon, an interesting new line of research had opened up after a discussion with a company based in San Francisco and this had kept Cornelius engrossed for the rest of the day. As he was leaving, he apologised to Ruth for being so grumpy and promised he would be back to his old self when he turned up for work in the morning.

The new research kept Cornelius so busy that the next day flew by. Ruth remarked that she was glad his disposition was improving.

Later that evening as he was getting ready for bed and just as he'd finished brushing his teeth, the doorbell rang. He put on his dressing gown and went to answer the door, thinking it might be the police with an update. If he'd been a little more alert he might have been suspicious, but he never believed lightning might strike twice. He opened the door and remembered no more until he woke in the cellar.

5

After what seemed like many hours the door at the top of the stairs opened again and the man who had brought him his breakfast returned. This time, instead of a bacon sandwich and a cup of tea, he was carrying a gun. In his other hand he had a small pair of snips, which he used to cut the cable ties fastening Cornelius to the radiator. Cornelius started to rub some life back into his wrists.

"I'd prefer not to have to use this," said the man, waving the gun, "but I will if you do anything stupid. We're going upstairs."

"By anything stupid, do you mean trying to stand up and falling over again? Because I'm not sure my legs are going to work." He dragged himself to his feet and wobbled uncertainly, then fell back against the wall. Shafts of pain shot up Cornelius' legs and he grimaced.

"You'll be fine once your circulation starts working again," said the man.

"I assume you speak from experience. Was it you who knocked me out?"

"Some friends of mine, the ones who brought you here. Just a little tranquillizer spray. I believe they used to use something similar in zoos to keep the big cats quiet."

"It may have escaped your notice but I'm not a big cat."

"Funny man."

"Who are you and what do you want?"

"You can call me Mr West and it's not me that wants anything. That'll be my boss. You'll find out as soon as you get upstairs. Let's go."

Cornelius walked towards the cellar stairs a little uncertainly, feeling much worse than Monday morning, after his previous encounter with the spray. He hoped this wasn't going to be a regular occurrence. He had to use his hands on the wall to make sure he didn't lose his balance.

At the top of the stairs he was directed along a bare hallway into a library. There were lots of shelves but no books, dust on all the surfaces and grimy sash windows. It was obvious the place had not been used for quite a while. Cornelius got the impression the house was probably very grand once. The man who called himself Mr West gestured towards a seat behind a desk at the far end of the room. On the desk was the stolen book. Cornelius sat and continued to massage his aches and pains, while staring thoughtfully at the book. Mr West took a phone from his pocket and made a call.

"Hello? Yes, it's me. I've got him here. Hold on."

He held out the phone to Cornelius, who took it and held it to his ear.

"Hello?"

"Good morning, Mr Pye. I'm very sorry to have inconvenienced you. I do hope you're feeling better after your ordeal. You'll be allowed to wash and brush your teeth presently, after which I'm sure you'll feel much better and ready to face the day, as they say. I'm assuming you want to know why I have had you brought there?"

"Who are you?" asked Cornelius.

"That's not something you need to worry about at the present," replied the voice on the phone. "If all goes well you will soon be released and you can carry on your life as normal, but first I would like you tell me how the book works."

"I'm sorry, I think you've got ahead of me somewhere. What exactly do you mean, how the book works?" asked Cornelius.

"Oh come now, Mr Pye, there's no need to play games with me. We both know this book has certain, shall we say, magical properties. I've known about its existence for many years. One of history's great lost books. It was supposed to have gone missing sometime after the death of your ancestor, Maccabeus Pye. Its re-emergence was first brought to my attention by an antique book dealer about fifteen years ago but, unfortunately, I never discovered the name of the owner. Then, miraculously, your aunt started making enquiries a few weeks ago about how much such a book might be worth. It had to be the same one, so I sent Mr West along to see your aunt to see if she could secure it for me. He discovered your aunt's hopes of acquiring it were slim to nil, but on the plus side, it transpired that her son, Mr Duncan, would be only too happy to open negotiations with your uncle. Sadly, as you probably know, your uncle wasn't amenable to selling, which left us in rather a difficult position, at least until your uncle passed away. My condolences, by the way."

He waited for Cornelius to respond but there was nothing. He continued.

"When I was informed your uncle had died I asked Mr Duncan to continue as my representative. After that, it was a simple matter to have him do what he does best and see if the book would reappear after the funeral. He told me he'd been to see you and you admitted that you had it."

"So after I refused to sell you decided to pinch it."

"Yes. Sorry, but needs must, Mr Pye. I've waited a long time to get my hands on that book. I'm not going to be thwarted any longer."

"Just a minute," said Cornelius, "how come after you took it you came back for me?" As he asked the question he realised he already knew the answer. "Oh, no, wait. I see. You have no idea what you're doing with it, do you? You thought you only needed the book and with your brilliant mind you'd easily be able to work out what you needed to do. How did that work out for you?" If Cornelius had expected his outburst of sarcasm might annoy, he was disappointed.

"Very good, Mr Pye. You've worked out my little problem, which has now become yours."

Cornelius looked at West, who was still pointing the gun at him.

"When I first took possession I began immediately to read through it, far into the night, hoping to find clues to its use. Unfortunately, I found nothing. It is, without doubt, Dee's own copy. There are many examples of marginalia in his distinctive hand throughout, but they refer only to the theorems on the pages. There is nothing that looks like any code I am familiar with. Codes and ciphers in the seventeenth century were in their infancy and much simpler than they are today. I have a good understanding of them but I couldn't get started. By four o'clock the next morning I had examined the whole book from cover to cover, looking for invisible writing, hidden text or anything secreted in the binding. There was nothing. I put it away and left it until the next day, hoping a fresh assault would bring results after a good night's sleep.

"The next day I started again but I began to notice I was feeling increasingly uneasy while I read. I thought it was just tiredness, so I pressed on. Finally, I got a headache which was so intense I had to close my eyes for a few minutes while it subsided. When I reopened them I found I was holding a copy of the 1955 Rupert Annual I had been given as a Christmas present when I was six years old. I had to concentrate very hard to get the image out of my mind. That was when I knew I was going to need you to discover the secret of the book."

"But then you realised you couldn't just ask me, having stolen the book in the first place."

"How much easier everything would have been if you'd accepted my original offer, Mr Pye. I could have offered you a nice commission to do what I'm asking of you now on top of what I would have paid for the book. When Mr Duncan came back to me for further instructions I decided we should strike while the iron was hot, so to speak, so I sent Mr West and his accomplices to pick you up."

Cornelius wondered if they had also taken the journal and his uncle's letter when they'd returned to the flat to kidnap him. He decided not mention them.

"Look, I'm sorry to disappoint you, but I really haven't a clue what it is you want from me. I have no idea what you mean by magic codes. It all sounds totally stupid."

"You're not going to tell me your uncle didn't discuss it with you?"

So they don't have the letter, thought Cornelius. Good.

"No, he never discussed it."

"Look, Mr Pye, I'm well aware of your background so I know you're not stupid. Please don't make the same assumption about me. I know the history of this book from the time it was the prized possession of Dr John Dee, one of Elizabeth the First's foremost advisers. It came into the hands of one of your ancestors, who knew its secrets and it appears now it has been secretly passed down through your family for hundreds of years. It's not just any old book, it contains some sort of code which could lead to vast wealth. You're asking me to believe your uncle said nothing about it to you? Well, be that as it may, you're still going to help me crack the code."

"How do you suppose I'm going to do that?"

"It's very simple. I'm going to keep you here until you do. You're obviously very bright or you wouldn't be working where you do. I'll give you all the materials you'll need to discover its secrets. I'm sure it won't take you long."

"And if I do manage to crack this code, or whatever, what then?"

"I'm not a nasty man, Mr Pye. I've already said I'll let you go back to your life"

"Minus the book, I suppose."

"Life can be very cruel, don't you agree? Now if you don't mind, I have a meeting in the City. Mr West will get you anything you need. We have a library full of books on ciphers and encryption. You can have limited internet access for research purposes but it will be monitored, so no messages to friends and family, I'm afraid. Good luck, My Pye, I'm sure you'll come up with the goods."

There was a slight pause, before the voice on the phone added, "You'd better."

After the call, West escorted Cornelius to a bathroom, where he was given the necessary items to enable him to wash and brush his teeth. Then he was taken back to the library. West opened a cupboard at the far end of the room and showed him an array of books, as well as writing materials, paper and a small laptop with a wireless connection.

"If you want to use the internet you'll need to ask. You can't access anything without the password, which I'll put in, then watch you until you've finished, at which point I'll log you out again. For that and anything else you need, bang on the door," he said, "I'm just across the hall." With a little smile, West wished him good luck and left the room, locking the door behind him.

Cornelius, with no real enthusiasm, ran his eye over the book titles. They all appeared to be concerned with codes and ciphers. He'd read a few books on the subject while at university so he had a good idea of the background but in the present case he had no idea where to start. He sat down at the desk and once again opened the copy of Euclid's Geometry, wondering why on earth his uncle and the people who had brought him here supposed there was a secret code. Back at his flat he'd been unable to find anything in Dee's weird scribblings to make anyone think huge wealth could be bestowed upon the reader.

Again though, as he turned the pages, he felt something tugging at his mind, something important, but he couldn't quite focus on whatever it was, a bit like trying to see a ghostly presence you only catch out of the corner of your eye and don't really believe in. He read once again through Dee's Foreword to the book, which even to a mathematician was fairly heavy going, couched as it was in unfamiliar terms and ideas. It yielded nothing. After an hour of flipping back and forth he decided a cup of tea might help and banged on the door.

"Hello! Do you think I could possibly get a spot of tea in here? And some biscuits – digestives for preference but anything will do."

West answered in the affirmative so Cornelius sat back down to wait. He must have drifted off for a few seconds because he thought he saw the book's pages turn by themselves and a voice said quietly, "Listen…"

With a bang the door opened and Cornelius snapped awake as West came in with a mug of tea. He was carrying a tin of assorted biscuits.

"These will have to do. I'll bring you some lunch in a couple of hours."

Ever polite, Cornelius thanked him and West left the room. The book was still open at the last page he'd been reading.

6.

Cornelius hadn't turned up for work and by lunchtime Ruth was getting distinctly worried. She hadn't heard from him since the end of the previous day, when he'd left in an optimistic mood, looking forward to continuing the promising research he'd been working on. It seemed to her he had recovered after the events at the beginning of the week but now she was worried in case something else had happened. They usually met up first thing each morning to go through the coming day and she'd had no text or email from him to say he would be late or wasn't coming in. He'd also missed a meeting they'd been scheduled to attend, one to which Cornelius had been looking forward, as he was expecting news about the battery project one of his teams had been working on. She'd emailed and texted him a couple of times but had no response.

Much against her better judgement, she phoned Angela to see if she knew anything. Angela was livid, as she had been trying to get hold of him since early morning. The arrangements for Barbara's party that evening had been changed and she wanted to make sure Cornelius knew about it. She was sure he had been sidetracked by something.

"This is exactly like him," she told Ruth. "There was one time I'd been shopping at Westfields with a girlfriend and I phoned and told him to meet me at that little wine bar by the Bush Theatre before going on to dinner. You know the one, where they have that yummy barman who mixed us those Negronis a while ago. Well of course he promised to set off straight away and he never turned up. I found out he'd stopped off at work to check on some experiment or other and completely forgot about me."

Ruth had to listen to Angela's complaints about him for a few more minutes before managing to make an excuse and hang up. Why couldn't he see that Angela wasn't good for him? She didn't seem to care about him at all. Film star looks weren't everything, although she suspected that like most men the sex kept drawing him back for more. Trying to dismiss mental images of Cornelius and Angela in the throes of passion she went to find Mr Singh to ask for an extended lunch break so she could go to his flat and check to see if he was okay.

"Of course, of course you must," said Mr Singh, "we ought to have him back here for the next planning stage. I do hope he's alright after what happened to him on Monday. Terrible business." Manmohan Singh was a boss in a million, she thought, another reason why working for Lightsource was such a joy.

"Thanks, Mr Singh, I'm sure he's fine," she said on her way out, stopping only to pick up her bag. She managed to hail a cab almost immediately and after settling back in the seat tried once more to get hold of Cornelius. Again, the call went to voicemail.

Luckily the traffic was light down the Holloway Road so it didn't take too long to get to the block of flats where Cornelius lived. She hurried up to the first floor and was about to knock when she noticed the door was very slightly ajar. Knocking anyway and calling out, in that awkward way English people do when they're entering someone else's place without permission, she walked into the living room and found it empty. She quickly checked the other rooms and found the same. In the bedroom she found the clothes he'd been wearing the previous day neatly folded on the bed, his wallet on the bedside table. The bed didn't look as though it had been slept in. Back in the living room she found his laptop on the coffee table, along with his phone and a bunch of keys. The rest of the room was tidy and nothing seemed to be missing. So it wasn't a burglary this time, she thought, but even Cornelius wouldn't leave the flat without taking his phone and keys.

Remembering her conversation with him from the previous day, she looked around for the clock, which sat on top of a bookcase, and saw his uncle's letter behind it. Not knowing quite why, but sensing the letter may hold a clue to what had happened to him, she put it in her pocket, then phoned the police to report him missing.

At first, the police were hesitant to do anything but when she told them he'd reported a burglary to them at the beginning of the week and now she was calling from his flat, which she'd found with the door wide open, they promised to send someone round.

"Are you his girlfriend?" asked the bored sounding lady on the other end of the phone.

Ruth hesitated, then said, "No, I'm a work colleague."

"Are you able to hold on there until someone can attend?"

"Will they be long?"

"Should be around half an hour, all being well. Luckily, it's fairly quiet out there at the moment."

Ruth thanked her and ended the call. After updating Mr Singh she went into the kitchen and made herself a coffee, then wondered whether she should read the letter. After a couple of minutes arguing with herself one way or the other she found herself reaching into her pocket and pulling it out. She read it through quickly, as though not wishing to be caught in the act. Then she read it again, much more slowly, as the full import of what she was reading began to sink in. She realised she had better not show it to the police. She didn't want them to jump to any conclusions about mad professors and magic books.

The letter had mentioned Maccabeus Pye's journal and she wondered if that too had been taken or if it was still somewhere in the flat. It didn't take her long to find the box under the bed. She took out the journal and the papers and transferred them carefully to her bag, then went back into the living room and sat at the table. No point leaving anything behind which might be connected to the book, she thought, in case they came back a third time. She realised with a shudder it might be a possibility and if they were coming, it could be at any time.

A knock at the door made her start. A voice shouted, "Hello, Police. Anyone there?"

"I'm here!", shouted Ruth as she opened the door to admit two policemen, one uniformed, one not.

"I'm Detective Inspector Evans," said the plainclothes half, 'this is PC Winter. "

The saying that policemen are looking younger then ever these days did not apply to PC Winter, who remained standing by the door, out of breath after the short climb up to the flat. She thought he looked dangerously unfit. On the other hand, DI Philip Evans, who had advanced into the room to meet her, breezed in like the junior partner of an estate agency. Ruth found it difficult to believe he was more than halfway through his twenties, although he had just turned thirty-two. To her eye, he was well dressed, good-looking, with fair hair and a dangerous half smile which might have affected her more if she hadn't been so keen on Cornelius.

"Are you the person who phoned about the break-in?"

"Yes! No! I mean, there was a break-in, but now there's a missing person."

"Come again?" said Evans.

"There was a break-in reported two nights ago, by Cornelius Pye, the person who lives here. A rare book was stolen and the police have been notified. Cornelius left work yesterday at around four o'clock and no-one's seen him since. He isn't answering his phone, which isn't surprising because it's there on the table. When I came round to see if he was alright the door was standing open. That's how I got into the flat."

"And you are?"

"Ruth Seaton. I'm a work colleague. We work together in Highgate, near the Gatehouse Theatre. I was worried about him. I mean, we all were, at work." She knew she'd started to blush and hoped the detective wouldn't notice.

"A work colleague. I see." He smiled briefly and Ruth smiled back, not having to wonder very much what it was he saw. "Would you like to fill me in on the details? We didn't get much of a background from the station."

She went through the events of the last few days, starting with Cornelius receiving the book, the oddness of him being sprayed unconscious after answering the door late at night, then waking up in the corridor outside his flat and discovering the book had been stolen.

"Can you tell if anything else is missing?" asked Evans.

"Not that I can see, but I wouldn't really know. I've never been here before." Once again, she felt herself blushing and wondered why. "As I said, his phone's on the table, so is his laptop and door keys. When I looked in his bedroom I found his wallet on the bedside table."

"Is there anywhere he might have gone in a hurry?"

"What do you mean?" asked Ruth.

"Well, supposing there was an emergency somewhere and he just rushed out without taking anything with him and he forgot to close the door behind him."

"Well, he can be a bit absent-minded sometimes but never about work. He's always been very conscientious about that. If there's a change of plan he always lets one of us know. It's not unusual to get a late night text from him if there's something he's just thought of."

She paused, then added, "His parents are dead. He was brought up by his aunt but she lives up north somewhere. I can't see him rushing up there without letting us know. He doesn't have any other close relatives. Anyway, he wouldn't get far without his phone and wallet."

"Do you have a number for this aunt?"

"No, sorry. I've never met her. He has a girlfriend, but I've already been in touch with her and she hasn't seen or heard from him either. They're supposed to be going out tonight to a birthday party. She won't be pleased if he doesn't turn up."

Evans eyed her, quizzically.

"She's a bit controlling," explained Ruth.

"Can you let me have her number? She might be able to throw some light on his aunt. Or he may have got in touch with her while we've been here."

She gave him Angela's name and number, then asked, "Do you think I could go now? I need to get back to work. I'm here on my lunch break."

"The station'll have your contact details, will they?"

"Yes, I gave them all that when I phoned earlier."

"Okay. Well, there's nothing much else we can do here at the minute. We'll be in touch if we find anything."

As she was leaving, Evans said, "What about keys? Does he have a spare set anywhere, d'you know?"

"I'm sorry, I don't."

"We'll go out together, then. We'll leave his phone and laptop here. You lock up and take the keys with you. Let his girlfriend know you've got them"

Ruth nodded.

"Can we give you a lift back to Highgate?"

"That's very kind, thank you."

"My pleasure", said DI Evans, with a smile.

When she got back she didn't want to alarm Mr Singh by saying she'd reported Cornelius missing. Mr Singh was, by nature, a great worrier and he had enough on his plate trying to raise the funds necessary to drive forward a new series of experiments. She decided to tell him she'd not found him at the flat but suggested maybe he was feeling a bit down after the funeral of his uncle, followed by the incident with the book and that the police thought he'd probably gone off to visit his Aunt Lucinda.

"I'm sure he's fine, Mr Singh, but you know what he's like, a little absent-minded."

"Yes, yes, of course. All these young geniuses are," he replied with a grin.

Ruth returned the grin with difficulty.

By late afternoon lunch was a distant memory and Cornelius was desperately trying to keep his eyes open. He had made no further progress, despite online research into the arcane writings of various medieval authors. He'd skimmed through the books they'd provided and read as much as he could online about the enigmatic Dr Dee, who struck Cornelius as sadly deluded. Lunch had been provided at around one, along with a scowl from West. Cornelius had tried to engage him in conversation, asking what he did when he wasn't kidnapping people and holding them prisoner in old houses but he was met with silence. Since then there'd only been a visit to the toilet to break the boredom.

He wondered what Angela would be thinking about his disappearance. She must have tried to get hold of him by now. She was going to be very annoyed if he didn't turn up to take her to her friend's party. He remembered the uncomfortable scene the last time he'd transgressed. And what about work? Ruth must also be wondering where he was, especially after not turning up for the meeting this morning.

He sat staring at the dirty window, noticing for the first time there was a coat of arms painted on the upper pane, but it was so faded he could barely make it out. It looked like a shield, with a boar's head in the middle, surrounded by three castles, one at each of the points. His thoughts drifted back to his uncle's letter and from there to the journal entry by his ancestor Maccabeus. What if the earlier episode with the book, where he thought he'd heard something, hadn't been a dream? What did Maccabeus say? He heard a voice seemingly by his side. There was no-one else in the house. Upon resuming his reading he once more heard a voice, which spoke one word, "Listen". What did he do then? Come on, Cornelius, think.

As he thought he caught once again the slightly odd feeling that there was something just outside his field of vision, trying to get his attention. He tried to see the journal in his mind's eye and then there it was.

> 'I relaxed myself and allowed all Thoughts to fly from my head so that there would be Peace and Tranquillity within. And then again I did hear its Voyce calling unto mee sayinge "Listen."'

Well, thought Cornelius, it's worth a go. It's no stranger than anything else that's happened to me recently. Uncle was sure he'd transported himself through the house once and it's a good enough explanation for what I thought I'd seen.

He made himself comfortable at the desk, closed his eyes and tried to clear his mind, but that was much more difficult to do than he'd imagined after all the events of the past couple of days. It brought to mind the old story about trying not to think about the word 'rhinoceros' when someone tells you not to. It's a Zen thing, he thought. One hand clapping, trees falling in forests, all that sort of stuff. His mind drifted back to the funeral and wondered why his uncle had chosen "Cool for Cats" to say goodbye with. He had a cat, didn't he, a big one. Black. Black cat. Name of what? What was its name? Joe something, was it? No, no good, can't remember, too long ago. Sitting in uncle's house. Top of the stairs. Warm. So warm. So drowsy…

"Hey!" said a voice.

Cornelius jumped and immediately became alert.

"Hello?", he said, tentatively.

Nothing. He gazed around the room but couldn't see who it was who might have spoken, if indeed, anyone had. He'd dozed off, obviously, and started dreaming. However, he decided to try again as he thought there could be just a tiny possibility he was on the right track. He settled back into the chair and closed his eyes and...

Nothing. The minutes slipped away, the room seemed to become very still. He started to drift, just on the edge of nodding off. He felt a warm, gentle cocooning as his body prepared for sleep. Suddenly, he was aware of a change but couldn't quite put his finger on what had just happened. His eyes opened wide but he remained completely relaxed. Something in his mind had just come alive, some sort of block had finally disappeared and he could think clearly for the first time in a long while. He closed his eyes again and tried to take stock of this new feeling. Was it worth asking the question again?

"Hello? Is there anybody there?" he said, with a half smile. As soon as he said it he felt stupid. It wasn't a séance. There was another few seconds of nothing before he heard a voice.

"Hello? Finally! I've been trying to get through to you for ages. You humans have got so much rubbish floating around in your head, it's like trying to shout through granite. If I actually had a throat it would be completely hoarse by now."

"What?" Once again he opened his eyes and looked around the room seeing no-one. Feeling excessively foolish and still half-believing the voice to be part of his dreaming state he spoke again.

"Hello?"

"Yes, I'm still here!" The voice sounded very grumpy.

"Excuse me," said Cornelius, "but who exactly might you be?"

"Ah. Exactly, eh? Now there's a story. Let's just say that at the moment I am the book you see before you. Not quite as straightforward as that, of course, but there's no need to rush things, especially given how long I've been waiting to have a decent conversation with someone. For now, you can call me Euclid. Oh, and by the way. There's no need to actually talk. In fact, it would be much better, given your current predicament, that you didn't. Just sub-vocalise, say the words in your head, and I'll hear you. No-one can hear me, either, so it's just our little secret."

"I can't believe I'm having an off-air conversation with a bloody book. Am I asleep?" he thought. Cornelius stood, stretched and yawned expansively. "It's been a long and stressful two days. In a minute or so I'll probably wake up in my own bed. Or perhaps not." He stood, to prove to himself he wasn't dreaming.

"If you want to wake up in your own bed you're going to have to bring your attention to bear on how you're going to get out of this room, for a start," said Euclid, tartly.

Cornelius jumped, as the words had been much clearer that time.

And now a bloody book is shouting at me! he thought. That's just perfect.

"And how exactly am I going to do that?" I'm talking to a book, I'm talking to a book. The words kept repeating themselves in his head.

"Well, if you'll just shut up and give me a minute, I'll explain. We're going to have to act fast before someone interrupts us."

"Do you mean to say you really can get me out of here?", asked Cornelius, sitting again and wondering if he'd lost the plot.

"Yes, if you'll listen and let me get a word in," replied the book testily.

Cornelius began to wonder what he'd done to deserve this, beyond all the events of the past few days, to be snapped at by a bad-tempered copy of The Elements of Geometry.

"I am not bad-tempered," said Euclid, "just a little impatient. After all, I have been waiting over four hundred years to have a decent conversation with someone who can actually hear me and just when I thought I'd managed it I end up with a babbling idiot."

"Whoa!", replied Cornelius, "can you hear everything I think? Isn't there a private bit you don't get access to?"

"Yes, but that's something you need to practice. You'll soon get the hang of it. Meanwhile just stay very quiet for a minute or two while I explain how we're going to get you out of this dump."

"You can do that?"

"I told you! Yes!"

"Well, lead on, Macduff," said Cornelius, sarcastically.

The conversation was broken by the sound of the door opening and the magic seemed to disappear as he became aware once more of his surroundings. The taciturn Mr West entered the room and walked over to where he was sitting

. He sighed heavily, hoping fervently he would be able to make contact with Euclid again, desperate to believe the whole episode had actually happened. West stood before him, a faint smile on his thin lips.

"My boss wants to know how you're getting on."

"As I told him this morning, I don't have a clue what I'm supposed to be doing and nothing's changed since then. This is a complete waste of both my time and his and I insist you let me go now. If he wants the book so badly tell him to make me a reasonable offer and it's his. Then I can go back to a normal life without having people like you continually knocking on my door and drugging me."

West narrowed his eyes. "The boss told me to tell you that if you don't come up with what he wants by this evening there'll be unpleasant consequences. Not for you, but I'm sure you wouldn't want your girlfriend to be..." He paused for a second, "inconvenienced."

"What do you mean by that?" shouted Cornelius, rising swiftly to his feet. "You'd better not do anything to hurt her."

"Up to you then, isn't it?" said West, with a thin smile. He turned and left the room.

7.

"Well," said Euclid, "we'd better get started, but first you need to calm down. You can't do anything in your current state."

"Calm! How do you expect me to be calm? You heard what he said. They're going to do something nasty to Angela if I don't give them what they want and how can I explain that it involves talking to a book!"

"Cornelius! Sit down, control your breathing and listen to me. I told you I'm going to get you out of here but you can't go anywhere unless you're perfectly relaxed. What we're about to do is not like hopping on a bus. It requires belief, concentration and a large dollop of inner peace. People have been known to disappear permanently attempting what I'm about to teach you so you need to pay attention."

Cornelius' heart rate went up another notch. "Disappear! Bloody hell, you really know how to make a person relax, don't you? Disappear where? What are you trying to get me to do?"

There was a longer pause than Cornelius felt comfortable with before Euclid replied.

"I'm not saying another word to you until you sit down and do as I say. If you want to get out of here you need to follow my instructions to the nth degree. Do I make myself clear?"

Cornelius stamped over to the window, banged a fist on the sash, then turned back to the desk. He let out a sigh, walked back to his chair and sat down. He stared at the book, marvelling that an inert object over 450 years old was his only hope of escape.

"Alright. Give me a couple of minutes. Although I don't understand how we're going to get out of here. There's only the one door and that goon is sitting behind it. The only way out of here would involve walking through the walls."

"Let me take care of the how, but first I need you relaxed. Everything will become clear. I'm sorry I mentioned people disappearing. It very, very rarely happens and even then we manage to get most of them back. Seriously, the dangers are extremely slight and even slighter if you're properly prepared for what's going to happen."

Cornelius arranged himself as comfortably as he could on the chair and breathed deeply until he felt his pulse slow down to something approaching normal. Euclid must have been monitoring him somehow as he began to feel a gentle probing in his mind.

"What's happening now?" he asked.

"I'm just making sure all the required neural pathways are connected and then we can begin. Place the book on your lap and close your eyes", said Euclid, quietly.

Cornelius did as he was told and was surprised to discover an array of vivid colours swirling around behind his eyelids.

"Are you doing that?" he asked.

"No. This is entirely your doing. I'll explain it all later, when we have a few moments. You can't actually see those colours with your optic nerve," explained Euclid, "they're on a far deeper level. What you need to do now is decide where you want to go. It has to be a place you're familiar with, somewhere you've been many times before, so you can visualise it with a good amount of detail. I suggest your home would be a good place in the first instance. It'll be a while before anyone realises you're gone from here and there won't be anyone there to see you turn up. We don't want to frighten the natives by having you appear suddenly in the middle of a shopping centre."

"Are you telling me I'm actually going to disappear from here and turn up at home?"

"Do you think it's not possible?"

"Well, I've spent the last half hour having a conversation with a book so I don't suppose anything should surprise me now."

"Keep concentrating on exactly where you want to be. When you've fixed on the place the colours will coalesce eventually into a representation of it. It might take a few tries before the image becomes fixed."

As Cornelius concentrated on his living room, the colours slowly resolved themselves, showing him standing beside the sofa, looking towards the bookcase, the edges of the furniture shimmering in and out of focus. He continued to concentrate and after a few seconds more the image stabilised

"OK. I think I'm there. I can see my room quite clearly now."

"Good, now this is the tricky bit and this is where you need to concentrate the most. Look a little beyond the room until you can see the colours you started with. They'll be moving around the same as when you began. You need to hold both images in your head."

Agonisingly slowly, the swirling colours returned until he could see both them and the room.

"Now, you need to find the blue and then try to forget all the other colours"

"Forget the other colours? How am I meant to do that?"

"It's easier than you think, but if you're going to keep questioning everything we can always stay here."

"Alright, alright. Keep your hair on. I'm just saying, that's all. Not as easy as it sounds." He tried to do as he was told and to his surprise, after a few moments the other colours subsided.

"Oh," said Cornelius, surprised, "I can see various blues," said Cornelius, "do I need to pick any specific one?"

"The darkest blue, the one that looks the closest to black. Can you see it?"

There was just a small area, no bigger than the dial of his clock on the bookcase.

"Okay, what now?"

"Now you must channel all your energies into that one colour. Again, there's no rush. Just take it steady."

He focused on the dark blue spot and it slowly grew bigger until it became the only colour he could see wherever he looked in his room. It was an odd feeling, being able to see his room as clearly as if it was a bright, sunny morning and at the same time looking into the deepest blue he could imagine.

"I think I've got it."

He felt the odd itch in his mind he'd come to recognise as Euclid.

"Just checking. Yes, I think you're there. Now we get to what you might call the magic. What you have to do now is stand, then imagine yourself walking forward. You just need to move a couple of steps. Then open your eyes."

On hearing the word magic Cornelius' heart suddenly started to beat a little louder.

"Careful, now. Let yourself relax again and when you're ready, do what I said."

He stood, clutching the book to him like a lifebelt, walked forward in his mind, one step, two. Suddenly, he sensed a change in the atmosphere and when he opened his eyes he saw he really was standing beside his sofa, looking at the bookcase. He looked down and noticed he was clutching the book to his chest.

"Did it work? Is this it?" He looked around him, disbelievingly.

"Nicely done, Cornelius. You're home."

He gave a huge sigh of relief, then promptly collapsed back in a heap on the sofa.

"That was brilliant! Thanks for getting me out of there."

"My pleasure," replied Euclid.

"But how did you do that?"

"I don't think now is the time for questions. I promise you, I'll answer all your questions but for now let's just concentrate on staying ahead of West and his cronies."

""Yes, agreed, but first, I think I need a cup of tea."

Later, after a fortifying tea, Cornelius decided he needed to leave his flat before West and his gang came looking for him. He had no idea where they had taken him, but judging by the quietness and the size of the grounds it was most likely somewhere outside London, so he reckoned he had a little time before anyone got to him. Plus, they might not even realise he'd gone yet.

He dressed, wishing he had time for a shower, but thankful he was out of his pyjamas. A query to Euclid as to whether he could take anything with him if he jumped again was answered in the affirmative. Anything he was holding onto would automatically stay with him so he stuffed another set of clothes hurriedly into his overnight bag. He was pleased to see none of his other belongings had been removed, so he packed his laptop and phone charger.

He checked his phone and saw there were a lot of messages, mainly from Angela but also a few from Ruth and one from Mr Singh. He decided to ignore them all until he had time to deal with them and placed his phone in his pocket along with his wallet. Then he remembered the journal and the letter from his uncle. He could find neither, which was puzzling because he was sure West didn't have them. And then he realised his keys were also missing.

"We really need to be moving, Cornelius," said Euclid. "Do you have any idea where you're going to go?"

"I think we'd be safe at my Aunt Lucinda's for a little while so we should have time to get our breaths back." He realised he was treating Euclid as another human being. "Er, I mean, until I get *my* breath back. It's over two hundred miles away so they won't think to look for me there. Can we go that far?"

"Of course, as far as you like, as long as you can visualise it correctly."

"OK. I'm almost ready." The mystery of the notebooks and keys would have to wait. Five minutes later Cornelius stood by his sofa with the bag in one hand and the book in the other and readied himself for another jump.

"I was just wondering. This thing about people disappearing."

"Don't worry. I never should have mentioned it. You did fine last time. Just do exactly the same again and you can't go wrong."

"Nevertheless –"

"Let's save the explanations until we have a bit more time, shall we?" said Euclid, tersely.

"Right. OK. Yes, let's go."

With his second attempt the process became a little easier. Two minutes later the flat was empty once more.

At about the same time, Ruth decided she couldn't stay at work a moment longer. She let Mr Singh know she was leaving early then headed out of the door and, to her near disbelief, managed to flag down a taxi. The usual early evening crawl had already started and it took nearly half an hour to do the three and a half miles to Cornelius' flat. From the cab she called Angela again and endured another strained conversation.

"Thank you very much for giving the police my number. Just what I needed, Inspector Plod bending my ear for half the afternoon when I had such a lot of work to get through. Jeremy was not happy, let me tell you." Jeremy was Angela's boss, not a pleasant man at the best of times. Probably just right for Angela, thought Ruth.

"Did you have his aunt's number?"

"Why you should have thought I had, I've no idea. Are you sure you should have reported him missing?" continued Angela.

"Well, yes, of course I should. No-one's seen him since yesterday afternoon and when I went round to his flat the door was open and his phone, his keys, and anything else he should have had with him were there."

"I wouldn't put it past Cornelius to go out and leave his door open. Like I said before he's probably found something incredibly interesting to do and everyone else can go hang. He'll walk back in as though nothing's happened."

"Perhaps you're right, but I thought I'd just nip round to his flat again and see if I can find his aunt's number. Maybe she knows what he's up to."

"I don't see why you should feel the need to go scurrying round there again." She paused, then hissed, "There's nothing going on between you two, is there?"

"Of course not!" shouted Ruth, "I'm a friend and I'm worried. I would think you should be worried, too."

"The only person who should be worried is Cornelius if he doesn't pick me up on time this evening. Tell him that when you see him." She hung up.

Ruth arrived at the flat forty-five minutes

after Cornelius had left. As soon as she entered she noticed the laptop and phone had gone. A quick check confirmed there was a dressing gown on the bed that hadn't been there before. There were no signs of the front door having been forced so she assumed Cornelius must have let himself in with a spare set of keys, then left again.

Puzzled, she sat down and tried to call him but the phone once again went straight to voicemail. How frustrating, she thought, but the good news was that he must be okay. She was just getting up to leave when the doorbell rang.

West entered the library with a mug of tea and was surprised by the obvious absence of Cornelius. Apart from the desk and chair there was nothing else in the room, nowhere Cornelius could be hiding. The door had definitely been locked, West still had the key in his hand. As a precaution he turned back to the door and locked it again before checking the locks on the windows, which were all intact, and making doubly sure Cornelius couldn't have hidden anywhere. There was no way out but through the door, which didn't seem possible as he'd been stationed in the room opposite with a direct view. Even making the tea wouldn't have taken him out of the line of sight.

He left the library and went to check the front and back doors, both of which were still locked. He ran up the stairs and checked the windows in each room, with the same result.

With a sigh, he made the call he was dreading, but couldn't put off any longer.

"Carfax."

"Hello, Mr Carfax, it's me, West. I'm sorry, sir, but Pye has gone. He's escaped."

There was a long silence before Carfax replied.

"How?"

"I don't know. He's just vanished into thin air. I took him in some tea a couple of minutes ago and he wasn't there. The room was definitely locked and the windows haven't been opened in years so he definitely hasn't got out that way. There's no other way into or out of that room."

"People don't just vanish into thin air, Mr West, so you'd better get looking for him. He can't have gone far on foot. He's wearing pyjamas and a dressing gown and he's got no money. You'd better hope he hasn't reached the village yet and talked some kind soul into giving him a lift somewhere. Send a couple of your lads to his flat, just in case he manages to make it back there somehow. He'll have to return there at some point to get some clothes."

"What if he's gone to the police?"

"That option wouldn't be in your best interests, Mr West." Carfax hung up.

West made a quick call to Dave Slinger, one half of the pair who had lifted Cornelius in the first place. He told him Cornelius had escaped and gave instructions to check out the flat, then keep it under observation.

"What about the girlfriend?" asked Slinger, "I thought we was supposed to be pickin' 'er up?"

"Forget about the girl for now. I need Pye back or I'm going to be in deep shit with the boss."

"Alright. I'll grab Jez and we'll 'ead over there now."

West spent the next thirty minutes driving at high speed around the lanes surrounding the house but had no luck. In the village he asked a couple of locals sitting outside The Wheatsheaf if they'd noticed a man in a dressing gown, but they were no help. He drove around for another half hour before giving up, returning to the house to wait for what he hoped would be good news from Slinger, who, at that moment had just rung the doorbell at Cornelius' flat.

8.

Ruth opened the door, fully expecting to see Cornelius, only realising her mistake when two large men pushed her back inside. One of them grabbed her roughly and clamped his hand to her mouth.

"No screams an' we won't hurt you," said the other man as he closed the door behind him. "Let's all calm down and we can wait until lover-boy turns up. What do you say, sweetheart?"

Wide-eyed with fear and shaking, Ruth nodded her assent. The one holding her pushed her along the hallway into the living room and forced her down onto the sofa before finally removing his hand and sitting down next to her. He smiled and blew her a kiss, which frightened her even more. The man sitting beside her had dark curly hair and a mullet. He was tall and wiry, with wide brown eyes. She thought he looked a little mad.

Behind her, the other one was punching numbers into his mobile. He was also tall, but his fair hair was balding and he looked like a rugby prop gone to seed. In her mind she christened them Fatboy and Slim.

"Hello? Yeah, it's me. We're in the flat... Yeah, I know what you said but we checked it out and didn't think anyone was in, then a few minutes after we got back in the car to keep watch we saw this girl goin' up the stairs. Well, we followed 'er up to see where she was goin' and she took some keys out and opened his door, so we thought, Hello, that's 'andy. It's the girlfriend."

He paused while he listened to the voice on the other end, then continued, "Yeah, I tried to get 'old of yer but it went through to voicemail, so we decided to give 'er a knock an' see what was 'appening, an' well, 'ere we are. What do you want us to do?" He paused again, then said, "Yeah, alright," and hung up.

"Give us your phone," said Fatboy, "we're going to send your boyfriend a quick text."

Ruth shook her head. Fatboy slammed his hand down on the coffee table and shouted, "Now!" She handed him the phone.

"Passcode?"

She told him. It might have been his idea of a quick text, but he spent a couple of minutes typing it out, one-fingered, using the backspace key more than once to correct himself. The text finally read that they had Cornelius' girlfriend at his flat and he'd better get himself over pronto, otherwise things could get nasty.

"Right," he said to the other man, "we sit and wait for now. You," he pointed at Ruth, "be a good little girl and go and make us a couple of coffees. Milk and two sugars."

She did as she was told and came back from the kitchen a few minutes later.

"The milk was off. I had to throw it away. You'll have to have it black." It was a lie, but a little victory.

After the initial shock, Ruth had calmed down a little and was furiously trying to figure out what was going on. Unless the police had returned and taken his phone and laptop, which was unlikely, Cornelius must have got away from these people and been to the flat to pick them up. So where was he now?

"Back on the sofa!" shouted Fatboy. She sat back down beside Slim, trying to keep as much distance from him as possible.

"Have you lost him?" she asked.

"Yeah, for now," said Slim, "but he's only been gone about an hour so he must be on his way here. Stands to reason, yeah? He's only wearing his pyjamas and a dressing gown." He laughed at the thought.

"Shut up, Jez," said the other.

"So I assume you're the ones who kidnapped him in the first place?"

Neither of them answered. Fatboy sat in a chair by the window, keeping a look out. The one she now knew as Jez had produced a copy of the Sun and was going through the racing pages, mouthing the names of the runners as he read.

Ruth bided her time, until about half an hour later, when she said, "So when you carried him off did you take his phone as well?"

Still no answer from either of them.

"Only, it was there on the table earlier today, along with his laptop." They looked at her, quizzically.

"Well, they're not there now are they? And if Cornelius hasn't been back to the flat yet that must mean the police have taken them."

"Why would they have them?" asked Jez.

"Because I reported him as a missing person earlier today. I met them here when they came round."

"Bollocks," said Fatboy, disbelievingly, "they have to be missing twenty-four hours before you can report 'em as missing."

"You know, that's what I thought, but apparently not. Google it, if you like."

"Well, so what if they 'ave been round, clever-arse. They're not 'ere now, are they?"

"You're not very bright are you?" said Ruth, with a smile. "You've sent a threatening text to his phone, which is in their possession. It won't take them long to find out where it was sent from."

"Oh, shit," said Fatboy, taking Ruth's phone out of his pocket and turning it off.

"A bit late for that," she said.

"We've got to get out of here, now!"

"Are we taking her with us?" asked Jez.

There was a sudden crash from the kitchen. Everyone turned to the source of the noise.

When Cornelius jumped from the flat he'd visualised the garden at the back of Aunt Lucinda's house. He reasoned that he couldn't just materialise in her house as this might cause her a bit of a shock. He peered in through the kitchen window and, seeing her at the table enjoying a cup of tea and a slice of cake, rapped gently on the window. Lucinda looked up, the cake halfway to her mouth. On seeing her nephew her eyes widened. She rose from the table and let him in.

"What on earth are you doing peering through the window, Cornelius? Come to that, what are you doing here at all? You never told me you were coming." She noticed the bag in his hand. "Are you staying?"

"Bit of a long story, Aunt Lu. The thing is, since you gave me that book I've had a bit of a torrid time." He paused. "Any chance of a cup of tea and a bite to eat? I'm starving. I've had not had much today."

While his aunt made him tea and whipped up an omelette he started to tell her what had been happening to him, from the time he'd left her at his uncle's house to when he'd been locked in the library. He wasn't sure what to tell her about the book and thought it best to broach the subject carefully, in case she thought he'd gone completely mad.

He took a couple of mouthfuls of the omelette and a sip of tea, then carried on.

"You know the letter Uncle Sedgewick left me? Well, it turns out he thought this book," he gestured at Euclid on the counter by the sink, "could talk."

After a short pause, he added, "It turns out he was right."

Aunt Lucinda eyed him levelly while he continued filling up with omelette.

"When I say talk, I don't mean it actually speaks. It, er, talks in here." He pointed to his head. "Not everyone can hear it, apparently. Something to do with having the right connections in the brain. You either can, or you can't, if you see what I mean."

"Are you telling me you've already discovered the thing your uncle was searching for? Good God, Cornelius, that was quick. He spent decades with that bloody book and he never cracked it but you've done it in, what, two days? Good job he's no longer with us, he'd have been miffed as buggery."

Cornelius smiled.

"But why have you come all this way to tell me? Couldn't you have just rung?"

"I know you're going to find this a bit difficult to believe, but five minutes ago I was in my flat."

He explained the events of the last couple of hours, while she stared at him, mouth open. When he'd finished he said, "I know this sounds like magic but believe me, it's all true. What do you think?"

"I think," said his aunt, "I need another cup of tea."

"Good idea," he said, "make that two. And a piece of cake, please, if there's any spare."

After she'd made the tea she placed a piece of cake before him then sat back down.

"When you say the book talks to you, what exactly do you mean? Is it someone communicating to you through the book?"

"Honestly? I haven't got a clue. I've not had a minute to myself all day. As soon as I know something you can be sure I'll pass it on. I've got a huge pile of questions I want answering myself, when I get the chance."

"I remember when Sedgewick first got his hands on that book after your father died. He was always a bit dotty, but highly intelligent. I never did find out exactly what work he did for the government but I do know he wasn't just a paper-shuffler. Anyway, once he had the book in his possession everything else just fell by the wayside. One time there was a big upset at work about some missing papers and soon after he told me he'd been asked to retire, which he did, because he said that would give him more time with the book. He used to drive me mad, talking about it and what would happen if only he could crack its secret. He was convinced it had some magical properties. He kept raving on about Maccabeus' notes being the key. Then he started buying all the chemical equipment. He was convinced the answer would be revealed to him in the form of some experiment or other. I never did understand how. Just one more bright idea he'd had, I suppose. That would have been around the time I first took you to stay with him. Ooh, I've just had a thought. It couldn't be Maccabeus talking to you, could it, through some sort of time thingy?"

Cornelius looked across the table at his aunt, surprised such a thought could even cross her mind. Mind you, no worse than what he'd just told her.

"No, it would have said if it was Maccabeus, rather than getting me to call it Euclid. It seems a bit too knowing to be a seventeenth century ancestor. It's more modern, somehow. I'm not quite sure how to describe it. Anyway, carry on."

"Where was I? Oh yes. Soon after that he seemed to lose interest but then there'd be a flurry every couple of years. He'd ring me up, sometimes in the middle of night, telling me he thought he'd solved some part of the mystery, but nothing ever came of it. I found out he wasn't well about six months ago when I got a call from the hospital in Barnes. They told me his housekeeper had arrived at the house and found him sitting at the bottom of the stairs with a badly twisted ankle. He said he'd had a dizzy spell and taken a tumble. They rushed him off to A&E and kept him in for a few days while the doctors ran some tests. They diagnosed a mild stroke.

"When he came out I arranged for him to have full time care but none of the carers lasted very long. He wasn't an easy man at the best of times and being a patient made him much worse. Eventually, about two months ago I took the job on myself and moved in with him.

Then, like I told you after the funeral, a few weeks before he died he made me take the book away and hide it, with instructions to pass it on to you. He told me your cousin Francis had been to see him, pestering him to sell the book to a client of his. Did you know Francis was a private investigator?"

"Yes. The last person, you'd have thought. He came to see me on the same mission."

"Did he? Sounds like his client might be the same man behind what's been happening to you."

"It would seem so."

"So what are you going to do now?"

"Haven't a clue. I've only got as far as thinking I had to get away from my flat and lie low for a day or two until I can figure out what's going on."

At that moment his phone beeped.

"Oh, bugger!" he cried, "I haven't had a chance to read any of my messages yet. They've been backing up since last night."

He checked his phone and saw all the messages from Angela and Ruth. He started looking though Angela's texts but they weren't particularly reassuring. There was a voicemail, informing him he needed to pick her up at seven instead of seven-thirty for the party. Then, more than a dozen texts asking him to confirm and threatening dire consequences if he didn't. The last, timed at four minutes past five, read, "Ruth thinks yv gone missing. I think yv gone walkabout. Better b picking me up at 7 or else!"

The texts from Ruth were fewer and less terse, apart from the last one. After an initial couple asking where he was and if he was alright he found himself reading the message her captor had sent.

'Were in ur flat with ur girlfriend. If you want her to stay looking pretty better come here quick. Don't call the law no funy business'

"Oh, shit," he exclaimed, "the people who kidnapped me are holding Ruth at my flat and they want me to go there, or else."

"Who's Ruth?"

"She's a work colleague, but why is she at my flat? The man at the house threatened to hurt Angela if I didn't do what they wanted so why are they calling Ruth my girlfriend? I'm confused."

"What are you going to do?" asked Lucinda.

"I'll have to do what they say and go back to the flat. I can't let them hurt her. She's got nothing to do with any of this."

"But you can't go bouncing in there without a plan. Why don't you call the police?"

"They said not to. I don't want to risk anything happening to her. If the police show up things might turn nasty. She might get hurt and it would be my fault."

"I can't see why you should think that."

"But I do, Aunt Lu. She must have gone looking for me because I haven't replied to any of her messages. We had some meetings planned for today and she was probably worried because I didn't turn up."

"I'll say it again. You can't go rushing in. You need to stop right now and think for a moment. You have no idea who these people are. They sound mentally unhinged."

"Yes, you're right. Let me consult with the book and see what it suggests."

He closed his eyes, more to stop his aunt talking than anything else.

"What am I going to do, Euclid?" he thought, "If I go back there with you we'll be back to square one except they'll be holding Ruth instead of Angela and I'll still have to give them something otherwise they'll hurt her."

"You don't have to take me back as the book. That's just a temporary housing. I can reside anywhere but I do need to be making physical contact for me to travel with you. Give me a moment while I transfer to your watch."

"So the book's just a book?"

"Yes, it always has been."

"So you could have left the book any time you wanted?"

"Well, yes, but it's not been as simple as that. Once we get this sorted out I'll tell you the full story."

"That would be very nice. Thank you."

"Don't thank me yet, we've got a bit to do first. We need a battle plan. Now, what's the layout of your flat?"

"As you enter from the hallway there's the bathroom on the left and beyond it is the living room. The bedroom's on the right by the front door and the kitchen is further down at the end of the hallway."

"Got it. He says "we" in the text so we'll have to assume there's at least two of them. And it can't be West because he couldn't possibly have got there yet. Let's hope there's no more. There's just the one main room so they've probably made themselves comfortable in there while they wait for you. They might have locked Ruth in your bedroom, so we should go there first. If she's there we can pick her up and return here and these people will be none the wiser. If not, we'll have to jump over to the kitchen and see if we can catch them off-guard. That's less of a distance than going from your bedroom and we'll need the element of surprise. As long as you're holding Ruth's hand and not her clothing we can bring her with us. All you have to do is walk through the door, grab her hand and we can be gone almost before they know it. Remember, we have the element of surprise."

"That's all very well," replied Cornelius, "but if Ruth's not in the bedroom and I have to get to the kitchen how am I supposed to snatch her in the few seconds before they figure out what's happening and then jump out? When we jumped from the flat to come here it took me a good five minutes of relaxation before I could move. I can't grab Ruth and just disappear. I'm going to need time to prepare."

"And you'll have it. If you have to jump to the kitchen, assuming no-one's in there at the time, you can take a few minutes to prepare again. All you have to do then is to hold off jumping until you've gone into the living room and got hold of Ruth. Remember, the step forward when you're about to jump is in your head. You just need to concentrate."

Euclid paused to let Cornelius take the plan on board, then said, "Are you ready?"

"No!"

"Come on, Cornelius. This is no time to waver about. You need to be a man of action."

"But I've never been a man of action. It takes me half an hour to decide what to pick from a menu."

"Do you want to rescue Ruth or don't you? I can't do it by myself."

"Okay, okay. I'll just need to let Aunt Lu know what's going to happen."

The exchange with Euclid had only taken a few seconds of real time and he found his aunt was still waiting for the answer to her question.

"I think we've got a plan," he said.

"We?"

"Yes, Euclid and I. That's his name. The book. Although I'm only assuming it's a he because the real Euclid was. We haven't had a chance yet to get better acquainted. Anyway, he's not in the book anymore, he's in my wristwatch."

"This Euclid. What is he?"

"At the moment, I haven't the foggiest idea. I've not had the chance to find out. Once I do, I'll bring you up to speed."

"Fine. Well, good luck."

"Thank you."

Cornelius stood there for a moment, looking lost.

"What do you do, just pop off? Or is it more like that squiggly stuff when they beam up in Star Trek?"

"There again, I've no idea. You'll have to let me know later, when I get back. I'd better leave the book here, if that's alright with you? It'll be safer with you for the time being."

"Of course."

He put the book on the table. His aunt picked it up and shoved it quickly into a drawer under the tabletop.

"With any luck I'll be in and out before anyone knows I've been there. I'll be fine, really," he said, with a certainty he didn't feel.

She took a set of keys from her bag and handed them to him

"Here, take these. They're the keys to Sedgewick's house in Barnes. You can't discount the fact they might know about me and come looking for you here. You're going to need a base to work from. You can come back here for your meals, though, if it helps, as long as you stay inside the house. Don't go back to your flat until you can find some way of getting these people off your back. Pop back later and let me know what happened."

"Thank you." He reached out and clasped her hands in his. She threw her arms around him and hugged him tight.

"I wish we'd never laid eyes on that bloody book. Be careful, Cornelius."

"I will, don't worry." They had a moment, aunt to nephew. "Now, I'd better get myself ready."

He sat back down, closed his eyes and breathed steadily for a few minutes as his aunt watched intently. Then suddenly, with no fuss at all, he wasn't there.

He materialised in his bedroom, looked around and realised Ruth wasn't being held there.

"Rats," he said, "we'll have to go with plan B."

"Remember what I told you, stay calm and concentrate."

"It's alright you telling me to stay calm. I'm not used to this sort of thing. Look at me, I'm shaking like a leaf."

He could hear voices from the living room, one he recognised as Ruth's. After calming himself once more he went through the preparations then jumped to the kitchen. As he arrived he heard someone shouting, "We've got to get out of here now!", which unaccountably caused him to take a step back and hit the table, knocking off the empty milk bottle Ruth had rinsed out and put there a little earlier. It landed with a crash on the floor, shattering instantly on the ceramic tiles and putting paid to plan B.

"Jez, stay with her!" shouted Fatboy as he rushed into the kitchen to find Cornelius looking forlornly at the broken bottle on the floor.

""Ow the fuck did you get in 'ere?" he asked.

"I'm very light on my feet," said Cornelius, with a sickly grin. A large hand wrapped itself tightly around his left wrist. Another propelled him towards the living room.

9.

Cornelius was searched and relieved of his phone, then bundled through the doorway and dumped unceremoniously on the floor by the television, opposite Ruth and Jez on the sofa. There was a shocked expression on Ruth's face and a puzzled one on Jez's.

"How the fuck did 'e get in there?" he asked Fatboy, who shrugged.

"Don't matter, we've got 'im now."

Jez looked back at Cornelius and warned him not to say a word. Cornelius put his hands up in a placatory manner. He looked over at Ruth and mouthed "Hello." She mouthed it back while looking at him, quizzically. Jez got up, walked over to where he sat and hovered over him, menacingly.

"You try any more funny business and I'll give you a slap first, then I'll give her one just to make sure you've understood. Is that clear?" Cornelius nodded.

"Oy, Slinger. Was 'e hidin' in the kitchen the 'ole time?"

""Ow the fuck do I know?" replied the one now identified as Slinger. "'E's skinny enough. 'E coulda bin 'idin' in a cupboard."

"Wot? All this time?"

"Well. mebbe 'e was under the fuckin' table. "Oo gives a toss? Jus' fuckin' leave it, o'right? Yer gerrin on me tits."

Slinger disappeared into the kitchen. Jez sat back down next to Ruth and scowled at both of them. She sidled away from him as much as she could but he reached out and grabbed her arm. "I thought you said the cops 'ad the phone." With a little difficulty she managed to pry his fingers off.

"I thought they had," she replied, huffily.

"Well, 'ow come we've just taken it off lover-boy, 'ere? 'E can't have got 'ere before you. We only got told 'e was missing about an hour ago."

She frowned. "Don't ask me. I'm just as surprised as you are."

"And where did you spring from? There was no-one in the kitchen when we got here." Cornelius looked at Jez but remained silent.

"There's something funny going on 'ere," said Jez, obviously now in a foul mood.

There was silence for a few more minutes. Cornelius brooded, wondering what to do next.

"Well," said Euclid, "to coin a phrase, that went well."

"I can do without the sarcasm. How was I to know there was an empty milk bottle on the table? It wasn't there the other day."

Slinger, who had been in the kitchen talking to West, came back into the room.

"We've to keep 'em 'ere 'til Mr West arrives, then 'e'll decide what's going to 'appen next. 'E sez 'e'll be 'ere as soon as 'e can."

"Christ, Slinger, I 'ope 'e 'urries up," said Jez, "I'm bloody starvin'. I ain't 'ad nuffin' since breakfast. What about popping out to get a bite to eat? There's a McDonald's on Highbury Corner."

"Yeah, okay. I'll go. You stay here and look after these two. You might need this, just in case."

Slinger pulled a gun from his jacket pocket and handed it to Jez. Pointing at Cornelius, he said, "Mr West wants 'im in one piece. 'E didn't say anything about 'er." He looked at Cornelius meaningfully then back at Jez. "You want the usual?"

"Yeah."

Slinger left the flat, slamming the door with a bang.

There was even more silence after he'd gone, then Cornelius said, "Sorry, Ruth, I've really messed this up, haven't I?"

"Not your fault. Thanks for trying to save me. It was very brave."

"Don't worry. I'm sure we'll get out of this okay."

"I wouldn't put money on it," said Jez, "now shut it, before I lose my temper."

"Any ideas, Euclid?" thought Cornelius.

"Well, the odds are slightly more in our favour with one of them out. I think I might have something that would work for us, but you'd have to be quick off the mark, no knocking things over this time."

"Alright, I'm sorry!" replied Cornelius, testily. "There, does that make you feel any better? What's the plan?"

"First of all I need you to make sure chummy here is looking towards your watch."

"Chummy? Where *do* you get your vocabulary from? The Sweeney?"

"Where I learned your preposterous language is not moot at the moment. You need to get yourself prepared to jump out of here. I suggest we go to your uncle's house for now. It might not be safe to come back here for a while. Then we can take stock and plan our next move."

"You're enjoying this, aren't you?"

"I've done nothing but sit on shelves for a few hundred years. What do you think? Now, are you ready?"

"I hope so. You're going to have to give me a few minutes to relax again."

"Fine. When you're ready, let me know. Don't leave it too long. We don't want the other one to come back."

Cornelius settled himself as best he could and waited until his heart was chugging at a moderate speed. He wondered if it would ever return to its normal rate.

"OK. I'm ready," he said, finally.

"Good. The important thing is to keep your eyes tightly closed. Make sure you can find Ruth's hand. When I tell you, put your hand up to your face and make sure your watch is pointing directly at Chummy. Shout out as loud as you can so he looks directly at you, then jump up and grab Ruth."

"Shout out?"

"We're trying to create a distraction. Just do as I say."

"Yes, master," replied Cornelius.

He relaxed as much as he could and concentrated his mind on the landing outside his uncle's study, the one where he'd sat all those years ago as his uncle came rushing up the stairs, clutching the book to his chest. He felt Euclid gently probing to make sure everything was right, then heard him say, "Now!"

He screamed. Jez and Ruth turned to look at him and an instant later there was a blinding flash of light from his watch. Even with his eyes closed tightly he could still see it. He reached over and grabbed Ruth's hand, then they were gone.

Cornelius was still screaming when they appeared outside his uncle's study. He opened his eyes and through the blind spots caused by the sudden explosion of light he noticed there was a problem. He could see Ruth next to him, holding his hand and screaming along with him. Unfortunately, Jez was holding Ruth's other hand. He must have reached out and grabbed it as the light blinded him. He still held the gun in his other hand but he let go of Ruth and used both fists to rub his eyes.

Sensing rather than seeing that the door to the study was open, Cornelius took the opportunity to push Ruth through it to safety and closed it, crying "Trust me!" as he did so. Jez shouted behind him, "What the fuck was that! I've gone blind!"

Cornelius turned back to Jez and, without really thinking about what he was doing, grabbed hold of the hand holding the gun and tried to wrestle it from him. Jez's reaction was to tighten his hold on the gun but this led to him pulling the trigger and a shot whistled close by Cornelius' left ear, almost deafening him. A scream came from Ruth as, with his other hand, Jez instinctively pushed him away. He let go of Jez, who took a step back in his efforts to disentangle himself. His foot went down onto nothing and he tumbled over backwards down the stairs, finally coming to rest in a heap at the bottom.

Cornelius' vision still hadn't fully returned so it took a few seconds of concentrated looking to see Jez wasn't moving. He ran down the stairs and kicked the gun away from Jez's open hand, then checked to make sure he was still breathing. He became aware of Ruth repeatedly shouting out his name.

"Coming!" He kicked the gun into the living room and closed the door, then ran up the stairs and into the study where he found Ruth backed against the window, hands frantically rubbing her eyes, sobbing, "Cornelius! Where are we? What's happened? Was that a gunshot?"

He reached out and took her hands in an effort to calm her down.

"It's alright. Relax. You're safe now. We're at my uncle's house in Barnes. It should have been just the two of us, but Jez came along for the ride. Thankfully, he's out for the count."

"Was that a gunshot?" she repeated.

"It was, but he missed me. I was trying to get the gun off him and in the struggle he missed his footing and fell down the stairs."

"But he shot at you!" Ruth screamed, terrified.

"Yes, but it's fine. He didn't hit me."

"What do you mean, it's fine? Of course it's not fine, it was a gun!"

As she was saying this she looked around, taking in her surroundings for the first time. She continued rubbing her eyes and looking around, not being able to work out where they were.

"But I don't understand. How did we get here? We were in your flat. Where are we now?"

He told her again.

"I still don't understand. How can we be here when we were there?"

"Er, you're not going to believe this –." He trailed off.

There was a silence while Ruth finally digested what Cornelius was telling her.

"Is this about your uncle's book?" she asked, in a voice that had just about stopped shaking.

"Yes. How did you know?"

"I was at your flat earlier today, trying to find out where you were. I was worried about you. I mean, we all were, at work. Mr Singh said I should go to your flat and check you were alright." She bit her lip. It was only a small white lie, she told herself. "I found your front door open so I went in. I noticed your uncle's letter behind the clock. I called the police and reported you missing and they said they'd send a couple of officers round. I know I shouldn't have done but while I was waiting for them to arrive I, er, I read the letter from your uncle. Sorry."

"No, don't be sorry. It makes things easier to explain."

"It all sounded so far-fetched. I've also got the journal. I found it under your bed. They're in my bag. Oh!"

"What's the matter?"

"My bag's still in your flat. And your keys are in it."

"I was wondering what happened to those. Well, never mind that now. When the other one gets back he won't be able to get in. How are your eyes?"

"Not too bad, considering. Luckily, I'd just closed them for a few moments because I could feel a headache coming on. It seems to have gone now, though. That's surprising."

"Sorry, I didn't know what Euclid was going to do. He just told me to get ready to move while he caused a distraction."

"Who's Euclid? Oh, you mean the book. Where is it? Where's the book?"

"Bit of a tale to tell. It's not really about the book. He's... Look, I'll explain later. First of all, I've got to work out what to do with Jez. I'm going to have to get him out of here before he wakes up, then get you to safety. Wait for me in the study. Lock the door if you want. I'll be back in a few minutes."

"What are you going to do?"

"Jez mustn't know where he was when he was here, if you see what I mean?"

"Be careful." She caught his hand as he turned.

"I will."

He went back down the stairs.

Ideally, Cornelius wanted to drop Jez off at a police station but that would involve explanations he was in no position to give. Wherever he chose to take him, he was going to have to do it quickly and it had to be somewhere where no-one would see two people materialise out of nowhere.

With a smile, he thought of the penguin pool at Whipsnade Zoo. It was half past six so the zoo would be closed. There might still be a keeper around but he'd have to chance it. He had a yearly pass for the zoo and he liked to go up there at weekends if he needed to think about his work. Watching animals was very calming, especially the penguins, and he could clearly see in his mind the location by the pool where he usually sat. When Jez woke up it would be a good ten minute walk from there back to the entrance, where he would then have to explain why he was still in the park after closing time.

"You're about to do a double jump," said Euclid. "You're getting quicker at preparing yourself now so there shouldn't be any problems but make sure you take your time on the way back."

"Will do. And thanks."

"For what?"

"For getting us out."

"Don't mention it."

He took Jez's wallet and phone and placed them on the console in the hallway, then took his shoes off and threw them behind him. No point making it easy for a man who'd been waving a gun around a few minutes since. Let's see how you get on without money, shoes and a phone, he thought. He readied himself, took hold of Jez's hand and vanished.

A couple of minutes later he was back at the top of the stairs. Now to get Ruth sorted, he thought. She hadn't locked the door of the study so he walked in, to find her sitting with her back to him at the huge desk, staring out of the window, presumably still trying to make herself believe she was no longer in Highbury. She was almost hidden by the piles of papers that had more than likely been there since his very first visit.

"Ruth, it's me," he said as he entered, "are you okay?"

She spun round in the chair and nodded at him. "I think so. I've still got some spots in front of my eyes but they seem to be going away. What did you do with Jez?"

"I thought he might fancy a trip to the zoo. I took him to Whipsnade."

"Whipsnade? How? Why Whipsnade?"

"So he can appreciate the peace and quiet when he wakes up. I used to go there a lot when I first came down to London."

"I think you've let him off a bit lightly, considering."

"Ha! Considering he's got no money, no phone, no shoes and no idea how he got there!" He grinned. She broke into a smile and Cornelius enjoyed the moment, surprised to find his heart had started beating more vigorously.

"We're going to have to go back to the flat to pick up your bag and our phones," he said, "I'm pretty sure Jez's mate put them on the kitchen table. After that, I think I need to get you home." After a pause, he added "And then I think I'm going to go to sleep for a couple of days."

"Well don't forget you owe me an explanation for all this. You certainly know how to sweep a girl off her feet." She blushed, then rose from the chair, came over to Cornelius and kissed him on the cheek.

"Thanks, Cornelius," she said in a quiet voice, "you're a true superhero."

"Don't mention it," he said with an embarrassed smile. "As soon as I know it myself I'll tell you the whole mad story. Unfortunately, you're second in line, as I've got to go back and update my aunt, who'll probably be worried sick by now. I was at her place when Slinger's message came through."

Then his jaw dropped. "Oh bollocks! Angela! I'm supposed to be picking her up at seven and it's nearly half-past. What's she going to say?"

"Can't you call her now and explain?"

He looked around, then rushed from the room and ran down the stairs to the console in the hallway, where in addition to Jez's things, he found the telephone. He lifted the receiver but it was dead. He rushed back up the stairs.

"The phone's been cut off. I'll ring her from my flat. I know she's going to be furious. She was counting on me."

"For God's sake, Cornelius, after what you've been through surely she can cut you some slack."

"You didn't read the texts she sent me earlier. On top of everything else, I have to warn her she might still be in danger of getting kidnapped, once they work out she's my girlfriend and not you."

A frisson of something passed through her. "I didn't let on to them I wasn't. They just seemed to assume I was so I let them carry on believing it. She might be alright." She grimaced. "I wouldn't want to be the kidnapper who went after Angela," she added quietly, through clenched teeth.

"What do you mean?"

"I think they'd be biting off more than they could chew if they messed with her."

Cornelius stood in thought for a moment, slightly taken aback by what Ruth had said, realising it was probably true.

"Anyway," he continued, "I still have to phone her, regardless. Give me a minute or two to settle myself, then we'll go back to my place."

When he was ready he reached out and took her hand. She looked up at him and their eyes met, causing Cornelius to look away. What would Angela say, if on top of everything else she found he'd been holding hands with another woman? He sighed.

"Ready?" he said.

"Ready."

10.

Dave Slinger returned to the flat with the takeaways and rang the bell. Getting no answer he tried again, then a third time, accompanied by a few bangs on the door while he shouted Jez's name. When he still didn't get a reply he called his mobile. No answer.

"What the fuck are you playin' at?" he shouted through the door. He banged again, waited a minute, then went back downstairs to the car, which by now had a parking ticket attached to the windscreen. He got in and dumped the food onto the passenger seat.

Shit, he thought, I'm going to 'ave to let Mr West know what's goin' on an I 'aven't got a clue meself.

He was just about to call when West's car pulled up on the other side of the road. He got out of the car and walked over. West rolled his window down.

"Blimey, you got 'ere quick," said Slinger.

"Less traffic than I thought there might be. Well? What's happening? Why are you standing out here?"

"I'm not sure what's 'appened, Mr West. That Pye geezer turned up and we got 'im quietened down nice an' sweet. We was 'ungry so I went out to get some grub an' when I got back I couldn't get back in. I was bangin' on the door about ten minutes an' I couldn't get no answer. Only thing I can think of is that they jumped Jez an' legged it, but I don't see 'ow. 'E's not the type to let a coupla civvies get the better of 'im."

"Oh, brilliant. Absolutely brilliant. So where's Jez now?"

"I dunno. I can't raise 'im. 'E must 'ave gone after 'em."

"So let me get this straight. Pye and his girlfriend have run off, we can't get into the flat and you've lost Jez. I don't fucking believe it. I give you a nice easy job to do and you blow it."

"I don't suppose there's any chance they're still in the flat?" said Slinger, hopefully.

"Well if they are they would have called the plod by now, wouldn't they? No, they've legged it alright. We'd better get off in case the cops turn up." West sighed. "What the fuck am I going to tell the boss. He'll be livid."

"Sorry Mr West," said Slinger.

"You fucking will be if we don't get them back. Clear off, go and get hold of your useless mate and find out what happened. Let me know as soon as you've got anything."

West wound his window up and drove off, leaving Slinger shaking. West was scary enough, but he knew very well that the boss, whoever he was, didn't have time for losers.

Back at the flat once more Ruth was surprised by how quick and seamless the transfer had been, as though she had done no more than walk from one room to the next. No weird noises, no flashing lights, just appearing as if by magic.

"How do you do that?" she asked.

"I'll tell you everything later, when I've sorted it out myself. All I can tell you is I had some outside help. Believe me, I'm just as bewildered as you are. I've not had five minutes to myself all day and I've still got so much to do before I can relax."

"Okay. Later then. I'll be looking forward to it."

They were relieved to find the phones on the kitchen table and Ruth's bag by the sofa. She handed over his uncle's letter and the journal.

"Why did you take the letter?" asked Cornelius.

"I don't know. I just thought it might be important somehow. After I'd read it I knew if someone else got hold of it they might make connections that you wouldn't want them to know. That's why I took the journal as well. It might have muddied things up with the police if they'd read it."

"Yes, thank you. It might have looked a bit weird for them to be reading about magic books."

"Oh, bugger! I'm going to have to call them, let them know you're okay. You're still listed as a missing person."

"No, hang on, don't do that. I don't think I could cope with the police just now, not after what's been happening today. Let's just leave it for now, give me a chance to get my breath back."

"Yeah, you're probably right. You deserve a good night's sleep after all you've been through."

"Not before I speak to Angela, though," he said with a sigh, "but let me get you home first."

"I've been meaning to ask. Can you go anywhere with, er, Euclid?" She felt odd, using the book's name.

"Apparently. The only requirement is that I have to have been to the location before so I can create an image of it to focus on. So, for me, not quite anywhere."

"Do you remember my flat, then?"

"Well, I hope so," he said with a grin, "otherwise we might end up in another universe!" He stopped grinning when he remembered Euclid's warnings about disappearing entirely. He thought it best not to mention the possibility.

When he finally got back to his uncle's house, after turning down offers of food and drink and promising to give her a call the next morning, he dropped his uncle's letter and Maccabeus' journal on the coffee table and flopped down onto what had been his uncle's favourite easy chair. He was exhausted but he knew he could no longer put off phoning Angela. He tried her number and it rang a few times before going to voicemail. He thought the pub where everyone was meeting must be noisy so he left her a quick message, apologising for not turning up and promising to fill her in the next morning with all the details of what had been happening to him.

He wasn't convinced it would be enough. It was a cop-out and he knew it. Very different to the way Ruth had reacted, he caught himself thinking, then realised he was being unfair on Angela. She hadn't been involved with everything that had been going on so had every right to feel aggrieved he hadn't been in touch.

"You ought to dump that one and take up with Ruth," whispered Euclid.

"Will you get out of my head! They're private thoughts!"

"I've told you, you need to work on it." Although Euclid didn't have a physical presence, Cornelius could tell he was doing whatever his version of grinning might be.

"Just leave me alone. It's been a long day. Two days. Whatever. And I still don't know who or *what* you are, but that's going to have to wait. I need a proper meal and a couple of drinks and I still have to phone Aunt Lu. She'll be worried."

There was no food in the house so Cornelius realised he was going to have to go and get supplies. As he walked to the front door he remembered the items he'd taken off Jez before transporting him to the zoo. He found the gun under the sofa and picked it up by inserting a pen into the barrel, so as not to leave fingerprints. In the kitchen He found a carrier bag and put that and the rest of Jez's belongings into it, then searched for the nearest police station. There was one not too far away, in Station Road.

At the police station he handed the bag to the desk sergeant, explaining he'd just found it in the street and it contained a wallet and some clothing. He didn't mention the gun. The sergeant thanked him and asked him to wait a second while he went into the back office to get a finder's form to fill out. Cornelius took the opportunity to slip away before any awkward questions could be asked.

He walked up to Church Road and bought enough food and drink to get him through a couple of days, along with a large Chinese takeaway to fulfil his immediate needs. Back in the house, he switched on the fridge and deposited the cold items. Luckily, the electricity hadn't been disconnected. He poured himself a large glass of wine and tucked into the takeaway.

He phoned Aunt Lu and put her mind at rest as he briefly brought her up to date with recent events. He didn't mention the gun. He could tell she was very nervous about what had been happening and he tried his best to calm her down.

"Really, I'm absolutely fine, just very knackered. I promise I'll pop over as soon as I can tomorrow morning. You can give me breakfast and in return I'll give you the full story."

"All right. You get yourself a good night's sleep, Cornelius and I'll see you in the morning."

After he'd hung up, he realised with a smile that the physical transference of matter between two points, something scientists had been researching for many years, one of the greatest gifts that had ever been bestowed on a human being, was now being thought of by him as 'popping over'. The phrase 'off you pop' had suddenly taken on a whole new meaning.

He looked around for his overnight bag, then realised with a groan he'd left it at his aunt's house. He couldn't face another journey back to his flat so he'd have to wear the same clothes again in the morning. Upstairs he found enough sheets and blankets to make up a bed in the room he'd had when he visited as a child. He didn't really fancy sleeping in his uncle's bed. After a quick wash and, as his toothbrush was also in the overnight bag he'd left at his aunt's, a good gargle, he finally drew the curtains against the evening sun and climbed into bed, dog tired.

"Euclid, we need to have a big talk tomorrow," he said, and promptly fell asleep. It was almost nine.

An hour later Dave Slinger reluctantly phoned West.

"Well?" he answered, tersely.

"I've just heard from Jez."

"And?"

"You're not goin' to believe this but he was arrested at Whipsnade Zoo. 'E's in the nick."

"What? Whipsnade? Why the fuck did he go up there?"

"'E 'asn't gorra clue. 'E sez there was a big flash of light at the flat an' after that everything was a bit 'azy. 'E remembers fightin' wiv Pye an' the next minute 'e's wakin' up wiv a fuckin' penguin givin 'im the eye through a fence. When 'e stands up 'e sees 'is shoes 'ave gone an 'is pockets is empty. The next minute there's a bunch of security guards turns up and grabs 'im so 'e belts one of 'em an' then they all pile in. They take 'im off an' put 'im in a room until the cops show up and cart 'im off. They've charged 'im wiv assault and trespass an' a couple of other things 'e didn't quite catch."

"Where is he now?"

"Luton police station. I phoned the brief but 'e sez there's nothin' 'e can do now until the morning."

West hung up, then just as reluctantly phoned Carfax to pass on the information, his ears still ringing from his earlier call with him.

"Interesting." said Carfax. "Our Mr Pye has hidden talents. He disappears from a locked room, then turns up at his flat forty miles away and overpowers one of your thugs, transports him to Whipsnade, rescues the girl and then disappears, all within the space of a couple of hours. This puts things into a different light. He's a lot more dangerous than I realised. Come to the office tomorrow morning at nine. Let's plan a little surprise, shall we?"

11.

When Cornelius woke the following morning he couldn't work out where he was. The room was in semi-darkness and seemed to be the wrong way round. His bed wasn't as wide as he remembered. He decided not to worry about it too much and drifted back to sleep again. Thirty minutes later he woke again with a clearer head. The events of the previous day slowly came back to him. He checked his watch and saw it was just before eight. He'd slept for almost eleven hours.

He dressed, went downstairs and made tea, then stared out at the long back garden, which stretched down to Barnes Common. A warm, clear Midsummer's Day in June, which meant it would probably be cold and wet by lunchtime.

I wonder what it's like in Bevagna right now, he mused. He remembered the house on the side of the hill, overlooking the little Umbrian medieval town, where his aunt had taken him a few years ago for a week's holiday. They'd stayed with friends of hers who had moved over there in the late 'nineties. It was a week of some of the best food he'd ever eaten, washed down with copious quantities of the local Sagrantino wine. He'd been meaning to return and explore further and hadn't yet got around to it. Or rather, he'd had no one to share it with.

I could just go and take a look, he thought. In fact, I can go anywhere I've ever visited before. The sudden realisation of what was now possible to him alone in the entire world caused a sudden light-headedness and he had to clutch at the window frame to keep from falling over.

"You've got a few things to sort out before you go swanning off to sunnier climes," said a voice.

"Will you stop doing that!" said Cornelius.

"If you will go leaking your thoughts all over the place I can't help but hear you," retorted Euclid. "I keep telling you, I haven't had a decent conversation in a couple of hundred years."

"And you're still not getting one until I've properly woken up. How do I screen you out? There are some things I'd like to keep private."

"Not so many now."

"Aaargh!" Cornelius shouted out loud.

"Alright, alright. I can't really do anything for you. It's something you have to practice for yourself. Try and imagine some sort of wall around your thoughts. If you want to speak to me open a door in the wall. See how that goes."

"Thank you. I'll work on it," said Cornelius without much conviction. "First though, I need to make a few calls. Then we must have our little chat and you can explain to me exactly who, or what, you are. After that we need to get to Aunt Lu's so I can shower, change and have breakfast."

"I'm looking forward to the chat," said Euclid, "but I don't think you're going to believe it."

"It was only yesterday I didn't believe in talking books. We've come a long way since then."

Euclid stayed silent.

He phoned Ruth to let her know he'd made it safely through the night. He could almost sense her smiling on the other end.

"What about the police," she said, "what do you want me to tell them?"

Another thing he had to deal with. He couldn't really put them off if they thought he was a missing person. He realised his story wouldn't make much sense to them but he had no other. Then there was Ruth to consider. She'd been kept a prisoner in his flat by two men, one of them wielding a gun. The police needed to know what had happened.

"I think we'll have to go in and let them know what happened at the flat, although we're going to have to edit the details slightly. I'll tell them I was kidnapped but managed to escape and when I finally got back to my flat I found you there but also that Jez and his mate were waiting for me. When the other one went out we managed to overpower Jez and escape."

"When you put it like that it all sounds a bit implausible, the two of us up against a couple of gangsters"

"That's the best I can do for the moment. Can you speak to the person you saw yesterday and arrange a time for me to go see him? In the meantime, I'll try and come up with a more convincing story."

"Okay, I'll call now and arrange something. What about work? You should give Mr Singh a call and ask for a few days off, to recover."

"Yes, good idea. Better do that now. He usually gets in around this time."

He called Mr Singh and apologised for not being in touch, that a few things had just got on top of him. After reassuring him he was feeling better, Cornelius arranged to take another couple of days off after the weekend, promising he would catch up on his return. He hadn't taken all of his holiday entitlement over the last year so Mr Singh had no qualms in giving him some time to make sure he was feeling fully himself again.

"Just make sure you come back fighting fit, Cornelius. Lots to do, you know."

"Yes, I know, Mr Singh. Thank you."

The next call was the one he was dreading, the call to Angela. Her phone rang a number of times before she finally answered. A harassed voice said, "What do you want, Cornelius?"

"Er, did you listen to my voicemail last night?"

"Yes, I listened but I was far too drunk to take much notice. Look, I'm in no fit state to listen to your sad excuses for not turning up last night. As far as I'm concerned that was the last straw. I realise now that I made a big mistake hooking up with you in the first place so I think we'd better call it a day."

"But, Angela, listen, it wasn't my fault –"

"I don't want to hear it, Cornelius. You know what last night meant to me but you'd rather go off on some wild goose chase. Well let me tell you, I'm not playing second fiddle to some old book. Goodbye, Cornelius."

"But –"

She hung up.

He sat looking at the phone for a minute or so, staggered at the unfairness of it all, then made one more call, to his aunt, to tell her he would be over for his breakfast and to expect him in her kitchen within the next hour or so, promising he would tell her the whole story, if he could understand it himself.

Then he settled himself into one of the comfy armchairs in the sitting-room.

"Right," said Cornelius, "chat time."

"I imagine you have quite a lot of questions by now," commenced Euclid, "so it would be better if I start at the beginning and tell you where I'm from, why I'm here and the events that led me to residing in Doctor John Dee's personal copy of Euclid's Elements for the last four hundred and forty-odd years. Leave the questions until I've finished or we could be here for quite some time."

"Fair enough."

"Before I start, I'd like to ask that you keep quiet about my presence, at least for now. There are a number of reasons why no-one should know I'm here. The reasons should become apparent."

"It would be nice to let my aunt know what's been going on, if that's okay," said Cornelius, "I think she deserves some kind of explanation after all these years. I'm certain she's not the kind to go spreading it around. I'd also like to let Ruth in on it as well, otherwise how am I going to be able to explain to her what happened yesterday? I think she has a right to know. They both believe by now that the book has been inhabited by some otherworldly force. Aunt Lu has seen me appear and disappear and Ruth has done some jumps. After everything that's happened it's going to be very difficult to explain any of that away."

"Very well, I'll allow those two, but no more. The boys back home might get a little miffed if they knew, but having been in contact with Lucinda and Ruth to some extent I think I can trust them to keep shtum."

"What? Shtum? Where exactly did you pick up that expression?"

"Are you going to stop me every five seconds?"

"I'm sorry. Please continue."

"Right, Thank you." After a pause that could only have been for dramatic effect, Euclid continued.

Euclid's Story 1

"I know you think I am probably an artificial intelligence of some kind, but you can forget that. Not even close. I have life, it just doesn't accord with anything your scientists have so far been able to explain. Not everything has to exist in only three dimensions, nor does life necessarily need to be carbon based. If you like, you can think of me as a mind without a corporeal presence. I could explain it by dragging in stuff about dark matter or dark energy but I'm sure you're much more interested in what I'm doing here, living in a book. When we have a little more time we can go into the nuts and bolts if you wish."

"Wait! You can explain dark energy and dark matter? That would be phenomenal. We've have been grinding our teeth over those things for years. This could change everything!"

"Whoa! Hold your horses, Cornelius. There's no way I'm going to explain anything in the detail you're hoping for, even if you could understand it. Getting to grips with how dark energy works makes quantum mechanics look as simple as learning that one plus one equals two. It's too big a technological leap and it would be impossible for you to explain away by saying you just stumbled on it by chance. I wasn't sent here to spill the beans, so you can't ask. If you're nice I'll give you a little pointer in the right direction, to get you started, but I have other things I need to sort out first. So, once again, can I continue, now?"

Cornelius sighed.

"Okay."

"Good. Please don't interrupt me until I've finished or we could be here all day."

Cornelius mimed zipping his mouth closed and Euclid began.

I arrived here from a planet which we call Farasta, approximately four hundred light years away. It circles a star in the Ophiuchus constellation, part of a multiple system of very young stars in the IRAS 16293-2422 cluster. It's very similar to Earth, although we are a touch lighter in oxygen, so you would need a little assistance with breathing should you ever visit.

There are two dominant life-forms on Farasta, one invisible, one not. I'm one of the invisibles, in case you hadn't noticed. Little joke. What we call ourselves can't be uttered by the human tongue, so to keep it simple, I'll refer to my own species as minds, as we have no physical presence in normal dimensional space. Each mind is part of a collective consciousness, acquiring and disseminating data, although we can each operate independently as and when required. We communicate with each other just as I am communicating with you now.

It has long been apparent that minds are not native to Farasta; we must have been placed there for some unknown reason, an experiment of some sort, perhaps. By what or whom, we simply do not know. Our memories go back to a point in history, our big bang moment, if you like, around three and a half thousand years ago, beyond which there is nothing but speculation. Somewhere in the galaxy there may be more of our kind.

We are unable to move very far unaided. For a while we were doomed to wander the planet, extremely slowly, incapable of interacting with any part of it. Our mode of travel involved hitching a ride with whatever animal happened to be passing, which meant we had little control over where we could go. Which brings me to the krai, a corporeal presence, similar in many ways to human beings. Suspiciously so, in my opinion, but that's a story for another day. The krai, and their ability to think creatively, became our saviours. They were present when our own records began and they very quickly achieved a level of consciousness where meaningful communication with them could be established, a process which we were able to refine. We helped them, they helped us. A happy accident? Probably not. One day we may know the truth. So together then, a mind and a krai form a symbiotic partnership.

In general, krai live for between seven and eight hundred years while we have a nominal lifespan of just over a thousand. As for dying, we never truly do so, but when our krai partners die we tend to retreat back into the collective. Eventually, even that small voice becomes silent, although its memories are always retained.

You are asking yourself, how do we replenish our numbers? I mentioned already about dark energy and matter. Collectively, we use this as a sort of breeding ground. We create ourselves, enough at a time so there is always an even balance of minds and krais.

Once we'd teamed up with the krai things became a lot easier for all concerned and in a relatively short space of time we had established a well-functioning society. Not without its troubles, to be fair, but all in all, a lot less bloody than the birth of your human civilisation. War between minds is unheard of. What would be the point? The krai, on the other hand, had to go through the territorial stage as part of their growing up process, just as you are still doing here on Earth, but theirs lasted only a few hundred years. Our melding managed to move them on, with just a few hiccups along the way. That's not to say there are no disagreements. Far from it. Factions exist on Farasta, just as they do here, but violence is never seen as the answer.

To the krai, we are their internet. We provide data processing and communication. In return, the krai offer the ability to physically connect to and interact with the world. An unforeseen, yet life-changing, bonus was the discovery by one pair that together they could teleport. What one pair can do is soon passed on to others. Within days our constricted world expanded massively in all directions.

The krai become aware of minds at quite an early age. They spend their childhoods learning how to use our resources and inevitably certain friendships are formed between those whose interests are of a similar bent. I know I said minds have a collective consciousness, but that doesn't stop us from being fiercely independent in our interests and enthusiasms. Upon reaching a certain age, analogous with your late teens here, krais and minds will start to pair up on a more formal basis. A mind can blend with any krai and we usually stay with the same krai for life. This is not through love, an emotion which has no meaning to us, simply a matter of practicality. At a later stage krais themselves will pair off, usually for life, to sort out the messy matter of procreation and child-rearing, not dissimilar to humans, but with much less angst.

My particular krai is called Tald. Like you, he can't see me but he is able to sense me in the same way as you do now. We inhabit the same space. Where he goes, I go. Intellectually, we are in many ways equals. My weaknesses are my krai's strengths and vice versa. Although each of us can exist separately, as I am doing now, true strength lies in our unity.

To keep things simple I'll refer to Tald as a male, although on Farasta things are a lot more fluid than they are here, even today, and certainly without all the accompanying hang-ups that you humans have to deal with. I came together with Tald just as he was finishing his initial schooling. Usually, minds and krai spend a couple of hundred years or so committed to whatever project takes our interest, in our case it was the exploration of new planets. On our return to Farasta he will pair off with one of his own kind and start his own family, after which we may either continue working together on new projects or just become involved in the day to day running of things in general.

As I said, a single mind cannot travel very far without assistance. Just jumping from the book to your wristwatch was an effort for me. Young krai are not born with the ability to jump from place to place. The distance they can travel alone is restricted by whatever transport is available. After pairing up with a mind, older krai are able, with our help, to jump anywhere on the planet, so there has not been the need to develop complicated transport systems.

Minds have no culture and we don't generate ideas. We are merely facilitators, but facilitators with an ambition. The discovery of our true heritage. On the other hand, the krai have impetus and look to the future. Together, we began to reach out for the stars.

We scanned the skies and came to the same conclusions as humans about the possibility of life elsewhere, but we discovered nothing for a very long time. Then, about a thousand years ago, we picked up signals emanating from a system about three hundred light years away, which finally confirmed that we were not alone. During this time we were focusing our attention on how to travel the vast distances required. We trod the same paths your scientists are doing now. We don't have a moon nearby so our first manned flight out of orbit took us to the moon of our nearest planet, a gas giant. It took just over a year. The first flight to the next nearest planet took nearly three. A lot of effort went into developing the drives in our spacecraft and eventually we achieved one eighth lightspeed. It was assumed we had gone as far as we could using velocity alone. We needed something a little quicker. The answer was, of course, the wormhole.

We are, by nature, a technological people. There is no religion on our planet, so we never had superstition holding back scientific research. Even so, it took nearly two hundred years before we managed to create and harness microscopic black holes that enabled us to establish stable wormholes between two points. I can tell by the turmoil in your brain that you want to ask questions. Have patience, please.

The first wormhole was opened between our planet and a spacecraft in a geo-stationary orbit no more than fifty miles above the planet. This went well, so we sent a ship to the planet we landed on earlier. You see what's coming next, I hope? There's no way you can make a wormhole exist remotely. Someone has to journey to the location of the desired exit point to create it. If our wish was to go to the stars, we still had to travel there by the usual, slow, method.

We were reasonably lucky in that the nearest star with a suitable planet for setting up a simple base was just two light years away. The first ship had a crew of two. It took eighteen years, most of it spent in suspended animation. Once there they set up a wormhole generator to create a travel portal back to Farasta. Their return journey was just like stepping through a door, almost instantaneous. They were welcomed back as heroes. A call went out for more volunteers and many answered, including Tald and myself. To our race, giving up a portion of our lives for such a project, anywhere up to a couple of hundred years, is no big thing. In fact, it is an honour to be allowed to participate.

That then became our modus operandi. Having identified a planet capable of sustaining life, or being able to be used as a hop to one that could, a vessel containing a krai and a mind would set off. When the planet was reached, the crew would undertake a survey. If uninhabited, a wormhole generator would be installed and a travel portal built. In the case of an inhabited planet like the Earth, the survey might take quite a few years before a decision would be made by the crew as to whether it would be safe to establish a station, or if it should be placed on a nearby planet, with a view to returning every so often to check on progress. Our prime directive insists that we must not interact with any civilisation until it has reached a technological level capable of accepting knowledge without causing harm either to themselves or to us.

After the survey the original crew would return home through the portal and be replaced, then the new crew would carry on from there to the next identified planet. In the meantime, any new uninhabited planet could be colonised simply by walking through the wormhole and setting up shop. By leapfrogging in this way we had managed, by the time I left Farasta, to set up permanent bases on thirty-two planets, with small way-stations on many more. That figure must by now be much larger, assuming all is still well back home.

By sending ships out in many different directions we ranged through the void. Years later, when we finally got to the source of the signals we had first detected, we found we were too late. That particular civilisation had died and the signals were residual, being sent from satellites and the like orbiting a planet that had been devoid of intelligent life for many thousands of years.

Eventually, we located another planet emitting signals and this turned out to be inhabited by a species calling themselves Allas, who were just breaking out of their own system. By the time we got to meet them, about fifty years before Tald and I left Farasta, the Allas had made contact with another species and were starting to build a trading association. We congratulated ourselves on our luck at finding not one, but two new species.

Our first contact with the Allas was benign and continued that way for a number of years. We traded technology with them and assumed we had discovered friends. Then, something changed. Perhaps a new regime, who knows? Without warning they turned on us. I suppose we were naïve, lulled by their apparent easy-going nature. Our background of almost permanent peace meant we were culturally unprepared for such deviousness in others. We simply hadn't realised they were in the throes of subjugating the other species they'd met. In a single day they attacked four of our colonies, killing everyone with whom they came into contact, hoping to gain access to our portals and so make their way to our home planet, where they no doubt expected to conquer us.

Fortunately for Farasta, the Allas had never been told that anyone wishing to travel through our portals could only do so if accompanied by a mind. When we'd entertained their trade delegations on previous visits we'd always gone through with them, our minds making the necessary preparations for their safety. It never occurred to us that we should tell them exactly how our systems worked. When they attacked us they assumed all they'd need do was step into one end of a gateway to our planet and out of the other. Approximately two thousand Allas entered the portals on the four colonies they'd attacked in a concerted effort to overwhelm us. They promptly disappeared, their molecules dispersed throughout the galaxy. Since then they have dogged our footsteps, seeking to capture an intact ship and make use of the wormhole-building systems each one carries. They still don't understand the extra refinement which would allow them to use our technology, but they have managed to create wormhole technology of their own, which is nowhere near as stable and can only be used over short distances. It is because of the Allas that I am now marooned here on your planet and Tald is missing, more than likely dead.

Earth is a world much like our own, with a similar atmosphere and climatic conditions, though with a slightly heavier gravity and a little more oxygen. Tald and I arrived in late 1580, having spent seventeen years travelling from an uninhabited planet orbiting Proxima Centauri. Our ship was quite small, with just enough space for comfort and an area equipped with a lab, for research. We also carried a small shuttle, accounting for about a third of its size, which could be used for trips to the surface.

Disappointingly, humans were not as far along the technological path as we had hoped, so it was our intention, after carrying out an in-depth survey over a number of years, to place a portal somewhere quiet, probably on one of Neptune's moons, which would enable us to return and check progress every now and then.

Europe became the focus of our investigation as it had the largest concentration of cities. We spent nearly a year in geo-stationary orbit over London, which we had chosen as our starting point. At first, we sent down tiny drones to record events from a distance. Then, when we felt confident enough, we visited, very discreetly, to get a first hand experience of life. This was not as straightforward as you may think.

As I mentioned before, a krai looks very similar to a human, so with a little work Tald could just about pass for a native of Earth, albeit one from a foreign country. Had we managed to return to Farasta I'm certain the similarities between krai and humans would have caused great surprise. Something to look forward to, I hope.

Standing at just over two metres Tald was much taller than the average person of the time but tales of giants were pretty much commonplace, so it would be no great difficulty for him to claim ancestry. The only major difference was his lack of human-like ears. Tald's were much smaller, so we managed to work up a couple of prosthetics. Even so, once we were walking among humans we were surprised by how many of them had various body parts missing, so the lack of a couple of ears would not have caused much comment.

Tald couldn't appear on the streets of London in a bright, clean spacesuit. At a time when England was alight with rumours of invasion anyone looking even slightly foreign was treated with great suspicion. Tald had to blend in somehow and for that he needed the correct clothes, so we devised a stratagem to acquire some but to do that we needed money, another unfamiliar concept.

The basis of currency in any land was gold. If you had enough of it, you could accomplish anything, so our first job was to find some. Not too difficult for us, as we understood the conditions in which it could be found and we were soon able to identify a number of places around the planet where gold was abundant. In addition, our shuttle was able to act as a very large metal detector, which made our work much easier. We needed to avoid people so we chose a site at what is now Coolgardie, in Western Australia, at that time undiscovered by Europeans. The nearest humans, an indigenous tribe, were over a hundred miles away.

Over the course of a couple of weeks Tald extracted and refined about twelve hundred ounces of gold, smelted into ingots weighing sixteen ounces each, enough to make Tald a very rich man. We returned to England and what we didn't need immediately we buried in the middle of what is now Epping Forest.

We then had to change some of the gold for coin of the realm. This was risky because the only way we could see of doing this was for Tald to appear to be someone he wasn't. In Elizabethan England there were no such things as bankers. We had to look for a merchant who specialised in currency exchange to help us out, preferably one who lived quietly and more or less alone. With the help of our drones we identified a suitable prospect, John Westwood, a comfortably well-off, god-fearing man with a good reputation, trusted by his peers. We watched him for a few days before finally going down to visit him at his home, one of a newly-built half-timbered row situated in a quiet street just off Lincoln's Inn Fields, a more salubrious part of town, where the filth in the gutters wasn't piled up quite so high. He was a widower, about forty years of age, whose son of fifteen he was training to follow in his footsteps. He also had a daughter who had married and moved out a few years before. He was looked after by a housekeeper and a small number of servants.

It was February and by early evening, even in the middle of the city, the darkness was all-engulfing, which suited us perfectly. Leaving our main craft in orbit, we were able to land our shuttle in the square just around the corner then leave it hovering just above the tree line, totally invisible.

The one thing you can't get from orbit is the smell of a place and let me tell you Elizabethan England stank to high heaven. Personal hygiene wasn't high on anyone's list of life's necessities. Some people thought bathing was akin to the worst excesses of Sodom and Gomorrah. Most people washed their whole bodies only once or twice a year. Even the nobility, who spent huge amounts of money on clothing and perfumes, only bathed perhaps once every couple of weeks. Add to that the smells from whatever ordure was flung out into the street or dropped there by practically everyone it's not surprising how much the place stank. Luckily, I wasn't affected but I know Tald felt almost physically assaulted.

A stealthy walk led us to Westwood's house, where Tald knocked on the door. As expected, it was the housekeeper who opened it and my first job was to encourage her see someone who might be the sort of person who would come calling on her master. Luckily, her eyesight wasn't very good and in the murk it was no great thing for me to bend her mind slightly so she saw Tald as a well-dressed and respectable gentleman.

"God grant you good evening. I am here to see Master Westwood on business. I am not expected but will you ask if he will see me?"

109

"Certainly, good sir. May I ask your name?"

"Edward Tald." We hoped such a name wouldn't seem too alien to our host.

We were shown into the parlour and a minute or so later John Westwood entered. As he had been told by his housekeeper that a gentleman had come calling he saw what he expected to see, with a little help from me. He was, however, a little wary.

"How can I help you, Master Tald?"

"May I offer you my apologies for appearing unannounced. I hope you don't think me discourteous."

"Not at all. Please be seated and take your ease by the fire." They both settled themselves.

"It is rather a delicate thing. I am newly landed in London after voyaging a few years in the Indies and do not know many in these parts. My family are from the northwest. I have heard good words said of you by a lordly gentleman of my acquaintance and am told you may be able to help me."

"May I ask who this gentleman is?" We knew from our researches that a recommendation was highly prized in these times. As we knew no-one, we could not lie directly. A little misdirection had to suffice.

"I am under an obligation not to mention his name, but I may tell you he lives no more than a furlong of here."

"Ah," said Mr Westwood, knowingly, thinking no doubt of the Earl of Southampton, who had a large house not too far away. He smiled. "Pray continue."

"I have a quantity of refined gold which I would like to exchange for coins of the realm. Would it be appropriate to ask this of you?"

Master Westwood relaxed at this point and stated he was certain he could help, at which point things flowed along nicely and arrangements were made for him to exchange the gold on our behalf. We had a good idea of its value so there was a short discussion on the terms, quite favourable to Master Westwood, as he well knew. Tald handed over enough gold to raise coins to the value of fifty sovereigns, a large sum of money for the time and hinted that further larger exchanges might be required, which pleased our good merchant very much. Business was business. It was concluded to everyone's satisfaction and the next evening we picked up an assortment of angels, crowns and shillings in a large leather bag.

Buying clothing for Tald was no less difficult, owing in part to the Sumptuary Laws, which set out what a person could and couldn't wear, according to their class or station in life. We chose a draper's shop in Cornhill for our purchases, again waiting until the quiet of nightfall before visiting. As before, I managed to disguise Tald's true form and Tald was able to convince the owner, with the help of a gold half-crown for his services, to close up for the night and devote an hour or two of his time to our requirements. The draper proved invaluable in navigating the maze of legislation, sending his boy out for other items such as shoes and hats, which eventually allowed Tald to appear as a wealthy merchant of the higher middle classes. He also provided us with an alternative set of clothing for a fictitious cousin, such as a doctor or other learned man might wear, which would enable Tald to approach the scientific community without raising suspicion. Finally, we were ready for the world, without charms and spells.

Our first visits to the streets of London during daylight were as the merchant Edward Tald and we were able to sample and record both the coarseness and refinements of Elizabethan life. Tald rented a small house and hired a couple of servants to look after him. We then spent nearly a month in the hurly-burly of the capital, documenting as much as possible before we got down to the real business of our mission, the scientists of the day. What we found when we arrived on Earth was a horrendous mishmash of conjecture, half-formed ideas and complete fantasy. Everything new was based on hearsay as there was no reliable way to confirm anything presented as fact. For example, someone had heard from someone else that a race of men known as Blemmyes had been discovered, who were said to have no heads, but had facial features in their chests. No-one thought to question this. Everyone believed the human body consisted of four humours and that hysteria in women was caused by a wandering womb. Nearly everyone, mainly because the church had told them, believed the universe rotated around the earth. Those few who doubted this were in danger of being excommunicated at least or being burned at the stake as a heretic at worst. Even so, everyone believed in the power of astrology to foretell the future and that the transmutation of metals could be achieved by a science known as alchemy.

Tald made an in-depth study of all the current sciences, preparatory to arranging meetings with various scientists and discussing their beliefs. Of particular interest to us was Doctor John Dee, who stood out then as no other. He was a leading figure in what was shortly to become the Age of Enlightenment, a mathematician at a time when that branch of science was still thought by many as being akin to magic. Sadly, like others of his profession, he was also a firm believer in astrology and alchemy. We formed a plan to visit Dee for which Tald would need to don his disguise as a man of science. He spent a few days completely immersing himself in the part. I had all the data he would need regarding current scientific practices and beliefs, he worked on perfecting the mannerisms and speech patterns of a man who had attended university and seen a little of the world.

Euclid's Story 2

On the evening of the eighth of March 1582, the day before our planned visit to Doctor Dee, we were on our ship, about ten miles above Mortlake. We had no idea whether the doctor would consent to see us without an appointment or letter of recommendation but we were confident that, with a little flattery, we would be able to influence him into dispensing with the conventions. Tald would present himself as a scholar from Oxford, eager to discuss mathematics and astronomy. He was already dressed in his doctor's clothing and was reading through various scientific books and journals he had picked up during our time in London.

Suddenly, proximity alarms began ringing and we discovered we were under attack by the Allas, who opened fire on us without warning. Unfortunately for them they discovered they had bitten off more than they could chew. Although we were mere beginners in the art of warfare, we were no longer vulnerable. After their initial act of treachery we had very quickly developed much more sophisticated weapons so even the smallest of our ships would be more than a match for whatever they could throw at us. Within minutes we had managed to destroy one of their ships and cripple another but just as we were about to unleash all hell on the third there was a mighty crash. Where Tald had been sitting there was now just a mangled mess. He had been thrown across the cabin with great violence and was now sprawled on the floor with blood pouring from a wound on his head. We had been rammed by the crippled ship. The collision had ripped a large hole in the side of our ship, damaging us beyond hope of repair and leaving us with no alternative but to escape in our small shuttle. Luckily, Tald was still conscious, though very woozy, and managed to fit his oxygen mask. Once in the shuttle we instructed our ship to self destruct and got away, mercifully cloaked from the remaining Allas. A few moments later there was a huge explosion, taking out their third ship, which had come alongside to board.

Minutes after he entered the shuttle Tald lost consciousness. The krai are a tough race, normally able to recover from injury very quickly. The cut on Tald's head didn't look too serious but his brain must have been damaged in the collision, something that wasn't immediately apparent as I fought to control the shuttle and bring it down somewhere safe to land. He regained consciousness a few minutes after we landed and managed to drag himself and his belongings out of the shuttle. He lay there unmoving in the darkness on the mud of the Thames, which was at low tide. I instructed the shuttle to hide itself beneath the river, with it the equipment we required to install a wormhole portal. Close by what is now The Royal Mid-Surrey Golf Club, there is a microscopic black hole, our only way of leaving Earth.

It was only then I realised I couldn't hear Tald, although he had regained consciousness and was moving around. I tried talking to him but there was no response. This was not good.

I have no idea what the Allas were doing so far from their normal hunting grounds. I've found nothing since then to make me think any other Allas have come looking for them. Another of life's little mysteries. As we later learned, Dee had stood in his garden watching the sky over south west London turn blood red. What he couldn't see, ten miles above the clouds, was the battle raging between our small ship and three larger ships, none of which were of this earth.

I'm not sure on what level Tald was functioning by then. He seemed to understand the need to get to safety and began to make his way towards the light of an inn, which lay a few hundred yards away. He must have been a surprising sight as he burst through their doors, taller than anyone else, with a black skull cap pulled down over his ears, long grey beard streaked with blood from the cut above his eye and his clothes and cape spattered with the mud of the Thames. Talk in the pub was all about the weird lights they'd just seen in the sky. Somehow, Tald managed to persuade the innkeeper to let him have a private room and we were shown upstairs by a horrified maid and left alone to recuperate. I kept trying to talk to him but got little response. He seemed to know something was going on as he looked around the room whenever I spoke but it soon became obvious that he couldn't hear me. Eventually, he fell asleep on the bed.

The next morning he washed the blood from his face and beard. He'd sustained some other injuries to his knee and back, judging by his careful movements around the room. He limped down the stairs and took breakfast. It was strange; he seemed to accept he was the person he portrayed, an Elizabethan man of science, sitting in an inn, looking for all the world as though he belonged there.

It was pure chance which led us to Dee's house. Around mid-morning, as Tald was sitting by the fire, he was approached by a soberly-dressed man of medium height, around 40 years of age, with quite a large girth, a bulbous red nose and grey chin whiskers around a foot long.

"Good morrow to you, friend," he said. "May I ask if you are on your way to meet Doctor Dee?"

"I might be," said Tald, guardedly, "why do you ask?"

"Well, there is only one reason gentlemen of our sort venture this way. We are seekers of truth, are we not? Benjamin Clerkson at your service, sir."

"I am honoured to meet you, Mr Clerkson. I am Edward Tald."

"A pleasure, Mr Talbot. I've heard something of you, have I not?"

Mr Clerkson, it seemed, was slightly deaf and had perhaps mistaken him for someone else. Something in Tald must have advised him not to correct the mistake. It might be better to be introduced to Dee as someone whose name might sound familiar.

"And what is it you have heard?"

"Why, that you are searching for answers to questions that puzzle many of us. Dr Dee is a fount of such knowledge. I have also heard he may be looking for someone to skry for him, as his current fellow is proving somewhat irascible. Indeed, if you have any leanings yourself towards that art I would be very glad to introduce you."

"I do lean that way, Mr Clerkson, most assuredly and would be glad of an introduction. I was thinking it may be presumptuous of me to call on him unannounced. Do you intend to go on there today? If so, we must go in company and see what we shall find. If you have no objection, of course."

"No indeed, I would welcome it and I am sure the good doctor would be very pleased to acquaint himself with you. It is a long hour's walk from here and I would be glad of decent conversation along the way."

Soon after this they rose and began the journey to Dee's house in Mortlake, discussing among other things the strange lights in the sky of the evening before, Tald falling easily into the role that seemed to be required of him. It was strange, listening to him, realising just how

115

much detail he had assimilated from his researches, so easily did he chatter away with Clerkson. For the first time I was conscious as to how far I was away from his thoughts. There was nothing I could do but go along for the ride and see what transpired.

Tald's leg was still very stiff so the walk to Mortlake took almost two hours. He had managed to purchase a walking staff from the inn-keeper's brother, a woodsman who lived nearby, but he often had to rest, sometimes five minutes or more. Luckily, it was a fine day and the feeble warmth of the sun hinted that spring might finally be on its way. Clerkson didn't seem to mind the slow going, I suspect it suited him equally as well. We finally arrived at the house of Doctor Dee at around two in the afternoon. Dee was in the garden at front of the house, tending his herbs and he watched us walking slowly towards him. He and Clerkson were obviously old friends and they greeted each other accordingly, clasping hands and patting each other about the shoulders.

"Well now, you are a sight for sore eyes, my friend. I'd been hoping you might turn up today. You may have heard already of my little trouble?"

"Yes, as you foretold, it is why I am come today."

"And who is this you bring with you?" inquired Dee.

"May I introduce to you Edward Talbot, a skryer of some repute, I do believe, who is also eager to make your acquaintance. We have travelled here today from The Bell, by Richmond, which is where we met."

"Welcome, Master Talbot," said Dee, shaking his hand. I sensed immediately that Dee's guard was up. I think Tald was also able to read him, as he tried his best to put Dee at his ease.

"I thank you most humbly," said Tald, with a smile and a slight bow. Side by side the two could almost be brothers. Each of them towered over Clerkson and both were dressed almost identically, a signature of their station in life. They even looked somewhat alike, although Dee's hair and beard were much greyer. He was at this time fifty-five years old. Tald, I imagine, must have looked to be in his early thirties. To a stranger they might have been father and son. It was quite uncanny.

"Are you a Talbot of the ancient Lancastrian line?" asked Dee.

Tald smiled gently, as though he'd been found out.

"I believe there may have been an ancestor whose blood was so favoured, but if so, it was long in the past."

"Blood is blood, Mr Talbot, and always runs true," replied Dee. Clerkson nodded vigorously.

"But you must have walked a long way today, and I saw as you limped towards me, Master Talbot, that you have suffered some hurt or injury. I'm sure you could do to rest. Come, let us enter into the house so you may refresh yourselves."

"I thank you kindly, Doctor. It is an old injury I carry and this damp weather makes it ache the more."

"I take it you witnessed the startling events of last evening?" ventured Clerkson. "What think you?"

"A very curious and serious thing, I deem, which warrants further discussion."

We followed Dee through a large gate set in the high wall surrounding the house. Upon entering, Dee called to his maidservant for beer and we followed him in and through a pair of double doors into his study, where we sat. With the doors closed the sound of Dee's young children was shut out. It was a warm, comfortable room and the well-tended fire was a welcome sight. Dominating the room was an imposing desk, a fine piece of oak, topped with green silk. Around it were several cushioned chairs, into which Tald and Clerkson were offered to be seated while Dee himself took the one behind the desk. All about the room there were stacks of books, There was little shelving so books had cascaded over onto the floor and onto every other conceivable surface except the desk, which was covered with piles of manuscripts and papers bundled with ribbon. It was well known that Dee had one of the largest private libraries in England, possibly in Europe, but in such a state of disarray I couldn't see how he could possibly find a particular book if he required it. In one corner was a full-length mirror partly hidden by more books, which I later discovered was known as the 'great perspective glass', a rarity then, most mirrors being just large enough to show one's head and shoulders and none too clearly. This one was extremely well made and must have cost a small fortune. Dee's little parlour trick was to have someone lunge at the mirror with a rapier, whereby they would be greatly shocked by a full size image of themselves lunging back in riposte. Quite childlike, really, but yet another instance of Dee's so-called magic. I wondered what the servants in the house thought about working for him, knowing the rumours that abounded.

Once settled in the room, I noticed with some alarm I was getting more and more distant from Tald. When I called out to him I could no longer get any response. I began to feel the enormity of being truly alone. Tald sat quietly, massaging the soreness in his leg.

After drinks had been brought in, Clerkson once more brought up the phenomena of the previous night. Dee was still puzzling over its meaning and what it might foretell, whether good tidings or no. He felt skies of that nature could bring nothing but bad news to the nation and he had already started to prepare a report for the Queen, who would soon be demanding an explanation from him. Dee's reputation was such that he was already expected to know exactly what had happened, and why. The three of them discussed this and other things for about an hour. Even though Tald had been an intimate part of the proceedings he seemed as vague as the others in his attempts at interpreting the event. Suddenly, Dee jumped up and apologised to his guests.

"Forgive me, I am such a bad host these days. Here I have been, blathering away and you have walked all the way from Richmond and must be near famished by now. You must both stay to dinner and I will go now to tell my wife, Jane, to prepare for two extra guests."

"You are very kind, Doctor Dee," said Clerkson, "I'm sure that would set us up very nicely for our walk back to Richmond."

Over dinner, which took place in another warm room overlooking the river, we were joined by Dee's wife. Towards the end of the meal talk turned to Barnabus Saul, Dee's erstwhile skryer, who, unlike his master, was supposedly able to communicate directly with spirits through a crystal ball. Saul, it turned out was the reason why Dee was so pleased to see Clerkson. Dee called this crystal gazing 'Optical Science'. He said he was unable to see such visions in crystals, regarding it as a failing within himself, which was why he had employed Saul, who had been living at the house for the last five months but who had disappeared the day before, much to Dee's annoyance.

"I think I may have an answer to that," said Clerkson. "He knew I was on my way here and fled, knowing full well I would advise you he is not to be trusted. I'm sorry to say you have been cozened, Doctor Dee. My sources tell me that Saul has been telling tales behind your back about what goes on here, that you have been making him scry against his will and he is weary of you as his master."

Dee pondered this and I saw his wife giving Clerkson black looks. I got the feeling talking about spirits was something which made her deeply uncomfortable.

"He came to me last week and told me he neither heard nor saw spirits anymore. I think it more likely he never did and he has had a good few months living high on my meat and drink and sleeping in a good bed in payment." He sighed deeply. "It must be well known by now I am easy prey to all sorts of rogues and scoundrels."

"Yes, just so," continued Clerkson, "he has been telling tales against me as well, that I was trying to replace him in your favour with another, though I had no intention of doing this. My journey here today was to assure you I am not about to foist some other n'er-do-well upon you. My meeting up with Master Talbot here was quite fortuitous, I assure you. Before this morning he and I were strangers and it was a most marvellous coincidence we were both heading in your direction."

At this point, and much to my surprise, Tald spoke up.

"I have been told of this Barnabus Saul also, by a magical creature, that he has cozened you both. It is well he has gone, else who knows what further charges he would lay against you. The injuries he has already done you in divers ways are very great. With all my heart I hope no further mischief will be done."

"My thanks to you both," said Dee, "I feel sure I shall hear nothing further of Master Saul."

Magical creature? Where on earth did Tald get that from? I couldn't figure out what was happening. After the meal, when Clerkson had gone to the jakes, Tald inquired of Dee if he could have a private word. Dee asked his wife to tell Clerkson they would be back presently, then they returned to the study.

"So, Mr Talbot, what is it I can do for you?"

"Say more what I can do for you, Master Dee. I have spent a considerable part of the last ten years accumulating as much knowledge of the ancients as I could. I am sure if you would but give me the opportunity I would do as much as I am able to further your knowledge in magic. Barnabus Saul has gone, but can it be mere coincidence I turn up here so soon after with the services you require?"

"Magic, sir," roared Dee, "magic? By God, sir, I don't do magic!"

He rose from his chair and looked for a moment as if he was going to ask Tald to leave but it seemed his anger was already over and he took command of himself once again. He sat and looked at Tald with those piercing blue eyes of his, as if asking, And what is it *you* want, I wonder? I wondered the same thing.

"No, Mr Talbot," continued Dee, a little more steadily, "I don't think at this moment I am ready to change, coincidence or no. A little more circumspection on my part is required, I think. We will not discuss it further."

"As you wish. I am sorry if I have mis-spoken." Tald was looking suitably contrite after Dee's outburst. "Rest assured my intentions toward you are well meant. Please forgive my clumsiness." Dee said nothing further and we returned to the dining room to find Clerkson and take our leave.

On the walk back to the inn we had to tread carefully in the darkness to find our way, Clerkson having but a small lanthorn with which to light us. For all Clerkson tried to engage Tald in conversation, he got little response. At the inn Clerkson bade Tald good night and continued on to his own lodgings in Richmond. Tald went immediately to his room and fell asleep on the bed.

I have to warn you, Cornelius, events from that moment on made very little sense.

The next morning Tald was up early and headed out towards Mortlake after taking breakfast. He still had his walking staff but I could tell he was moving much easier. I had tried talking to him again and again since he woke but got no more response than Tald flicking his hand around his head, as though I were some sort of invisible fly. I had been hoping whatever other damage had been done to Tald would heal as quickly as the injury to his leg. Without him I was helpless and I had the first intimations that we could be stuck here for a long time, waiting for mankind to become technologically adept in order to put him right. Without Tald to do the physical work there was no way of setting up a portal to get us back home.

After a much quicker walk than the previous day, Tald reached Dee's house at about ten o'clock. He knocked on the door and was admitted by the maidservant into the living room, where Dee appeared a few minutes later, a scowl on his face.

"I thought I had made myself perfectly clear, Master Talbot. I am not looking to replace Master Saul at the moment. I have much else to take up my time and I am not interested in vulgarly accounted magic tricks."

"May I please prevail upon you, Doctor Dee, to let me speak and set things right between us. I see now I left a bad impression with you yesterday and once again I crave forgiveness. It is not magic tricks I pursue, either, but if you will permit, I am willing and desirous to see or show something in spiritual practice."

"And how would you do that, good sir? What I desire is something of a higher plane altogether and I think that may well be beyond your comprehension."

Tald was silent for a moment, then said in a quiet voice, "Tell me what it is you seek."

Dee was slightly taken aback by the tone of Tald's voice. It was a little trick Tald had discovered for himself while conversing with other humans in his disguise as the merchant, something that made them do what they could to please him. I hadn't thought much of it at the time, as it was helping us get our job done, but coming as it did now it seemed a little strange, as though he didn't realise he was doing it.

After a few moments of contemplation, Dee whispered, "For a long time I have been desirous to have help in my philosophical studies through the company and information of the blessed angels of God."

Well, I thought to myself, how are you going to do that, Tald? All he knew about religion came from the few books we had managed to acquire for our research.

"I apologise for my frail understanding and I assure you, Doctor, I fully understand the seriousness of such a venture. Let me scry for you and if I do not come up to your expectations I will leave and you will never see me again."

There was a long moment of silence, during which Dee looked at Tald intently, as though trying to decide if it would be a good idea. Then he nodded.

"Come with me."

He led Tald into the study and from a wooden trinket box that sat on the window-sill he took out a round crystal about the size of a ping-pong ball, sitting on a little silver base and set with a small silver cross on its top. Think of the Orb that is part of the Crown Jewels, only much smaller and a lot less ornate. This he placed in a small wooden frame on his desk that acted as a sort of cradle which held the crystal about three inches above the desk.

"I am credibly informed," said Dee, "that to this stone are answerable several good angels. I was once instructed by a skryer to call for the good angel Anachor to appear in this stone. I will leave you with it and trust Anachor gives you answer. I will go into my oratory next door to prepare myself in prayer."

Tald immediately dropped to his knees, all trace of his lameness gone, which I could see surprised Dee. Tald then began, as far as I could work out, to pray. Dee withdrew and Tald continued his muttering.

Minds do not get headaches. We don't feel anything in the way of pain, it's not possible. We are nothing more than intelligent energy, but at this point I felt certain I was getting one. I felt that if I had had a head I would have wanted it to explode and frighten Tald back to his true self. I sensed a great raging within myself and experienced what I thought at first was some kind of out of body experience, quite paradoxically seeing myself in two places at once. For the first time in my existence, I was truly frightened. Then something snapped. One moment I was part of Tald, the next I was looking up at him from a book on the desk, Dee's copy of Euclid's Elements of Geometry.

For me, this was a unique and shocking new development. A krai and its mind are not supposed to be separated once they've been joined. A lot of time and effort goes into making sure a krai and a mind choose each other. They never, to my knowledge, spontaneously separate. Unless I could get Tald to snap out of whatever was going on and let me back in I was stuck to this book, totally helpless.

Why I had come to rest in the book was a mystery to me at the time. I have since determined that some unconscious part of me looked for an escape route and concluded that the book, as an easily portable object, might be carried around and certainly, in those times, looked after very carefully. Books were very valuable commodities. Then the full horror of my situation hit me. I could be stuck like this for years, far away from home with a race which still thought stars were fixed to the night sky like giant sequins, while Tald somehow returned to Farasta without me. He could summon the shuttle himself just by calling for it. The shuttle would be alert to his presence and respond. He could set up the gateway and return home. For me, there would be no way of getting back home without help.

What made it worse was that there was no guarantee a rescue party would come looking for us. We had no particular date set for when we would return. If, eventually, anyone did set off in search of us it would be years before they arrived. Assuming anyone finally did get here, they would be able to home in on the beacon being broadcast from the shuttle but they'd be looking for a krai, not a book. I could only make contact with any would-be rescuers if they came close enough, within a range of two or three miles but they wouldn't be able to locate Tald without me being with him. Anything more than three miles would mean trouble. That's about the limit of a mind's range. With Tald in his current condition he wasn't going to be looking for them and if this book that I now inhabited moved very far from Dee's house I might be missed altogether. I desperately needed to get Tald back to the pod and into stasis so we could wait to be picked up, however long it took.

I remember thinking then that things couldn't get much weirder, only to be proved wrong when Tald got up from the floor and gazed directly into the crystal on the desk. He started spouting a mixture of Farastan and English, partly words from the Portal technical manual and partly words which I recognised as being drawn from ancient writings known as the Pseudepigrapha which, like the Apocrypha, had once been part of the bible and in which Tald had recently been immersing himself in order to explore this strange new phenomenon, religion.

About fifteen minutes later Dee came back into the room to find Tald staring intently into the crystal ball. Tald exclaimed loudly that he could see a vision of the angel Uriel. I could see Dee was shocked. Whatever he was expecting from Tald, it wasn't this. Uriel was one of God's high angels and should have been beyond any mortal's reach. Tald's eyes looked like they were on fire and he was waving his arms around like a madman.

"Ask him this, Master Talbot," shouted Dee, "are you one of those that are answerable to this stone?"

Tald raised himself to his full height. "I am," he said, recovering his composure and presumably now speaking as the angel Uriel.

"Are there any more there beside you?"

" Michael and Raphael. But Michael is the leader."

Then Dee shouted back a most unexpected question. I was expecting something along the lines of a philosophical enquiry. Instead, he asked, "Is my Book of Soyga of any excellency?"

This, it turned out, was a book owned by Dee, full of astrological tables and lists of spirits, purported to be related to the Book of Enoch, a long lost treatise which was supposedly a record of the language that God had taught Adam. He had parted with a huge amount of money to secure it but was yet to be convinced of its worth.

"That book was revealed to Adam in paradise by the good angels of God."

Dee was almost crying with joy at this news.

 "Will you give me any instructions, how I may read those Tables of Soyga?"

"I can, but only Michael can interpret it."

"I was told that after I could read it I should live but two years and a half." I could hear the fear in Dee's voice as he said this. It was obviously not in his plans to perish so soon.

"Thou shalt live a hundred and more years." At this Dee breathed an audible sigh of relief.

"What must I do, to have the sight and presence of the blessed Angel Michael?"

"Summon and invoke our presence with sincerity and humility. This is the ultimate concern of Michael. Michael is an angel who lights your way. And his truth is not revealed by power and force."

Suddenly, Tald slumped down to the floor, apparently exhausted by his efforts, while Dee fawned over him like a lost lamb, helping him onto a chair and grasping his hand. The session was at an end.

What Tald hoped to gain with all this mumbo-jumbo I had no idea, but a few hours later they were at it again, this time Tald explaining to Dee how to create a Holy Table upon which his crystal, or shew-stone, was to be placed. Tald then revealed to Dee how to write down letters from the angelic alphabet and place them all around the edges of the table and add word squares at certain points on it. The so-called angelic alphabet was Farastan, which meant that somewhere inside Tald's fevered mind he still retained some knowledge of who he was.

When night came, Tald was given Barnabus Saul's lately vacated room and he retired, exhausted. A servant was despatched to the inn to collect his meagre possessions and settle his account. That left Dee alone in the study with me. He sat at his desk and I looked out at him from the book in which I had been imprisoned. It struck me I might somehow be able to talk to Dee directly and I tried very hard to make the same connections in his neural pathways as I did with you, to let him hear my voice, but I got no positive response. Suddenly he picked up the book, meaning I supposed, to place it on one of his bookshelves in another room. What I didn't want was for me to be moved away from whatever was going on between the two of them and forgotten about so I put all my energies into making him return me to the desk.

I did something similar to the trick I pulled in your flat when I blinded your two new friends, but not quite as intense. I hadn't had much practise at that point. The flash of light certainly caught his attention and as he looked at the book I managed to convince him that he could see the centrepiece of the Holy Table, a square of angelic letters as described by Tald, on the cover. This display was enough to make him replace the book on the desk with great reverence, where it sat, with me attached, allowing me to record any future meetings in his study. He even placed the cradle containing the shew-stone on the book, which was where it stayed for all future actions. Without meaning to, an unwanted side effect of my action confirmed to Dee that Tald really was talking to the angels.

The sessions between Tald and Dee continued, on and off, over the next couple of months, with things getting more and more weird. Near the end of April Tald recited a set of seven ridiculously complex tables to Dee, said to come from the Archangel Michael, which took Dee nearly three hours to write down.

After this particularly gruelling session, Tald said, "I have been commanded by Michael to go forth and marry, something which I have no inclination to do as it would be contrary to my vows."

The implication was that Tald was a Roman Catholic priest, a very dangerous person for Dee to give shelter to, especially as he was known to be a close advisor to the Queen. Religious tension was running very high and Dee would be damned by association if it was discovered that he was harbouring a priest.

In May, we had an unannounced visit from Charles Sledd, one of Francis Walsingham's men. A spy, in other words. Walsingham was in charge of England's national security and rabidly anti-Catholic. Immediately after Sledd had left, Dee and Tald had a violent confrontation, Dee trying to ascertain whether it was still safe to carry on. Afterwards, Tald became morose and refused to help Dee with any further sessions. A couple of evenings later, I heard Dee and his wife, Jane, having a blazing row in the kitchen, she accusing Tald of deceiving both Dee and herself.

"He's just like all the others Clerkson has brought here, honest learned men he calls them and they've just used you for their own ends and you, like the great blind fool that you are, you're taken in by their honeyed words and promises of godly revelations, bewitched beyond all reason. He'll be the death of you!"

She was still at it the following morning, calling Tald every nasty name she could think of. During all this time Tald was still refusing to scry, which only added to the tension. A few days later Jane rode off to Cheam to visit her father and they were left alone together in the house.

"I don't know why she has taken against you so greatly," Dee told Tald when they were in his study once more, "but perhaps now she has left for a while we may return to our godly purpose."

Tald was having none of it. He seemed to be suffering some great depression. Once again, I tried to reach him and for a moment I swear I'd succeeded, because he shouted, "Go away!", which Dee took as relating to himself because he huffed out. Tald left the study soon after and I could hear him banging around upstairs. A few minutes later the front door slammed. Tald had gone.

When you're sixteen light years from home, stuck in the middle of nowhere with a man who thinks he communicates with angels and you've just lost the only person who can help you get back, I don't think anyone could blame me for feeling just a tiny bit panicky. I hoped this was just a spat, a little lovers tiff, soon mended, but it was nearly a week before Tald returned. Where he'd been I had no idea. He stayed a few days but no angelic sessions took place, which annoyed Dee greatly. Tald did seem somewhat calmer and for a day or so, a strained sort of peace reigned. Then Tald said he was going away again, to track down some important books he'd heard might be for sale. Dee argued strenuously against his going but Tald told him that on his return he would resume the sessions. They parted on reasonable terms, with Dee even going so far as to give him a little money to help him on his way. This time he didn't return until sometime in July, nearly two months later and without the books. Once again, there was a row, but they made up again after Tald convinced Dee he now knew where the books were and he would be able to get hold of them quite soon. He left again the next morning.

I can only speculate as to what was going through Tald's mind at this time. He seemed to be at war with himself. I thought perhaps he was starting to see glimpses of his true self, which I took to be a good sign and left me hoping he might be on the mend. Not so.

It was November before Tald turned up at Dee's door again and he was shown straightaway into the study. I had given up all hope of ever seeing him again and had been desperately trying to get Dee's attention during this time, but I might as well have been trying to get a reply from one of the other books in the room. I thought then that maybe it wasn't possible to connect with humans.

"Master Talbot," said Dee, entering a minute or so later, "how good to see you again." I wasn't sure, by the tone of Dee's voice, that he meant a word of it.

"And you too, Doctor Dee, but I must tell you my name is not Talbot," said Tald. "That was an alias I needed to use because there have been pursuivants looking for me. I did not know if I could fully trust Mr Clerkson. My true name is Edward Kelley."

I imagine Dee was as taken aback as I was at this strange confession. What had Tald been doing that had caused him to change names? Another question with no answer. Tald walked over to the window and gazed out.

"When I was living in Bristol I was conducting some alchemical experiments. It has long been an interest of mine and I was working with someone I thought could be trusted." He sighed heavily. "The fool was only interested in how much gold I could make. I showed him I could do so by creating for him a few ounces from a pewter tankard but when I told him I wasn't interested in such petty

127

sideshows he turned against me and falsely accused me of coining and forgery. I have recently had word he has withdrawn his allegations so it now seems safe to resume my true identity."

"Well, Master er...Kelley. I am glad to have you safely returned." Dee was quiet for over a minute, while the two of them gazed at each other. It was like a scene from a romantic film. I could have sworn I saw tears in Dee's eyes. Finally, he said, "If you are feeling well again would you be able to assist me as a scryer once more?"

"You must know, Master Dee, that doing so causes me great fatigue, which leads, as you have found, to irascible behaviour in me and for which I humbly apologise. However, in light of the great work we were discovering I would gladly resume, albeit at not such a great pace as before, if you will have me."

"By all means. It would do my soul good to converse with the angels once more. I feel certain that great things are yet to be revealed."

And so the sessions started again, days and days of Tald gazing intently into the stone, describing to Dee what he saw. Dee, sitting there entranced as he painstakingly wrote down every utterance. I don't know what Tald really saw, but the flow of Farastan being passed off as the language of the angels never ceased, so on some level he had retained all his past knowledge.

After about a week of these interminable and quite frankly, extremely boring sessions, a strange thing happened. Tald had summoned up a spirit called King Camara. Camara, you should know, was in reality one of Farasta's greatest scientists, who had died a few thousand years earlier.

As Tald explained to Dee, this Camara was saying, "One thing is yet wanting. A meet receptacle, a stone. One there is, most excellent, hid in the secret depths in the uttermost part of the Roman Possession. Be of good comfort. Lo, the mighty hand of God is upon thee. Thou shalt have it. Dost thou see, look and stir not from thy place."

Tald pointed toward the window.

"I see nothing," said Dee.

"Thou shalt prevail with it, with Kings, and with all creatures of the world." Tald motioned towards the window. "There upon the mat by that stack of books, a stone as like a blackbird's egg, most bright, clear and glorious. Go toward it and take it up."

Dee went toward the window and looking down saw something on the ground. It was small and round. He picked it up and I could see a dark crystal in his hand, about the size of a large marble.

"Let no mortal hand touch it, but thine own. Praise God."

I could see straight away that the crystal was an integral part of our portal equipment, used to create wormholes. We'd brought it with us from Farasta and without it we couldn't return that way.

I knew he didn't have it with him when we first landed after the battle, so Tald's possession of the crystal could mean only one thing. He had called the shuttle from the bottom of the Thames and retrieved it. All pilots have the mental ability to navigate and manoeuvre spacecraft in case anything should happen to a mind, but raising and opening the shuttle was a fairly intricate operation, something I would normally be called on to do, as it is much more difficult to do this from outside the shuttle and from a distance. I hoped Tald had had the presence of mind to return it to its resting place, out of sight of any humans. Why he had decided to do this and give the crystal to Dee I had no idea, unless he meant in some way to show he was just as capable of supplying magical artefacts. Such crystals in those days would have been very rare and consequently, very expensive. That particular crystal, I knew, had no flaws at all, which would have greatly increased its worth. Dee was overwhelmed by its sudden appearance, as he assumed it had been presented to him directly by the angels, albeit through the medium of Tald's scrying.

The next day, Tald left the house yet again and didn't return again until March 1583, a matter of four months. He brought with him a scroll and a small amount of what looked to be red soil, which Tald explained had been found with the aid of magical creatures just outside Blockley, a small town in the Cotswolds. The scroll turned out to be some sort of treasure map, with some odd symbols and even odder cryptic writing, not Farastan this time so presumably some mumbo-jumbo from the ancients. The red soil was supposed to be a sample of the fabled Philosopher's Stone.

Once more they started their interminable sessions and if you want to discover the root of my short temper I suggest you look to this time as its breeding ground. On and on and on, day after day of the most amazing claptrap and the gullible Dee sucked it all up and then asked for more. Yet another so-called celestial alphabet was produced by Tald's visions, which was taken to be the written language handed by God to Adam, but which I could identify as one of the old alphabets of Farasta. After this there was a break until 6th April, when once again Uriel appeared to Tald.

"In 40 days must the Book of the Secrets and key of this world be written," he exclaimed, portentously.

This was followed by an excruciatingly long passage of lines from the Book of the Secrets, all in an old Farastan language, which turned out to be an extremely boring and interminable peroration by an ancient philosopher whom Tald had studied when he was younger. Who knows from what hidden recesses in his brain he managed to dredge up this rubbish.

A few days after this we were blessed by a visit from the Queen of England herself, who just happened to drop by on her way to Greenwich. I never got to see her, of course, because she didn't enter the house. After the visit I could see that Dee was very pleased with himself. He told Tald she'd more or less promised to find him a sinecure at court, which should finally make him financially comfortable and enable him to pursue his studies without worrying how he was going to care for his family.

The next day, they were talking to the angels again, with Dee writing down everything Tald uttered. I remember one line distinctly because it was one of the few things that afforded me any amusement among all the dreariness.

'Arney vah nol gadeth adney ox vals nath gemseh ah orza val gemáh, oh gedvá on zembáh nohhad vomfah olden ampha nols admácha blah, blah, blah,' which I recognised as being from an old self-help guide for those unlucky in love. This could loosely be translated as a cure for heartache. The premise was that pain might be eased by making a long journey which would transfer the ache to one's feet.

The dictation of the Adamic language, with its many lists and tables, went on for more days than I care to remember, with Tald getting increasingly aggressive until one day he screamed and began moving around the room as though seeking a hiding place. He told Dee he was being attacked by four spirits who appeared to him as labourers armed with spades. Large red welts appeared on Tald's arms where he was fending them off while trying to hide behind a stool. Dee took up Tald's old walking staff, which had been left in a corner after his second visit and started swinging away like a madman at the spirits he couldn't see, until eventually Tald said they had disappeared.

Later, he told Dee he needed to get away from the house. He felt he was wasting his life and wanted to get a decent job and earn a proper living, to become, as he put it, a good and proper man. He said he was burning up, that his bowels felt as though they were on fire. I then discovered, shockingly, that while he'd been away Tald had somehow found himself a wife and was now married. It was this that seemed to be causing Tald so much grief. Not only that, but this new wife, Joanna, brought with her to the marriage two infant children and he didn't know where they were all going to live. Amazingly, Dee invited them all to stay with him, which they did soon after. Tald told Dee he didn't know why he had married her in the first place.

"I cannot abide my wife," he said. "I love her not, nay I abhor her."

The feelings appeared to be mutual. I discovered later he had been paid to marry her to give her children legitimacy. After they had moved in both Joanna and Jane Dee took sides against him. Argument followed argument and so the long days wound wearily on.

Soon after this, Dee had a clandestine visit from a Polish prince, Albert Laski. Most of what I know of Laski is hearsay, as the meeting was confined to the living room and subsequent meetings were held at other locations. Apparently, he was very taken with the good doctor. I found out later that he had designs on the Virgin Queen and was laying the groundwork for an amorous assault.

Dee wanted to ask the spirits about some questions posed by Laski, regarding the King of Poland and Laski's own pretensions to the throne. According to Tald, Raphael replied that he would grant him his desire. The next day, presumably because Tald had returned, Joanna left for her father's house, taking the children with her.

More spirits appeared over the following few days, with one, a little girl known as Madimi, supposedly making some kind of familial connection between Laski and the Queen through common ancestors dating back to Edward the Fourth, a hundred and twenty years before, although when pressed by Dee, Madimi didn't explain further.

Another spirit, Murifri, warned them that 'Hell itself is weary of Earth,' however, there was a chance of salvation, which again led to Laski.

"Do you see what this means?" said Dee, "an epochal change is imminent and Elizabeth and Prince Laski are to be the spearheads, as was foretold by the Fiery Trigon. We must make ready to receive the divine message so we might reveal it to them."

It suggested to me, on the other hand, that Laski and Tald were in cahoots.

These Trigons were astrological events which influenced the earth in a repetitive cycle through fire, air, earth and water. It was thought that every thousand years, when Jupiter and Saturn, in 'a great conjunction', entered the sign of Aries, a Fiery Trigon would be heralded, bringing about momentous changes. Previous events were said to have coincided with the Great Flood, Moses receiving the Ten Commandments and the birth of Christ, which was heralded by the Star of Bethlehem. Altogether, there had been six fiery trigons since the time of creation, a matter of some six thousand years earlier according to the church. They were only out by fourteen billion plus. The last was said to have coincided with the reign of Charlemagne, some eight hundred years after the birth of Christ.

On the third of June an unknown man called at the house. He said he came to warn Tald that a warrant had been issued for his arrest in connection with coining. Dee was worried that if Tald was arrested then all of this good work in the service of God would come crashing down around his ears.

"I'll stand by you, Edward," said Dee, "and together we'll see our great enterprise to its conclusion. I have a cousin, Richard Young, who is a member of the judiciary. Let me ask him what can be done."

"I thank you, John. You are indeed a good friend to me."

The next few days saw both men on tenterhooks, as the pursuivant sent to arrest Tald was expected at any time. In the end no-one came, so it appears Dee's words with his cousin must have had some effect.

I heard nothing further about the charges laid against Tald. Whether Dee's cousin really had managed to intervene and settle things, or whether Laski had something to do with it, which was, I thought, much more likely, given he had the ear of the Queen, I never found out.

Three days later another new book of angelic revelations was revealed by a spirit named Galvah. This was to be the Liber Logoeth, or the speech of God, which for some reason threw Tald into all sorts of hissy fits, crying out to Dee that he didn't believe what he was being told by the spirits and that he couldn't carry on. It seemed to me that Tald's grip on reality was being loosened daily by the sessions and I couldn't see it carrying on much longer. Something had to give.

Dee had invited Prince Laski for a session with Tald, hoping to impress him, I suppose, with what they were doing. Dee was running out of funds and needed to find someone to be his patron. Laski was known to be wealthy and had ingratiated himself at Elizabeth's court. A future king of Poland as patron to Dee would have been perfect.

At the session Tald informed Laski his guardian angel was present. Over subsequent sessions he was told by the spirits that although the Queen loved Laski faithfully, the same couldn't be said of Robert Dudley, the Earl of Leicester, while William Cecil, Elizabeth's first minister, hated him and couldn't wait for him to return to Poland.

Another spirit warned Laski that Cecil and the spymaster Sir Francis Walsingham considered him a traitor. Dee was further alarmed to hear he himself was also under investigation and his house would most likely be searched. After the session, Dee broached the subject of leaving England, to escape what might happen next. Tald didn't seem unduly worried. The next day, Dee had to visit London to meet with Laski. He didn't return for a week. Tald was in the study when he returned, busy packing his books and papers into a large travel bag.

"Edward, what are you doing? Are you leaving me here before we have finished our great works?"

"I cannot stay any longer. They have told me that if I tarry here I shall be hanged and if I go with this prince they will cut off my head."

Dee eventually persuaded him to stay but once again, there was an uneasy peace in the house, with neither man directly talking about what might be happening.

At the end of July the Queen visited again. A day later a courier arrived with a letter from Sir Walter Raleigh, which spoke of Elizabeth's good disposition towards Dee. With it came a small parcel containing forty gold angels, which was desperately needed.

I didn't see much of either man throughout August. In September, Dee busied himself making a complete catalogue of his books, for the first time placing them on the shelves, where possible, in some sort of order. A couple of weeks after, with no more sessions that I knew of, the whole household, including Tald's wife and children, left the house, bound for Poland.

That was the last time I saw Tald. Everything I have learnt from that date is hearsay. There are differing accounts as to how he supposedly met his end. In 1595 he was imprisoned in Hnevin Castle, about fifty miles northwest of Prague and it was there he supposedly died two or three years later, either of injuries while trying to escape or by self administered poison in front of his wife and children. My own theory is that Tald is still alive. It would take a lot to kill a krai as their bodies have marvellous recuperative qualities. Broken bones would mend within a few days, any poison in his system would have been neutralised almost immediately. No, I think by now something must have happened to jolt him out of his fugue state and he is now some sort of lost soul, eking his way in a strange world, not knowing that he is waiting to be rescued.

Euclid's Story 3

Now let me tell you how the book ended up in the hands of your ancestor, Maccabeus Pye.

John Dee left his house in Mortlake on the twenty-first of September 1583. I have no idea why he didn't pack his copy of Euclid along with all the other paraphernalia he'd been using in his communications with the angels, especially as he'd grown so used to having the book form part of his rituals. Either he wanted to travel as lightly as possible or he was afraid of losing the book. As far as I could tell he took no other books of any kind. I discovered much later that in order to finance the journey Dee had mortgaged his house to his brother-in-law, Nicholas Fromond. He also entrusted to him his library of almost three thousand books, a vast number of papers and many scientific instruments of great value. In hindsight, this was a very bad decision. Family, eh, what can you do?

For many years the story went around that soon after Dee had left England an unruly mob had burst into his house and ransacked it in the belief that he had been practising black magic there, even that he was raising the dead. The truth was that Fromond, eager to make a little extra from his dealings with Dee, had handed over the keys of the house to a privateer named John Davies, who then began to plunder it, removing valuable scientific apparatus, including two globes given to Dee by Mercator and a large number of books, one of which was the copy of Euclid I inhabited. Fromond and Davies disposed of the scientific equipment so diversely most of it was never recovered. They sold many of the books to a man who was once a pupil of Dee's, Nicholas Saunder, at whose house I resided for nearly thirteen years.

Saunder considered himself something of a scientist and scholar. In reality he was a bit of a chancer, a second-rate con man who was in financial difficulties for much of his adult life. As with so many others since, I tried to reach out to him but got no answer. I watched him as he bleached out Dee's name at the front of each of the stolen books. He then wrote his own name over the top, You can see in the books which have survived how badly he did even that simple job, Dee's name is still easy enough to read in most cases. Considering his financial situation I thought he might have tried to sell the books immediately but they all remained on the shelves in his study while I was there.

I wish I could say he came to a bad end but he was knighted in 1603 and lived another forty-three years. During the time I spent with him he had to sell a couple of his properties to keep himself out of debtors prison. Typically, he blamed other people for his troubles, but his wild money-making schemes always fell flat and he was constantly having to borrow money to keep himself afloat. That's probably why he finally decided to sell off Euclid's Elements.

Over the years a considerable number of rumours had circulated regarding the loss of Dee's library and scientific equipment. In particular there had been a great deal of speculation concerning the whereabouts of Dee's supposed book of spells. As far as I'm aware, there was no such thing. A man who had once been a servant at Mortlake had talked of seeing the Elements on Dee's desk on many occasions, with the crystal ball sitting on top in its little stand. From this came the idea that they were one and the same, with the spells magically hidden in its pages.

In 1595, using this story as his starting point, Saunder supplied rumours that the book contained a secret spell which would bring huge riches to whomever could decipher it. When these rumours came back to his own ears he identified a likely mark, a notoriously dim nobleman, to whom he wrote a letter, tailored to tempt him. The letter stated that five years earlier he had come into possession of the book, the former property of a distant kinsman, a nobleman who had successfully used it to find the location of El Dorado, the fabulous city of gold in South America. In addition, the book had magically transported him there and back. This nobleman and his magnificent riches had now left England to enjoy his wealth in sunnier climes, but before he'd left he'd sold the book to Saunder, stating that the spell could only be used once. He dropped large hints in the letter as to who the supposed nobleman had been, still vague enough to refer to several different people.

The book, of course, had supposedly cost Saunder a small fortune but he was willing to sell it, for a small profit, because, as he put it, '*I had not the wit to realise the spells therein, not being of sufficient knowledge as those that have called this science their masters, nor the monies to pursue such knowledge.*'

In February 1596, Saunder sold the book for £75, just under £13,000 in today's money. Not a bad return for something that had probably cost him no more than a few shillings. The man who bought the book, and me along with it, was Sir Richard Ruddle. He was an idiot who was given quite a large allowance each year by a rich uncle on the assumption he was making his way at Court. About three months before taking possession of the book his uncle had passed away and he inherited a large estate and fortune. Sir Richard then became hellbent on frittering away his vast wealth on his consuming passion, alchemy. The man had the attention span of a goldfish. He quite quickly lost interest in trying to decipher Dee's supposed spells and sold the book before the year was out.

After that the book and I passed through the hands of a succession of dealers until I finally came to rest with Maccabeus a few years after Dee's death in 1609. Maccabeus had known Dee briefly in the late 1590s. They both had an interest in alchemy, Maccabeus the young scholar eager to question the master, Dee flattered anyone still thought his words and ideas to be worth anything. He told me he remembered Dee talking about his lost copy of Euclid and how it seemed to have some special significance for him in his actions with the angels.

Maccabeus was a quiet and tidy man, who lived in a fine house in Lime Street, close by Leadenhall Market, with his wife, Anne and his seventeen year old son, Roger. Two other children had died in infancy. He was a merchant trader and a junior member of the newly formed East India Company, which was set up to trade in silks and other fine fabrics from Asia, pepper, cloves and nutmeg from the East Indies and more recently in the burgeoning tobacco trade. He was comfortably off, but not rich. Two recent ventures he had invested in had not come to fruition but luckily he had other irons in the fire, notably in the wool trade, from which he gleaned a regular income. He had managed to purchase the house where he was living but his ambition was to buy a large house in the country and retire in a few years time. He had been born in a small village near Winchester, where his father was a steward at a large estate and Maccabeus was aiming to return to the same area.

In January 1612, when he was thirty-eight years old, he discovered a copy of Euclid for sale at a local book dealers and he had arranged to see it with a view to purchase. Upon opening the book to the flyleaf he was thrilled to see the name Saunder and, just visible below, the name John Dee, in Latin. Certain that the book had originally belonged to Dee he was very pleased to be able to make the purchase for a good price.

After years of silence, first with Saunder, then Ruddle and a succession of others after him, Maccabeus finally became the first human with whom I successfully communicated. I could sense his openness from the very first time he held the book. Thinking back to that first evening, I must have frightened the life out of him. After a hearty dinner he'd retired to his little study and settled himself in his favourite chair by the fire, meaning to inspect his new acquisition. His wife and son were visiting his mother-in-law in the country and he'd given his servant the evening off so he was alone in the house. As he read, I tried to attract his attention but I could sense his mind was too active to be receptive. I decided to wait a little, until he became more relaxed. He read for about an hour, then started to become drowsy. He was on the verge of drifting off when I reached out to him with just one word.

"Listen," I said.

I must have used a little more force than I'd meant to as he stood abruptly, the book crashing to the floor. I thought he was going to have a heart attack, which would have set me back yet again. After a few seconds he seemed to recover and went running about the house shouting for his servant, in case it was she who had returned and spoken. When he found himself completely alone he returned to his chair and sat down, having decided he'd imagined it. He started to read again and when I sensed he'd relaxed I tried again, gentler this time.

"Listen."

This time he seemed to realise that the voice he was hearing had something to do with the book, as he proceeded to inspect it closely, at one point putting it close to his ear. He then placed the book back down onto his lap, sat back and closed his eyes. I could sense his mind relaxing and I was able to enter and make some connections. When I thought he was ready I tried again.

"Listen, I have something to tell you."

"Speak, book," he said, "and let me know your mysteries."

I was surprised at how unsurprised he was. Most men of his time would have run from the house, babbling about witchcraft. I knew then I had come into the possession of someone very special.

And so I started to tell him, in very simple terms at first, who I was and how I had got there. I had to be careful because his mind would have been quite unprepared for some of the concepts I could admit to him. I told him at first I was a sort of spirit, originally conjured up by Doctor Dee and placed in the book as an otherworldly assistant to help him communicate with the angels, knowing Maccabeus had knowledge of this aspect of Dee's work. His view on this was that it was all a fantasy.

"Angels, forsooth. Now why would angels bother themselves with us poor mortals?"

"You don't believe in angels, I take it?"

"I'm not saying I do or I don't, if you follow me." I could sense he was being cautious. A man could find himself in a lot of trouble for questioning characters or events in the bible.

"What I think is that Dee's need to believe made him far too trusting of what other fellows would tell him, especially Edward Kelley."

"Did you know Kelley?" I asked.

"No, not I, but I heard enough tales from others. It was bruited he was a forger, a coiner, and he was once put in the stocks, which was when he lost his ears. But if you were in the house at Mortlake perhaps there are things about him you can tell me."

"Perhaps," I said, "but tell me what you know of him first. I would be interested to find out what happened to him and Doctor Dee after they all left the house to travel overseas."

He didn't have much to tell me.

"Apart from the usual rumours that seemed to follow Dee wherever he went, I can only tell you he returned from the continent without Kelley in 1589, much maligned and out of favour, although he did eventually manage to restore his good standing with the late Queen. Of the whereabouts of Edward Kelley, all I know was what Dee told me when I met him one time at his house in Mortlake after his first sojourn in Manchester in 1598. They had parted company in a town called Trebon, somewhere in Southern Bohemia. Kelley had gone on to Prague and Dee had returned home.

"From others I learned later that Kelley was hailed as a great alchemist in Bohemia, where he turned base metals into substantial amounts of gold and for which he had been knighted by the king there. Walsingham, and later Cecil, who at one time had been trying to hang him, were now making desperate attempts to get him to return and do likewise for the Queen. Needless to say, they were unsuccessful and by all accounts the Queen hadn't been pleased they'd let him slip through their fingers.

"I saw Dee a number of times when I was a bit of a dabbler in alchemy, but that's a rich man's game and at the time I was still finding my feet in the world so had to let it pass. A couple of years later Dee returned to Manchester, where he died in the spring of 1609."

I told him something of the sessions between Dee and Kelley, but didn't tell him who Kelley really was. For a man with an early seventeenth century mind he was very quick to grasp new concepts. He had already formed his own opinions about certain things and I was able to enlighten him about others, such as the real state of the heavens. He saw himself more as a natural philosopher than a man of religion so he was pleased to have it confirmed that planets circled the sun and that the sun itself was just one tiny part of a larger universe. He had already read Copernicus and discussed the heliocentric theory with like-minded friends. He had even heard of Galileo and his discovery in 1610 of the moons of Jupiter. When I told him there were other planets even further away he was not surprised. I think it pleased him to be in receipt of knowledge which was either so far undiscovered or being held back by the church as being heretical.

These were the sort of conversations we were hoping to have had with Dee almost thirty years earlier in order to nudge earthly technology in the right direction. Unfortunately, Maccabeus wasn't in any position to be able to influence the great thinkers of his day, knowing no-one who moved in those particular circles and being more of a dabbler than a great thinker.

I liked Maccabeus and after having been alone for so many years it felt good once again to be engaging with someone. He was wonderfully receptive and open to new ideas and our first conversation went on long into the early hours.

A few evenings later he was once again sitting beside the fire in his study with the Euclid on his lap. By this time, his wife and son had returned from the country and I had the chance to observe his family. Anne was everything a dutiful wife should be, kind and good-tempered, with a keen sense of humour which I could see Maccabeus treasured.

The son, Roger, was a clod and I knew his father despaired of him, although loyally he never uttered a word. Roger's only interests in life were gambling, killing small animals and chasing women. He hated living in the city and was forever nagging at his father to let him live in the country so he could carry on being a complete nuisance. Maccabeus didn't have the money to afford to indulge his son in this way so he was trying to get him to take an interest in the family business but Roger would have none of it. His only ambition in life was to be a country gentleman and I could tell he was close to breaking his father's heart.

Perhaps it was this need to appease his son which caused Maccabeus to ask if I was able to help him in his business affairs.

"What would I be able to help you with? Bear in mind, I am but a spirit."

"If you dwell in the spirit world perhaps there are ways you could help me. I have interests in the north of England and I am concerned that my factor there is taking advantage of my goodwill to line his own pockets. Perhaps you would be able to go to him and find out the truth of the situation."

"Oh, Maccabeus, if only I could, but I am bound to this place and that book. I can only leave this house if you take it with you."

"Yes, I see," he replied, somewhat despondently. "No matter. My apologies for trying to use you to my own advantage."

He looked so sad then that I couldn't resist.

"How would it be if you could be transported there instantaneously? Then you would be able to deal with this person directly". He laughed out loud and asked if I thought it was he who was an angel, rather than me.

"Do you realise quite how far it is to Bradford?" he added.

"No I do not, but I will ask you the question again. I'm not known for my wild sense of humour."

"You are serious, then? It can be done?"

"It can, depending on certain conditions."

"Ah, here comes the catch," he said.

"It's not a catch, exactly, more of a precondition on the one hand and a willingness on the other."

I knew he was turning over the proposition in his mind. We had, after all, only known each other for a few days and he didn't know how far he could trust me.

"Would you be able to explain further?" he asked.

"Is there somewhere in Bradford you can picture easily in your mind, somewhere where your sudden appearance would not be noticed by anyone?"

He thought for a minute or two and then confessed he knew of no such place in Bradford, having been there only once, but he had visited relations in Sheffield a number of times and knew of a secluded old churchyard close by The Bishop's House where he would sometimes go and sit.

"From Sheffield to Bradford is but a matter of four or five hours ride."

"Well then, if you can visualise that churchyard quite perfectly we'll be able to travel to Sheffield. Knowing the location with great clarity is essential. It would be best to go very early in the morning so there is less likelihood of anyone else being around. From there you should be able to hire a horse for the rest of the journey."

"So we can be in Bradford within a single day?" He looked doubtful.

"Not only that but once we are in Bradford it will be much easier to return here directly and it can be done in the blink of an eye, but it is imperative no-one sees you arrive or leave. Such a sighting would not go unregarded and you do not want to be had up on a charge of witchcraft."

"It would be an adventure no other man has ever had, I'll warrant."

"You would be correct to assume so," I said, "but you do realise no-one can ever know about it. Not your wife, not your son. It is not witchcraft, but others would think it so, which is why we must proceed in absolute secrecy. This is a precondition I must make, to protect you as well as myself."

"Even if I told anyone I'd never be believed, but I accept your terms, gladly."

"Good. So now we have it settled, when would you like to go?"

"I will have to make preparations but I can see no reason why we shouldn't leave the day after tomorrow. But you mentioned willingness as the other condition?"

"Yes, the willingness of your inner being to believe that this journey can be done. It is no small thing and I am sure it is beyond the comprehension of many to even contemplate. Without your own commitment we can go no further. I will merely tell you how this feat can be managed. It is you who must decide if it can be done, you alone who will step forward. I think it would be advisable if we were to make a few trial runs here in the house. Can you make sure everyone is out of the house tomorrow morning?"

"Yes, it can easily be arranged. Everyone will be at church in the morning for Prayer Service. I was there last Sunday so my absence won't be commented on just this once if I excuse myself on the grounds of a slight discomfiture in the gut. It probably won't be so far from the truth. We should have around two hours to ourselves."

"That will be perfect."

The next morning a noticeably excited Maccabeus waved his family and servants off to church then came back into the study for his first lesson. After I explained what he had to do and the dangers of not paying attention there was no hesitation. I made sure the correct neural connections had been made and that he was clutching my book close to his chest. Then I asked him to visualise his bedroom and explained the steps he'd need to take to get there. It took him a little while as, at first, he couldn't grasp the concept of being able to see two things at once, the room he was in and the place where he wanted to be. We had to go through that step a couple of times before he got it. When he'd finally mastered it he had some problems overlaying the image with the colours. When he'd solved that I couldn't get him to take the imaginary step forward.

An Elizabethan's thought processes were so much different to yours, Cornelius. They tended to think of things being absolute. Imagination wasn't something to toy with carelessly. I thought it might never happen but eventually, he took a step forward and found himself standing in his bedroom, staring out of the window at his little garden. At this point he passed out. Luckily, he fell straight backwards onto the bed.

When he came round a few moments later, he sat up and, believe it or not, began to cry.

"Congratulations, Maccabeus. How did that feel?"

"Did I truly get here just by thinking about it?"

"Well, with a little help from me, yes, you did. Are you ready to try again?"

"My mouth is very dry. I think I need a drink."

"Very well, compose yourself for another jump and let's go to the kitchen and get one."

And that's just what we did. After the drink he had to sit and rest a while as his legs were too wobbly to allow him to stand. He managed one more jump before his family returned from church. The rest of the day he went around with a slight smile on his face, which he put down to the effects of wind when his wife questioned him about it.

By six o'clock the next morning we were ready to leave the house, the copy of Euclid, with a few other items, in a large leather bag. Maccabeus had told his wife he would be away for the day, perhaps two, leaving it sufficiently vague and mentioning business in St. Albans. He left the house and stood outside his front door, which was enclosed by a small porch. In the darkness he was unlikely to be seen. Assuming our journey was successful we would return to his house just after dark and return to the exact same spot.

Maccabeus remembered his lessons well and a few seconds later we were in the old churchyard of St Leonards, close by the Bishop's House. No-one was around to see him appear, which was a good thing, as he let out a loud yell of delight when he confirmed we had arrived at the correct place. It took a good ten minutes before I was able to calm him down. A short walk took us to The Bull, a comfortable looking inn, where after a leisurely breakfast Maccabeus was able to hire, at considerable expense, a post horse and guide to take us to Bradford, a distance of just over forty miles. The guide would return the horse to Sheffield. These were the days when only rich people had carriages and most people travelled on foot or begged lifts from carters. Going on horseback meant we could more or less guarantee arriving by early afternoon, giving Maccabeus plenty of time to conduct his business.

I won't bore you with the details, except to say his factor almost fainted from fright when Maccabeus knocked on his door and asked to see the books. Upon finding various discrepancies the man was promptly dismissed and his deputy was installed in his place, with the warning he could expect further unscheduled visits in the future, in order to keep him on his best behaviour. Maccabeus enjoyed himself immensely. By late afternoon he was ready for a large slice of game pie at a nearby tavern. Afterwards, he sat by the roaring fire with a large glass of hot punch and a few pipes of tobacco until darkness fell. He left the tavern and walked around the town until he found a secluded spot and then we returned home. The next morning he told me he'd hardly slept with the excitement of it all.

I agreed to go with him to his place of work, a table at the Nag's Head Inn in Bishopsgate, to see if there were any other ways I could be of use to him, but it soon became obvious that, apart from accumulating data, I could give him no further advantage. This was the original office of the East India Company, which was more or less in its infancy and business was conducted on the basis of speculation, gossip and what King James needed to keep him sweet. They hadn't had much luck in the last couple of years. Two vessels that set sail for the East Indies in 1607 had been lost. A further two vessels had left the previous March and they'd so far had no word of them.

I couldn't do much to help him in his business, so I told him about the gold.

If you remember, we had a stash of gold we'd hidden in a clearing in Epping Forest. Because of its isolated position, a good few miles from the nearest hamlet, we had used this clearing to enable Tald to become accustomed to Earth atmosphere and gravity. After our initial exchange of gold into currency through John Westwood, there were still around eleven hundred ounces buried in a hole beside a prominent oak tree. Approximately thirty-two kilos, worth around eight million pounds in today's terms. Enough for Maccabeus to live very comfortably for the rest of his life. Without Tald, the gold was useless to me and by that time it didn't look likely that he would ever reappear.

"Do I take it you want me to have your gold?" he asked.

"Well, I don't particularly have any use for it," I told him.

"And what do I have to do for it?"

"Beyond digging it out of its hiding place, nothing. It has no value to me and you could make good use of it."

"But I can't," he protested.

"Why not?"

"I've done nothing to earn it."

"Neither did we. It was just lying around on the other side of the planet. No-one owned it. We simply picked it up." I was trying to keep it simple.

"We?"

And that's when I had to tell him that Edward Kelley was really a being named Tald who came from another planet and that he and I had worked in partnership until his unfortunate disappearance. I have to say he took it rather well, considering.

"That's why I was so interested in what happened to Edward Kelley," I explained.

"But what will be the outcome if this Tald should make his way back to you?"

"After thirty years it seems unlikely, but if he did and found himself in need of gold he would have no problem acquiring more."

He went quiet for a few minutes and I could see he was struggling to understand. Finally, he seemed to come to some sort of decision.

"In the eventuality I agree to go along with this, how could I account for it? I can't just come into possession of so much gold and say I'd found it. Buried treasure belongs to the king. It would all be taken from me."

"Then we must come up with an appropriate story."

And we did. First of all, we concocted a story which I hoped would account for why Maccabeus was in possession of so much gold. I would be with him to answer any awkward questions which might be raised. I then asked him to make an appointment to see John Westwood, if he was still alive. It turned out he was.

Maccabeus wrote a short letter, introducing himself as a member of the East India Company and asking for a meeting. Westwood replied, setting a date and time and a few days later, at his home, he welcomed Maccabeus graciously and invited him to sit by the fire. After the preliminaries he asked why he needed to talk with him in particular, as he no longer kept up with the day to day affairs of the office as his son was now in charge.

"You once did business with a man named Edward Tald," said Maccabeus. "He came to you some thirty years ago and asked you to exchange some gold for him. Do you remember?"

Westwood closed his eyes and a silence followed. I was afraid the old man had gone to sleep. Then he opened his eyes, leaned forward towards Maccabeus and said, "Yes, yes, I remember now. A strange affair and one that puzzled me at the time. We had one dealing and he promised there would be more to come but I never saw him again. I haven't thought of him for many a year. He told me I came recommended by a titled neighbour but discreet enquiries failed to produce anyone who had ever heard of him. A man of mystery, certainly. Is he still alive then?"

"Alas, no," replied Maccabeus, "but I am now come on behalf of his son, also called Edward Tald, who is a close cousin of mine." I could sense Maccabeus flinching at this fiction. "For the last twenty years he has resided in the Americas, where he is deeply invested in the gold trade. I suppose you have heard of the fabulous city of El Dorado and other such fantastical tales?"

Westwood nodded and continued to watch Maccabeus intently.

"What I am about to tell you must be kept between us, as it is a great secret. If it becomes widely known it may lead to his life and those of others being threatened. There are many men who would kill to gain knowledge of the gold mines he controls deep in the hinterland of Guyana. Now Master Tald wishes to retire and return home to England but before he does he must transport his gold to England and find a safe harbour for it here. He has tasked me with the mission of making it so."

"A fine tale, Master Pye, but what does this have to do with me?"

"You exchanged gold for his father all those years ago, turning it into coin of the realm. It would please me greatly, by way of settling the outstanding business he promised, if you would do the same again."

"I'm afraid what you ask is not possible, Master Pye. As you know, it is my son who takes care of business now. I merely provide him with advice. Sometimes he accepts it and sometimes he doesn't."

In the days leading up to the meeting, at my suggestion, Maccabeus had already investigated the son and found nothing untoward, but he would have to be convinced to do the deal and it would be one more person who knew our secret. We agreed between ourselves that our choice was no choice at all.

"Would your son, then, consider this business, if you were to advise him of its peculiarity?"

"I would have to consult with him and accept his answer as non-negotiable. Are you able to return, to give us time to consider this proposal? Perhaps we can meet again in a few days time."

"It seems we must," said Maccabeus. "I would much rather deal with you directly, but as you vouch so for your son, and rightly too, then I will gladly agree." Both men stood and shook hands by way of farewell.

"One more thing, Master Pye. How much gold would be involved in this transaction?"

"I think it may be more than one transaction, considering the amount involved. Master Tald is a careful man and will not ship the entire consignment in one go, but overall there would be well over one thousand ounces."

"One thou-!" Westwood dropped into his chair again and let out a gasp of wonder. "Truly, he has discovered El Dorado."

"Until we meet again," said Maccabeus.

Four days later we were back at John Westwood's house, seated by the fire, but this time his son in was attendance. Henry had been well briefed by his father and had done his own homework on Maccabeus. He knew Maccabeus' income almost to the last penny and had discreetly sought references from some of his colleagues at the Nag's Head. Maccabeus, of course, had conducted his own investigation into Henry Westwood and found nothing untoward. I liked him immediately and sensed he would be true to his word in his dealings with us. Luckily, he accepted our story without me having to intervene, so we got down to the nitty-gritty.

Our story was that Edward Tald would be shipping over to the care of Maccabeus a quantity of gold, amounting to between eighty and 100 ounces, every three to four months, dependant on when trading vessels visited Guyana. The gold would be hidden in barrels of molasses so as to escape attention. Maccabeus would then hand over the gold to Henry, to be converted as before, for which Henry would be paid a five per cent commission, a nice little earner for doing very little. Our intention was that the intervals between each exchange would be fairly sporadic, with at least a couple of consignments being 'lost at sea" or 'seized by pirates', for authenticity.

To get the gold I guided Maccabeus to the clearing in the forest, an easy two hour ride. He, armed with a shovel, dug up the first portion and carefully covered his tracks. That first time we had the horse, so had to ride back with the gold, which was quite nerve-racking as they were lawless times. Luckily, vagabonds rarely challenged men on horseback so we made it home safely. All subsequent trips were done using Maccabeus' new favourite mode of travel, in and out within an hour.

In the end, we exchanged just over eleven hundred ounces of gold over a four year period. Because the amounts came in incrementally every three or four months and because Maccabeus was a cautious man who didn't flash the cash, no-one suspected a thing. He had a large iron bound coffer in his study, where he kept his valuables and he strengthened that with the addition of two extra locks. He let it be known that every so often an investment had paid off, to account for the gradual improvements in the family's lifestyle.

His wife commented at one point that his business seemed to be prospering and he told her his luck had changed for the better when he'd purchased Doctor John Dee's copy of Euclid's Geometry. He couldn't explain to her exactly what was going on but he did impress upon her how important it would be to look after the book in case anything ever happened to him.

"It's magic," he told her with a smile.

"Magic, how can that be? It's just a book."

"Yes, but it's a book that once belonged to a great man, a magician who once advised the late Queen." He noticed the worried look on her face. She'd had quite a strict religious upbringing and had sometimes told him she feared for his immortal soul. He tried to soothe her misgivings.

"No, no, no, my dear, not real magic. Nothing to worry about. I just mean it has become my good luck charm. Look what has happened since I purchased it at the beginning of the year. I've a feeling that life is going to be even better for us now and we'll soon have enough for that home in Winchester we've talked about."

"All this talk of charms troubles me not a little, Maccabeus. You should not tempt the devil by such utterances."

"Now, now, let's have none of this. It's just a book after all and no harm can come of it. Come, let me have a smile to show we are friends again."

Anne smiled, but I could see she was troubled. She needn't have worried. Maccabeus did finally retire five years later and they moved to their grand new home and lived there happily for a further twelve years until she died of a fever in 1627. Maccabeus survived her by two years. On his deathbed he told his son Roger all about me and the book but I don't think he was really listening. Roger inherited the bulk of Maccabeus' fortune and gambled most of it away before dying himself five years later, of mercury poisoning, which was used to cure his syphilis. Your uncle's letter mentioned it was bubonic plague that led to his demise but that was a Victorian invention to make family seem a little more respectable. Luckily for you, he had a son, otherwise I would not be here now. He had looked after his father as madness overwhelmed him. That was when the story of the magic book was born.

Part 2

Friday 22nd June

15

After a minute or two of complete silence, Euclid asked, "What do you think?"

Cornelius let out a long sigh.

"I don't know where to start. Really, I don't. Until this morning I'd hardly even heard of John Dee, apart from the fact he was supposed to be some sort of magician."

"It's all documented between him and Edward Kelley, except that no-one ever suspected Kelley was an honest-to-goodness alien. Dee kept a diary, you can access it on line. All that weird stuff about angels and books in God's own language is true, as far as it goes. Tald must have picked up on what Dee most desired and somehow attempted to make it come true for him. I can see no other explanation. Then after a time, he must have come to believe it himself. I need to find out what happened to Tald. If he's still alive I need to get him home. It's been a long time."

"Can I help?"

"Gladly. First of all we need to raise the shuttle from beneath the Thames and make sure I can create the gateway to enable us to get back to Farasta. That might not be so easy. The crystal Tald gave to Dee was an essential part of the equipment. We'll need to get it back. I know the whereabouts of one of Dee's crystals, he had three or four, but I don't know whether it's ours. It's in the British Museum."

"The British Museum?" said Cornelius. "How are we going to get it back from there? We can't just walk up and ask for it to be returned."

"No," said Euclid, "I don't suppose we can. It looks like we'll have to liberate it."

"You mean steal it?"

"Can't see another way, although it goes very much against the grain to be carrying out a criminal act, even though it did once belong to us. But first of all, we need to visit the museum and make sure. It might not be the right one, but judging by the photos I've found on the internet, it looks very much like it."

"What's so special about this particular crystal? Wouldn't something of a similar size work?"

"No, I'm afraid not. The crystal's lattice is what makes it work, anything slightly different would be useless. Originally, our crystals came from a very particular part of our planet. We were eventually able to manufacture them artificially but it's not possible here. They contain a very precise amount of impurities that affect the colour and an even more precise displacement of ions which bend light by two different amounts, producing a double image. It's caused by discrepancies in the binding forces that hold the atoms of the crystal together. The forces are stronger in some directions than others. When light passes through the crystal, it is split in two due to the asymmetry in the crystal's structure, resulting in the particular double image we require."

"So, a trip to the British Museum, then. But first, I need to see Aunt Lu and give her a quick version of what you've just told me. Then a trip to the cop shop to let them know what's been going on. Perhaps we can leave the museum trip just for now. I mean, it has been over four hundred years, I don't think one more day is going to make much difference now."

"Yes, you're probably right." said Euclid.

Cornelius phoned to let his aunt know he was on his way and moments later he appeared in her kitchen. She was standing at the sink with a mug of tea, looking out of the window. She hadn't noticed his appearance so he coughed gently and said good morning. She whirled round and drew a deep breath in. Tea shot out of the mug and slapped onto the floor.

"Bloody hell! That was quick. I'm not sure I can get used to this." She put the mug down and got to work on the tea spill.

He apologised, smiled and asked if there was any chance of having a shower before breakfast.

"I can't remember the last time I felt clean. I was so tired when I finally got to uncle's house last night I forgot to turn on the immersion heater. Then this morning I was busy getting the life history of an alien."

"What?"

"It wasn't the book that was magic. Magic never entered into it. And it was nothing to do with Maccabeus, except it was him who came across the book in the first place. It may surprise you to know that since fifteen eighty-two until yesterday it's been inhabited by a visitor from another planet."

"An alien? An actual living, breathing alien?"

"Well, not exactly. You can't see him and I doubt that he, if it is a he, ever drew breath. Apparently, I wouldn't be able to pronounce his real name, so we're going with Euclid. There are lots of other things I don't know yet but I'm doing nothing else until I've had a shower and put myself outside of one of your breakfasts. Would that be OK?"

She smiled. "The full Monty?"

"Oh, yes!" How is it, he wondered, that his aunt could provide all the ingredients necessary for a full English breakfast at the drop of a hat?

After a shower and a welcome change of clothes he came back to the kitchen feeling closer to normal. While he ate the gigantic breakfast he gave her a brief resume of his conversation with Euclid and did his best to answer her questions.

"Is he here now? Could I talk with him?"

"I don't know. You could try. He says he tried to reach out to you when you were at Uncle Sedgewick's but got no response. He generally has a feeling for who will and who won't respond, something to do with brain patterns. Do you want to give it a go now?"

"Yes, I'd love to," replied his Aunt.

Cornelius took her through the routine as he'd learned it but it was obvious after a few minutes that there wouldn't be a connection.

"Sorry," said Euclid, "'there's nothing there."

"Yes, I'm sorry, too," said Cornelius. He explained to his aunt that it wasn't going to work.

"He can't communicate with most humans. After our ancestor, Maccabeus, there was no-one else until me. He thought he was nearly there with Uncle Sedgewick but apparently uncle could never get himself into a calm frame of mind, except just the once, many years ago. It was while I was staying at the house as a boy, but that was a fluke, really. Never happened again, no matter how hard uncle tried."

"Yes, I remember that, I think. He was as high as a kite for days afterwards. That was probably when he began to go a bit loopy, not that he needed much of a push."

Cornelius felt sorry for his uncle, being so close to establishing contact with an extra-terrestrial. He wondered what would have happened if he had.

"What about these other lot? The pirates who attacked Euclid and his friend. Have they just disappeared?"

"He says it's a good question and one to which he currently has no answer, nor will unless he can make contact with his own people. His opinion is that they are still keeping watch over earth every so often to see what happens with us but they've probably been keeping a low profile since our technology has been good enough to spot them. They might have been responsible for the outbreak of the first UFO sightings near the end of the war, although he thinks it's hilarious anyone would claim to be kidnapped by them. He reckons they're not really the type to be curious about humans, much more likely to kill them for fun. His best bet is that they're waiting until we've got something worth pinching, then they'll hit and run but Euclid doesn't think we'll have anything they'll want for many years yet."

Just after breakfast Ruth called to say they were due at Hornsey Road police station at twelve-thirty. She'd told Mr Singh she was going to meet Cornelius and make sure he was okay after his ordeals of the past couple of days and asked if she could have an extended lunch break. Cornelius praised Mr Singh and suggested they should get together half an hour before to run through their story. They arranged to meet at a coffee shop on the Seven Sisters Road.

Over coffee, they ran through the previous day's events. There seemed to be no way to make the story any more plausible so decided they'd have to play it by ear.

"I took all of Jez's things to a police station last night so they'll have found the gun by now."

"I wonder what happened to him after you took him on his little trip."

"I'm hoping we'll find out now." He grinned at the thought.

He brought Ruth up to date on the background to Euclid.

"As if you weren't fascinating enough, now you're friends with an alien," said Ruth with a grin.

Cornelius blushed and Euclid said, "Well, what are you waiting for, idiot? She's mad about you. Give her a bit of encouragement."

"I can't. What about Angela?"

"What about Angela? Didn't she just dump you? Be honest with yourself. You only took up with Angela because she flattered you that night at the party and the sex was better than you were used to, but let's face it, any sex at all was better than you were used to. Nowadays all she can do is criticise. She doesn't believe a single word you've told her about being burgled or kidnapped, whereas Ruth here thinks you're a knight in shining armour for saving her. You can't go wrong."

"I really am going to have to work at this keeping you out of my head thing."

"Well, it's up to you, but you know I'm right."

Ruth spoke up. "Hello? Are you still with me?"

"Sorry. I was just having an argument with my alien friend."

"What have you got to argue about? You've only known him twenty-four hours."

"It's complicated. He keeps listening to my thought processes when I don't want him to."

"I'd love to have a word with him myself, if only to say thank you."

"I don't see why you shouldn't, but you need to be very relaxed before he can make the initial contact. Maybe we can find somewhere quiet later and try it."

"I'd like that," said Ruth.

"So would I," said Euclid, "maybe I could finally have a conversation with someone with a bit of sense."

"If you mention one word to her about me and Angela I'll throw you in the river."

"My lips, as they say, are sealed. I know how to keep a confidence."

"Thank you." Cornelius wasn't convinced.

At the police station they were shown into an interview room, where they were joined a few minutes later by DI Evans. After greeting Ruth with a friendly smile he turned to Cornelius.

"So, you're the famous Mr Pye everyone's been looking for. Would you mind bringing me up to speed? I'd be most interested to hear where you've been. I know your colleague here has been very worried about you. You seem to be leading a very exciting life at the moment." There was more than a hint of sarcasm in the detective's voice. Cornelius shifted uneasily in his chair.

"I'm not sure you're going to believe much of what I have to say. Even to me, it sounds a bit implausible."

"I'm not going anywhere, Mr Pye. Take your time and start from the beginning."

Cornelius told the story from the time he'd received the book until when he'd been locked in the library. At this point, he claimed he'd escaped through an insecurely locked window sometime during the afternoon. Then he'd made his way back to his flat only to find Ruth there, being held by two men, one of whom, a man called Jez, was armed. He told how they'd managed to overpower Jez when the other man went out for food and he'd taken refuge at his uncle's house in Barnes after first seeing Ruth safely home.

"Did you see the person or persons who sprayed the tranquillizer at you, either time?"

"No, sorry, I can't say I did. I didn't get the chance."

"So we have nothing to connect the men waiting for you in your flat with your abductors?"

"I suppose not. Sorry."

DI Evans thought for a while. "I'm not saying I don't believe your story, Mr Pye. It's fairly obvious that much of what you've told me did happen, but maybe not quite as you described it. There are some elements that just don't add up. First of all, we've got a bunch of kidnappers, one of whom tells you his name and none of whom bother disguising themselves. And then you say you were in your dressing gown when you answered the door, just before you were kidnapped. You then escaped from where they were holding you, a big house somewhere in the country. How did you get back to your flat with no money, no phone and looking like an escapee from a secure unit?"

"I was really lucky, I got a lift a few hundred yards down the road."

"You got a lift? In your dressing gown? Really?"

"Yes, there was a pub just down the road and someone was just getting into his car, a middle-aged man. With a small dog. I told him I'd been rehearsing a play in the village hall round the corner, but my friend, who had given me a lift there, had gone off earlier in the car with all my things and hadn't returned when the rehearsal had finished. I told him I'd been waiting for him for nearly an hour. The man was going all the way to central London so he was able to take me almost to my doorstep.

"Well, that was lucky, wasn't it?"

"Yes, I thought so," said Cornelius, nervously.

"You didn't happen to get his name, I suppose?"

"Er, no. The subject never seemed to come up."

"And then you got back home where you managed to overpower an armed man? How did you manage that?

"Um, I managed to get his attention and Ruth hit him over the head with an empty milk bottle she found in the kitchen. She'd been out there making tea, you see."

"So, once you'd overpowered this armed man why didn't you phone the police?"

"We were worried he'd wake up again, so we ran."

"But not before you dressed?"

"Ah, er, no, I did that earlier, when I arrived at the flat. They let me change out of my dressing gown."

"How nice of them."

"Yes, I suppose so. Then after I took Ruth home I went to my uncle's flat in Barnes. I was so dog-tired I couldn't cope with being questioned about it last night." Well, that last bit's true, at least, thought Cornelius.

DI Evans smiled at them then excused himself and left the room.

"Do you think he believed us?" said Ruth.

"Not for a moment," replied Cornelius, "but he can't disprove any of it." He took her hand without thinking and gave it a squeeze. The door opened and Evans came back into the room. He put two photographs on the table in front of them.

"Recognise this man?" he asked, pointing to one of the photos.

"That's one of the kidnappers," said Ruth, "that's Slim, I mean Jez. And this other one is the man who was with him, Slinger."

"Slim?"

"I'd given them nicknames before I found out their real names. Fatboy and Slim. Jez was Slim."

"Yes, I see. Jeremy Wilson, a man well known to us. The other man is Dave Slinger, his usual accomplice. Another hard man. You were lucky to get away from these two."

"Well, like I said, this Dave Slinger had gone out to get some food," said Cornelius.

"You'll be interested to know the police were called to Whipsnade Zoo last night and your chum Wilson was arrested. He had nothing in his pockets and more interestingly, no shoes. He says he doesn't know how he got there. Quite annoyed he was, so they tell me, punched one of the zoo's security guards, which was why he was arrested. He's just finished serving three years of a six stretch for GBH. Only been out a couple of weeks so it looks like he's just broken the terms of his probation. We'll be detaining him until Monday, when he'll go up before a magistrate who'll decide whether he goes straight back inside. Also last night, an unknown person handed in a carrier bag at the police station in Barnes. He ran off before the sergeant could get a name. The bag contained Wilson's wallet and shoes and also a gun, which had recently been fired. We're checking the prints on the gun but I'm reasonably certain we'll find they belong to Wilson. You were in Barnes last night, Mr Pye. Know anything about these items?"

"Me? No, of course not."

"No, somehow, I didn't think you would."

Ruth gave Cornelius a quick glance, then looked down at her feet.

"There's a lot here you're not saying, Mr Pye, and to be frank, the timings don't make a great deal of sense. Wilson's things were logged in at Barnes only about twenty minutes after he was picked up at the zoo, so unless you were in two places at once…" DI Evans tailed off, leaving the thought unsaid.

"That's not really possible, is it?" said Cornelius.

"No, Mr Pye, that's not possible, but there's something you're not telling me. What I don't understand is what this book has to do with all this. You say the book's quite valuable and it was stolen from you. But a few nights later the same people who took the book came back and took you as well. Why?"

"Why what?"

Evans let out a sigh. "Why do you think you were kidnapped if they already had the book?"

"Oh, I see. The book was once owned by Doctor John Dee, who used to dabble in magic. He was an advisor to Elizabeth the First. I'm told it's quite valuable. There are a lot of scribblings in the margins. West's boss believed the book contained clues to some hidden treasure or something. When they couldn't work out the clues for themselves, they took me, thinking I knew how to figure them out. I had no idea what I was supposed to be looking for and I told them so, but they didn't believe me."

"Are you seriously trying to tell me now that this is all about some lost treasure?"

"I'm just relaying what I was told by the person on the phone," said Cornelius, "as mad as it seems."

"Can you describe this Mr West?"

"Yes, of course," said Cornelius and proceeded to do so.

"And where's this book now? Did you bring it away with you after you escaped from this unknown house somewhere in Radlett."

Cornelius shrugged. "No. I didn't get chance to pick it up in case West came back in. I was expecting them any second. When I realised the window could open I just legged it."

The room went quiet. DI Evans stared pointedly at Cornelius. Cornelius stared back, somewhat furtively. He knows we're not telling the truth, he thought. Ruth stared at the floor and wished the interview would end. She was also uncomfortable with not being completely honest but knew the truth wouldn't be believed, which might make things even more difficult for Cornelius. Unable to endure the silence a second longer, she spoke.

"So, what happens now."

"Well, Mr Pye, if I can borrow a key, we'll get a forensics team to go over your flat to verify that Wilson was there, along with Slinger. See if they can work out what really happened."

Cornelius took the spare off his key ring and handed it over.

"Try not to touch anything until after they've been. I've put out a call to get Slinger picked up and I'll have them both brought over here, see if we can find out who these mysterious master criminals are. A right little conspiracy we have on our hands, it seems to me. The problem is, with Slinger having popped out and Wilson appearing in a zoo thirty miles away, it will be a bit difficult to get any charges to stick, seeing as how they just seemed to leave you both in your flat. They're going to claim they just came round to have a chat about something."

"Oh," said Cornelius, "when you put it like that I can see your difficulty."

"Yes, it'll be their version of the events against yours, I'm afraid." said DI Evans with a wry smile. "Let me have some contact details for each of you and if anything develops I'll give you a ring. You'd better pop off now and leave us to investigate further. Thank you for coming in, sir, miss. Oh, and if you do happen to remember anything else, you will let me know, won't you?" He nodded to them and after saying goodbye they hurried out of the station.

"He definitely didn't believe us, did he?" said Cornelius.

"Would you, with that story? I suppose it's his job to be suspicious."

"He fancies you. I saw him," he teased, "he could hardly take his eyes off you."

Ruth punched him on the arm, then smiled and went red. He smiled back.

"What now?" he asked.

"I think I'd better be getting back to work. Mr Singh's been very good giving me time off but I don't want to push it too much."

"No, I suppose not."

She spotted a black cab and hailed it.

"Ask her out for a drink," said Euclid.

"Stay out of it!"

"Go on, ask her. She's standing there waiting for you to say something, trust me."

"Er, do you fancy a drink this evening? I mean, if you're not doing anything else. But I'm sure you're busy. Of course you are, Friday night and all. I expect you've already got other plans."

"No, no particular plans. I'm supposed to be meeting some people for a drink." Cornelius said, "Oh," and sighed.

"But I can easily rearrange. I'd like to see you tonight. You promised I could meet Euclid."

"See?" he said to Euclid, "It's you she wants to talk to."

"Rubbish," said Euclid.

"Do you want to come round to my place?" said Ruth, "I could make us a bite to eat. About seven?"

"That would be great, thanks. I'll knock at your door. I mean, I won't suddenly turn up in your flat like last night."

"Seven o'clock, at my door then. Do you remember how to get there by normal means?"

She smiled, then jumped into the cab and sped off with a wave through the back window.

Ruth's flat was situated above a parade of shops about ten minutes walk from Muswell Hill, at the southern end of Alexandra Park. There was an entrance next door to an estate agent's shop. Cornelius turned up on the stroke of seven, with flowers in one hand and a bottle in the other and with some difficulty rang the bell, which was at head height. Ruth opened the door a few moments later and there was an awkward moment when Cornelius should have kissed her on each cheek but he found himself flummoxed and presented her with the flowers and wine instead.

"Oh, how sweet, I love cornflowers." She turned to go back up the stairs and he followed her up and into the kitchen, where she found a vase for the flowers, then put them on the windowsill where they caught the early evening sun. He had no idea they were cornflowers, he just knew they were his Aunt Lucinda's favourites.

Although Cornelius had been to Ruth's flat twice, once for the party and once again to drop her off after the rescue, he'd never really had time to take it in. At the party the place had been filled with other people and furniture had been moved around or pushed back to make room. Breakages occur at parties and Ruth hadn't taken any chances. Anything with real meaning had been stowed away. The previous evening had been a very short visit. They'd arrived and stood looking at each other awkwardly.

"Right, then," said Cornelius.

"Right."

"Good night, then."

"Good night. And thanks." She'd smiled at him and then he'd left, feeling like an idiot.

Looking round at the flat now, Cornelius felt as though he'd found a safe haven, somewhere he would find it easy to settle into. It was warm and comforting and filled with everything that made Ruth what she was. He realised that, compared with this, his own flat was just somewhere he used for life's essentials. It was sparse and clinical and it lacked any lived-in feel. He knew things needed to change.

Ruth snapped him back to the present.

"I really can't wait to meet your invisible friend," she said, then smiled. "I nearly said your imaginary friend." Cornelius smiled back. "So anyway, I thought I'd better just keep it simple. I got a couple of steaks with all the trimmings and there's a homemade tiramisu to follow. This wine will be perfect." She held up the bottle he'd brought, opened it and poured out a couple of glasses.

"Cheers," she said, handing him one.

"Cheers, yourself. And thank you for cooking."

"You haven't tasted it yet."

"I'm sure it will be perfect."

As far as Cornelius was concerned, the dinner was better than perfect. He marvelled at how relaxed he felt, so different from the way he felt with Angela, where he seemed to be continually on trial.

They moved from the table and sat down next to each other on a sofa that seemed designed to push them closer together.

"So," he said, "time to introduce you to the alien in my life. The best way is to sit back and get as comfortable as you can."

"Please, God," he thought, "let them be able to communicate."

"No good getting God involved," said Euclid.

"Will you please stop listening in!"

"Will you please stop broadcasting every single thought!"

Ruth settled back into the sofa with a glass of wine in her hand and closed her eyes. Cornelius felt an almost overpowering urge to lean forward and kiss her and was just moving his head towards hers when Euclid interrupted.

"Hold on there, Romeo. This is my big moment, not yours. You can do all that canoodling business when I've finished."

"Canoodling! Where on earth did you dig that one up from?"

"Hush, I think I have contact."

"That was fast."

Ruth's eyes suddenly opened wide and she sat forward.

"Hello?"

"Hello, Ruth. Welcome to the party. My name, for all intents and purposes, is Euclid. My real name is unpronounceable. You don't have to speak out loud for me to hear you but as Cornelius can hear me as well at the moment it'll be best if both of you spoke normally so we can have a three-way conversation. We wouldn't like to leave him out would we?"

Ruth shook her head. "No, that wouldn't be right, would it." She smiled at Cornelius.

"Can I just point out that he can be a right sarcastic sod," said Cornelius.

"And can I just point out that, as I've already explained to lover-boy here, I haven't had a decent conversation for over four hundred years. Perhaps I'll fare better with you."

"It would be my pleasure," she said, trying to stifle a laugh. "I really didn't think my first conversation with an alien life-form would be anything like this."

"I don't suppose Cornelius has brought you up to speed yet with what happened to me?"

"Give me a break!" shouted Cornelius, "I've hardly had a chance. I knew nothing about it myself until this morning."

"Fine. Well, let me tell you what I told him. Hold on a second. I just need to connect a few neural pathways."

A few minutes later, Ruth knew everything Euclid had earlier told Cornelius.

"Wow! What happened there? It's like I just read an entire book in about five seconds."

"You didn't do it so fast with me this morning," said Cornelius.

"We had plenty of time this morning," said Euclid, "and I thought you might get a bit bored if you had to listen to the whole thing again. Did you get all that?" he asked Ruth.

"Yes, fine," she said, a little breathlessly. She took a large sip of her wine then sank back further into the sofa. "Wow!"

"As I've already explained to Cornelius, we're connected mind to mind. If there are things you don't want me to know you need to try and ring fence them. For my part I will give you some privacy and try not to be too nosy but if you go shouting things out I can't help but hear you. Understand?"

"Yes."

"That's more warning than he gave me," said Cornelius. "His people skills are obviously improving." He explained the rhinoceros conundrum to her, which made her smile. I like that smile, he thought, I want to see more of it.

"So, what happens next?" asked Ruth, "You have to find Tald?"

"Yes," said Euclid. "From what I can gather on the internet Tald, as Edward Kelley, was last seen in the town of Most, which is in the Czech Republic. He was being held there in the castle. That will have to be our starting point."

"Wait," said Ruth, "you can access our internet?"

"Well, of course. I can access anything that's broadcast. I wouldn't be much use to Tald if I couldn't provide communications and data when he needed it. I have to say, though, your internet needs a thorough cleaning. So much rubbish you have to sift through before you get down to the truth."

"And what about before that? Radio? TV?"

"I can't believe how long it took you lot to discover radio! I was stuck in a book, out of sight and out of mind, for hundreds of years, with no way of gleaning any information, when suddenly I started hearing voices I didn't recognise. Voices, moreover, which didn't live in my house. There was wireless telegraphy before that, of course, but that was all just dots and dashes. It took me a little while to work it out but most of it was useless to me. When radio started in earnest, in 1922, my world started to come alive again and I began to find out what had been happening in the outside world while I'd been stuck on a library shelf in a musty old book. Television was glorious. It meant I could see around the world, in a manner of speaking. Your trip to the moon in 1969. How proud you all were. If I'd been able to meet those scientists then, who knows what might be happening by now. Ho hum!"

"He's joking. He knows he's not allowed to interfere. Anyway, to get back to today, we have two objectives. One is to get hold of the crystal and two is to find Tald. Easy" said Cornelius with a grin.

At that moment his phone rang.

"Hello?"

"Cornelius?"

"Oh. Hi, Aunt Lu."

"Cornelius, there's someone here who would like a word with you."

There was a brief silence before a voice said, "Now listen very carefully, Pye."

It was the voice of Dave Slinger.

16.

At about the same time as Cornelius was being given the brush-off by Angela, West was in a spacious but discreet office overlooking Finsbury Circus. He was sitting in the hot seat, across the desk from the sharply dressed and well-manicured Alfred Carfax.

Carfax conformed to many of the stereotypes which might be expected of a successful businessman. He was thin and slightly balding, his steel-grey eyes peering out from behind very expensive rimless spectacles. He had a face that wasn't born to laugh. At most, a small smirk might appear when a hard fought deal went through or when one of his competitors found themselves in a tight spot. None of this seemed to bother him too much. As long as he got what he wanted. No-one knew very much about Alfred Carfax and that's exactly the way he intended to keep it.

His office was Victorian in style. Dark wood panelling, glass-fronted bookcases and grim-looking filing cabinets surrounded an impressively large mahogany desk, complete with blotter and solid silver Georgian inkstand. The only nods to modernity were the large computer screen positioned to one side and his mobile phone on the blotter. In the outer office he had one secretary who had been with him for many years. She didn't particularly like him but he paid her extremely well and she knew enough to keep her mouth shut, even though she was thankfully unaware of most of his shadier deals.

Born in 1959, the son of well-to-do upper middle-class parents with whom he'd had little contact for many years, Carfax had always had an aptitude for profit, from school playground deals involving lunch money to rather more involved dealings in the City, where he became a stockbroker in the early nineteen-eighties, just in time to enable himself to become stinking rich very quickly. He managed to ride the dotcom bubble perfectly, jumping out with negligible losses days before it burst. He started buying property as the market in London took off and by the middle nineteen-nineties had accumulated a fairly large portfolio based around the up and coming areas of Notting Hill and Islington. Further forays brokering deals in the early 2000s saw him take advantage of the newly emerging PFI market, which is when he moved most of his holdings overseas. His current assets were in the region of four hundred million pounds.

He began to cultivate the great and the good, firstly through old school contacts (Eton, naturally) then through donations to deserving political causes. Fairly secretive, even from an early age, he guarded his personal life jealously but began compiling dossiers on everyone with whom he came into contact. As a result he was known to few but able to influence people in positions of power on a wide variety of decisions affecting the country.

And on another level, Carfax was a criminal, pure and simple, with interests in those areas of illegality which produced the most money, mainly drugs and people trafficking.

Carfax's own view of himself was at odds with what he did for a living. His great passion was hunting down and acquiring rare or lost books, manuscripts and written ephemera. He had been chasing a copy of William Shakespeare's supposed lost work *Cardenio* for many years and believed he had uncovered enough evidence to prove its existence, though not where a copy might be found.

He had also been pursuing *Inventio Fortunata, or The Discovery of the Fortunate Islands*, by an unknown Franciscan monk from Oxford. It was known that the monk gave Edward the Third a copy sometime around 1360 and legend had it there had been an additional five printed. All copies eventually vanished but in 1364, another Franciscan described the contents of *Inventio Fortunata* to Flemish author Jacob Cnoyen, who later published a summary of what he had been told in his own book, Itinerarium.

All copies of Cnoyen's book also went missing—but not before the great cartographer Gerard Mercator had read it. In 1577, Mercator wrote a letter to John Dee, which included a quote from its description of the North Pole. Dee had replied that he knew the book, but didn't mention whether or not he owned a copy.

This connection then led him to the purchase of a bundle of correspondence between Dee and Edward Kelley, written after Dee had returned home and found his house ransacked. There were a number of missing books mentioned in the letters but unfortunately nothing that identified the missing Cnoyen.

In one of the letters Dee complained at length about his missing Euclid. Carfax's interest was piqued by references to the book's 'strange emanations' and the mention of Dee's crystal which had been used in conjunction with the book to enable the communications with the angels. Carfax discovered Nicholas Saunder's part in the aftermath of the robbery and began to focus his investigations on him. It took Carfax nearly three months before his inquiries bore fruit, uncovering the letter written to Sir Richard Ruddle, describing the riches harvested from the famed El Dorado using Dee's copy of Euclid. All the evidence pointed to Sir Richard suddenly coming into great wealth at around this time, although the actual reason for this had been lost. Why Carfax believed in this story of lost gold is a mystery. Perhaps some romantic streak in his nature that had no other outlet. He was, surprisingly for such a hard-hearted man, a sucker for tales of the supernatural. Whatever the cause, a fire had been lit and Carfax was determined to hunt down Dee's Euclid and discover the key to this supposedly unlimited wealth, but the trail was cold again until Cornelius' Aunt Violet's enquiries to the book trade.

Her first enquiry had been some five years earlier, when Sedgewick had told her the book was special. That enquiry had left whispers in the book trade that it might still exist, whispers which naturally came to Carfax's ears. What came with the whispers was the story that the book might have been passed down through the generations. Along with the whispers, a name, Pye. He checked the name in connection with Dee's and found his first real clue. A young man called Maccabeus Pye had once assisted Dee in his researches into alchemy.

Armed with this name, Carfax poured all his resources into finding him. He researched Maccabeus' family tree and found his son Roger and his grandson, Thomas, but then the enquiries ran into a dead end. The records were lost, or destroyed, or the family had moved from London. What he did discover was that Maccabeus had dealings with a merchant, a man named Henry Westwood. In the vaults of the banking firm Henry's father John had founded over four hundred years earlier he discovered a book of accounts. There, he finally found what he was looking for. Every four months or so transactions pertaining to large amounts of gold shipped from Edward Tald, of Guyana, to one Maccabeus Pye. Luckily for him, bankers never threw anything away. Confirmation, if it were needed, of all his theories.

After which there had been silence, until just less than two weeks ago when word came of Aunt Violet's second foray into the world of antiquarian books. This time she had left her details with the bookseller, who had tipped off Carfax for a nice finders fee, which is how Mr West had found his way to her house. For Cornelius, it was the start of all his present troubles.

"So. Where are we?" asked Carfax, looking intently at West.

"I had a word with his brief, Mr Briggs. He says Jez is still being held by the police on a suspected firearms charge. The things that were taken off him when he disappeared were handed in at a police station in Barnes last night in a carrier bag, along with his gun. It's got his fingerprints on it and it's been recently fired. Jez couldn't give him any explanation about what had happened at the flat. All he remembers, he says, is a blinding white light, followed by a tussle with Pye, during which the gun went off. After that it's a blank until he woke up in Whipsnade Zoo. He'll be up before the judge on Monday, after the police have made a few more enquiries and then, more likely than not, straight back inside for violating his parole requirements. He's only been out of nick for a fortnight."

"You say his belongings were handed in at a police station in Barnes?"

"Yes, Mr Briggs got that bit of info from the desk sergeant in Luton, where they're holding Jez. They were handed in by someone matching Pye's description not long after Jez had been booked in. Whoever did it ran off before they could get a name."

"But he's being held in Luton. How on earth did his things get to Barnes so quickly? And why Barnes? That's the other side of London. It's nowhere near Highbury or Whipsnade. Curiouser and curiouser. Perhaps our Mr Pye has unlocked some of the book's secrets after all."

"What, do you think he's using some sort of magic to move things around?"

"Well, I'm struggling for any other explanation at the moment." Carfax sighed, got up from the desk, walked to the window and stood for a moment, looking out over the square. He turned back to West.

"And what about his accomplice, Slinger, is it?"

"Dave," said West.

"I don't intend ever being a close personal friend of Mr Slinger," exploded Carfax, "so his first name is of little importance to me." West squirmed in his seat. Annoying Mr Carfax wasn't a good idea, as other people had found out to their cost.

"Sorry, yes, Slinger."

"So where was he when his friend was being transported to the zoo."

"He'd just popped out for a while, to grab some food."

"That was very useful of him. And where is he now?"

"He's lying low. The police know he's a close friend of Jez's, er, Wilson, and word from our friendly DC is that they're actively looking for him now as well."

"Then perhaps we need to get Mr Slinger out from under their noses for a while. I'm sure he'd appreciate that. I've got a little baby-sitting job for him up in the deep and grimy North. Do you think he'll be able to handle a sixty year-old woman? It won't be too much for him?"

"I'm sure he'll be fine," said West, with a certainty he didn't quite feel.

"He wants me to do what?" queried Slinger, "go up North? Is 'e 'aving a fuckin' laugh? Me? Go up North?" It would be true to say Dave Slinger was not comfortable anywhere outside the M25, unless it was the Costa Brava, where many of his friends and accomplices had gathered over the years. In his view, people in the north spoke funny and ate weird food, like black pudding and haggis, stuff no self-respecting Londoner would touch with a bargepole. The North was a foreign country to Slinger, it even more foreign than Spain.

"It's just for a few days, while the heat dies down. Pye's disappeared so the boss wants us to put a bit of pressure on his aunt to draw him out. She'll have his phone number. You'll be baby-sitting her while we get what we want from him. I'm sure he'll be much more pliable when he knows she's in a spot of bother."

"But up North? It's the back of fuckin' beyond up there."

"Fine. Stay here. I'll get someone else," growled West, "I'll tell you what, I'll phone the boss now and tell him you don't want to go."

"Whoa! Jussa minute, I never said I wouldn't go. Only, you know..."

Slinger knew he was defeated. Work for the boss was steady, lucrative and not particularly onerous. Added to which, people who upset him tended to disappear off the radar.

West grinned. "That's better. Now you've had your little strop shall we get down to the details?"

By six-thirty that evening Slinger was pulling into the Woodall services on the M1, a little way south of Sheffield. He was not in a good mood, having just spent over an hour in a traffic jam somewhere near Nottingham, caused by a lorry shedding its load, ironically enough, of prefabricated sheds. Combine this with the usual extremely heavy Friday afternoon traffic out of London and monster roadworks just north of Luton and it had already taken nearly four and a half hours from Tottenham, where he'd picked up the hire car. The road sign welcoming him to South Yorkshire was like some demonic bad joke.

Added to which, the aircon had died. On one of the hottest days of the year so far the inside of the car was like an oven. He'd turned all the vents he could find into the off position but the car was still blowing hot air in from somewhere by his feet and the seat warmer was stuck in the ON position. Even though he had all the windows open he was uncomfortably aware he was sitting in a puddle of his own sweat. He'd already taken off his jacket and loosened his tie and was now wishing he'd thought to wear shorts. It was a so-called smart car, fully controlled by a computer system that would have baffled Einstein. Computers and Dave Slinger did not get on. He'd just about mastered his phone but still couldn't do all the fancy things he heard other people talking about. He'd only just managed to get the fingerprint thing to work. Whatever happened to proper cars, he thought angrily. At one point in his life he'd been a trainee mechanic, before the lure of easier money had drawn him away, but that had been in the days before on-board computers.

His satnav was showing he still had another hour and twenty minutes before he reached his destination, but he desperately needed a rest and sustenance. A burger, a large coffee and possibly a shower were essential before he felt up to progressing further into bandit country, as he was now calling Yorkshire.

The more Dave Slinger thought about Cornelius Pye, the more he wanted to perform extreme acts of torture on him and all his family for getting him into this state. Slinger's creed was simple enough. People like him and Jez were put on God's good earth to make sure

172

people like Pye did as they were told. This usually worked out well and it had made him a well-respected man in his manor, Finsbury Park. People came to him for help with difficult situations and Dave would hire himself out for a reasonable sum, or slice, as it was referred to by his circle of friends. For the past couple of years he had been mainly working for Mr West and a right tidy wedge he'd been picking up. When Jez got out a couple of weeks back he'd managed to get him on board. Most normal people were intimidated by him and Jez and rightly so, he thought. They made a good team and Mr West had predicted great things for them both. And then this nonce Pye had come along and put the kibosh on it.

What had happened to Jez was unforgivable, thought Slinger. How could a little pipsqueak like Pye overcome somebody as street savvy as Jez? It didn't bear thinking about. They'd be a laughing stock if the lads found out. And how the fuck did he manage to get Jez from Highbury Corner to Whipsnade *and* take his socks and shoes off him? Pye must have drugged him somehow. I should've searched that sly little git properly when I first found him in the kitchen. Speaking of which, I still haven't worked out how he got in there. We'll have to have words about that when we meet up.

Another thing annoying Dave Slinger were the instructions from Mr West, concerning Pye's aunt.

"She must come to no harm, do you hear me? No rough stuff," said West, 'the boss wants her in good health for when you call Pye. He doesn't hold with hurting old ladies unless it's absolutely necessary. Some kink in his make-up, I expect, but he pays the wages so you do as you're told. Understand?"

"But what if she gets all snarky and won't play?" he'd countered.

"Then you can start breaking things in the house, if you like. Put your foot through the telly, smash some ornaments. That'll make her sit up and take notice. She's just one little old lady. She won't give you any bother."

Slinger wasn't convinced. His mum was a little old lady but he knew she'd fight back tooth and claw if she was cornered. His dad had told him she'd once put paid to one young villain's chances of having a family with a swift kick to the goolies and all he'd done was accidentally bump into her in the pub and spill her drink. According to his dad, the lad's apology wasn't contrite enough. A breed apart, were women, according to Dave. He'd never understood them, which was why, at the age of fifty-two, he had two failed marriages behind him.

An hour later, his burger and coffee finished and the air-conditioning in the services having dried him off somewhat he returned to the car to complete his journey north. The evening was cooler now but he still needed the windows down in the car. He rejoined the M1, only to stop once more in heavy traffic after he'd gone less than a mile because of roadworks on the approach road to the M18, where he needed to turn off towards Hull. He finally pulled up outside his destination at half past nine, seven and a half hours after setting off. He got out and put on his jacket then reached in and lifted his travelling bag off the front passenger seat. He locked the car, and looking around to make sure no-one was watching, walked up to Lucinda's door.

Lucinda was in the kitchen, making her final cup of tea of the day, when the doorbell rang. She knew no-one who would turn up at her front door at this time of night, except in an emergency, so she was quickly on her guard, the earlier conversation with Cornelius still fresh in her mind. She went first into the living room and looked around for some sort of weapon. Just in case. Her eyes lit on a large glass paperweight, not the usual round kind but a flattened version. It had an engraving of the Humber Bridge on it and had been a leaving present from her last job before retiring. She'd been meaning to take it down to the charity shop for ages but now it looked like it might finally come in useful. She thanked the fates she was wearing a fairly voluminous dress with large pockets in the sides. She dropped the paperweight into one of the pockets and went to the door, where she slipped on the security chain and opened the door. Peering through the side she saw the large, dishevelled, sixteen-stone muscular outline of Dave Slinger.

"Yes?"

Before she could say any more, Slinger threw himself at the door with all the force he could muster, which tore the chain from the door frame. She jumped back to avoid the door swinging towards her and fell over backwards onto the floor. Slinger stepped in quickly, dropped his bag on the floor and closed the door behind him.

"You should know," he said, "that most security chains are fuckin' useless unless they're fitted by a proper company. Yours wouldn't have stopped a fuckin' boy scout."

"Who the hell are you?" shouted Lucinda from the floor. "Get out of my house. NOW!"

"Up you get," said Slinger, looming over her, grabbing her arm and pulling her roughly to her feet, "let's go in and have a little chat." He started to propel her towards the kitchen, deciding it would be better to keep away from the front of the house.

"Jus' behave and you won't get 'urt. Do you follow?" He pushed her down onto a chair by the table.

If Slinger had expected a meek and tearful reply at this point he was sadly disappointed.

"You'd better get out of my house now or you'll be wishing you'd never been born," snarled Lucinda, standing slowly and looking him straight in the eye. He slammed the table so hard she jumped in spite of herself.

"Sit down!", roared Slinger. "If you don't shut up and behave I'll give you such a slap you'll wake up in the middle of next week wondering what 'appened." On the last word he lifted the table to one side and upended it. There was an almighty crash as the table and everything on it hit the floor. There was nothing now between her and Slinger. In spite of this, she glared at him for a few seconds, before slowly sinking back down onto the chair. Slinger felt better, now he'd made some noise and vented a bit of his anger on the table. He really, *really* wanted to hurt her, but knew if he did there'd be consequences.

"What do you want with me?" asked Lucinda.

"With you, nothing. It's that long streak of piss nephew of yours what we want. You're our insurance policy to make sure 'e does as 'e's told. Now, where's your phone?"

"Well, it was on the table, before you had your little tantrum. It's there behind you, if it's still working."

Slinger picked it up and handed it to her. "Call 'im," he growled.

"Make me," she replied.

He walked over to the kitchen worktop and opened a few drawers until he found what he wanted, a bone-handled carving knife. Lucinda looked around, searching for a way to escape. He noticed and put himself between her and the door, then advanced towards her, took a handful of hair, yanked her head back and held the knife at her throat. Lucinda grabbed the sides of the chair in terror.

"Please," he whispered, menacingly, his face a couple of inches from hers, "don't make it any 'arder than it already is. I 'aven't had the nicest of days so far. I've just spent nearly eight hours coming up to this god-forsaken shit'ole of the world in a so-called smart car with the 'eater on full, so I'm hot, tired and thirsty. I don't know how much more I can take before I snap. Do you understand me?"

She looked at him, eyes wide, trying to avoid his hamburger breath.

"I said, do you understand me?" he shouted into her ear.

"Yes," she croaked. She knew when she was beaten.

"Now, are you going to make that call or not?"

She nodded, carefully.

"Good. Now I'll tell you what. You make me a nice cup of tea with some biscuits. You do 'ave biscuits?"

She nodded again.

"Chocolate?"

Another nod, almost imperceptible.

"Lovely. Let's just relax and we can start all over again as pals. Alright?"

"Mm." A small noise in her throat.

He let go of her. Slowly, she stood. Her legs were shaking but she managed to control them enough to allow her to walk over to the kettle and begin making tea.

"I'll be watching you, so don't do anything stupid," said Slinger, settling himself into the chair she'd just vacated. "Mine's milk and two sugars."

When she'd poured out two mugs of tea and filled a small plate with chocolate digestives Slinger stood and set the table back on its legs. She put a mug and the plate of biscuits in front of him. He put the knife down on the table. Her eyes followed the movement.

"That's better. Civilised now, ent we?" said Slinger after a noisy slurp of hot tea. "Don't get no fancy ideas about this," he said, tapping the knife with a finger, "that wouldn't be smart, would it?"

His bulk seemed to take up most of one side of the table. Lucinda stood as far away as possible from him, with her back against the sink. She considered throwing her mug of tea at him but didn't know what that might achieve, apart from a momentary feeling of joy. The aftermath didn't bear thinking about so she restrained herself.

"What is it you want?" she asked.

"Well now," said Slinger, "that's more like it. See 'ow well we're getting on now? No need for all that palaver before, was there?"

She sipped her tea, keeping her eyes on him at all times.

"Your nephew 'as annoyed a very important person, someone who was only tryin' to be nice to him and when that type of person get's annoyed there's consequences, right?"

"What's Cornelius supposed to have done?"

"Don't you know? 'E 'asn't spoken to you?"

"Not since the funeral, no."

"Funeral? What funeral?"

"His uncle. He died a few weeks ago. I went down to the funeral in Mortlake."

"Ah, so that'll be where 'e got the book from, is it?"

"What book are you talking about?"

"See. There we were, getting along all nice and now you're tellin' me porkies. You know very well what book. The book what all this is about. This person I work for is very keen to get 'is 'ands on it and your nephew with it. Don't ask me why. I'm just 'ere to make sure it 'appens and like I said, you're our insurance policy to make sure 'e behaves 'imself until it's all sorted. You'd better get used to havin' me around for a few days, until all this blows over. Then I'll be off and it'll be like I was never 'ere an' I for one will be very happy to be away from 'ere an' back on me own patch, where I belong. I fuckin' 'ate the North."

Slinger finished his tea and ate a few more biscuits. He took his own phone out of his jacket pocket and sent a quick text to West, telling him he'd arrived and was in the house. He placed it on the table, then he stood, picked up Lucinda's phone and the knife, walked over to her and handed her the phone. He then went over to the cutlery drawer and took out all the other knives and sharp objects he could find, scanned the room for anything else that might be used as an offensive weapon, opened the back door and threw them all out into the garden. He locked the door, pocketed the key and stood in front of her.

"Better safe than sorry," he grinned. Lucinda finished her tea, then placed her mug in the dishwasher, under Slinger's steady gaze. She was reaching for the mug and plate on the table when he stopped her.

"S'alright. You can play housewife later. Phone call first."

"What am I supposed to say?"

Jus' tell 'im there's someone wants to speak to 'im, then 'and the phone to me. Can you manage that?"

She nodded and dialled the number.

17.

"Now listen very carefully, Pye. Do you know who this is?"

"I've got a fairly good idea, yes."

"Good. Then you know I'm not gonna fuck around. I don't know what you did to my mate Jez and I'll personally settle up with you over that once this little shenanigans is all over, but I want you to think very carefully before you start pullin' any tricks with me. Gorrit?"

"Yes, got it."

"Cos any funny business on your part an' your aunt will be makin' a visit to the local A&E an' she may have to stay there a very long time. Do I make myself clear?"

"Yes. Extremely."

Cornelius had sunk back onto the sofa, his face white. Ruth was looking at him quizzically, mouthing the words, "What's up?"

"It's Dave Slinger. He's at Aunt Lu's," he whispered. Ruth went the same shade of white and grasped hold of his arm. He put the phone on speaker so she could hear, then signed to her to stay quiet.

"You still there, Pye?" asked Slinger.

"Yes, yes, I'm still here. What do you want with my aunt?"

"She's the reason you're going to be a good little boy an' do everything I tell you."

"If you hurt her, I swear I'll -." He couldn't finish the sentence because he didn't know what he'd do.

"You'll what? Come after me? Beat me up? Ooh, I'm shakin' like a leaf," said Slinger sarcastically. "Listen, sunbeam, the day I can't handle a little shit like you 'll be the day they put me in the ground. Now, are you going to listen or do I have to make some noise at this end?"

"Alright. Calm down. Aunt Lu's got nothing to do with all this and I'm sure she's scared enough so please leave her alone and tell me what it is you want me to do." Cornelius was trying very hard to stay calm himself but he could feel Ruth's hand shaking where she was holding onto him, which made him feel even more nervous.

"Now you're seein' sense. I thought you would, once you knew I meant business. This is what you're going to do."

Dave Slinger was feeling pleased with himself now things were going to plan. He would have liked to have put his boot through the television, as Mr West had suggested, but the old dear didn't have one in her kitchen and he couldn't be bothered to drag her through the house looking for one, just to prove a point. No matter, the look on her face when he'd upended the table had been nearly as good and she was now standing against the sink again, meek as you like. Control, that was the key. Show them who's boss and they'll do anything to keep you happy. Same with this Pye geezer. Once he'd realised what was what he'd soon backed down. Now, at last, after the shit day he'd had so far, he was beginning to enjoy himself a bit. Just got to get the instructions from Mr West understood by Pye then he could relax a bit, maybe get a curry delivered and a few beers, like a regular Friday night. He turned his attention back to the phone.

"You've got twenty-four hours to work out how that fuckin' book works. No ifs, buts or maybes, understand? You phone me back to say it's done and I'll arrange to 'ave you picked up by Mr West. He'll drive you out to where you were before and you'll prove to him you've sorted it. Once 'e's happy, 'e'll let you loose an' call me 'ere. Then I'll leave your precious aunt to 'er own devices and make my way back home to civilisation. Any questions? I do 'ope the answer's 'No.'"

"I don't have the book," said Cornelius, "I er, I took it to the bank this afternoon, for safe keeping." He wondered if it was still in the table drawer where his aunt had put it after he had left it with her. It was going to be very difficult to retrieve it with Slinger in the house as well, if it came to it.

"Not my problem, is it? Twenty-four hours."

Slinger hung up. The thought of curry and beer had been on his mind during the last part of the call and he had developed a raging thirst with all the talking he'd been doing. He spotted the fridge, walked over to it and opened the door, looking inside for a cold drink, hopefully even a beer. In doing so, he made the first mistake of his visit. He turned his back on Aunt Lucinda. Lights exploded before his eyes and to use the local parlance, he went down like a sack of spuds.

In Ruth's flat, Cornelius was in agonies.

"What am I going to do? It's all my fault. I should have realised they weren't done with us." He turned to Ruth. "I've already put you through it and now this. Aunt Lu must be scared stiff."

"It's not your fault, Cornelius, you couldn't have known this would happen."

"Calm down, both of you," said Euclid, "we need to think. It's no good getting your knickers in a twist, it's not going to help anyone."

"But you heard him. He'll hurt Aunt Lu if I don't do what they say," shouted Cornelius. "Even if I get the book to them how am I going to explain you? You already said West's boss couldn't hear you and it's odds on West can't either."

Just then, Cornelius' phone rang again. He saw who was calling and answered immediately, expecting to hear the voice of Dave Slinger once again. Instead he heard his aunt breathe his name.

"Cornelius?"

"Aunt Lu?" he shouted. "Are you alright?"

"You need to get over here right away. I think I've killed him."

"What?"

"What's happened?" asked Ruth.

"She says she thinks she's killed him." He turned back to the phone and once again, put it on speaker. "What do you mean, killed him?"

"When I heard the doorbell I wasn't expecting anyone and I knew that if you were going to turn up you would have warned me and after everything that's happened I had a feeling something might be wrong. So on my way to answer the door I nipped into the living room and slipped a glass paperweight in my pocket. Then, after we got off the phone from you he decided he was thirsty and he went to the fridge. That's when I hit him."

"Oh, Aunt Lu!"

"Probably not dead. Ask her if she's got any rope," said Euclid, "she'll need to tie him up before he comes round."

Cornelius relayed the request to her.

"Yes, I've got a ball of string in one of the kitchen drawers."

"Okay, you start tying him up and I'll be there in a couple of minutes."

He ended the call.

"What about me?" asked Ruth, "can I help?"

"I'd really rather you didn't. I've involved you too much already. If anything goes wrong it would be all my fault. I'm hoping we can get something sorted before he sees me and I don't want to risk him seeing you as well."

"Well, hurry back and let me know what's happening."

"Thanks. I won't be long, hopefully." He took her hand and gave it a squeeze.

He calmed himself and imagined his aunt's kitchen. He decided that, with a body on the floor and his aunt presumably pacing up and down, the safest place to materialise would be just outside the kitchen door. When he found himself standing there he looked through the glass. His aunt was standing with her back to him, by the sink. He tapped gently.

"Aunt Lu?"

He saw his aunt stiffen momentarily, then she turned to face him.

"I can't open the door, Cornelius. He locked it and put the key in his pocket."

"Okay. Give me room and I'll come through." He willed himself three feet forward, a lot easier when he could actually see the spot he was aiming for. He gave his aunt a hug, then realised she was still holding the ball of string. He looked at her, quizzically.

"I'm sorry. I couldn't bring myself to go anywhere near him," she said. "What if I've killed him?" Slinger chose that moment to let out a low moan and shifted slightly.

"No such luck." He smiled at her. "Quick, Aunt Lu, we need to get him tied up. Then we can decide what to do next."

Luckily, Slinger was face down on the floor, but it still took a bit of pushing and pulling to manoeuvre his arms behind him. His aunt held Slinger's wrists together while Cornelius wrapped the string around. For good measure he looped the string a couple of times around one of the table legs then finished off with a couple of tight knots back at the wrists.

Slinger groaned again and shifted slightly on the floor.

"Where's his phone?"

"That one, on the table"

Cornelius picked it up and inspected it.

"It's fingerprint protected," he said, "let's see if we can get him to open it."

He knelt down and pressed an index finger onto the screen. Nothing happened, so he tried with the index finger on the other hand. Success this time. He went into Settings and removed all the security features, then placed the phone in his pocket. He raised a finger to his lips to make sure his aunt didn't say anything further and beckoned to her to follow him, picking up his aunt's phone on the way. They went into the living room and sat next to each other on the sofa, holding hands.

"If he wakes up, I don't want him to know I've been here," explained Cornelius in a low voice. "I'm tempted to disappear him somewhere, like I did with his mate, but that leaves too much to explain. There's still Slinger's boss and the person he reports to in turn. They're a lot cleverer than this one so I don't want to give them too much to think about. Now that I've got into his phone I can see what calls he's been making, see if I can find a way to his boss. I think the best thing for you to do now is call the police and tell them he broke in and threatened you. Better tell them they'll need an ambulance as well. They shouldn't take long to get here. I'll wait until they arrive before I go."

He handed her the phone and she dialled. When the call ended he asked what had happened. His aunt was remarkably calm and he marvelled as she explained the events of the evening.

"I'll say it again," she said, finally, "your uncle was a fool. He was supposed to keep that book a secret but it sounds like everybody and his dog knows about it."

"Too late now, Aunt Lu."

"Do you want to take it with you? I'd feel safer if it wasn't here."

"Of course. I'll take it to Ruth's and we can hide it somewhere."

"Who's Ruth?"

"I told you before. Someone I work with. A friend," said Cornelius, as nonchalantly as he could, not daring yet to admit it could me more.

"Oh," said his aunt, eyeing him keenly, not fooled for a second. "Good." She disappeared into the kitchen, returning a few seconds later with the book.

"What will you do now? You need to be extra careful because they'll still be after you."

"Don't worry. I'll try and sort something out."

They heard sirens and seconds later saw blue lights flashing through the window.

"Bye, Aunt Lu. Take care. I'll probably be back tomorrow at some point. I'll text you beforehand."

"'Bye, love. Thanks for your help. And say hello to Ruth for me." As they hugged, there was a sharp rap at the door and someone shouted, "Police!"

"You'd better get yourself off," she said, then went to let them in.

Back at Ruth's he dropped the book onto a chair and gave her a quick thumbs up and a smile. She came over and hugged him tightly.

"What happened? Is your aunt okay?" She released him and he gave her all the details.

"Thank God you're alright," she whispered and hugged him again. "I was really worried." Cornelius was happy to continue the hug, but Euclid interrupted them.

"Sorry, children, we've got work to do. Two of the bad guys may be out of the picture but they were just foot soldiers. The real brains and his lieutenant are still out there and we don't have much info on them at the moment. Slinger's phone is going to be a good place to start."

Cornelius hadn't yet released Ruth.

"Sorry, Euclid, but you're going to have to wait a minute until my heart rate returns to normal. Ruth's helping me."

He couldn't see her face but he heard her giggle. They stayed that way a few more seconds, then broke apart and looked into each others' eyes. Cornelius' heart fluttered once again, in a good way this time. They smiled at each other, then sat down on the sofa.

"Have you quite finished?" asked Euclid.

"For the time being," answered Cornelius, still smiling. "Ruth, do you think you can hide the book somewhere?"

She jumped up. "I'll find somewhere for it," she said. "What about a drink before we start. I don't know about you but all this excitement has made me thirsty." She noticed the empty bottle. "I'll open another one," she said, disappearing into the kitchen. He heard the pop of a cork, then she reappeared and began filling their glasses.

"Now have we finished?" said Euclid.

They both nodded and took a drink.

"So, as I was saying, we need to find out who the big boys are before they come back at us. Let's get into that phone."

A quick check of Slinger's contact list revealed nothing interesting. There was no listing under West. Most entries seemed to be members of Slinger's family and friends. Dots, Lols, Gavs and Tracys, interspersed with entries for garages, pubs and betting shops. They checked his SMS messages and found the last entry, *"I'm here and inside. All under control"*. The name of the contact was Bunce.

"Bunce?" asked Cornelius.

"It's a slang word for money," said Ruth, 'maybe it's some little in-joke. Your Mr West must be the one who pays him."

"Possibly derived from the word bonus," said Euclid.

"Yes, you'd know, wouldn't you?" replied Cornelius. He turned to Ruth. "Did I tell you he's a big fan of cop shows like The Sweeney?"

"I don't think I've ever heard of that one," she replied.

"Oh, what a sheltered life you've lived," said Euclid. " Now can you both please pay attention?"

"Yes, mum," giggled Cornelius.

Euclid sighed. Cornelius wondered how an entity without breath could do that. He decided it was time to get serious again.

They looked next at Slinger's emails and discovered Bunce was actually Bunce Security. A number of emails from them contained details of jobs, mainly of the door security variety, to be carried out at various clubs across London. These emails had stopped abruptly six weeks earlier, about the same time more cryptic text messages started. When they returned to the Bunce texts Cornelius wasn't surprised to find one dated the seventeenth of June, the day the book was stolen, giving his address and a time. There was another, dated a day later, which simply read *"Pick him up."* Finally, there was a text with his aunt's name and address.

"We have to find out a bit more about this Mr West and Bunce Security," said Ruth to Cornelius, "assuming they're one and the same. He's the only link we have now to his boss, the man you spoke to on the phone."

"I would think so," replied Cornelius. He got his own phone out and did an internet search. "They don't have their own website but they're on a listing site, with an address in Tottenham and a local phone number. We could give them a call tomorrow and see if we can get any more information but there may not be anyone there over the weekend. One thing we can't do is hand the phone over to the police. They'll make the same connection as we're doing and bring him in for questioning before we get a crack at him."

"What are we going to do if we do manage to track him down?" asked Ruth, "he's not likely to tell us what we want to know, is he?"

"I think you can leave that to me," offered Euclid. "Assuming we get close enough, I'm sure I can persuade him to tell us all, quite voluntarily. And he will get close because Cornelius is going to tell Slinger he's cracked the code and Slinger is going to arrange for Cornelius to be picked up tomorrow morning by Mr West."

"And how are we going to do that with Slinger in a prison cell?" asked Cornelius.

"We don't need Slinger, because we've got Slinger's phone." Comprehension dawned.

"But we'll need to act fast, before West gets the news Slinger's been pinched. With a bit of luck Slinger will be kept at the hospital overnight. That's the usual procedure for a head injury so he may not be able to get word out about what's happened until they take him to the police station. So first thing tomorrow morning we send him the text and with any luck he'll send one back with details of the pick up."

"What if West phones instead?" asked Ruth.

"Yes, it is possible," replied Euclid, "but going by these other text messages it looks like he prefers to text the important stuff, presumably so Slinger doesn't make a mistake. Not the brightest candle in the box, is he?"

Ruth frowned. "You can't ask Cornelius to do this. It's dangerous."

"I'm sure I'll be fine," said Cornelius, uncertainly, not feeling particularly brave.

"That's the spirit," said Euclid, "Of course he'll be fine. I'll be with him"

"We'll set up the meeting with West, then you can take this phone back to your aunt." said Euclid, "Get her to hand it over to the police. She can say she found it after Slinger was taken away. I'd say it contains enough evidence to put him away for a goodish while."

Cornelius checked his watch and was surprised to see it was only ten thirty. So much seemed to have happened since he'd got out of bed that morning.

"Er, it's getting late. Perhaps we should think about wrapping things up."

"Yes," said Euclid, "big day tomorrow. You probably need to get a good night's sleep."

He walked over to Ruth and put his arms around her. She responded and they stood there, silent for a moment. Cornelius spoke first.

"Thanks for everything. I've had a fabulous evening. Perhaps not the one I thought it would be when I first arrived."

"Thank you for coming. When I woke up this morning I never guessed I'd be conversing with an alien. Apart from when you went to your aunt's I've had a really lovely time."

They looked at each other, still in an embrace.

"I'd better say good night."

"Good night, whispered Ruth. She looked up at him. He looked down at her. There were only a couple of inches in it. Then, inevitably, they kissed. For quite a long time. Then she whispered, "You don't have to go."

Euclid, thankfully, was saying nothing. Cornelius was concentrating on keeping him out of his head by thinking about rhinoceroses. It seemed to be working. He could feel his heart rate increasing again. He couldn't remember the last time he'd felt so good.

"Are you sure?"

"I don't think I could sleep for a while, after all that excitement."

"Oh," said Cornelius. "Funnily enough, I was thinking the same thing."

18.

The next morning was another bright, clear day over London and in Cornelius' heart. He opened his eyes to see the still sleeping Ruth next to him. Everything tingled and he sighed ecstatically, a stupid grin on his face. He stroked her shoulder gently and she woke and looked at him.

"Hello," he whispered.

"Hello, back." They cuddled, and things would have progressed nicely, if not for an interruption.

"Good!" Euclid's voice rang out, shattering the early morning peace. "Finally, you're both awake! Chop, chop! We've got lots to do."

"Oh no," groaned Cornelius. He'd been looking forward to resuming where he and Ruth had left off in the early hours. From her exasperated sigh it was clear she'd been thinking along the same lines.

"Come on!" exhorted Euclid, "It's nearly eight o'clock. Time to get started. Lots to do."

"But it's Saturday," complained Cornelius, "I was looking forward to a bit of a lie in. We didn't get a lot of sleep last night."

"Sorry, children, but we need to get our plan into action before West gets acquainted with the facts about his buddy, Slinger. I did mention this last night."

"I don't suppose you can make tea, can you?" asked Cornelius.

"Don't be facetious."

"Come on," said Ruth, "let's not annoy the brother from another planet. We don't want him zapping us with a deadly mind ray because we wouldn't get up." She rose from the bed and pausing only to slip on a dressing gown, left the room.

"I'll get the kettle on." she shouted.

Cornelius watched her go, sad and happy at the same time.

"Thanks for staying quiet last night. I really appreciate it."

"No problem. I could see how much it meant to you. But now you've addressed your primitive urges we really do need to get a move on. Do you think your aunt will be up yet?"

"I don't know." said Cornelius, rising from the bed, "She's usually up by now. I'll give her a ring."

He hunted around for his clothes, which were scattered over a wide area, then joined Ruth in the kitchen.

"Hello, beautiful," he said, kissing her once again.

She wrapped her arms around him. "Hello, handsome."

They smiled at each other. The kettle boiled awhile.

After a breakfast dogged by Euclid's persistent calls to hurry, Cornelius phoned his aunt.

"How are you this morning, Aunt Lu?"

"Still a bit shaky, to be honest. Yesterday must have affected me more than I realised. I didn't sleep too well and I was awake early."

There was a noise from Euclid, which sounded like "Ha!"

"I'm not surprised. I'm so sorry I've brought this on you."

"You have no need to apologise, Cornelius. It's not you who set all this in motion. At least there's one less player in the game now, after last night."

"Oh yes, Mister Slinger. How was he when the police came?"

"The idiot was away with the fairies," said his aunt crossly, as she remembered the incident. "He had no idea why he was sitting on the floor of my kitchen, surrounded by police and a concerned young paramedic. He couldn't even tell them who he was and I didn't know his name. They identified him after finding his driving license in his wallet. At first, I think the police had the impression he was someone I knew and I'd attacked him for no reason. It was only when I showed them the broken security chain and the bundle of knives outside the back door that they began to take what I was saying seriously. I suppose it might have been my fault. When I phoned them I just said I thought I'd killed him but didn't explain further."

"Oh, Aunt Lu, I'm sorry."

"I've told you, you've got nothing to be sorry about. Anyway, the ambulance crew eventually got him strapped to a stretcher and carried him out, handcuffed to the trolley. He still didn't know what was going on, he kept shouting, "What am I doing here?" After he'd been taken away someone made me a cup of tea and sat me down. A young policewoman interviewed me and I told her about what had happened to you and how this man had barged his way into the house, threatening to beat me up if you didn't do what you were told. And then I explained what I'd done. She told me she'd probably have done

189

exactly the same in those circumstances, so that made me feel a bit better. Up to that point I was feeling a bit like a criminal myself. But he had the audacity to break into *my* home."

"It can't be a nice feeling. I still think of it as my home as well."

"It will always be your home, you know that."

"I know."

He arranged to return Slinger's phone later that morning, then said his goodbyes and hung up. He looked across at Ruth.

"I'll need to go back to Barnes to have a shower and brush my teeth, find some clean clothes. I'll be back in half an hour or so. Will you miss me?"

"I'll yearn for you, tragically," she replied.

"I'll try and make it fifteen minutes." He leaned over and kissed her. He took a minute to compose himself then vanished. A little over twenty minutes later he was back, refreshed and changed.

"It's weird how you just disappear and reappear. One second you're there, the next you're not. It's almost mundane, blink and you'll miss it. And there's no sound. I keep expecting to hear some sort of sound effect, but there's nothing."

"Let's discuss this when we've got more time," said Euclid, impatiently, "at this particular moment we need to send our message to West."

"What do you suggest?"

"Well, from a quick read through of Slinger's text messages, he keeps them short so we only need to send the basics. The main thing is to try and get his style right, so we don't raise any suspicions."

"Okay," said Ruth, "how about something like this."

She picked up the phone, opened the app and typed "*Pye just call. He says hes cracked it.*"

"Looks good to me," said Cornelius.

"Yes," agreed Euclid. Simple and to the point. Let's try that." She pressed send.

"Fingers crossed," she whispered.

In his hospital bed, Dave Slinger was just coming round. He'd been having the strangest dream. He remembered flashing blue lights and sirens blaring, then lots of people in surgical masks peering at him and shining lights into his eyes. He was aware of a heavy ache at the back of his head, which made him feel a little sick. He opened his eyes and closed them again quickly when the room started reeling. What room? Not one he'd seen before. He tried opening them again and the room wobbled into focus. He was in a room by himself, lying on his back, propped up on a couple of pillows. Hospital, he thought, I'm in a hospital. I must have had an accident. There was something unmistakable about hospitals, like nowhere else. He closed his eyes again to keep the light out.

He tried to remember what had happened. He was definitely driving a car yesterday, a very hot car. But where was he going? He recalled being on the motorway but didn't know why. He vaguely remembered being unhappy. Had he had a smash? There was a service station, burger and chips, a traffic jam. Maybe he'd been rear-ended. That would explain why his neck was aching so much. Whiplash. He must have gone out like a light when he was hit.

He tried calling out but got out nothing more than a dry croak. No-one came. He opened his eyes again, very carefully and moved his head to one side. He was hooked up to some kind of machine. A cable led from it to his index finger, where it was fastened with a sort of clip. He had expected it to be making a noise but it was silent. Slowly, he moved his head to the other side and saw a bedside cabinet with a pitcher of water and glass on top. He tried reaching out his hand but it would only move a couple of inches. There was a sort of clinking noise when he did so. He looked down and discovered he was handcuffed to the bed.

Ah, he thought, what have I done now? He noticed there was a large button by his handcuffed hand. He pressed it and waited. Did I kill someone with the car? I don't remember hitting anything in front of me. Couldn't have been a pedestrian, I was on a motorway, they're not allowed.

The door opened and a nurse came in, Slinger caught a glimpse of a police uniform behind her, hovering at the door.

"Hello there," said the nurse, quietly, "how are you feeling?"

He croaked again and looked over at the water. She poured some water into the glass then held it to his lips while he drank. All he could see was her face. She's gorgeous, he thought.

"What happened?" he asked.

"Can't you remember?"

191

He tried to shake his head, then realised moving it was causing a great deal of pain.

"No."

"You were hit on the back of the head."

"Was it a car?"

"No," she smiled, "why do you think it was a car?"

"I was on the motorway. In a car," he added, for clarification.

"No. It wasn't a car. It was a paperweight."

"A paperweight? In the car?" Slinger was becoming confused. He didn't remember having a paperweight with him in the car. He didn't even own a paperweight.

"No, not in the car. In the house."

"What 'ouse?"

The nurse smiled again, such a beautiful smile, he thought. "I'll get the doctor to come and look at you. Alright?"

He tried to nod his head but the pain hit him again. The nurse turned and went to the door. Again, he got a glimpse of the police uniform. I'm in big trouble, he thought.

After she'd sent the text Ruth disappeared into the bathroom, leaving Cornelius sitting at the table looking at the phone.

"It's been twenty minutes," he complained. Surely he's seen it by now."

"Maybe he's still asleep," said Euclid.

"Yes, like we could have been. Well, not asleep, but you know what I mean."

"Are you going to moan about it all day?"

"No." He paused. "Not all day. But in the normal way of things today would have been extra special, a day of getting to know each other. It's a beautiful, sunny day. I could be going for a walk in the park with the girl of my dreams. Instead, I'm going to be running out at a moment's notice to meet yet another lunatic who wants to hurt either me or someone I know."

"Girl of your dreams, eh? That's a bit sudden."

"Well that's how it happens, isn't it? All of a sudden, and now I'm on edge, alright. I'm a bit scared."

"Yes, I understand," said Euclid, "I'm sorry, I really am, but I didn't know it would pan out this way. Although I did say she fancied you, didn't I and I was right."

"Yes. You were right. Thank you. I don't suppose I would have got up the nerve to ask her out yesterday if it hadn't been for you giving me a hard time." He smiled at the memory.

Euclid changed tack.

"It might be an idea to give DI Evans a call after you've dropped Slinger's phone off. Let him know what happened at your aunt's house. Although he'll find out soon enough, I suppose, when news reaches him about Slinger's arrest."

"Should we mention what we've found out about Bunce Security and West?"

"No, I think we should keep it under our hats for now. You know what the police are like. They don't want amateurs getting in the way. The problem is, if we don't get to West before they do, we might never find out who his boss is. If he's arrested he'll just clam up and we'll be back to square one."

"You're still doing it, aren't you?" laughed Cornelius, ""He'll clam up!" Which particular cop show did you get that phrase from?"

"I think it might have been 'The Rockford Files.'"

Ruth came back into the kitchen and they met each other like long lost lovers. After surfacing for air, she asked, "Tea? Coffee?"

"Tea would be wonderful."

"Do you ever drink coffee?" she asked.

"Rarely," said Cornelius, "usually just on holiday. They can't make tea to save their lives anywhere abroad, so it's usually the safer bet."

Slinger's phone buzzed. A message from Bunce. It read, *'Tell him outside the office. Midday. No funny business or else.'*

"The office?" shouted Cornelius.

"He must mean the place in Tottenham, Bunce Security's office," suggested Ruth.

"Let's hope so, or we're screwed," said Euclid. "We've got an hour and a half to find out."

Dave Slinger was dozing when a doctor opened one of his eyes and shone a light into it.

"Uh, what," he muttered, disorientated once more.

"Just follow the light, please." said the doctor, as he moved the light from side to side. Slinger did his best.

"Good," said the doctor, "now, can you tell me your name?"

"Dave."

"Just Dave?"

A pause, then, "What?"

"I mean, what's your surname?"

"Oh, right, yes, er -" He paused, thinking hard. "Slinger," he said at last, "Dave Slinger."

"And can you remember what happened to you, Dave?"

"I was hit on the back of the head. The nurse said it was a paperweight, but I didn't have one in the car."

The doctor, whose name tag Slinger could now read as Patel, turned to a nurse at the end of the bed.

"Definitely concussion. He's still a bit confused. I'm not surprised, really." He turned back to Slinger.

"We've checked your x-rays and your skull is intact, but you have got a pretty bad case of concussion. We're going to keep you in here for a few days and keep an eye on you. Do you understand?"

Slinger nodded. He was surprised to find the action a lot easier to do than the first time he'd come round. The pain in his head had subsided. They must have dosed him with painkillers at some point.

"Do you not remember being in someone's house when this happened?"

"In someone's 'ouse?" parroted Slinger, "What do you mean, 'in someone's 'ouse?'"

"Can I question him now, doctor?" asked a voice from somewhere in the room. Slinger raised his head and saw the policeman again.

"Not yet, I'm afraid. Let's leave it a couple of hours, see how he gets on. We have to tread carefully when there's been trauma to the head." The policeman pulled a face and left the room.

"Can I ask a question?" inquired Slinger.

"Of course."

"Do you know why I'm handcuffed to the bed? Did I do something?"

"I'm afraid I can't answer that, Dave. I'm sure the police will let you know all about it a bit later. They're outside, waiting to interview you. But for now, I need you to get some rest."

"Thanks," he said, as he drifted back to sleep.

Cornelius texted his aunt to say he was on his way, then appeared in her kitchen by the back door once he'd seen she'd read it.

"Hello? It's me."

"In here," shouted his aunt from the living room. He went through to find her in her favourite armchair, feet up on a footstool, browsing through a copy of The Times.

"How are you doing?"

"Improving, I think. I've got someone coming round to mend the door after lunch, hopefully with something a bit more substantial than what was on there."

She stood and gave him a hug, which he returned.

"I'm sorry you've got mixed up in this."

"You need to stop apologising. I told you, it's not your fault. Anyway, I think I gave as good as I got and the police have told me I'm not being arrested for attempted murder or anything." She smiled. "That was a joke, Cornelius."

He returned the smile.

"The police phoned about ten minutes ago to let me know that the animal who broke in is still in the hospital, suffering from concussion and temporary amnesia. They're saying he can't remember being here or anything about what happened last night. They're still waiting for the doctor's permission to let them interview him. I told them I'd found the phone. There'll be someone coming round to pick it up, before midday, they said."

He handed the phone over to her.

"We've managed to make contact with his boss. We sent him a text, pretending to be Slinger, to say I'd cracked the code and as far as we know, he thinks Slinger's still here with you. I'm being picked up at midday, supposedly so I can show him what I've discovered, but Euclid's hatched a little surprise for him. We're hoping we can find out who he works for before the police get hold of him."

"Please be careful, Cornelius."

"I will. I promise. Sorry, but I have to get back. We don't have a lot of time before the meet. Are you sure you'll be okay?"

"I'll be fine, Cornelius. It'll take a lot more than that idiot to get the better of me. That'll teach him not to turn his back on a defenceless old woman."

In the hospital, Slinger surfaced once more and as he did, the events of the previous evening came back to him.

"Oh, fuck," he exclaimed, loudly to the empty room.

He needed to let Mr West know what had happened because a penny to a pound Pye would know by now his aunt was no longer being threatened. He realised he was going to be in deep shit but the alternative, not saying anything and hoping it all went away, was probably not a good option. He reached for the button and pressed. A minute later the nice looking nurse came into the room.

"I need to make a phone call," he shouted, urgently, "get me my phone."

"Now just calm down, Mr Slinger, I'll go and get Doctor Patel for you."

"Well, 'urry up. I've got to make a call. It can't wait."

The nurse left and returned a few minutes later with Doctor Patel. Just behind him was the policeman.

"Hello, Dave," greeted the doctor, "How are you feeling now? You do look a lot more chipper."

"I'm fine. I've got to make a phone call."

"Whoa, slow down. I need to examine you."

"I don't need examining. I need a phone," shouted Slinger. Attracted by the noise the policeman entered the room.

"How's the memory, Dave? Is it all coming back to you now?"

"My memory's fine. Just get me my bloody phone!" He started to rise from the bed but was pulled back by the handcuffs. The policeman pushed him back down onto the bed.

"Calm down, mate, calm down."

Slinger subsided.

"She bloody hit me, didn't she? She hit me! That's assault. I want to press charges."

"So, you remember what happened now do you?"

Slinger looked at the policeman and realised there was no turning back now. He nodded.

"About bloody time," said the policeman. "David Slinger, I'm arresting you for threatening behaviour and criminal trespass. No doubt, we'll find other charges once we get you down to the station. You do not have to say anything but it may harm your defence if you do not mention when questioned, something that you later rely on in Court. Anything you do say may be given in evidence. Do you understand?"

Slinger nodded again.

"Can I make a phone call?"

"Certainly not."

"Well, can you phone my brief and tell him what's happened, then? There's a card in my wallet with his details. My mum will be worried if she doesn't hear from me."

"You carry a brief's details with you? This won't be your first offence then, Mr Slinger?"

This time Slinger shook his head. He knew he should have never agreed to come up north.

19.

Cornelius arrived at the appointed place ten minutes before midday, with the book in a rucksack over one shoulder. The office of Bunce Security was closed and didn't look as though it had been open for a while. Through the glass of the door he could see a heap of circulars, free newspapers and a half hundredweight of assorted flyers advertising pizzas, fried chicken and kebabs piled up behind the letterbox. Between this door and the next-door shop he noticed an array of small brass plates attached to the wall, each one with a different company name, including, Cornelius noted, Bunce Security LLP, Bunce Leisure LLP, Bunce Travel LLP and Bunce Financial Structures LLP. Interesting, he thought. Mr West seems to be a man of many talents. He remembered reading a report in a newspaper recently about LLPs, that many of them were fronts for money laundering. He thought it might be an interesting thing to look into so he took a photo and sent it to Ruth, with the message *"Interesting?"* followed by four x's, which he changed to three in case four was a bit over the top, then changed back to four and thought, what the hell. He sent it, then he waited. A few minutes later he received a text back, with the message, *"I'll follow it up. xxxx"*. Four x's definitely not over the top then, which made him feel even happier than he already was.

After returning to Ruth's from his aunt's he found she had been out to a local bakery and returned with a bagful of assorted Danish pastries.

"Ah, second breakfast," said Cornelius. He saw Ruth's puzzled expression and explained. "Hobbits. Lord of the Rings. They always have a second breakfast."

"Ah," she echoed. "Sorry, hobbits are not something I'm familiar with. I thought it might be an idea to give you something before you leave. Unless things get wrapped up quickly you might not get time for a proper lunch."

Cornelius was staggered by her thoughtfulness and told her so. He was further staggered by the thought he'd known Ruth for so long and had never really considered she would be interested in him until the last couple of days when she had somehow, entirely of her own volition, become entangled in his life.

In truth, Cornelius had been struck by her the first time they had met almost a year earlier, when he'd started work at Lightsource, but his innate shyness had led him to believe he stood no chance of making any impression and he didn't want to spoil their working relationship so soon after meeting her, so he'd settled on just being pleased to be in her company.

When Ruth had finally managed to get him to come to her party, a couple of months previously, he'd gone with the serious intention of telling her exactly how he felt about her. When he arrived she had been so busy making sure everyone was happy and had drinks and food he never really got the chance to start a meaningful conversation. The longer he was there the more his resolve drained away. With the last of his courage finally dashed when she was called away following the explosion in the kitchen he decided it had not been a good idea to start with and gave up his quest as a forlorn hope. At that precise moment Angela had happened and, mesmerised, he'd been unable to escape. When it dawned on him Angela was speaking to him voluntarily and was flashing him that smile of hers he'd felt extremely flattered and very awkward. He'd seen Ruth coming back into the room a little later. She'd looked at him and he'd sort of smiled at her, trying to convey without words that he'd be eternally grateful if she came and rescued him, but she'd turned on her heels and disappeared from the room. That was the last he'd seen of her. Come to think of it, he remembered with some embarrassment, Ruth had been very distant with him when he'd gone into work on the Monday after the party. It must have been three of four days before she said more than good morning to him. But no, it couldn't be, could it? No, surely not, but that would explain... He sighed and mentally kicked himself. What an idiot!

For as long as he could remember he'd been making a mess of his love life. His history of involvement with the opposite sex was littered with false starts, mix-ups, misread signals and missed opportunities, so much so that apart from one period of three months, with a girl he'd met at a Fresher's Ball, all of his other liaisons had fizzled out in a matter of days, a week at the most. The girl from the Fresher's Ball, Jennifer, a law student, had only lasted so long because neither of them had been brave enough to admit they'd made a mistake. After the first couple of days it was apparent they had nothing whatever in common with each other apart from an interest in sex. They hadn't so much broken up as drifted apart and afterwards would be highly embarrassed if they found themselves in each other's company. The six weeks he'd been seeing Angela was the longest he'd stayed together with a girl since then.

Angela had been a conundrum for Cornelius. It was the first time he'd ever been targeted by a member of the opposite sex and he'd had no idea how to handle the situation. She was such a forceful personality that the very idea of just saying no had been impossible for him and he'd found himself like the proverbial rabbit, in the headlights of her attention to the exclusion of all else. They'd left Ruth's party within the hour and ended up back at her flat, having the wildest sex Cornelius had ever experienced. Whatever else Angela may have been, she wasn't shy. Subsequent meetings tended to follow a similar pattern and Cornelius had found it intoxicating for a while. Then came the introductions to her circle of friends and he began to feel less of a boyfriend and more of a pet, shown off for her friends to admire. He still hadn't worked out what had attracted her to him in the first place. Eventually, it dawned on him that the sex, good as it was, had been just sex. What they had never really done together was make love. Nothing like what had happened last night with Ruth.

With that memory his thoughts turned back to Ruth and he wondered what she was doing now. He realised he'd never felt quite like this before. He sent another text, *'Missing you already xxxx'*, then panicked in case she thought he was being too clingy, then relaxed when she replied *'Me too xxxx'*. Where the hell was West? Why couldn't they just get this over with so he could be with her again? He checked his watch. A minute to go.

"Are you sure this is going to work?" he asked Euclid, not for the first time.

"Relax. It'll be fine."

The plan was a simple one, according to Euclid. When he'd finished his second breakfast they'd sat down and discussed the plan of action.

"West is going to be cautious," began Euclid. "One, because you've already escaped from a locked room and two, because of what you did

200

with Jez Wilson. He's a lot more intelligent than Dave Slinger and he'll have been trying to work out how you managed both of these things. He probably assumed when he first met you that you'd be a bit of a pushover, so he's not going to make the same mistake again, especially if he thinks you really have cracked my so-called code."

"I thought I'd just need to get close enough to grab him and take him off somewhere and dump him. I was thinking maybe Death Valley," said Cornelius, who was pretty sure he could visualise the car park at Zabriskie Point, where he'd visited with a tour company group the year before. It would be about four o'clock in the morning at the moment. There'd be no-one around to see them suddenly appear and West would be stranded in the middle of America with no passport and no explanation as to how he got there.

"That sounds dangerous." replied Ruth. "You said before he had a gun."

"No, Cornelius, you are not going to 'just grab him'. We need to interrogate him and for that we need him calm. A little more finesse is required, I think. Do you remember when I told you about Tald's meeting with the merchant?"

"Yes, you made him see what you wanted him to see, or what he expected to see."

"Precisely. And you're going to have to do the same thing with our Mr West."

"Me?" exclaimed a startled Cornelius. "How am I supposed to do that?"

"Well, when I say you, I mean me, channelled through you."

"Thank god for that."

"We have to make him believe he's seen some genuine magic which can't be easily explained away. We need one extra prop, which we can download from the internet, a copy of Dee's Liber, the book containing the tables and instructions on reading the Enochian language."

"The what?" interrupted Ruth.

"It's supposed to be the language of the angels, as told to Adam."

"Right."

"Just do and say what I tell you and we should be able get what we need."

Ruth opened up her laptop, found the book, downloaded it and sent it to the printer.

"And what will you do with him afterwards?" asked Ruth. "You can't just let him go." The same thought had occurred to Cornelius.

"By the time we've finished we should have enough on him to be able to turn him over to the police and let them take care of him."

"Oh, that's no fun," growled Cornelius, "can't I take him to Death Valley? Please?"

"No," replied Euclid, "the fewer unexplained events the better. We don't want to advertise the fact you're involved in supernatural phenomena or anything of that sort so I suggest we let the police force do the job they're paid for."

"That reminds me," said Ruth, turning to Cornelius, "I haven't called DI Evans yet."

"I'm sure he'll be very pleased to hear from you," he teased. Ruth punched him on the arm.

"Behave, you!" she threatened with a smile, as she picked up her phone. The call to DI Evans was brief and Ruth relayed the gist.

"He said he'd been informed late last night that Slinger had been picked up. The details were sketchy because Slinger was still unconscious but he was tickled pink to learn your aunt had clobbered him. He said Slinger would never live it down once people in his manor found out he'd been overpowered by an old lady and he couldn't wait to go and tell them. I mentioned that your aunt had found his phone this morning and he said he'd call the police in Hull to find out the latest. I asked him if he'd found out anything about West but he just said that things were progressing and he'd let us know."

"Well hopefully we'll be able to hand him over this afternoon. Once the police have West's phone they'll be able to tie him in with Bunce and Slinger. Then there's just the mysterious bossman to sort out. So what's next?" asked Cornelius.

"Just about time to go," answered Euclid.

Cornelius asked Ruth if she had anything he could put the book into and after rooting around in a cupboard handed him a small rucksack.

"I want it back," she said, "and you with it. Just be careful, Cornelius, I mean it. No heroics."

"I'm not really the heroic type," he replied.

"Oh yes, and what about the other day against a man with a gun?"

"A fluke. Nothing more. If it hadn't been for Euclid we'd probably still be in my flat."

"Well, no flukes today. Promise?"

"Yes, I promise."

They took a few happy minutes to say goodbye.

Cornelius glanced at his watch again. Twelve-twenty. He was getting irritated. Maybe West wasn't coming. He didn't know how long he should stay before deciding it was all off. What if they were at the wrong place? What if he'd heard from Slinger? If he didn't turn up now they were back to square one. Euclid told him to relax, but that was easier said than done. He took a small bottle of water from the rucksack and had a drink.

A few minutes later, after Cornelius had checked his watch twice more, a black transit pulled up alongside him and the passenger window wound down. West leaned over from the driver's seat.

"If I find anyone on my tail when I'm driving, you'll be sorry."

"Don't worry, no-one's going to be following. Let's just get this over with." Cornelius made to open the passenger door.

"No, no. In the back, Pye. Got a little surprise for you." West gave him a big grin. With foreboding, he went to the back door and climbed in. The rear of the van was cut off from the front by a hardboard partition which had a small opening into the driver's cab. As he closed the back door he heard a noise. After the bright sunshine outside it took him a few seconds for his eyes to become used to the dim light. He saw someone sitting on the floor of the van, a girl with long blond hair, hands tie-wrapped in front of her, with another longer tie-wrap from there looping around the framework of the van so she couldn't move more than a few inches. She was also gagged. With a start, he realised it was Angela. She was dressed in her jogging gear, vest, shorts and trainers. She must have been coming back from a run when West grabbed her. Cornelius assumed he had used a gun to force her into the back of the van. He couldn't see Angela giving in meekly. She took lessons in tae-kwan-do and wouldn't have hesitated to put her skills into practice. She'd told him, with great pride, about sorting out some man who had followed her home from the pub one night, so he knew nothing much scared her.

"Make yourself comfortable, Pye," came West's muffled voice from the front, "we've got a goodish drive ahead of us. And leave that gag on our guest, or I'll thump you good and hard. I heard enough from her when I put her in there. I was honestly shocked to hear some of the words that came out of her mouth. I prefer to drive in peace if you don't mind." West laughed, put the van into gear and pulled away into the traffic.

Cornelius sat down opposite Angela, horrified. What could he say? It seemed as if everyone he knew was being dragged into his affairs.

"Sorry," he said.

Angela was trying to say something and from her red face and body language he knew it wasn't complimentary. Furious would be an understatement. Incandescent was nearer the mark. He wondered why on earth West had done it. Did this mean he'd discovered what had happened to Slinger? As the journey continued Angela kept trying to talk to him and he got more and more embarrassed. Finally, he could stand it no longer, threat or no threat.

Very quietly, he said, "Listen, Angela, I'm sorry. I don't know why you're here. If you promise not to shout at me I'll take the gag off, alright?"

She let leash another couple of sentences he couldn't understand but guessed the meaning of.

"Angela, please, calm down. I'm going to take the gag off now so don't shout. Okay?"

She looked at him with venom in her eyes, then finally subsided with a growl and nodded her head. He leant over and removed the gag, which didn't look very clean and felt oily. It had probably been in the back of the van for quite a while.

"What's going on, Cornelius?" she hissed in a low voice. "Who's that fuckwit in the front?"

As usual, he felt tongue-tied in front of her and just opened and closed his mouth a couple of times.

"I'm waiting," she said, dangerously.

"It's a bit complicated," he began. "You remember that book my uncle left me?"

"Go on."

"The one that got stolen?

204

"Yes, yes, I remember, for fuck's sake," she said loudly. He shushed at her, frantically. She regarded him with what might be described as a death stare, but then whispered, "What about it?"

"Well the people who stole the book came back and kidnapped me. That's why I never turned up for Barbara's party. I tried to tell you on the phone. Anyway, I managed to escape but since then things just seem to have got out of hand. First of all, Ruth was held hostage at my place. Then when I helped her escape someone went up to my aunt's and held her hostage, but luckily she battered him with a paperweight and now I'm supposed to be handing the book over to this guy, Mister West, he calls himself, although it's probably not his real name, so that they'll stop making my life a misery and now I find they've kidnapped you and I don't know why."

Cornelius, strangely, was very close to tears. Angela, however, seemed unmoved.

"Are you serious?" she hissed again. "Because of some stupid book I'm trussed up in the back of a dirty old van with you and some fucking psycho. Do you have any idea where I'm meant to be today?" Cornelius shook his head. "I'm supposed to be at Royal fucking Ascot, being entertained in a private box, dressed in a brand new dress and an insanely expensive fucking hat I bought especially for the occasion. By now, I should be drinking copious amounts of champagne, watching the Royal Family sitting within spitting distance and shouting at the gee-gees. Instead, I'm tied up in this shitty old van listening to you rabbiting on about your stupid fucking book, being driven god knows where on a Saturday afternoon by a madman who's probably going to shoot me before the day's out." How Angela managed to convey all this in just a whisper astonished him.

"Sorry," he repeated. "I don't know what else I can say. I'm sorry your day's been ruined."

"You're *sorry*? Is that all you can say?"

Although Cornelius was genuinely sorry, he was beginning to wish he'd left the gag on.

"What are we going to do, Euclid?"

"It's an added complication, Cornelius, but it shouldn't really change our plan. We've just got to hope Angela doesn't get too hysterical. I want West as calm as possible when we work our bit of magic."

"Perhaps I can ask him to leave her in the van when we get there," said Cornelius, then immediately regretted saying it. It wasn't Angela's fault. They'd just have to hope things turned out alright.

"I'm sure we'll think of something," agreed Euclid.

"Look, Angela, if we both just stay calm, we'll be fine. I just need to hand over this book and explain a few things about it to West, then we should be able to leave unharmed."

"You'd better be right."

They sat in silence until the van finally pulled up. The back door opened and bright sunshine flooded the interior.

"Out you get, Pye. Just stand to one side and keep quiet until I get madam out."

Cornelius jumped out and did as he was told as West climbed in. He looked around and saw they were in the private grounds of a large Victorian mansion, built in the Arts and Crafts manner, with grey brick, leaded windows, high gables and tall chimney pots. It looked vaguely church-like and was, presumably, the house where he'd been kept the first time he'd been kidnapped.

"I thought I told you to keep the gag on," shouted West from inside the van.

"I couldn't leave her with that oily old rag over her mouth. She promised to stay quiet. You didn't hear her, did you?"

"Well, she'd better stay quiet or someone's going to be sorry." West used a penknife to cut the long tie-wrap holding Angela to the van and seconds later she was standing beside Cornelius with a sullen look on her face. The tie-wraps were still around her wrists. West pulled a small revolver out of the waistband of his jeans.

"No sudden moves. Alright?" They both nodded. He led the way to the front door and unlocked it, then ushered them in ahead of him.

After the heat of the day outside, the coolness of the house came as a bit of a shock. It was obvious from the stillness it had been uninhabited for years. In its day it must have been quite an impressive place, with lots of light oak and William Morris wallpaper. Now, the rooms were mainly empty, what little furniture had been left behind was covered with dustsheets.

They were motioned forward by West and they entered the room Cornelius remembered from his last visit, the library.

"Well, here we are again," said West, "just like old times."

206

"Why have you got Angela?" asked Cornelius. "She's got nothing to do with all of this."

"Oh, Pye, you didn't think I'd fall for all that pony with the text messages did you? I knew last night that that idiot Slinger had got himself carted off by the police." He smiled at the surprised look on Cornelius' face. "That's the advantage of working for someone like my boss. He's got people all over the place. As soon as Slinger's name went into the police computer one of his contacts sent an alert. A couple of quick phone calls and we had the whole story. Absolutely fucking pathetic. Ah well, that's what you get for employing idiots. Out of the goodness of my heart, I gave him and his dozy mate a couple of jobs. He's my brother-in-law, so my wife was always on at me to help him out. Well, he's on his own now and good fucking riddance. I never liked him, but you know women. Yadda-yadda-yadda in your earhole until it's easiest just to give in."

West smiled.

"So why did you respond to the text?"

"Well, we still wanted the book and whatever the book's supposed to do. I couldn't believe it when that text arrived. Manna from heaven. But I didn't know what your game was, so I thought I'd get myself a little extra insurance, hence the presence of madam here." He gestured towards Angela, who growled at him.

"I knew that other girl wasn't your girlfriend. Just another little fuck-up by Dave and his associate. So I went after the real thing this time. If you want a job doing and all that."

"Argh!" shouted Angela, who turned and kicked a chair.

"Cheery sort, in't she? Swears like a trooper. Put up a bit of a fight as well before I showed her the gun. That calmed her down a bit but, fuck me, would she shut up?" He turned to her and said in a dangerous tone, "That's why she got the gag and she'll get it again if I hear another sound."

"You could at least untie her, she's not going anywhere."

"She'll stay exactly like she is. Serves her right for being such a mouthy cow."

If looks could maim and terminally injure it was obvious what Angela was thinking.

"So what happens now?" asked Cornelius.

"I'm puzzled. Pye. Why did you arrange the meet? You had your book, your aunt wasn't in any danger. What did you hope to gain?"

"I just want all this to be over. People around me," he waved his arms at Angela by way of example, "are getting sucked into this and I want it to stop. I thought if I just volunteered to meet you we could sort it out between us and no-one else would need be bothered by you and your goons. And now you've brought Angela into it, so that didn't work out for me, either."

"You've got it with you, I assume? The book's in the rucksack?" Cornelius nodded. "Well, we're back to square one, then, aren't we? You settle down and crack the code, or whatever it is and then you're both free to go."

"For fuck's sake, Cornelius," said Angela, "give him what he wants and we can both get out of here."

"I did ask you to keep quiet," said West to Angela, "but on this occasion I'll let it go. It is in your interest as well, I suppose."

"It's not as simple as that," said Cornelius.

"What do you mean?"

To Euclid, Cornelius said, "What am I going to tell him?"

"Tell him you really have cracked the code but it's going to take a little time to explain. You have to make sure Angela is calm while we go through the procedure I outlined earlier. I need to have West completely relaxed so I don't want her winding him up."

"The code, as you call it, is sorted, but it's going to take me a while to set things up. There are various incantations to go through before I can show you anything, so I need to get into a relaxed state of mind. At the moment my heart's going at a rate of knots."

"Okay. I'll leave you alone for twenty minutes while you get set up. That had better be long enough. I'm missing my footy for this, so there'd better be something for me to see, understand? My boss is getting very annoyed that things have dragged on for so long and I've found out it's not a good idea to let him get annoyed. Do you follow me?"

"Yes, I follow you," said Cornelius.

West took hold of Angela's arm. "I don't know how you got out of this room the last time you were here, but I'm sure you wouldn't want to leave without your girlfriend this time." West looked at the two of them pointedly, then turned and marched Angela out of the room, locking the door behind him.

20.

The brass plates intrigued Ruth, who remembered reading somewhere how LLP companies could be used for pursuing illegal operations, such as money laundering, with very little interference from the UK government. As she quickly discovered, an LLP, or Limited Liability Partnership, is a type of legal structure for businesses, lying somewhere between a traditional partnership and a limited company, the main difference being that LLPs don't pay corporation tax. Instead, each LLP member counts as self employed and should complete an annual tax return. However, if the LLP is registered to a company that is in turn owned by one from overseas, that tax is not collected in the UK. The almost nonexistent regulation and financial policing of LLPs has turned Britain into the capital of international organised crime.

Setting up an LLP is easier than joining a library. Fill in a form with some basic details of two or more members in the LLP and send it off with a cheque for £40 to Companies House. There are no checks, no requests for ID.

Ruth turned her attention to the companies shown on the brass plates. Choosing Bunce Security as a starting point she looked it up on the Companies House website. There were two members listed, Graham and Margaret Jesney, both registered at the same address in Luxembourg. She tried another, Bunce Travel, and wasn't surprised to find the same members listed. Both companies had been formed on the same date in 2010. A check on a third company revealed the same details. When she searched for the Jesneys and the Luxembourg address she came up with Eternal Hope Consultancy Services, part of a group of four companies registered in the Cayman Islands as The Safe Harbour Syndicate Inc.

She had no idea yet if any of this would lead anywhere but she thought it was wise to be prepared. She phoned a close friend of hers, Cathy, who worked for a large firm of accountants in the City and asked her if it would be possible to find any further information about Eternal Hope. She told Cathy that the firm had approached Lightsource and she was curious to know more about them. Cathy promised she'd get back to her after the weekend.

It may be nothing, thought Ruth, but you never know.

"I was rather hoping he'd leave Angela with us," said Euclid after the door had closed. "Now we'll have to try and control what both of them see, rather than just West. A little trickier given your ex-girlfriend's rather volatile nature. However did you get involved with her in the first place? She doesn't really seem to be your type."

"It's a long story, one which I'd rather not recount at the moment." Cornelius wasn't sure if he was getting better at putting the wall around his thoughts, as Euclid had suggested, or if Euclid was just being polite in letting him think that. Either way, it wasn't a discussion he was keen to have because, in light of what had happened over the last couple of days, the whole episode troubled him more than somewhat. "Tell you what," he suggested, "why don't you run over this plan of yours once more, just to make sure I've got the hang of it."

"Cornelius, I have perfect faith in you, so long as you stand in front of him and look as though you know what you're doing. I'll do all the talking through you but it will look to him like it's you. You just need to start waving your arms mysteriously when I start the incantations. People are always more convinced when you put on a show. Once he's convinced he's looking at the real thing, I'll be able to get inside his mind and find the information we need. You'll be fine, relax."

"I hope so."

Following Euclid's instructions, Cornelius placed the book on the library table and opened it to a page covered with John Dee's handwritten notes, the idea being that there was a hidden codeword among them which referred to a certain passage in the Liber, which when spoken out loud would turn base metals into gold. Euclid told Cornelius that the incantation he was intending to use was actually an instruction from his ship's flight manual on the cleaning of air scrubbers, that Tald had related to Dee all those years ago.

"What metal are we going to use for the transmutation?" queried Cornelius.

"I was thinking of using the leading in the windows. It should give us the perfect lead to gold effect, with the added bonus that it can't be moved or too easily inspected."

Cornelius placed two chairs to one side of the table and another opposite them, where he sat and waited for West to return. He drank the last of his water from the bottle and placed it on the floor, out of the way. He was glad that Ruth had provided a second breakfast but he was in dire need of tea.

Eventually, the door opened and West walked in, still with gun in hand, pushing Angela ahead of him. She sat down on one of the chairs, West remained standing.

"Are you alright, Angela?"

"Just peachy, Cornelius," she replied. She looked every inch the sullen teenager, slouched on the chair, her legs straight out in front of her, chin down and eyes looking up at him. If it hadn't been for the tie-wrap around her wrist her arms would have been folded. She kept flicking glances at West. Cornelius prayed she wasn't planning anything rash.

West leaned over the desk towards him. "I hope you're ready, Pye. I've got things to do today."

"I'm ready."

"Come on then, show us what you've got."

Cornelius relaxed as he felt Euclid take control of his voice. He leant back slightly in his chair and placed his hands on the table. West glared at him.

"What do you know about alchemy and the transmutation of metals into gold?"

"Enough to know it's a load of old bollocks," grinned West.

"Yes, it was, at one time. The ancients didn't understand that lead and gold were two completely different atomic elements. At the time, they were believed to be hybrid compounds and therefore amenable to change. Unfortunately, they were restricted in the processes they could use. Nowadays it's quite possible. All you need is a particle accelerator, a vast supply of energy and an extremely low expectation of how much gold you will end up with."

"Is there a point to this?"

"Well, that depends. Your boss believes that this book," Cornelius spread his hands over the table, "offers a completely different solution to the way the old scientists went about things. Different, because the process was given to John Dee directly from angels."

"Are you winding me up?"

"You wanted me to come here and prove to you I've broken the code. I'm here now to show you what is possible and why your boss is

212

so interested. I want you to sit down, please, relax and concentrate. Bear in mind what your boss has sent you here to do because you're going to have to go back to him and show him how it's done. He wants great riches. This book and the tables in this other document," Cornelius picked up the Liber and placed it in front of West, "will show him the means to do it."

Cornelius noticed that Euclid had used the word 'boss' three times already. He knew it to be a deliberate ploy to make West think about his employer. The room had taken on a charged stillness. Sharp rays of sunlight streamed in through the windows, highlighting dust motes in the air, which now seemed to be stationary, almost as if time had stopped. No-one was moving. Perfect.

"Before we begin, we need to find a metal which can be changed into gold, lead for preference." Cornelius made a show of looking around the room, then focused his attention on the windows. As they'd hoped, West looked there too and pointed.

"There's lead in those windows. Change that."

"Very well. I tried this earlier today and managed to change an old toy soldier from lead to gold, so it should work there."

"You didn't bring it with you, then?"

"Would you have believed me if I'd just shown it to you?"

West shook his head.

"No. You want to see it with your own eyes. That way you know you've not been fooled. There's no way I could have known where we'd be today so there's no chance I could have set this up in advance. Shall I carry on?"

"Don't let me stop you."

"The process I discovered," continued Euclid through Cornelius, "after many hours of painstaking research, came about after I found a strange error in one of the calculations Dee had written in the margins of the book, here." Cornelius duly pointed it out to West, who leant in closer. It was a calculation that had puzzled him when he'd first gone through the book back at his flat. Anyone with a background in mathematics would have thought it was strange so Euclid wasn't leaving to chance West's understanding. Out of the corner of his eye he noticed that Angela hadn't moved and seemed totally uninterested in the proceedings.

"Yes, I see. I think," said West, who leaned in further to take a look. It was obvious he didn't have a clue.

"It was that calculation which led me to this." Cornelius then showed West an image in the Liber labelled '*The Great Table*' and pointed at random to one of the curious letters. "This is the letter denoting the divine name of Lazdixi. When we look up Lazdixi in the Liber we find the following incantation, relating to transmutation."

At this point, Cornelius closed his eyes, raised his arms in supplication and started the incantation in a voice barely above a whisper.

"*Ol sonuf vaoresaji, gohu iad Balata, elanusaha caelazod sobra zod-ol Roray i ta nazodapesad, Giraa ta maelpereji, das hoel-qo qaa notahoa zodimezod, od comemahe ta nobeloha zodien, soba tahil ginonupe pereje aladi, das vaurebes obolehe giresam.*"

All Cornelius could think of at this point was air scrubbers and was finding it difficult not to laugh at the ridiculousness of it all. Euclid reminded him to pay attention, everything was going to plan and he was inside West's head. It wouldn't take much longer to get the information they needed. Cornelius looked at West and saw he was spellbound. He brought his hands together as though in prayer.

"For the next part I need to be touching the lead." Cornelius walked over to the nearest window and placed a finger on the lead in one of the panes.

"*Zodacare, eca, od zodameranu! Odo cicale Qaa; zodoreje, lape zodiredo Noco Mada, Hoathahe IAIDA!*"

At first, nothing happened. Cornelius held his breath and prayed to whatever gods he thought might be listening. Then came a sort of grating sound and West leaned closer and saw that the lead was moving slightly, almost writhing, as though it had turned to liquid. Then slowly, from the point at which Cornelius was touching it, the lead started to send out little streaks of gold to each corner of the pane, which then started to thicken, until eventually all the lead in that particular pane shone golden in the bright afternoon sunshine.

"Nice!" said Cornelius to Euclid. "In fact, it's beautiful."

He looked at West, who was standing there open mouthed. He reached out to touch it.

"It's really gold," he breathed. "You really can do it." He smiled at Cornelius, who almost felt sorry for him. It was at this moment Angela chose to strike. She stood quickly and lashed a foot at the gun in West's hand. It flew into the air and landed a few feet away, by which time Angela had landed two more blows on him, one foot sideways on, into his kidneys, the heel of both hands following up and striking him on the chest, causing him to fall backwards against the wall, winded. The fact that her wrists were still tied together didn't seem to be affecting her.

"Cornelius, grab the gun!" shouted Angela as she prepared to strike again. He looked around for it but couldn't see where it had gone.

West was a street fighter. Although the first few blows had caught him off guard it didn't take him long to recover. He pushed Cornelius away and went for Angela. Cornelius dropped down onto one of the chairs, which he then fell off.

The problem with Angela's fighting technique, good though it was against a similar type of opponent who played to the same rules, was not so effective against someone who had fought dirty all his life. She'd made the mistake of not kicking him between the legs during her first flurry.

As Angela's foot came up once again West caught it, twisted and pushed back, causing her to fall backwards. West followed up very fast and dived down on top of her, pinning her arms to the floor. He was a bit out of condition, so instead of staying where he was his momentum and Angela's arching back caused him to topple over alongside her. Angela was quickest to her feet and tried this time to hit the sweet spot in his trousers but was slightly off the mark and West rolled once again and came to his feet facing her. She lunged at his face but he batted her arms away and moved forward to headbutt her, catching her on her ear, which caused her to yelp. He followed up with a punch to the stomach and a kick to the legs, which dropped her once again to the floor.

"Cornelius! The gun!" Cornelius was still on the floor. He looked around and saw it beneath the table. He started to slide towards it but felt a tug on his shirt collar as West grabbed him, lifted him off the floor and threw him at the table, which he hit with a nauseating crunch before sliding off onto the floor. In the meantime West had pushed the table towards where Cornelius had ended up, reached down and picked up the gun. He turned to Angela in a blazing fury.

215

"Not another move, or else!" Angela was still on the floor, so she stayed there, beaten.

"Nice try, sweetheart."

On the other side of the table Cornelius stood slowly, checking for damage. He was relieved to find himself all in one piece.

"Euclid! What are we going to do now?"

"It depends on how much control I've still got. Go and stand opposite him."

"He's got a gun!"

"I know, but maybe he hasn't."

"What?"

"Just do as I say. Let me do the talking and follow my lead."

Cornelius did a mental shrug then did as Euclid suggested, positioning himself in front of West.

"Sorry about that," said Euclid through Cornelius, "I didn't know she could do that."

"She's *your* girlfriend," responded West.

"No, she's not!" interrupted Angela. "Haven't been for days."

"Oh, sorry," said West to Cornelius, with a smile. "Dumped you, did she?"

"Something like that," said Cornelius. "I hope this doesn't interfere with our arrangement." He nodded towards the windows and crossed his fingers behind his back. West looked at the windows for a few seconds, before turning back to Cornelius.

"If she moves a muscle I'm going to put a bullet in her. As for you, I think we're good. I just need those spells you did and the books, then I'm out of here."

"Good," replied Cornelius, pointing towards the gun in West's hand, "so you won't need the banana then."

"Banana?"

"That banana. In your hand."

West looked down at the hand which held the gun and saw the banana. He looked up at Cornelius, puzzled, then back to his hand, then back again at Cornelius.

"It's not a banana, it's a gun," insisted West.

"A gun? No, silly, that's not a gun. That's a banana."

"It's a gun!"

"If that's a gun, where's the trigger?"

West looked back at the banana in his hand, trying to work out where the trigger could be. Angela was watching him in disbelief. She could see the gun, but then again, she could see the banana.

"Come on, Mister West, if that's a gun why don't you pull the trigger?"

"For fuck's sake, Euclid," thought Cornelius, "don't push it. I don't want to get shot."

"Don't worry, Cornelius, you can't get shot with a banana."

Cornelius looked back at the gun in West's hand and even he couldn't distinguish between gun and banana.

"I'm going to suggest he puts it down," said Euclid, "and then I'm going to make him fall asleep so I can get what we need, then we can get out of here."

But Euclid hadn't reckoned with Angela. With a sudden leap from the floor she kicked the banana from West's hand and, moving quickly, followed its arc to the floor where she caught it expertly before it hit the ground. As she rolled, West came alive and went after her, but Angela spun around with the gun in both hands and squeezed the trigger. If West hadn't stumbled slightly he'd have lost a vital part of his anatomy. As it was, the bullet flew past, grazing his ear. West reached out, grabbed a chair and threw it towards Angela before she could get a second shot off. She rolled again to avoid the chair, by which time West had gone through the door. Angela got to her feet and started after him, with Cornelius close behind her. They heard the slam of the van door and the engine starting as they came through the front door. West had the van in reverse in order to turn back down the drive. Angela fired again and the driver's window shattered. Luck, once again, was on West's side as the bullet flew past his nose this time. He put the van into gear and screeched away down the drive. Angela shot again, hitting the driver's side wing mirror, which exploded into fragments. Then it was gone. Everything had happened in seconds, but even so, Cornelius was annoyed with himself when he realised he hadn't managed to get the registration.

"Don't worry," said Euclid, "I've got it."

Relieved, he turned to Angela.

"Fuck me!" he said, "where did you learn to shoot a gun?"

"I'm not just a pretty face," replied Angela, smiling. "Daddy used to be the chairman of a gun club so I was brought up around them. I've been shooting since I was five. Got medals. I'd have done better if my hands hadn't been tied. I'm out of practise, though. I missed him three times. Do you think you can get these off me?" She held up her wrists.

"Not unless we can find something inside. There's a kitchen somewhere." He smiled at her. "You must have scared the living shit out of him." Cornelius was glad she was on his side. "I know you probably won't believe me," he said, "but everything was under control back there, I had him sort of hypnotised and ready to go to sleep, but thanks anyway. You weren't to know. I tried to tell you earlier but West took you with him out of the room before I got a chance. I really, really appreciate it."

"What do we do now? I've no idea where we are, do you?"

"I haven't the foggiest, sorry." Looking around they could see only fields beyond the house's grounds. He knew he could get her home in a flash but he couldn't let her know that and he couldn't leave her here by herself.

"I guess we'd better call the police."

"That bastard's got my phone in his van. Do you have one?" Cornelius nodded.

"It's in my rucksack. We'll find out where we are, then you can use it if you want to."

"Yeah, thanks, but you know how it is. All my contacts are on my phone. I couldn't tell you what anyone's numbers are, apart from my parents', but I don't want to call them. They'd only worry. I'll leave that story until I get back."

They turned and walked back into the house. As they went Cornelius asked Euclid the burning question.

"Did you get anything?"

"Very little. A name. Carfax. I didn't manage to get any further details because Emma Peel took over. Twice! I know what this Carfax looks like, from West's mental picture of him, although it's not really going to help very much if we can't find him."

In the kitchen they found a bread knife and Cornelius was able to hack through the tie-wraps. Back in the library, Angela made a bee-line for the windows.

"How did you do that? Change the lead to gold. I mean, I saw it happen, but now it's gone."

"Hypnotism."

"And the gun? I saw a banana, I really did but something told me it was still a gun. You hypnotised both of us? Wow! You are one cool customer, Cornelius."

"I needed some information from him, but it didn't quite work out."

"Did I fuck it up? Sorry."

"No, it's fine. He might leave me alone now if he thinks I can make him see things. And if he thinks he might come up against you again."

Cornelius retrieved his phone and called the police. He gave them the van registration and the location of the house, which turned out to be less than a mile from a village called Matching Tye, a couple of miles to the east of Harlow. He had trouble convincing them of the village's name, but they got there in the end and promised to be with them shortly.

They righted the table and chairs, then sat down. He called Ruth and gave her a brief description of the afternoon's events. Even over the phone he could sense an iciness as soon as he mentioned Angela's name.

"Is she there now, in hearing distance?" asked Ruth.

"Er, yes," he replied, feeling slightly uncomfortable.

"Then you'd better wait until you get back before you give me all the gory details. At least you're still alive, which is the main thing."

She hung up and Cornelius knew their next conversation was going to be tricky.

"That was Ruth, then?" asked Angela.

"Oh, er, yes. How did you know?"

"Probably the mention of her name more than once during the conversation. I take it you've joined forces?"

"Yes. Sorry." Cornelius somehow still felt guilty, even though it had been Angela who'd dumped him.

"No, no. It's me who should be apologising to you. And to Ruth. I haven't been very nice to either of you, have I."

"What do you mean?"

"Remember her birthday party, where I trapped you in the corner and spirited you away?" Cornelius nodded and she continued. "That was me getting my own back on Ruth for something I thought she'd done to me. Only she didn't."

"What?"

219

"I'd had my eye on this guy for a couple of weeks. I knew he liked me but I was playing a bit hard to get. All part of the fun, you know? I was pretty sure he must have realised. Anyway, a few days before the party I'd arranged to go to dinner with some friends, knowing he'd be there and by then I was ready to let him work his magic. But he didn't show up. Ruth was supposed to be at this dinner as well, but she didn't show up either. When I texted him later to find out what had happened to him he didn't reply, which was odd, because he'd normally reply to my messages straight away. I heard nothing from him the next day and I was beginning to put two and two together when Barbara called me and confirmed what I'd been starting to suspect, that he and Ruth had been seen together that night in a bar somewhere. I guessed that Ruth was quite keen on you because she told me she was happy she'd finally got you to come out. So the next night, at the party, I decided to take my revenge."

Cornelius didn't know what to say, so said nothing. He'd got a little stuck at the phrase, "Ruth was quite keen on you", so he almost missed the last sentence. Angela continued.

"I just wanted to get back at Ruth for what I thought she'd done. I probably wouldn't have pounced on you if I hadn't thought you were quite cute. Anyway, it wasn't until a few days ago I found out Ruth was entirely innocent. It was Barbara who'd been out with him that night and she used Ruth to throw me off the scent. So, sorry, Cornelius. It's my fault love's young dream didn't get started at Ruth's party."

"Oh, er, thanks for telling me. You didn't have to. Really, thanks. It's not surprising if that's what you'd been told. I can't blame you for anything, really. Just one of those things."

"I quite enjoyed going out with you, Cornelius. You're different to all the other men I know. I don't think it would have lasted, though, even before all this business with that damn book. Mind you," she looked him in the eye and smiled coquettishly, "you have to admit the sex was pretty hot!"

He blushed. "Yes, I will definitely admit that. Thanks for letting me know. It's a weight off my mind to know were still friends. I'm glad."

"Yeah, me too, but do me a favour. Don't mention any of it to Ruth. It won't sound good coming from you. It's a conversation that I have to have with her. I'll leave it a while, a week or two, give you both a chance to catch up on the time you've missed." She stood, then so did he and she hugged him. He hugged back.

"Thanks, Angela. You've been great today."

"To be honest, I quite enjoyed it in the end."

They heard cars on the gravelled drive, the slamming of doors and the stamping of feet. Suddenly, two policemen wearing body armour appeared at the door to the library pointing rifles at them.

"Down on the ground. Now!" one of them screamed. "Throw the weapon towards me and put your hands behind your heads!"

Angela hadn't realised she'd still been holding the gun all this time. She threw it towards the officers and complied, as did Cornelius, who shouted, "We're the good guys! I'm the one that called you."

"Stay where you are! Don't move!" replied the shouty policeman. His colleague moved forward and picked up the gun, then they both stood over Cornelius and Angela, with their rifles pointed towards them.

"Do you have any other firearms?" said Shouty.

"No," they chorused.

A policeman and a policewoman entered next and began body searches.

"Clear!"

"Clear!"

Another policeman entered, plainclothes this time.

"Alright, you can get up now. Sorry about all the drama, but when guns get mentioned on emergency calls we usually play safe, just in case. I'm DI Roberts. We'll take you back to Harlow first off, for a bit of a debrief and then we'll see about getting you back to wherever it was you came from."

The two armed officers left the room as Cornelius and Angela stood.

"That's probably the scariest thing that's happened to me today," said Cornelius.

21.

They spent nearly two hours in the police station in Harlow. As a kidnap victim, Angela was treated sympathetically and handled gently. Before her interview she decided she should call her father after all, as she discovered that the police didn't give people lifts home, except in emergencies, which this now wasn't. After she'd assured her father she hadn't been harmed he told her he'd come and pick her up. Luckily, she still had her door key in a small purse in her shorts.

The police told them that West's van had been spotted, abandoned outside Theydon Bois tube station. West was still on the loose. Angela's phone had been found on the front seat of the van and she would be able to pick it up from the police station in Cheshunt on her way home.

Cornelius got a rougher ride. He was having great trouble explaining why he'd decided to meet up with West at all if his aunt was not now being held hostage by Dave Slinger.

"You're telling me," said a disbelieving Detective Sergeant, 'that you arranged to meet this West character, even though you didn't need to, just to make him stop harassing you and your family? You've been kidnapped by him, your girlfriend was threatened by his two sidekicks, your aunt was taken hostage and today your ex-girlfriend was taken prisoner in broad daylight and bundled into a van. Why did you think he'd stop coming after you after all this?"

"To be fair, I didn't know about him taking Angela when I arranged the meeting."

"For God's sake," spluttered the DS, "these are dangerous criminals you've been messing around with. Two of them have been inside for committing violent acts. Didn't you think it might have been better to talk to us?"

Cornelius stayed silent.

"I still don't understand what it was they were after. You said this book," the DS pointed to it on the table, "then, once they'd got the book they wanted you as well. Why?"

"I told you, they thought there was a secret code in the book that pointed to some sort of treasure. I've been trying to persuade them there's no such thing."

"But your friend Angela says you were trying to hypnotise West into believing there was. Seriously? You thought hypnotism was going to work against a man with a gun?"

"I was trying to find out who he works for. The man behind all this."

"Oh! I see. You were after Moriarty! Who do you think you are, Sherlock Holmes?"

There was more in the same vein. Eventually, the DS left the room. Ten minutes later he was back.

"I just spoke to DI Evans, whose case this is. Thank god it's not me, that's all I can say. He suggested you go and see him for a little chat, tomorrow please at one o'clock. I would say he's been very polite because it's not really a suggestion."

"But tomorrow's Sunday."

"Strangely enough, crime doesn't stop for the weekend, so most of the time neither do we. Although sometimes I wonder why we bother when we have the likes of you running free. Now go home and behave."

After their interviews, Cornelius and Angela sat together in the waiting area by the front desk until her father picked her up. He'd met her parents a couple of times. They had a nice house in Kings Langley where they'd visited for barbecues. When he arrived he hugged his daughter, then turned to Cornelius with a stern look.

"Hello, Mister Miller."

"So, we've got you to thank for all this, have we? My wife is worried sick."

"Leave him alone, daddy," said Angela, "it wasn't his fault. Well, not entirely," she said with a grin. We can give him a lift, can't we?"

"No, it's fine, honestly. I'll get the train."

"Come on, let's get you home," said her father, before Angela could persuade him otherwise.

"Bye, Cornelius, look after yourself."

"Bye, Angela, you too."

They hugged and gave each other a quick peck on the cheek, then she was gone. Cornelius realised he was feeling a little apprehensive about seeing Ruth again. There was a bit of a problem and its name was Angela.

"Don't worry," said Euclid, "I'll show her edited highlights of exactly what happened, leaving out the bits about Angela's apology. It'll be as if she were there and easier than you trying to explain it. You should be glad if she's jealous. Shows the right spirit."

"Yes, you're right. Thanks for that."

He texted Ruth to say he was on his way back, picked up his rucksack and headed outside. The police station was in a quiet location behind a shopping centre. To the right of the building was a side street with warehouses on the other side. No houses and no pedestrians in sight. He started walking along it, then vanished.

Immediately on his return, Ruth flung her arms around him.

"I was so worried!"

This was going better than Cornelius had expected, so he hugged her back and kissed her, hungrily. She broke off and held him at arms length, looking him straight in the eye.

"Now, what's all this about Angela."

"I, er -"

Euclid broke in and did as promised in about a fiftieth of the time it would have taken Cornelius to explain.

"Oh," said Ruth, "I suppose that's alright, then. Who'd have thought Angela had it in her? I knew she did Tae-kwan-do but not to the extent that she could actually use it. And her outlook seems to have improved since I spoke to her on the phone."

"She's not so bad when you get to know her."

He felt Euclid do one of his impossible sharp intakes of breath and realised he'd said the wrong thing.

"It might be best if you didn't get to know her any better," said Ruth darkly. Then her mood changed. "Tea?"

""Please!" he gasped.

"Then after that, you might fancy a bit of a lie down, after the rigours of your ordeal."

"I'm not tired,"

"Silly," she replied with a smile, locking her arms around his neck.

"Ah," he said and smiled back.

"So, all we've got is a name. Carfax," said Cornelius, "and we know what he looks like." They each had the image Euclid had shared with them. Cornelius and Ruth were sitting on the sofa together, enjoying an early evening glass of wine, going though the events of the day.

"He looks a bit like Arthur Slugworth," said Ruth, "the man who tries to bribe the children with sweets in Willie Wonka and the Chocolate Factory. The original film, not the remake."

"Sorry," replied Cornelius, "I've never seen it."

"What? Your upbringing has been sadly incomplete. I've got the DVD, we can watch it sometime."

"Yes, yes, later," interjected Euclid. "I also got some impressions from West. He's based in the City, near an open green space. Not an office block, somewhere quite discreet."

"Narrows it down a bit, I suppose," said Cornelius.

"It might tie in with the photo you took of the brass plates. I did a bit of digging into some of the names." She told them what she had discovered. "We'll have to wait until Monday for any more information, though."

"Well, now that West is on the run and his henchmen are in police custody we might have a bit of breathing space," said Euclid, "so I suggest we pay a visit to the British Museum tomorrow to have a look at John Dee's crystal and case the joint."

"He's doing it again," laughed Cornelius, "Sweeney talk!"

"Alright, then. Discover what their security's like. Whatever, we need to go and look at the Museum's crystal and determine whether or not it really is ours."

"I suppose it won't be stealing if it was actually yours in the first place," said Ruth.

"It's a moot point. If it's the same one, it was given to Dee by Tald. Look, I only need to borrow it for a very short time, to power up the portal. Once it's operating we can return it."

"So," said Ruth, "a trip to the British Museum. I haven't been for years."

"Yes, but first we have to go see DI Evans. If it wasn't for him I'd probably still be in Harlow."

"What time?"

"One o'clock."

"Well, at least we don't have to get up early tomorrow. Euclid?"

"No," he responded, " you can have a lie in."

"Good," said Cornelius, "so that just leaves the little matter of where we're going to eat this evening. I haven't had a proper meal since second breakfast!"

On Ruth's recommendation they booked a table at a Greek restaurant just off Muswell Hill Broadway, about a fifteen minute walk. After a quick visit to his flat to shower and change they went on their first date as lovers.

Detective Inspector David Evans was in a good mood as he welcomed them into his glass-walled office the next morning. Cornelius hadn't been looking forward to the visit so was pleasantly surprised at not being shown into a dingy interview room and given a dressing down. Evans offered them drinks and talked lightly about the good weather and asked them about holiday plans until a uniformed constable brought in tea, coffee and biscuits.

When the door had closed he took a quick sip of his coffee, then said, "So, Mr Pye, I hear you've been playing detective. I gather you didn't make a hit with the Essex constabulary. Their DS was spitting feathers when he phoned me. Wanted to know whether I thought it was a good idea letting you wander around loose on your own."

Ruth bridled. "That's a little unfair. Cornelius is more than capable of looking after himself. If it hadn't been for the sudden appearance of Angela -". She broke off, not really wishing to bring her erstwhile rival into the conversation. Too late.

"Ah yes, Angela. I need to go and have a little chat with her, have a word about her exuberance with guns. I believe she's now the ex-girlfriend?" He stressed the ex. Cornelius nodded. "And I take it that you two...?" He pointed to them both. They both nodded this time and looked at each other sheepishly.

"Right. Just so I'm clear." Cornelius thought he sounded disappointed.

Evans opened a folder on the desk and scanned it in silence for a minute or so.

"So. To sum up this little caper so far. Dave Slinger and Jez Wilson pinched a valuable book and later kidnapped you," he pointed at Cornelius, who affirmed, "presumably on the orders of this Mister West, who in turn works on behalf of some unknown criminal mastermind." Cornelius thought there was more than a hint of sarcasm behind the last two words. "You then escaped, only to find that Wilson and Slinger were holding this young lady," he nodded at Ruth, "hostage at your flat. You managed to get in without them knowing and when Slinger had gone off for some food you overpowered Wilson and escaped. Is that correct so far?"

"Yes," replied Cornelius.

"Then, for some inexplicable reason, Jez Wilson decides to take a trip to Whipsnade in his bare feet where he gets himself arrested. His personal belongings, including a recently fired gun, are handed in soon after at a police station in Barnes by an unknown person, whose description uncannily matches yours. Now I have to ask this, because I'm baffled, although I'll be surprised if you give me an answer, but how do you think Jez Wilson, who has no memory of going anywhere at all after being in your flat, ended up in Whipsnade Zoo?"

"I honestly can't say," answered Cornelius, pleased with himself at this sophistry. Euclid had asked him not to mention it to anyone, so he didn't.

"Okay. A bit much to ask, I suppose. The next bit of this story begins with Dave Slinger's little odyssey to your aunt's house, again presumably on the instructions of West, the idea being to put pressure on you to hand yourself and the book over to West and force you to give up its secrets. But their little plan bit the dust when your aunt found a novel use for one of her nick-nacks and friend Slinger ended up in the hospital. Am I getting this right so far?"

"Yes," said both Ruth and Cornelius together.

"We now come to another one of those inexplicable happenings. You make contact with West and set up a meeting. Can you tell me, please, how you managed that?"

"What do you mean," asked Cornelius.

"Where did you get West's phone number from?"

"From Slinger's phone. Aunt Lu found it after he'd been taken to the hospital."

"And you got her to go through Slinger's phone until you found a likely looking contact, which just happened to be West's. You then got your aunt to send a text to West arranging a meet. Correct?"

"Is this leading somewhere," asked Ruth.

"Oh yes, Miss Seaton, it most definitely is. Just bear with me a second. Now, Mr Pye, you've already told me your aunt found Slinger's phone after he'd been taken to the hospital. Correct?"

"That's what I said."

"Tell me, Mr Pye, is your aunt a whizz with phones? Is she some sort of hacker?"

"No, of course not."

"I thought not." DI Evans paused, for dramatic effect. "So can you tell me how she managed to circumvent the fingerprint security on Slinger's phone?"

"What?"

"I had a chat with Slinger after he was brought down here, yesterday. He may not be very bright, but one thing he knows how to do is set up the security on his phone. He was absolutely adamant it was turned on when he last saw it. In his line of business things like that are important. But when we received it from your aunt the security had been turned off. Do you have an explanation?"

Cornelius and Ruth exchanged glances.

"No?" asked DI Evans.

"Not really," offered Cornelius. "Maybe he'd turned it off for some reason and forgotten."

"I'm not normally one to believe anything some low-life like Slinger tells me. Like they say about politicians, if I can see their lips move I know they're lying. But in this case, for some reason, I think I do. So the question I ask myself is this. Should I have one of my colleagues up north go round to your aunt's and get her to explain how she managed it? What do you think?"

"I'm pretty sure she wouldn't have a clue what he was asking her. My aunt's not really up to date with technology."

"You see my problem, here, I hope. We've come up with another of those inexplicable things that seem to be a feature of this case."

"I don't know what to tell you," said Cornelius.

"No, I'm sure you don't. So shall I tell you what I think happened? I think your aunt panicked and phoned you just after she'd clonked Slinger on the head. You saw your chance to get to West and got her to open up the phone using Slinger's thumbprint or whatever. Then she hid the phone until after everyone had gone and it was safe to use it. Am I right?"

Cornelius said nothing.

"Very simple to prove. We just dust for fingerprints. In the normal course of events, your aunt's prints would be randomly scattered over the phone. She picked it up off the floor and put it on the table, then handed it over the next day. If, however, we find multiple instances of your aunt's index finger all over the screen -" He left the sentence hanging, waiting for Cornelius' reaction. Cornelius suddenly realised that if they dusted for prints they'd find an unknown set, which would lead to further complications for his aunt. He could feel the sweat breaking out on his forehead and he was certain DI Evans had noticed.

"Well, what do think? Should we ask your aunt?"

"No! No need," spluttered Cornelius, "you're quite correct. I asked her to do it so I could get West's number."

"So you could play hero." A statement, not a question.

After watching Cornelius squirm uneasily for what seemed like an hour but was probably no more than a few seconds, Evans continued.

"Anyway, moving on. When you got the reply from West agreeing to the meeting, you thought he didn't know what had happened with your aunt and Slinger, so I imagine you were quite surprised to come across Miss Miller in the back of his van."

"It was a bit of a shock, yes. As I told your colleague in Harlow, West told me he had inside knowledge, I'm assuming from someone on the force."

"Yes, we're looking into that. Annoying, to say the least. I'm hoping it's no-one working out of this office. I've known most of them for a good few years now and I'd like to think they're all trustworthy." He paused to finish his coffee.

"Now we come to the great feat of hypnotism and your attempt to find out who's really behind all the shenanigans surrounding you and this book. Is that something you picked up recently or have you always been able to do it?"

"It's something I've been interested in for a little while," said Cornelius, cautiously.

"Could you hypnotise me, for example? According to this report you made West think you had turned lead into gold and that his gun was a banana. Maybe you could make my coffee cup turn into a bottle of whisky."

Euclid jumped in. "It might be to our advantage for him to believe you really can hypnotise him. He'll be more likely to believe your story if he's had a practical demonstration."

Cornelius was alarmed. "Are you joking? What if it doesn't work?"

"Give me a second," replied Euclid, "let me see how amenable he might be." There was a short pause before Euclid said, "Let's give it a try. Again, let me speak through you."

Cornelius turned his attention back to the inspector. "Okay. A practical demonstration. I need you to relax. It'll take a few minutes. When I think you're ready I'm going to count down backwards from five." He looked around the office, which was decorated in the modern office style. The desk had a simple varnished beech effect top on four chrome legs. The chairs were Ikea's finest, functional and spare. Nothing was more than a few years old.

"When I get to one I want you to close your eyes for my count of five, then open them again."

Evans grinnned. "Will you have magically disappeared?"

"At the moment, nothing would give me greater pleasure, but no. You'll notice a bit of a change in the room."

"Do you not do the thing where I'm supposed to get sleepy?" asked Evans.

"I'm not a stage hypnotist," replied Cornelius, "all I want is for you to relax, okay?"

"Okay."

Cornelius waited a few minutes while Evans relaxed, then started to count down. When he reached one the inspector closed his eyes while Cornelius counted back up to five, then opened them again.

The first thing Evans noticed was that the glass walls of his office had turned opaque. He saw a set of hunting prints on the wall in front of him. He looked left to where the filing cabinets should have been and saw a large built-in bookshelf, crammed with leather backed volumes. Next, he noticed the large ink blotter on the large antique desk in front of him. He leaned back in his chair with a gasp and clutched at the deep mahogany arms, scrolled at the ends and inlaid with rosewood. He was in his old headmaster's study, perfect in every detail, except he was sitting in the place that would have been reserved for the quiet old man who once inhabited this room. On the other side of the desk Cornelius and Ruth saw the room exactly as

Evans was seeing it, thanks to Euclid. Ruth was amazed at the clarity and depth of detail in the vision. There came a greater appreciation of Euclid's abilities.

Finally, with an emotional quiver to his voice, Evans spoke. "I'm officially impressed. This is amazing."

"If you open the top right-hand drawer of the desk," suggested Cornelius, "you'll find a diary. I want you to take it out and look at the name imprinted on the cover. It reads Doctor John Giles, MA (Oxon)." Evans did so.

"But how can you do that? How did you know his name? I never told you."

"You think you didn't. You wanted a demonstration. Does this convince you?"

Evans nodded, his mouth open in wonder as he tried to comprehend what he was seeing. The array of pens on the blotter, including the fat, black Mont Blanc he remembered so well, the small brass desk lamp with the green shade, a pile of assorted books to one side, including a Dickens and a P.G. Wodehouse.

"I want you to close your eyes again for a count of five. When you open them again you'll be back in your own office. Ready?"

He closed his eyes for the required time. When he opened them again he was staring at his coffee cup and the plate of biscuits on his own desk. He shifted around in his chair, unwilling to believe he was in his office.

"That was incredible. I never realised such things could be done so easily."

"It's not always easy," replied Cornelius.

"And why my old headmaster's office?"

"You must have had a strong attachment to him. I merely suggested somewhere you'd find comfortable."

"Yes, he was a very kind man," said the inspector, quietly. "My father died when I was still at school and he sort of appointed himself my official guardian. He's retired now. We still keep in touch."

Cornelius felt a pang of jealousy, having found no father figure in his life. Ruth stayed silent, realising she should not have been able to see someone else's memory. She felt like a trespasser. Finally, Evans roused himself.

"So, your plan was to hypnotise West, which I agree now you could do, and get him to tell you who his boss is, but Miss Miller jumped in and spoilt it. Correct?"

"Yes." Cornelius and Euclid thought it would be unwise to mention the name they'd gleaned. Evans, they felt, was very sharp and it wouldn't take him long to realise that Angela hadn't mentioned anything.

"But you'd worked on him enough to make him believe he was holding a banana, rather than a gun. A banana that Angela was also able to see. That's a pretty powerful skill you have there, Mr Pye." He turned to Ruth. "I'm hoping he hasn't been trying it out on you, Miss Seaton."

"I'm pretty certain not, Inspector, but if I thought he had..." She turned to Cornelius and smiled, leaving the thought hanging.

"It looks to me then, that you've come to a dead end and as far as I'm concerned that's a good thing. The police are not too keen on civilians, no matter how talented, taking matters into their own hands. Things could have turned out very badly for you and Miss Miller against an armed man. I'm hoping you're now going to refrain from doing anything further?"

"I don't see what else we can do," replied Cornelius.

"Good. That will put my mind at rest. You'll be pleased to know forensics found some nice prints in your flat, so with everything else Slinger and Wilson were responsible for it looks like it might be a while before they see the light of day again. As for Simon Anthony West," this was the first time they'd heard his full name, "he's been tied into all of the proceedings involving the other two, along with the kidnapping of Angela Miller and various firearms charges. He's on the run so hopefully he'll no longer be a bother. As for your Mister Big, we can't find anything yet that might help us, but with his little gang off the streets he's going to find it a lot more difficult now to be a nuisance. However," the inspector paused, "if you do hear anything I want to be the first to know about it, alright? No more heroics. If you want to play at being detectives, buy yourselves Cluedo and do it in the safety of your own home. Am I making myself clear?"

"Extremely," said Cornelius.

"Of course, Inspector," agreed Ruth.

"I still don't see how Jez Wilson got to Whipsnade, but I'll figure it out, eventually."

Good luck with that, thought Cornelius.

"Right then." He opened a drawer, pulled out the spare key to Cornelius' flat and handed it over. Cornelius thanked him.

"Then if that's all, I'll wish you a pleasant afternoon. Doing anything nice?"

"Yes, a trip to the British Museum," said Ruth, taking Cornelius' hand, omitting to mention the plan to steal Doctor John Dee's crystal ball.

The news of Saturday's events at Matching Manor wasn't slow to reach Carfax, thanks to his contact in the police. For his security, the email he received shortly after five pm had been bounced through a couple of proxy servers and forwarded with a change of address before it reached him. As he read through the details he found himself beginning to admire the luck, tenacity and madly odd strategies Cornelius was employing in his attempts to foil him. A worthy opponent, he thought, a nice little challenge to take the edge off his general boredom. He didn't get a lot of enjoyment out of life so he welcomed the opportunity this current venture provided.

He wasn't too bothered about the loss of Slinger and Wilson. They were idiots who had been outmanoeuvred by a boy and an old lady. Plenty more where they came from, he thought. However, he was disappointed with West, who up until the last few days had been a capable and dependable lieutenant. He couldn't understand how West had lost Cornelius in the first place and then fallen for such a bizarre trick at their next meeting.

In the normal scheme of things a simple job like this would have been wrapped up within a couple of days, yet here he was, a week later and still no further on. Whatever had possessed West to kidnap the girl? And despite having a gun she had bested him and even shot at him while he made his escape. It was total madness.

He supposed West was lying low somewhere, licking his wounds for the moment. They'd be having a very pertinent conversation if and when he did get in touch. West was paid well enough and had proved himself loyal, but if he was caught he knew it was in the best interests of his health to say nothing. Not that he knew very much anyway.

Carfax treated his employees using the mushroom theory - always keep them in the dark.

The things that puzzled Carfax now were rapidly growing into a list of *hows*. How had Cornelius escaped from the Manor in the first place? How had he suddenly appeared at his flat, overpowered Wilson and rescued the girl? For that matter, how had he got back to his flat so quickly from the Manor? And how had Jez Wilson ended up in Whipsnade? Why Whipsnade? And finally, how had Cornelius managed to set up the meeting with West so quickly after Slinger had been put out of action by the old lady, using Slinger's phone to send a text?

It was the Whipsnade thing that bothered him the most. It was just so unlikely. According to West, it was also bothering Jez a great deal. Wilson had told his lawyer what little he remembered.

"There was this blinding flash of light an' I just shot out me arm and grabbed one or other of 'em, the girl I think. After that, I couldn't see a bloody thing but I ended up grappling with Pye an' then the gun went off. I knew I'd took a step back and then I felt meself falling over backwards but I carried on going down, which was fuckin' impossible, right? 'Cos there wasn't nowhere to fall down to in his flat. Then I hit me head on something on the way and the next thing I knew I was waking up in Whipsnade, eye to eye with a fuckin' penguin."

Which, Jez had told the lawyer, was another impossible thing, because he knew that Slinger had left the flat just after six and less than an hour later he was being booked into the cop shop in Luton. Summing up, his exact words had been, "It's not 'umanly possible, is it?"

No, thought Carfax, it's not. There's something going on here that I'm missing. It's time I took a closer look.

Like any aspiring Sherlock Holmes, he marshalled the facts at his disposal. There weren't many. He knew where Cornelius lived and worked. He knew Ruth Seaton was employed at the same place and was also in his flat when Slinger and Wilson had got there. His inside contact had told him it was she who had reported Cornelius missing. But why her, and not his girlfriend, Angela Miller? He realised there were many things he didn't know, but that could be corrected. He picked up one of his phones and dialled a number.

"Hello? This is Trevor at BPI. How can I help you, Mr Jones?"

"I need you to follow someone for me and I'll want the information as quickly as possible. I'll send you the details. Use as many bodies as you need. The usual terms. And be discreet."

"Of course, sir. I look forward to receiving your instructions."

22.

If a visitor goes up the steps to the British Museum, carries on through the hallway into the Great Court and stands for a moment or two to admire or decry what they've done with the place in the last few years, then bears left past the book shop, they will find the door to Gallery One, noted on the museum's map as The Enlightenment Gallery. Previously known as the King's Library, it is unlike any other gallery in the museum. Rather than being concerned with one particular time period or culture the objects within range from the prehistoric era to the beginning of the nineteenth century. One person binds all these objects together; the great Victorian collector, Sir Hans Sloane. What began as a personal cabinet of curiosities evolved to become the foundations of the British Museum.

Once inside it might appear as though this gallery is home to a random selection of objects, but in fact it has been carefully curated to evoke an eighteenth-century museum experience. If our visitor walks through the door to the centre of the gallery, turns left and walks a few steps, they will come to a large display cabinet on their right containing artefacts once owned by Doctor John Dee. Along with a black obsidian mirror and four magic discs, three made of wax and one of gold, there is a small stand which holds Dee's shew stone, a slightly brownish coloured rock crystal ball, a little over four centimetres in diameter.

"Is that the one?" asked Ruth.

"Yes," confirmed Euclid, "that's it."

Cornelius looked at it intensely, wishing it could somehow magic itself into his pocket. He hadn't realised it would be so small. He had the idea it would resemble a typical fortune-teller's ball such as might be seen at the seaside or the fairground. How was it possible to see anything at all in something that size?

"I know it's not going to be difficult to materialize in this room, not that I'm looking forward to it, but how am I going to get it out of the cabinet? I can't break it open."

"It's quite simple, Cornelius. Think about it for a moment," said Euclid, patiently.

Cornelius thought, then realised he didn't like what he was thinking, but it turned out that Ruth was thinking the same.

"He can put his hand through the glass, can't he," she said. "If he can materialise anywhere then there are no barriers, so if, in his mind, he moves his hand towards the crystal, he should be able to grab it." Cornelius gave a small shudder.

"What's the problem?" asked Euclid. "Ruth is perfectly correct. There are no barriers where materialization is concerned."

"I know," countered Cornelius, "it's just the thought of it. Pushing my hand through a pane of glass, it makes me feel a bit queasy, quite honestly."

"I'll do it," said Ruth.

Cornelius was horrified. "What? No! I can't let you do it. What if you're caught?"

"What if *you're* caught? Same thing. Then *I'd* worry. Or are you saying girls shouldn't be allowed to do these things?"

"No, of course not. It's just, well..." He couldn't think of an objection which didn't involve being thought of as sexist so he said nothing. Chivalry counted for nothing these days, he mused.

"Anyway, you've been having all the fun, popping here and popping there. I've only done it once, when I had no say in the matter. Not that I'm ungrateful, but I'd like to try it myself."

"Don't worry," broke in Euclid, "there'll be plenty of opportunities for both of you. Apart from sorting out Carfax we still have to find out what happened to Tald. In the meantime, I'm going to raise the shuttle from the bottom of the Thames and retrieve the generator. If I can't do that I'm stuck here anyway. But Ruth's right. She's only travelled once with me. She should experience it properly. It's only fair."

Ruth was thrilled. Cornelius realised he'd been selfish and a little immature and apologised.

"Of course you should do it."

"I'm glad you've got that settled," said Euclid. "Now make sure you can visualise where you need to be when you return while I check what sort of security is in this room and if I need to do anything about it. Then we can go."

Once back at Ruth's flat they planned their next step, the raising of the shuttle.

"Where will you set up the portal?" asked Cornelius.

"A good question," replied Euclid, "and one to which I've given quite a bit of thought, because it needs to be somewhere quite private. It was only yesterday I realised I knew the perfect spot."

"Where?" asked Ruth.

"Just outside the village of Matching Tye."

"The old house!" cried Cornelius. "Yes, it's perfect. It's not been lived in for years and it's set in its own grounds. We won't be overlooked."

"Exactly. Pity we won't be able to thank our old friend Mister West for introducing us to the place," replied Euclid, sarcastically.

A quick internet search identified it as Matching Manor, rebuilt in the eighteen-nineties on the site of a medieval manor house. A satellite view of the property revealed that it stood in its own grounds, hemmed in by trees. Cornelius already knew the house couldn't be seen from the road and there were no For Sale signs anywhere, indicating that, although empty, it was unlikely to be open for viewings. Another trawl of estate agency sites confirmed this. At Ruth's suggestion they paid a small fee to a website which would make the title deeds available. They were unsurprised to discover the current owner was listed as The Eternal Hope Property Trust, another link back to Bunce and the office with the brass plates. Euclid was delighted.

"We can raise the shuttle and take it straight to the Manor under cover of darkness. I'm sure it won't be too difficult to hide once we're there."

"You mean, we get to take a ride in a spaceship?" asked Cornelius, in awe, visualising Han Solo's Millenium Falcon.

"You need to tone down your expectations," warned Euclid. Ruth was lost for words, just thinking about it.

"So, we move the shuttle tonight. Then, when we've dealt with the Carfax problem and found Tald, we borrow the crystal from the museum and set up the portal. If all goes according to plan we can return the crystal within the hour and no-one will be any the wiser. Does that meet with your approval?"

"Doesn't the portal need the crystal to keep running?" asked Ruth.

"No. The crystal just initiates the process."

They agreed wholeheartedly with the plan, both itching to start. "Good," said Euclid. "So first, we need to get to the shuttle."

According to Euclid, it was located about twenty metres offshore from the Kew Riverside Walk, just north of the Royal Mid-Surrey Golf Club and more or less opposite Syon House on the opposite bank of the Thames. Luckily, in the intervening years no houses had been built directly overlooking the area. The raising of the shuttle would have to be done under cover of darkness, which would mean sometime after eleven, and late enough to ensure there were as few people around as possible. The quickest route was by tube to Richmond, a walk to Twickenham Bridge, then drop down onto the riverside and head north. On Sundays the last train to Richmond arrived at seven minutes past midnight, which was perfect. A leisurely stroll would get them to the required spot by around one o'clock. Once the shuttle was retrieved and moved to its new home at Matching Manor, returning home would require no time at all. If all went well they would be back before two. Although Cornelius was still on leave from work, Ruth was expected in, but there was no way she was going to miss out on this expedition.

They decided to leave around ten thirty to make sure they didn't miss the last tube. They finished eating by nine so Euclid suggested that this might be the perfect time for Ruth to practise jumping. He transferred himself from Cornelius' wristwatch to the necklace Ruth wore most of the time. As she was already aware of Euclid and the mechanics of what she was about to do, it didn't take too long before she'd made her first jump, from the kitchen table to the sofa. Then from there to the bedroom and back again.

"I could really get used to this method of travelling," she said. "Imagine if everyone could do this. Go anywhere you want without the hassle, instantaneously. No more commuting to work, no more waiting around at airports."

"Yes, but then think of all the people who'd be put out of work, all the airline staff, car makers, tube drivers, anyone in fact involved in getting you from one place to another. And what would you do about criminals and terrorists, if they were allowed to go wherever they wanted? I'm afraid it would be chaos."

"Aw, come on, Euclid, it's just a daydream," said Cornelius.

"I know. Sorry to be a wet blanket, but something like this would radically alter your entire culture. I'm not supposed to give gifts like this to the human race. The two of you have this by accident, because you're helping me get back home. You know you can never tell anyone else about this, don't you?"

They both nodded.

"And when I've gone you'll no longer be able to do it anyway. It's only my presence which enables this."

With all that had been happening over the past few weeks, neither of them had really thought too far ahead. It hurt to realise that one of the greatest gifts ever given to mankind would have to be given back and that Euclid might be gone from their lives forever.

After they had both pondered this for a little while, Cornelius was the first to speak.

"I've never thanked you, have I? I mean, really thanked you for everything you've done. Since Maccabeus, I've done things no other human being has ever done before. Now Ruth gets to do them too. And tonight we're going to fly in an actual spaceship. It's something we'll remember for the rest of our lives."

"Once you've gone back home will you ever return?" asked Ruth.

"I don't know," replied Euclid. "I've been gone a long time. I've no idea what's been happening on Farasta. But if I can, I will. I promise. After sitting around doing nothing for such a long time I've suddenly had a great deal of excitement in a very short time. I've come to life again and I have you two to thank for that, so it goes both ways."

"Thanks, Euclid, for everything," said Ruth.

The journey out to Richmond would have been boring under normal circumstances, but the knowledge of what they were about to do made it intensely exciting. In addition, Cornelius was getting to spend even more time with Ruth. He couldn't believe his luck but was conscious that if it hadn't been for exceptional circumstances things might never have got to this point. His usual shyness with the opposite sex would have kicked in yet again.

With a lot of preamble and umming and aahing, he mentioned this to Ruth during the journey. She gave him a look of concern, much as a mother might give an idiotic son who'd just dropped his ice-cream on the floor. She placed a finger over his lips and whispered in his ear, "Rubbish."

"It's not rubbish. I've never been very good in those sort of situations. I only went out with Angela because she practically kidnapped me and I didn't want to say anything to her in case it hurt her feelings. At your party, I was really hoping to speak to you, but I bottled it."

"You idiot, Cornelius! Why do you think I tried so hard to get you to my party? I knew you liked me and I knew you needed a bit of encouragement and you would have got it if Angela hadn't butted in while I was dealing with a full-scale emergency in the kitchen."

"All that time. Wasted! If only I'd realised."

"Doesn't matter now, does it? We got there in the end. That's all that matters."

"Yes," agreed Cornelius, with a glint in his eye, "and when we get back we can make up for lost time."

"Whoa, hold your horses, cowboy! By the time we get back it's going to be the wee small hours and I have to get up for work."

"Oh," replied Cornelius, suddenly downcast.

"But we can make up for it all the more tomorrow evening," she promised.

He brightened again. "Promise?"

"Promise."

After Turnham Green they were the only ones in the carriage so they canoodled at length until the train juddered to a halt at its terminus.

The walk from the station to Twickenham Bridge took twenty minutes at a leisurely pace. Away from the road it was pitch black and they were glad to have brought powerful torches to light the way. Another half hour brought them to the spot Euclid had specified. There were lots of shrubs and bushes growing between the walk and the river but there was a small patch of grass between them and the golf course, which Euclid said would be big enough for their purposes. The time was a couple of minutes to one. Thankfully, they'd seen no-one else on the way.

"What now?" asked Cornelius.

"Now," said Euclid, "is where I find out if the shuttle is still there and if it is, will it answer my call. I've been listening for it's presence and I think I hear it, but it's right on the edge of my perception. Hardly surprising, after all this time. I'm going to need all my powers of concentration to get it ashore. Feel free to talk among yourselves for a minute or two."

Instead, they stayed quiet, holding hands nervously in anticipation, their torches off so as not to attract attention. Apart from the low background roar of the city, which never went away, there was very little sound, just the occasional rustle of leaves as a faint breeze stirred the trees. London is never completely dark but Cornelius couldn't think of anywhere else in the city as dark as this. The cloudless sky meant there was no orange glow from the streetlights. The moon had set an hour earlier.

After a few minutes they noticed a small change in the sounds from the river, which increased very slowly until they could hear the water bubbling. There was a sudden splash and the sound of water raining down. Looking up they could just make out a black object, only because, as it moved, the stars in the background winked off and on as it passed over their heads, still dripping water. They involuntarily stepped back a few paces to avoid getting soaked. Then the object settled onto the patch of waste ground beside them.

"Okay," said Euclid, "that went a lot easier than I expected."

With some difficulty, because the light seemed to slip round the sides, they shone their torches on the object, which was much smaller than either of them had imagined.

"You travelled *how many years* in that?" asked Ruth.

"No, no. This is just the shuttle, although our actual ship wasn't much bigger."

"It's tiny," whispered Cornelius.

"What did you expect?" asked Euclid. "It only has to hold one person until they're rescued."

The spaceship's shuttle was about the size of a small transit van, rhomboid in shape but with all the edges rounded. They had to concentrate hard to focus on it, their eyes seemed to slide off its surface. It bulged out slightly at each end but looked impossibly sleek. It reminded Cornelius of an old Airstream caravan, except there were no wheels. It hovered about a foot above the ground, it was completely black and had no adornment or marking except where one side had been damaged, presumably during the fight with the Allas.

They walked all the way around it but could see no sign of doors and windows, nor any means of propulsion. It was also completely dry, suggesting water could not cling to its surface. Without warning, an aperture opened before them with a quiet hiss. As they stared into the doorway the darkness within slowly grew brighter and at last they could make out a few interior details.

"Don't just stand there gawking," said Euclid, "in you go, before someone comes."

There was a small step up and then they entered, more than likely the first humans ever to board an alien spacecraft. As they moved forward the door closed behind them and the lights brightened. The interior was even tinier and the two of them seemed to take up all the available space. Before they could fully comprehend what they were seeing there was a shout.

"WHAT!" It came from Euclid, so loud they almost dropped to the floor in anticipation of who knew what disaster.

"What?" echoed Cornelius, as Ruth shouted, "What's happened?"

"The cryo unit! It's active." They felt Euclid urging them to look directly in front of them, where a coffin shaped box was emitting a gloomy blue light. A small red light was flashing lazily above one end.

"It's Tald! He's here. He's still alive!"

They took a step towards the unit. At one end was a small window and through it they could see the face of Tald, once known as Edward Kelley, scryer to Doctor John Dee.

"I've just interrogated the ship," Euclid told them. "It informs me Tald returned here in May 1602. He didn't have the crystal with him so he couldn't return home. He had no idea what had happened to me so he put himself into suspended animation until such a time as either I returned or the ship was found by our own kind."

"So he's been here ever since?" said Ruth, "Over four hundred years. Wow!"

They were both still staring at Tald in awe. An actual living, breathing alien.

On a ledge just to one side of the cryo unit Ruth caught sight of something totally out of keeping with the rest of the ship. A brown leather pouch about the size of a coffee mug. She realised she could smell the leather.

"What's this?" she asked.

"Ah," said Euclid, "that'll be the gold. Open it up and have a look."

Ruth loosened the draw string and started to tip the contents into her hand. She stopped pouring when the first few gold coins dropped out and looked inside.

"There must be a small fortune in here." She held out her hand to Cornelius, who looked in amazement at the assortment of Elizabethan coinage, as clean and fresh as the day they were minted.

"You'd better hold onto it, Cornelius," said Euclid, "Tald and I won't be requiring it now."

"But we can't take this!" he cried.

"We need to go, now!" said Euclid, urgently. "There are some people heading towards us. Probably just a couple of dog walkers, but I don't want the ship to be seen by anyone. Hang onto something while I lift us."

Ruth poured the coins back into the pouch and tightened the drawstring, then handed it to Cornelius. They each hung on to an arm of the single pilot's chair as the door closed. There was no sound but from the odd feeling in their stomachs they knew they'd shot upwards very quickly, then come to a stop. As the shuttle started moving the internal lights went off and a window became visible in the direction they were travelling. They knelt down either side of the chair and looked out as they began to fly over London at great speed.

"We'll be at Matching Manor in a little over six minutes," said Euclid.

"Won't we be picked up by radar or anything?" asked Cornelius.

"Not a chance. We're flying quite low and the ship has various ways of avoiding detection. Radar pings would slide around us, as though we didn't exist."

"Very handy. Could do with something like this on the motorway," said Cornelius.

Within minutes they were flying past the radio mast on Alexandra Palace, close to Ruth's flat, then all too soon they landed in the gardens behind the Manor. It was pitch black outside. The window disappeared and lights came up once again.

"So what now?" asked Ruth. "Are you going to wake Tald?"

"No, I don't think that would be wise. The process takes a couple of days and after all this time I think I'd rather do it where there are medical facilities available, which means getting him back home. The cryo unit is intended for use in emergencies. It only has basic diagnostics so I don't want to take any chances. If Tald has any serious injuries greater minds than mine can take care of him. There's nothing else we can do tonight, so I suggest we head back and return in a couple of days time. In the morning, Cornelius and I will start to investigate the mysterious Carfax. Hopefully, your friend Cathy will be able to supply us with some information we can use."

"I don't know about anyone else, but I'd like to take a break from all this and get my life back to normal," said Cornelius, "at least for a few days. I'll do the research tomorrow but on Tuesday I'm going back to work again. I've been away long enough and it's not really fair on Mr Singh when there's nothing wrong with me."

"I see no harm in waiting until the weekend before carrying on," replied Euclid, "it's been a hectic few days." Ruth nodded her assent.

"Bedtime, then," said Cornelius.

23.

When they'd returned the previous evening they'd tried to sleep, but it had been difficult as each of them kept going over in their heads what had happened. The next morning the alarm went off at seven. Ruth got ready for work, Cornelius got up in sympathy and made breakfast. After a very strong coffee a sleepy Ruth kissed him goodbye and left just after eight.

"I'll chase Cathy if I haven't heard anything by mid-morning," she said as she closed the door.

Cornelius didn't yet feel comfortable alone in Ruth's flat so he decided to return home to start the investigation into Carfax. His flat seemed oddly quiet and there was little to suggest the events of the previous week had ever happened, apart from the shattered milk bottle on the floor of the kitchen. He checked the fridge and cupboards, decided he needed to stock up on a few items and went shopping. Forty minutes later he was back in front of his computer.

A search on the Companies House website revealed forty-seven separate companies using the name Carfax in their titles, with fifteen having an officer of the same name, an officer being either a director or financial secretary. He printed details of them all as a starting point. Each one would have to be looked at individually to see if they could throw up any clues, a boring task. He ran further searches on the company names Ruth had uncovered, but couldn't find any links between them and Carfax. The man was certainly mysterious. He wished Angela had held off attacking West for just another few minutes. That's all Euclid would have needed. After an hour and a half of not getting very far, Cornelius asked Euclid if there was anything he could do to help.

"I remember you telling me you could pick up radio and view television channels. I was just wondering if you could do anything with phones?"

"I wish I could help, but no. There's far too much noise in the air where phones are concerned. I can scan the airwaves and listen in but I would have to know what I was listening for. When radio started there was nothing else getting in the way of the signal, so it was relatively easy to find something of interest and listen. Television was more complicated because of the addition of vision but again, it only used a limited amount of bandwidth when it started and it was easy to assemble the various feeds for the different channels. It got much more difficult when satellite tv started, but even then I was just receiving a single stream of data, which could be picked apart. To me, that's all free to air. Landlines have always been difficult to access because they use dedicated cabling. I could pick up on the calls coming into your uncle's house because of the proximity of the cable, but I couldn't really get into the system. Nowadays, with mobile phones it's even more difficult because there are millions of calls a day. I would need to be within about a kilometre of a mast before I could even start to differentiate calls, but it wouldn't help if Carfax didn't come through that particular mast, even if I knew when he was making a call. If we could get a phone number for him, landline or mobile *and* if you were to call that number from your phone, then I could probably pinpoint his location, but I think getting to him that way is a very long shot. Sorry."

"No, don't be sorry. You've done far too much for me to ever need to apologise. I didn't think it was going to be so difficult to track him down. It means we're relying very heavily on Ruth's friend coming up with something."

"What about getting in touch with your cousin Francis? He may be able to help."

"Good idea! I'd forgotten all about him." A quick search revealed the card Francis had left, stored behind the clock on the bookcase. His next step was to make himself a cup of strong tea, in order to fortify himself before calling.

"Hello. Duncan Investigations," Francis' bland voice intoned.

"Francis. It's Cornelius. You came to see me about the book."

"Yes, hello Cornelius. What can I do for you? Have you decided to part with it?"

"No, I'm afraid not." He was sure he heard a sigh from the other end. "There have been a few complications since I last spoke to you."

"Oh, I'm sorry to hear that," replied Francis.

"Thank you. The thing is, I need your help. It's about your client. I'm trying to find out who he is."

"Oh, I'm afraid I can't help you there. Client confidentiality, you know."

"Yes, I appreciate that. Very commendable. But you might change your mind after what I've got to say. If you're not already sitting down you'd better do it. It may take me some time."

"Okay," said Francis, doubtfully, "I'm sitting."

Cornelius told him the story, or as much of it as he could without involving aliens and talking books. Essentially he gave Francis the same details he'd given the police. When he'd finished there was a long silence on the phone.

"Hello, Francis, are you there?"

"Yes, yes, I'm here. Sorry, I was just sort of digesting what you've just told me. I had no idea there was a criminal element involved."

"Yes. It looks likely you were never going to get your commission."

"No, I see that, now. How very annoying. For you, I mean." As far as Cornelius was concerned, 'annoying' was an understatement.

"So, if you could help me out?"

"Ask away, Cornelius, I'll see what I can do."

"I'll pay you for any information, obviously."

"No, no. Don't worry. You're family, after all. What do you want to know?"

"The man who came to see your mother. Was he your client or just someone acting for him?"

"No. He told me he was acting on behalf of the client." Cornelius cursed quietly.

"So you never found out the name of the man who was hiring your services? You never met this client, or had any dealings with him directly?"

"No, sorry, not so much as a phone call. Everything was done by his agent, the man who came to see us."

"And the name of this agent, was it West? Tall, balding man with glasses?"

"Yes, that sounds like him, but he called himself Gregson. How did you know?"

"Well, I'm sorry to have to tell you, but he's the one behind most of the criminal activity."

"Oh, my!" whispered Francis. Cornelius imagined him putting a hand to his face as he said this.

"Did he mention anything at all about who he was working for?"

"No, not really. Just that he was a collector of rare books. If I remember correctly, he said something like, 'You know what it's like with these old City boys. No family to spend their money on so they take up a hobby.'"

"That's interesting. And how did you get paid for your retainer?"

"He arranged to meet me in the City, on a bench in the gardens at Finsbury Circus to be exact. Said it was handy for him. He paid me two hundred pounds in cash, which I thought at the time was a bit unusual. I like to keep everything above board, you see. The taxman and so on. I see now that he probably didn't want to give me a cheque in case it could be traced back anywhere."

"No, he wouldn't, would he. Shame. Well, thanks a million, Francis, you've been a great help. Please give my regards to your mother and let her know I may be in a position to do something for her very soon."

"That's very kind of you, Cornelius. I'm sure she'll appreciate that. Good luck with your search."

Cornelius ended the call and was musing on what he'd been told when Euclid broke in. "He's a bachelor, he's a collector of rare books and he most likely works in the City, possibly in the Finsbury Circus area, as that seems a slightly out of the way place for West to meet your cousin. It's a start."

"Yes," agreed Cornelius, "but we can't just go wandering around the City in the wild hope we spot him. We need something a little more concrete."

He ran another search through Companies House. None of the companies associated with Carfax had an address in or close by Finsbury Circus. Then he had a brainwave and began again, this time using the names of Graham and Margaret Jesney. Bingo! One hit, a company called Hope Springs Consultancy, with an address in Finsbury Circus.

"That has to be it. The link. It can't be a coincidence. Let's see what we can find out on the internet."

There was nothing. As far as the World Wide Web was concerned, it didn't exist.

"Now that is weird. I think we should go take a look."

"Good idea," agreed Euclid.

Just as Cornelius was about to leave, his phone rang and an email pinged in his Inbox. It was Ruth.

"Hello, gorgeous," he said, "did Cathy come up with something?"

"She did, but it's not much. The group of companies that includes Eternal Hope Consultancy Services are all owned by a company called Safeharbour, registered in Panama . They have one office registered in London, Hope Springs Consultancy, under the names of our old friends, the Jesneys."

"Don't tell me, they have an address in Finsbury Circus."

"How did you know?"

"I'm not just a pretty face, you know."

"Who told you that?"

"I think it might have been you, actually, last night."

"And I think *you* might have been dreaming!"

" Anyway, I've been doing a bit of digging at this end." He explained the call to cousin Francis which had pointed him in the right direction. "Your information confirms what I've just discovered. We were just on the way out when you rang. We're going to have a look around, see if we can find out a little more."

"Check your inbox. Cathy sent me all the details so I've forwarded them on to you."

"Thanks. I'll have a read on the way."

"Please be careful," said Ruth.

"I will."

There is nothing else quite like Finsbury Circus in the City of London. There are no shops, cafes or public houses, so tourists and vehicles are rare. It is an oasis of quiet, hidden between Moorgate and Liverpool Street stations, consisting of a large oval shaped garden surrounded by office buildings of various ages, which can be approached from the east, west or south. The garden was home to a bowling club before modern times intruded. In 2010 Crossrail took over a substantial part of it to drill a massive hole down to a section of tunnel where they created platforms for the new Elizabeth Line. Crossrail finally departed and what's left is simply a grassy space, surrounded by large trees, with a bandstand at one end. The bowling club found new premises close by the northern end of the Rotherhithe Tunnel and never moved back when work had been completed.

Cornelius crossed the road from Moorgate Station and entered the Circus from the west. He found what he was looking for on the south side, a massive curved office building built in the neogothic style beloved of the Victorians. Imposing doors with colourful leaded windows and brass handles opened to reveal a large hall and staircase, with marbled floors and acres of Doulton tiles below oak panelling. On one side of the entrance he spotted the signage which signified occupancy. He found Hope Springs Consultancy listed on the third floor, office number thirty-six.

Rather than use the lift, Cornelius walked up the imposing staircase to the first floor, where it gave way to something less grand for his journey up to the third.

"This must be the place," said Cornelius. "It's very quiet."

From the landing a carpeted corridor stretched to either side. He turned left, following the sign for thirty-six and eventually found himself standing before an imposing set of double doors, with brass door knobs and plates, the name of the company painted in white on the left hand door and *Reception* painted on the other.

"What now?" asked Cornelius, nervously.

"Let's find out if our Mr Carfax is in."

"Are you sure about this?"

"Of course. What can he do? He's just one man and I very much doubt he's prone to argy-bargy. He's a man who likes to keep his hands clean. He hires other people to do the dirty work for him. If anything goes wrong, they take the rap. He's Mr Invisible."

"I'm still not keen on bearding Mr Invisible in his lair."

"Don't you want to find out what this is all about?"

"Well yes, but I'd rather he just left us alone."

"Come on, Cornelius, stiff upper lip and all that."

"It's alright for you to talk. He doesn't know you're here."

"What's the worst that can happen? He's not expecting us, so we have the advantage."

Cornelius opened the door cautiously and stepped through, finding himself in a well appointed reception area, with a large Chesterfield sofa on one wall, a coffee table in front of it piled with various out of date business magazines and a desk by the window with a large computer screen on one side. Behind the desk sat a formidable looking middle-aged lady, who reminded him of his Aunt Violet. A single door opposite the sofa led, no doubt, to Carfax's inner sanctum. The lady, Carfax's personal secretary, looked him up and down. What she saw didn't seem to impress her.

"May I help you?" asked the secretary, staring at him intently.

"Er, I'd like to see Mr Carfax. Please."

"And do you have an appointment," she replied icily, knowing very well he didn't.

"No, I'm afraid not, but if you could give him my name I'm sure he'll want to see me. It's a personal matter."

"Well, I'll try," she sighed, hopelessly, "but it's highly unlikely. Name?"

"Cornelius Pye."

"Cornelius Pye," she repeated slowly, in a tone which suggested she didn't believe him. She picked up the phone and tapped a button.

"There's a Cornelius Pye to see you."

After a few seconds the look on the secretary's face turned to astonishment.

"Are you sure?" she said, disbelievingly. She put the phone down. "He says he'll see you. He has something to finish off, which should only take a couple of minutes. You're to go straight in when he buzzes."

Cornelius smiled at her triumphantly and sat on the Chesterfield.

"Try and keep him talking, Cornelius," said Euclid. "I'll find out what I can."

A minute or two later, the switchboard buzzed and the secretary nodded at him. He walked through the door and came face to face with his persecutor for the first time.

"My, my. This *is* a surprise." A smiling Carfax leaned back in his chair and clasped his fingers together over his stomach. It was not the smile of a man who got much practise at it. "Come in, young man, take a seat." He waved at the chair on the other side of the desk. "We meet at last, as they say."

"Did you think I wouldn't find you?" asked Cornelius.

"I have to say I'm very impressed. I try to make it difficult for people to find out about me. I do so like my privacy."

"Yes, I'd noticed. You'd rather get other people to do your dirty work for you."

"Dirty work, Mr Pye? I've no idea what you're talking about."

252

"Oh, I think you know full well. You went too far when you involved my family and friends in all of this."

"All of what?" There was a puzzled look on Carfax's face, then he smiled again. "Are you recording this conversation Mr Pye? Are you hoping to extract some sort of confession from me so you can turn me over to the police?"

Cornelius said nothing. Carfax continued.

"I'm sorry to disappoint you but I've done nothing wrong."

"You may tell yourself that, but we both know your involvement in this is much deeper than you admit to. You can't tell me that during our previous conversation you didn't know I was being held against my will." Carfax made no reply to this accusation. "No matter, your thugs are both locked up now and your main man is on the run, but I suppose you already know that from your contact in the police force."

"Oh, you mean Mr West and his brainless associates. It's no matter to me. Easy come, easy go, as they say." He paused to let his last statement sink in. If he was hoping for a reaction he was disappointed. Cornelius noted he didn't deny his source.

"Yes, I admit I asked Mr West to carry out some instructions on my behalf in order to acquire your copy of Euclid's Elements. Unfortunately, it appears he misinterpreted my requests and took things a bit too far. I don't see how I can be held responsible for his misdeeds. I must say, I was very impressed with your little display of hypnotism. That did make me chuckle, but I must warn you, such trickery will have no effect on me." If Carfax had chuckled, thought Cornelius, it was probably the first time in his life.

"I'm not recording this conversation Mr Carfax. I don't need to. I just came to tell you it's over. I want you to leave me alone. I might have been willing to part with the book once, if you'd kept everything clean, but there's no way on earth I'll part with it now."

"In case you didn't know, I'm a bibliophile. I collect rare books. Apart from anything else, I want to own the Euclid for it's own sake, so my offer still stands. One hundred thousand pounds for the book and a few hours of your time."

"Not a chance. Anyway, you're wasting your time. There's nothing there. No codes, no magic, nothing. It's just a book. Don't you think that after all this time one of my ancestors would have discovered something?"

"But one of your ancestors did just that, didn't he? Maccabeus Pye. The man who first acquired the book for your family. He knew its worth, didn't he?"

"What do you mean?

"Oh, come on, Mr Pye. Do you think I haven't done my homework?

"I have no idea what you're talking about."

"Don't you?" said Carfax, disbelievingly.

"You've gone to a lot of trouble chasing a pipe dream, it's just an old family story with no basis in fact."

"A pipe dream? Oh no, it's no pipe dream. There's hard documented evidence. I'm sure you know all this but let me run it by you, see where I might have gone wrong. We know for a fact the book originally belonged to John Dee, that it was stolen from his house in Mortlake, along with most of the rest of his library. It's long been known that Fromond and Davies sold a lot of the books to Nicholas Saunder but there's a gap of a couple of years before he got his hands on the Euclid. I have a letter that Saunder sent to Sir Richard Ruddle, claiming he'd bought the book from an unnamed nobleman, who had suddenly become very rich, attributed to a secret found in Dee's book. It took me a while, but I finally tracked down the nobleman in question and it all fits. From scratching around for a living he suddenly acquired huge wealth, seemingly from nowhere. Are you with me so far?"

"This man's as mad as a box of frogs," said Euclid to Cornelius. "There was no nobleman. Where does he get his information, The Boy's Book of Conspiracy Theories?"

"That could just have been a coincidence," said Cornelius to Carfax.

"Alright. Then is it also a coincidence that Ruddle himself came into a fortune soon after buying the book from Saunder? And later still, when your ancestor Maccabeus Pye acquired the book he also became extremely wealthy. Three coincidences suddenly start looking a bit suspicious wouldn't you say?"

"But Maccabeus was a member of the East India Company. It's not surprising he was quite well off," countered Cornelius.

"His wealth didn't come from the East India Company. I've looked into your ancestor quite thoroughly and I've discovered his little secret. In the archives of Westwood & Mercer, a merchant bank in the City, I found transactions that showed him receiving regular

254

shipments of gold from a man named Edward Tald, who supposedly lived in British Guyana. Tald is quite an unusual name, so you'd think it might be quite simple to track him down. Surprisingly, there's quite a lot of information on the people who lived and traded there during the early seventeenth century, if you know where to look for it. But no Edward Tald. According to the bank's archive the shipments left Guyana as regular as clockwork, spanning a period of just over four years but there are no ships leaving there that tie in with any that reached England. The shipping records are quite extensive, if you want to check. Ergo, Maccabeus received his gold from somewhere else. What I then found, surprise, surprise, was an account in your ancestor's name at another London bank, that showed extremely large deposits, on a regular basis. How do you account for that, Mr Pye?"

Irritatingly, Carfax smiled once more and gestured with his hands, inviting Cornelius to speak. Disconcertingly, that part of the story was true.

"You have to give him credit," said Euclid to Cornelius, "he's done a very thorough job of discovering the truth about Maccabeus. Hard to fault that. Most of the other stuff is just coincidence but you can see how it might appear to someone who wants to believe in tales of instant wealth. No wonder he's so sold on finding out the book's secret. Pity for him he's not only barking up the wrong tree, he's not even in the right forest."

"He's not going to give up, is he?" replied Cornelius.

"I doubt it. Monomania like his won't just go away of it's own accord. The only thing I can think of is to try and give him what he wants, but I don't see how at the moment."

"No response, My Pye?" asked Carfax, jolting Cornelius back to his presence. He suddenly realised he'd been staring at him during the conversation with Euclid. He shook his head, somewhat bewildered.

"Well, if that's all I think it would be best if you were to leave now. I'm a busy man and you must have somewhere else to be. So nice to have had this little chat."

Carfax leaned forward across his desk and glared at Cornelius.

"A word of advice, though. I normally get what I want."

"Then prepare yourself for disappointment." Cornelius replied. He held his glare for a couple of seconds longer, then turned and left.

Back outside in the corridor Cornelius asked Euclid if he'd discovered anything helpful.

"Not a sausage, if you'll excuse the phrase. His mind's like a closed book. I think the only reason I got through to him last time was that he was tired, after poring over the book for hours. Even so, it was hard work. He's as tight as a drum."

"We'll have to come up with something to stop him," said Cornelius. "There must be something we can do."

"There's sure to be *something*." agreed Euclid.

There was no-one in the corridor so they returned home without troubling public transport.

Ten minutes later, one of Carfax's phones rang. He looked at the caller id. West. Interesting, he thought, as he answered.

"Mr West, so good of you to call. I sincerely hope you've got an explanation for the shambles you've left behind."

There was a pause before West spoke.

"Mr Carfax. Promise me you'll let me strangle Pye with my bare hands. I'm going to get even with that little - " There was a sharp crackling on the line and Carfax missed the end of the sentence, although he didn't need to guess what had just been said.

"Yes, yes, you can do what you like once I've got what I want. Where are you? The line is awful. I can hardly hear you."

"I'm at the Manor, on the top floor. Reception's a bit patchy. I can see down the road from up here, make sure no-one's sneaking up on me."

"What on earth are you doing at the Manor?"

"I didn't have anywhere else to go that was safe, so I came back here. I reckoned the cops wouldn't think to look here again. I phoned one of my cousins and he let me borrow his wife's car. I can trust him. He's going to come up here now and again to bring me food and stuff. I had to dump the van. I knew it wouldn't take long for the cops to spot it."

"So tell me what happened."

With breaks for apologies every thirty seconds, West explained as best as he could the events of Saturday afternoon. Carfax listened without comment until he'd finished, then sighed heavily.

"Have I made a big mistake employing you, Mr West?"

"You know I haven't let you down before, Mr Carfax, but this Pye, he's not human. I can't explain it but its like he's got some sort of guardian angel sitting on his shoulder. Whatever we've thrown at him he's just brushed it off."

There was another meaningful pause from Carfax. West felt the warm summer air around him turn cold.

"I do have something you might be interested in," he said, hopefully.

"And what might that be?" snapped Carfax.

"So, about half one this morning I was woken up by some noises out in the garden. I looked out and I could see a couple of figures moving around, flashing torches. I thought at first it might be the police, come back for a sniff around but it didn't seem likely. Then I wondered if they might be poachers."

"Yes, yes, get to the point."

"I was going to open the window and shout down at them, scare 'em off, but then I noticed one of them was a girl. Anyway, before anything else happened the lights went off and they just disappeared, like they'd never been there at all. I didn't hear any cars driving off so God knows where they went. They can't have been on foot. I watched out for about twenty minutes in case they came back but nothing happened so I went to sleep. Then, this morning I went out for a look around, see if I could work out what they'd been doing, and I found this sort of container in among the trees where they'd been."

"Container? What sort of container?"

"Well, that's the thing. I've never seen anything like it. It's completely black, about the size of a tranny van but it's got no doors or windows. There's no way in. No handles, no locks, no nothing. It's completely smooth all over. Funny thing is, if you put your hand on it you can feel it sort of vibrating."

"And you don't know who was out there?"

"I know you'll think this is a bit mad, but I'd swear it was Pye."

24.

Being back at work was an odd experience for Cornelius. The work was no different and he had no concerns about catching up. The office hadn't changed in any way. Everything was just as he remembered; tables, chairs, workbenches all in the same places, familiar faces flitting in and out, the usual chats in the kitchen while teas and coffees were being made. Mr Singh was his happy, smiling self, on his rounds to check on the progress of this or that project. Everyone had welcomed him back, asked after his health and sympathised over the burglary, just the right amount of fuss for the first hour or so before settling into the everyday pattern. But two things were very different. Cornelius thought of them as Thing One and Thing Two, bringing to mind the two characters from The Cat in The Hat.

Thing One was his relationship with Ruth, which had changed beyond all measure. They'd had a chat about it the previous evening over dinner in her flat.

"Did you mention anything at work about us?" asked Cornelius.

"I just said you were thinking of coming back tomorrow. I don't want anyone making a fuss over us. You know what offices are like for work romances."

"Mm. Best to keep quiet about it for a while, do you think? Keep it professional," he said with a smile.

"Yes, for now at least, while we've got this other stuff going on. I think it would be better if we let the dust settle before telling anyone."

"But you know I want to shout it out to the whole, wide world, don't you?"

"I want to do the same," agreed Ruth with a grin, "but there'll be plenty of time after we've dealt with Carfax."

"You're right. You might get fed up with me, anyway. When I'm not consorting with aliens I'm not all that interesting, really."

"I'm sure I'll see through you soon enough," she teased. They both knew their relationship was in no danger of ending anytime soon. Cornelius returned home later that evening. They'd decided, for appearances sake, that it would be best for now to arrive at work separately.

By late afternoon the secret was out. Although they'd both tried, it was almost impossible not to smile at each other when they thought no-one was looking. They touched whenever they could, just brief strokes in passing to satisfy themselves that, yes, it is true, we are seeing each other. He stole a quick kiss in an empty corridor. It was enough. The invisible system which measured personal space in their office was alerted, the jungle telegraph started sending signals and by the time they were packing up for the evening it was common gossip, which they had no choice but to acknowledge. They were officially an item. Mr Singh said he knew it was going to happen sooner or later and told them how delighted he was.

"Some people are just made for each other and I knew when I saw the two of you together that this would happen. Congratulations!" His enthusiasm embarrassed them, making them feel like a couple of newlyweds.

One less thing to worry about, then.

Thing Two was Euclid.

Before leaving home Cornelius hadn't been able to decide whether or not to leave Euclid behind, feeling that it might be a little distracting to have him, metaphorically speaking, peering over his shoulder throughout the day. When he mentioned this to Euclid he was surprised at the response.

"You want to do *what*?"

"I don't want you to be bored while I potter around at work all day."

"Bored? Why on earth should I be bored? I've had four hundred years of being bored. What I need now is to get out and about and do the job I was supposed to do in the first place. Where better to do that than at the cutting edge of technology? Anyway," he continued, "I want to come into contact with ordinary, everyday humans. The only ones I've met so far, apart from a few notable exceptions, have been kidnapping, burgling or waving guns around. I need to see what normal people do each day."

"Well, if you're sure?"

"Of course I'm sure. If I reported back to Farasta what I've learnt so far they'd get the impression Earth is Mad Max country and best left alone. I happen to think the human race is worth a closer look. So yes, please, Cornelius, take me with you."

So he did and was delighted when Euclid stayed quiet throughout the whole day. No sarky little quips, no jumping in to ask questions. Nothing. At times it was so quiet Cornelius eventually felt obliged to ask Euclid if he was still there.

"I'm observing, Cornelius, as promised."

On Tuesday evening Cornelius and Ruth left work together and decided to go back to his flat, where he offered to cook dinner, in return for Ruth's hospitality and to prove that, yes, he was capable of cooking and looking after himself. They went by tube as they found no convenient moment alone which enabled them to jump. They had dinner and Ruth stayed the night. In the morning she took Euclid and jumped home for a change of clothes. They travelled into work separately. It wouldn't be possible to jump to work. There was no knowing who might be around.

On Wednesday evening they hung back to let the building empty before finding a quiet corner to disappear from, this time back to Ruth's. They ate out and the next morning Cornelius jumped back home.

Thursday and Friday were further variations on the theme, except on Thursday evening, where he took Ruth to visit his aunt, who was pleased beyond words to meet her. Lucinda fussed over both of them throughout the visit, leaving Cornelius slightly embarrassed after the regaling of stories from his youth. Ruth was delighted that she had been made to feel so at home. They both relaxed as the week progressed, putting off for as long as possible having to think about the Carfax problem.

Carfax was on edge. His uneasiness had started the moment Cornelius had left his office, just an odd little twinge of nervousness but enough to notice. The conversation with West only increased his unsettled nerves. On Monday night he hadn't slept well. A nagging headache failed to go away. On top of that, he imagined a couple of cats were having some sort of battle in his stomach.

On Tuesday morning he phoned West and gave instructions to expect him at the Manor just after lunch. He lived in a small village just north of Harlow, about a five minute drive from the station where he normally caught the train into Liverpool Street. He could get to the Manor in less than fifteen minutes. Once there, West showed Carfax the strange, brooding black box tucked amongst the trees. He could almost sense its presence and he didn't like it, which added to his twitchiness. West had described it perfectly. He walked around the thing two or three times, trying to get a handle on what he was seeing but got the weird sensation his eyes were just sliding off it whenever he tried to focus. There was no obvious way into whatever this was. It had no wheels so he couldn't work out how it had got there, unless it had just dropped from the sky, but it was under a group of trees, which showed no sign of being disturbed by large items crashing through their branches. He pushed it. It didn't move. He felt like kicking it but decided that would look like a sign of weakness in front of West. He ended up saying, "Mmmm," as though he were figuring it out, but he hadn't got a clue.

"This has to be something to do with Pye, hasn't it?" said West. "It must be. Every other weird thing that's happened this last couple of weeks has been connected to him. Why should this be any different?"

Carfax didn't answer, but turned and walked back to his car.

"Keep a close watch. If anyone turns up here, anyone at all, call me straight away."

West assured him he would, pleased to be back in his boss's good books.

The rest of the week passed without Carfax's symptoms improving. On Friday evening they got worse.

This isn't possible, he thought, as he read through for the umpteenth time the report he'd received from the investigation agency. When it had first appeared in his Inbox he'd read it thoroughly and on reaching the end he'd phoned Trevor at BPI to query it.

"I know it looks odd, Mr Jones, but that's exactly as it happened. I've had eight of my top operatives assigned to this so I know it's right. If it was just one of them I'd have queried it, because it didn't look right to me, either, but all eight of them are telling me the exact same story. They can't account for the gaps, so unless these two can turn themselves invisible I don't know what else I can tell you. Even if they could they wouldn't have known they were being watched, so why bother?"

"And your men, you trust them? They couldn't have been got at to turn a blind eye?"

"Not a chance. I'd stake my reputation on it. Like I said, there's no way they could have been clocked. They're too good at their jobs. You know me, Mr Jones. I've been doing these little jobs for you for nearly twenty years now. One of the men I used on this surveillance has been with me nearly as long, none of the others have been with me for less than three years. I have to admit, most of them told me separately they were embarrassed about this. Two of them told me they couldn't accept payment for their time because they thought they'd been conned and can't believe they fell for it. They're professionals to the last drop."

"Alright, I believe you. I know I'm dealing with a very tricky character here, so thank your team. Tell them they did their best and I won't hold it against either you or them. I know there's something odd going on and I haven't figured out what it is yet. But I will, of that I'm absolutely certain."

The problem with the report was the gaps. He read through the salient points of the report yet again, trying to grasp its hidden meaning.

> *'Monday, 6am. Start of surveillance. Subject Cornelius Pye (CP). CP lives alone. Home address details supplied.*
>
> *Two-person teams; drone and fixed camera surveillance used at appropriate points to cover entrance to building and first-floor flat overlooking secluded garden to rear. 9:20am CP exits residence and visits local shops.*
>
> *10:10am returns to residence.*
>
> *1:15pm exits residence; tube to Moorgate, then on foot to Providence Building, south side of Finsbury Circus. Enters building 1:57pm.*
>
> *CP not seen to exit building.*
>
> *CP not seen to return to residence. Fixed camera in garden shows no activity inside until 3:12pm when seen at kitchen window. Three further sightings until 6:30pm then nothing further until 11:15pm when lights are turned on and CP sighting confirmed.*
>
> *11:25pm Lights out. Overnight team confirm no further movement.*
>
> **Unable to account for CP's movements between 1:57pm and 3:12pm.**

* * *

Tuesday 8:02am CP exits residence; bus to Highgate; arrives Lightsource Research 8:46am. Confirmed Lightsource Research place of work. Address supplied.

12:25pm exits Lightsource; buys sandwich and returns.

6:11pm exits Lightsource accompanied by female, identified as Ruth Seaton (RS), co-worker. New person of interest. Home address details supplied. CP & RS return by bus to Highbury Corner, visit local shops.

6:54pm enter CP residence.

11:35pm Lights out. RS does not leave residence. Overnight team confirm no further movement.
* * *

Wednesday 8:14am CP exits flat alone, operative 1 follows CP, bus to Highgate; arrives Lightsource 8:54am. RS does not appear; operative 2 waits for RS; 9:03am RS arrives Lightsource, spotted by operative 1. Confirmation from Operative 2 - **RS did not leave from CP residence!!!**

Extra team allocated to RS residence. Mews to rear of residence utilised for additional remote camera surveillance.

6:35pm Lightsource building locked by keyholder. Neither CP nor RS were observed leaving the building.

7:35pm CP and RS seen leaving RS residence. Neither seen to enter. Meal at Hana Suchi, Muswell Hill; return to RS residence 10:12pm.

Unable to account for CP's movements between 6:35pm (or even earlier if not at place of work) and 7:35pm.

11:25pm Lights out. **CP did not leave RS residence.** *Overnight team confirm no further movement.*

11:26 - 11:37pm **Lights on at CP residence!!!'**
* * *

The results for Thursday and up to Friday afternoon followed the same bewildering pattern. Either one or the other *'persons of interest'* had somehow evaded surveillance, which, considering the number of operatives involved (eight) and all the other gadgets which had been employed, should have been nigh on impossible, especially as neither of *'the persons'* had any reason to think they were being followed.

Carfax thought hard. What am I missing? Add this information to what I already know. Pye escapes from a locked room at the Manor. He appears as if from nowhere in his flat, surprising Slinger and Wilson. Wilson turns up miles away in Whipsnade with no explanation of how he got there. No, go back. *He appears as if from nowhere.* Hold on to that thought. Can it be possible? Look at the report again. Wednesday, 11:25pm, presumably, he's still in Muswell Hill with his girlfriend. The lights go out and almost immediately they go on in Highbury, which must be at least three miles away. And what was it West said the other day. If it *was* Pye and the girl, *they just disappeared.*

There's only one conclusion. When you've discounted all other factors, whatever is left must be the truth, no matter how fantastical. Cornelius Pye can instantaneously transport himself from one place to another.

No! That's not possible!

Is it?

Is that the secret of the book? Not that there's some arcane way to make vast sums of money but that once you know how, you can transport yourself miraculously to anywhere in the world in the blink of an eye. And not just transport yourself, but take others with you. Like Wilson. And things. Like gold! Is that how Maccabeus Pye came into all those riches? He somehow discovered the whereabouts of an El Dorado and, using some sort of arcane knowledge, was able to take himself there, scoop up handfuls of gold and transport himself back home, all in the blink of an eye.

Really? Can that be how it happened?

Yes, that explains everything, the escape from the Manor, the trip to Whipsnade, the journey between Muswell Hill and Highbury in just a few seconds. Say it again. Cornelius Pye is able to teleport. And if that's true, I have to get him to tell me how it's done? Imagine the possibilities!

The gall of him! To turn up at my office, knowing if he got into any kind of trouble he could just wish himself away to safety. And he even threatened me! Alright, Cornelius Pye, now I've learnt your little secret I can plan my counter-attack. I'll have that secret from you if it's the last thing I do.

If he'd thought about it, Cornelius might have been unsurprised to find himself under surveillance by Carfax, but he would certainly have been surprised that DI Evans too had ordered him to be placed under observation. Evans was troubled by various aspects of the case. He didn't think for a moment Cornelius was lying to him, but on the other hand, he knew he wasn't being told the full story. He had also developed a bit of a soft spot for Ruth and was disappointed he hadn't been able to make more of an impression on her, but it was obvious from seeing them together that his was a lost cause. That being said, he didn't want to see her getting hurt because her boyfriend was so headstrong.

Evans had wanted to assign an Obs team immediately after his meeting with Cornelius and Ruth, but it was Tuesday morning before he managed to get even one officer on the case. The officer arrived in Highbury soon after eight and took up a position on the corner of the street. He was there less than a minute before he spotted Cornelius leaving home. As he set off in pursuit he noticed someone get out of a parked car further down the street leading to St Paul's Road. The car drove off and the person, a woman in her late thirties, he guessed, fell in behind Cornelius. Coincidence? He didn't think so. His suspicions were confirmed when the woman followed Cornelius all the way to his place of work in Highgate, then got into the same car which had dropped her off. He watched the car position itself to get a good view of the building Cornelius had entered.

As the week progressed it became clear that a large team had been assigned to follow Cornelius and Ruth. Evans, after much pleading with his boss, had only managed to get three officers assigned, none of whom were allowed to work beyond eight pm. The car spotted on Tuesday morning was traced to a company based in Tottenham, Bunce Investigations, which tied into Dave Slinger's phone.

Evans' research into Cornelius' background had shown nothing out of the ordinary. No criminal record, no dealings with the police whatsoever. Not even a parking ticket. Then all of a sudden he's burgled, kidnapped and held against his will on account of a book he inherited from a dotty uncle, He escapes his kidnappers (how?) and somehow manages to rescue Ruth from Slinger and Wilson. His aunt is paid a visit by Slinger, famous for extra gratuitous violence. Who knows what might have happened if she hadn't managed to put him in hospital first? Then he and his former girlfriend outwit another criminal in a house in the middle of nowhere and he comes up smelling of roses yet again.

The only smell I'm getting is fishy, he thought. He's hiding something. I don't know what but I intend to find out, before things go horribly wrong. Cornelius Pye might be well-meaning, but he's an amateur and amateurs are notoriously dangerous. If there is some sort of criminal mastermind lurking in the background it would be better for everyone concerned if the police took him down.

At a little after seven on Friday evening, just as he was leaving the office and looking forward to his first weekend off in a month, his mobile rang.

"Is that DI Evans?"

"Speaking."

"It's Cornelius here, Cornelius Pye. Have you got time for a quick chat?"

"Yes, of course. What's going on?"

"Well the thing is, Inspector Evans, Ruth and I haven't been totally honest with you."

25

A shell-shocked DI Philip Evans stood in Ruth's flat and looked around, first at Ruth, then at the room, then at Cornelius, who was grinning like the Cheshire Cat, and finally back to Ruth again, who moved forward, took his hand and guided him to the sofa, where she gently sat him down. He stood up, then sat down again. He looked around the room once more. He didn't appear to be completely in control of his body.

"Can I get you a drink, Inspector?" asked Ruth, quietly.

"Call me Phil. Please. I mean, yes please, a drink."

Cornelius went into the kitchen and returned with a large glass of red wine.

"This okay?"

"Perfect." He reached out for it like a man being given water at an oasis. He glugged half the glass then finally relaxed back into the sofa. His eyelids never closed. He was worried that if he blinked things would change again.

"I don't believe this," he said to Ruth, then turned to Cornelius. "What just happened?"

The answer to 'What just happened?' began on the terrace outside Kenwood House, where Ruth and Cornelius had been having lunch. Ruth had mentioned she was feeling guilty about spending all their time concentrating on Carfax, when it was Euclid who had the real problem.

"Euclid and Tald have been stuck here for over four hundred years. Let's think about that for a moment. Tald needs medical treatment and they both need to know whether the troubles with the Allas have been resolved. It's time they went home."

Cornelius was stunned. "Oh, my God!" he cried, "What have I been doing? You're right. Of course you're right. I've been an idiot."

"No, no, you just got carried away, that's all. A lot of things have happened in the last couple of weeks and you've been right in the middle of it so your perspective has been a little skewed."

"Skewed? Blind, more like. Euclid, you should have said something. This isn't about me. It never was. We need to get you home!"

"That's very kind of you, Cornelius, but I don't want to leave you in the lurch."

"Don't you worry about me. I'll cope. Ruth and I will cope together. We should be worrying about Tald. He must have family on Farasta. They'll be worrying about him."

"They would be relieved to know he was safe, certainly, but are you sure you don't want me to stay?"

"Euclid, I would love for you to stay. Who wouldn't want a real live alien living with them? Look what's happened since you got here. I've found the girl I love! Nothing could be better. Compared with that Carfax is just a fart in the wind. No, you need to go back."

"Let's have a talk when we get home tonight." said Ruth, "See what needs to be done." Ruth had the makings of a plan but she wanted the rest of the afternoon to think about it.

"Shall I start?" asked Ruth, once they'd settled down with drinks back at her flat.

"What did you have in mind?" answered Cornelius.

"If we're going to send Euclid and Tald home this weekend we're going to need some help after they've gone. Carfax is still going to be a problem and we're not really equipped to deal with it. I think we should ask DI Evans for help. If we could get him properly onside I'm sure he'd be able to advise us."

"How do you mean?"

"What if we told him exactly what's been happening, about Euclid, Tald and the shuttle? If he knew the whole story he'd be much more likely to take us seriously. So far, he's viewed us as liabilities, getting in the way of proper police work, but he doesn't know why all this has happened and he doesn't know about our secret weapon."

"I'm not sure I'd want you to tell him," said Euclid. "I'm supposed to be keeping a low profile. I was hoping you two and Aunt Lucinda would be the full extent of it."

"But without your part in all of this it leaves Cornelius looking like what the police have accused him of, acting like an amateur detective. We're way out of our depth. Besides, DI Evans is quite smart. I'm sure he doesn't really believe half the things we've told him."

"She's right, Euclid. Once you're gone we can't get much further without some extra help and the DI does seem friendly."

"Yes, Ruth is right. You both are," agreed Euclid, "The forces of law and order need to deal with Carfax. Whatever evidence we provide will have no standing in a court of law. It's all hearsay. He needs to be taken down by someone in authority."

"Well, I'm glad that's sorted," said Cornelius. "That just leaves how we're going to convince him of your existence. He's not going to take our word for it."

"I've got an idea about that, as well," said Ruth. "Let's hope he's still on duty."

Five minutes later, after Ruth had outlined her plan, they put it into action. Cornelius picked up his phone.

"Is that DI Evans?"

"Speaking."

"It's Cornelius here, Cornelius Pye. Have you got time for a quick chat?"

"Yes, of course. What's going on?"

"Well the thing is, Inspector Evans, Ruth and I haven't been totally honest with you."

"I had a feeling that might be the case," replied Evans. "Do you want to meet up and tell me about it?"

"Are you still in your office, Inspector?"

"Just about to leave."

"Is it quiet there? I'd rather people didn't see us together, considering there's still Carfax's mole unaccounted for."

Evans looked out into the squad room. There was one officer at his desk, facing away from him. He relayed the information to Cornelius.

"Okay, good," said Cornelius. "Now I want you, please, to draw the blinds so no-one can see in."

"What on earth for?"

"Because I'm going to show you something that proves what we're going to tell you is the absolute truth. If I don't do it this way, you're not going to believe a word we say."

"You're not going to hypnotise me again, are you?"

"No, certainly not. And just to be clear before we go any further, you weren't hypnotised the last time we met. Apologies for that, but you'll realise why very shortly. What I'm about to show you may take you a while to process. So, can you close the blinds?"

Evans sighed and decided to play along. Anything to get to the bottom of this weird case.

"Okay. That's done."

"Now sit down at your desk and I'll be with you in a moment."

"What? What are playing at? Are you outside now?"

"Are you sitting down?" asked Cornelius, forcefully.

"Yes! I'm sitting down."

Cornelius appeared on the other side of the desk. Evans pushed himself back from the desk and stood up.

"How the hell -"

"This is the first part," said Cornelius, holding up his hands in an attempt to calm the DI.

"How did you do that? What -"

"Are you ready?"

"Am I ready for what?"

"In magic, this next bit is called the convincer. But I can assure you now, there's no magic involved. Shake my hand." Cornelius held out his right hand for Evans to shake. Evans looked at it as though fearing a trick.

"Please?" asked Cornelius. "I promise we'll explain everything."

DI Evans nerved himself, then took Cornelius' hand.

And found himself in Ruth's flat.

Once he had recovered a little, it didn't take them long to tell Evans the complete story, including the meeting with Carfax in his office. When they'd finished he asked for another glass of wine and then sat there, quietly, trying to absorb what he'd just heard.

"So, what do you think, Phil?" asked Cornelius, with a cheeky grin. Ruth was smiling too and she leant forward to listen to the answer.

"Well, assuming I haven't gone mad and assuming also you weren't lying about not hypnotising me, then I have to say things are finally making sense, although how I'm ever going to explain this to anyone else is beyond me."

"Ah, there's the thing." said Ruth, "Euclid requires that you never mention this to another living soul. He's not supposed to be here. You can't mention this to anyone, otherwise they'll look at you the same way you would have looked at us if we hadn't shown you beyond doubt what Euclid is capable of doing."

"I was afraid you might say that." He took another drink before continuing. "This Euclid, he's here now, but I can't see him?"

"Correct, but he can see and hear you." replied Cornelius.

"But I'm not going to be able to have a conversation with him myself. Is that right?"

"Sorry. So far, it's only the two of us." he said, indicating Ruth. "He's tried to talk to you directly but wasn't able to. It's the way your brain's wired. Same goes for most of the planet, according to Euclid. For some reason we're wired slightly differently."

"That's a shame. I would have liked to have met an alien."

"Look on the bright side," said Ruth, "if everything goes according to plan you'll get to see the shuttle go through a portal. You deserve that much, at least."

"I shall look forward to it. In the meantime, what is it, exactly, that you need from me?"

"Protection against Carfax after Euclid and Tald leave."

"I'm not sure what I can do."

Ruth responded. "Once Euclid leaves, Cornelius and I will have to deal with Carfax. We'd feel a lot better if we knew we had someone with authority on our side, a sympathetic ear, someone who understands why we've been acting like we have. At least now you know what we're up against."

"We've realised there's no easy way to get Carfax off my back while he thinks he has a chance of coming into possession of a mountain of gold," continued Cornelius, "He's very careful, so there's nothing substantial connecting him to anything that's happened to either of us."

"Where's this famous book now? Is it here? I'd like to at least have a look at the thing that's caused all this trouble for you."

Ruth left the room and returned carrying the book, which she placed in his hands. He started to leaf through it.

"It's fascinating," he said. "Doctor John Dee's own book. I love these pop-ups. A shame it couldn't have come to you under better circumstances."

"I've decided to take it to Sothebys tomorrow and put it up for sale. That takes it out of the equation. After that, we're going to have to come up with some sort of plan to deal with whatever Carfax throws at us after Euclid has gone."

"Are you sure you want to do that?" asked Ruth. "It's a family heirloom."

"Well, it is and it isn't." replied Cornelius. "If it hadn't been for the bit about being a magic book it would probably have been sold off years ago. I'd rather it went to someone who'd appreciate it and I can put the money to good use. Uncle Sedgewick's house in Barnes needs a lot of work doing to it and I'm sure Aunt Violet would appreciate a share. She needs cheering up."

"I hate to be the bearer of bad news," broke in Evans, "but someone, I'm assuming it's Carfax, has been having you followed."

"What?" cried Cornelius. "How do you know? I've not noticed anything."

"You wouldn't. They're professionals. I only found out because I started having you followed as well or no-one would have been any the wiser."

"You had us followed as well?"

"Yes! I couldn't trust you to stay out of trouble and I knew there was something you weren't telling me. I was right, wasn't I?"

"Who are they?" asked Ruth, ignoring Evans' question.

"A company called BPI, Bunce Private Investigators."

"Bunce! I don't believe it."

"Have you heard of them?"

Cornelius laughed. "You tell him, Ruth. You're the expert on the secret world of Carfax." Ruth explained about the other companies they'd found, to the DI's obvious interest.

"The sneaky old sod," was his conclusion. "I knew about Bunce Security from Slinger's phone, but not about the rest of them."

"His name doesn't appear anywhere unless you go looking for it. Cornelius only found out about the other companies by accident."

"I'll pass this onto the Finance team, see if they can shed any more light on his dealings. We'll get him one way or another."

"You see," said Cornelius, excitedly, "that's exactly why we need your help."

"But in the meantime," countered Evans, "you're still being followed. They're probably camped outside somewhere right now, waiting to see what you do next and wondering if you're even in here."

"What do you mean?" asked Ruth

"The curious thing about following you two is the anomalies. When I got reports back from my team, there were gaps, where you'd seemingly disappear and suddenly turn up somewhere else. I've only had a team of three or four following you, off and on, so the gaps weren't as obvious and now you've told me about the jumps it makes sense. Carfax, on the other hand, has had the luxury of two full teams of at least four watching you twenty-four seven since at least last Monday. The gaps where you jump from here to there are going to be screamingly obvious to him. Who knows what theories he's going to come up with but you can be certain he's having you watched like a hawk, waiting for the right moment to strike."

Cornelius looked at Ruth in horror. "We can't let him find out about tomorrow night. We have to get Euclid and Tald safely away."

"We're going to have to be extra careful," she replied.

For the next fifteen minutes the three of them formulated a plan to make sure Carfax's minions wouldn't be able to follow them, after which Cornelius stated he was getting hungry.

"I booked a table just down the road at a Lebanese restaurant," he said. "Would you care to join us, er, Phil?"

"I can hardly walk out of here if no-one's seen me walking in. I think it might be better if we're not seen out in public with each other. Then I can remain your secret weapon."

"Right, good thinking. I'd better get you back the way you came, then. I'm afraid I'm restricted to places I've physically been, so back to your office?"

"That will be fine. Thank you." replied the inspector. "It's a great way to travel," he added.

"Better make the most of it." said Ruth, sadly. "After tomorrow night everything will be back to normal."

The next morning Cornelius called Sothebys and arranged to meet one of their rare book experts. In the afternoon they travelled by tube to the auctioneers and handed the book over. The lady he dealt with inspected it in minute detail and professed herself thrilled. She asked him if he had any provenance and he handed over his uncle's letter and the journal. She read the letter then looked at him, pityingly. Cornelius shrugged. "He was a touch eccentric, I'm afraid."

"Yes," she replied, "I can see that."

She continued with the journal and when she had finished she broke into a grin.

"Looks like the eccentricity was inherited along with the book!" Cornelius smiled at her. She handed back the documents and continued. "It all looks authentic enough. If you could provide a few more details about your uncle so we can confirm everything. I'm sure it's all fine but we do need to satisfy ourselves. You understand, I'm sure?"

Cornelius nodded. The lady entered everything into her computer, then printed off a receipt.

"Our next Rare Book sale won't be until the autumn, so it will give us plenty of time to advertise. Will that be alright?"

"That'll be fine, thanks. I'm not in any hurry. Thank you for your time."

"A pleasure," she replied with a smile.

"Well, that's that," said Cornelius to Euclid. "How do you feel about saying goodbye to the other Euclid after all this time?"

"A touch nostalgic, I think, but at the same time, glad to be away from it now. It did feel a little like a prison sometimes. I hope someone gets to enjoy it as it should be enjoyed."

As they turned to leave, Cornelius and Ruth both did their best not to notice a rather dowdily dressed middle-aged lady fiddling about with brochures behind them, certain she was trying to catch what they said.

That evening, after a leisurely dinner in Ruth's flat, which had become the centre of operations, they prepared themselves for the main event. They were feeling distinctly nervous, not helped by the fact they had limited themselves to one glass of wine each, in order to keep clear heads.

"This is it, then," said Cornelius.

"This is it," echoed Ruth.

They embraced and kissed, each hoping to give the other courage.

"It won't be 'it' unless you two get a move on," said Euclid.

"You know," said Cornelius, "I won't miss you interrupting our romantic interludes. It's only just ten o'clock. Phil won't mind me being a minute or two late."

"Sorry," replied Euclid. "I think I'm as nervous as you two."

"We understand, really," said Ruth.

"Here we go, then," said Cornelius, and promptly disappeared. A minute later he was back with Evans.

"I don't think I'll ever get used to this. Hello," he said to Ruth. He looked around the room, just to confirm he was where he thought he was.

"Ready for the awfully big adventure?" she asked.

"I can't believe I'm going to see a spacecraft."

"I only wish we could take you up in it. I'd love go up once more. The last trip was over almost before I could breathe and all in darkness, so we couldn't see very much."

"Before we go, I've got a bit of news," said Evans. "I was doing a bit of digging into your arch enemy and I found out he's married, with a son."

"You're joking!" chorused the other two, almost in unison.

"I kid you not. I was as surprised as you two. They live in a large house in a village just north of Harlow. Been married ten years. The son's eight. He goes to a private school just outside Ware. According to local gossip, it's not a very happy marriage. They're rarely seen out and about, but she and her son do go to the church each Sunday. Apparently, she hardly ever cracks a smile and always turns down the opportunity to serve on any village committees. She told the woman from the paper shop that her husband likes his privacy. They don't even have a local cleaner. They use a contract firm based in Hoddesdon."

"Poor thing, " said Ruth. "Fancy having him for a husband. I can't imagine him playing the happy father, can you?"

Cornelius could sense Euclid wanted to get started.

"Yes, but sad as it is, I think we need to get going or a certain someone is going to get grumpy." He shouldered a rucksack containing three torches, a large bottle of water and extra clothing in the event it turned colder. They didn't know how long they might be there.

"Phil? If you want to grab Ruth's hand," he said, taking hold of the other. As soon as they were joined they jumped to the large front doors of Matching Manor, which was the easiest place for Cornelius to visualise. If he'd tried to focus on the shuttle, with its weird way of bending the light, they could have ended up somewhere from which there was no way back. The thought made him shudder. He wondered what had really happened to the Allas that had tried to sneak through the portals. No-when, he said under his breath.

"Almost correct," said Euclid, picking up on it. "When you start dropping through different dimensions all sorts of strange stuff happens."

There was still a small amount of natural light to see by but they took the torches from the rucksack and headed off into the Manor gardens, where the shuttle lay hidden. Cornelius and Ruth knew roughly where they had left it but they were almost upon it before Evans realised it was there. There was an odd absence of light where it sat and the beam from his flashlight seemed to bend slightly where it was pointed directly at it. Finally, he could make out its shape against the dark background. He stopped a few yards away, uncertain whether he should approach any closer. They all stood in silence for a moment. Cornelius was the first to speak.

"Odd, isn't it, the way the light won't stay fixed on it? It hurts your eyes until you get used to it."

"It's so small!" gasped Evans.

"We need to stand back a little so Euclid can move it into the open. Then we can get started."

As they stepped back the shuttle rose a foot into the air and sailed majestically to a spot in the middle of the lawn, about twenty-five yards away, where it hovered expectantly a foot above the grass. As they walked towards it they saw the door open and a bluish light radiated out.

"Part one complete," said Euclid to Cornelius and Ruth, "I need to get on board to check all is still well with Tald before we move on."

"Is Phil allowed on board?"

"I don't see why not."

Cornelius turned to Evans. "After you, Phil."

"What, me? Are you sure?"

"Yes, we have to check on Tald. You can have a peek at a real alien. Unfortunately, we can't talk to him but this is better than nothing. Careful in there, it will be a little cosy with the three of us."

After receiving the surveillance report on Friday evening and coming to the astonishing conclusion that Cornelius was able to jump instantaneously between two points, Carfax had phoned Trevor at BPI and arranged for some equipment to be sent to his house.

"You can call off your hounds. They won't be necessary any longer. Pye has found a way to avoid you."

Next, he phoned West and told him to expect his arrival.

"Is that container still sitting there?"

"Yes," replied West, "but no-one's been sniffing around since I told you about it."

"They'll come soon. I'm sure of it."

As soon as the equipment arrived from BPI and were loaded into his car, he drove over to the Manor where, with West's help, he littered the grounds with microphones and miniature HD cameras, concentrating on the area around the shuttle. In West's room on the top floor of the Manor they set up a computer and two screens to run the CCTV program.

"I don't want you to take your eyes off that screen," barked Carfax.

"I can't manage everything myself. I'm going to need to sleep at some point."

"Well, get someone you can trust to help you. Your cousin, maybe? I want to know the second anyone trips any of those cameras."

"But you haven't put any facing the road. We'll get more warning if we can see someone approaching."

"Take my word on this," said Carfax. "When they come, they will not be coming by road. Do you have a gun?"

"Not now, no, but I won't need a gun to break Pye's scrawny neck."

"You'd better take this," said Carfax, handing over a Beretta semi-automatic pistol and a box of ammunition. "Where Pye's concerned I don't want to take any more chances. Call me as soon as you see them. I can be here in twenty minutes."

And so it was that, by the time Cornelius, Ruth and Evans had walked round to the shuttle, Carfax was on his way.

Evans was suitably impressed with both the inside of the shuttle and the medical pod containing Tald. He was already a little light-headed with what had happened so far and being aboard an actual alien craft - with a real live alien, admittedly in suspended animation - made his legs turn wobbly, so he was glad to sit for a moment on the only seat. After Euclid had checked Tald he told Cornelius where to find the equipment they needed to erect the portal. Evans stayed aboard the shuttle, still taking it all in, while Cornelius hefted the surprisingly light toolbox-sized container off the shuttle. He and Ruth were guided by Euclid to a spot about twenty metres away, in the centre of the lawn.

"Always well to give ourselves plenty of room. Now, press that little indentation on the top to open it and take out the equipment."

Cornelius did as he was asked while Ruth looked on. He found a small, square black box and two short metal poles mounted on circular bases. Acting on instructions he handed a pole to Ruth and they placed them on the ground about three metres apart.

"You need to open the box," said Euclid. "Just press down on the top, where you see the little squiggle."

As he did so, the box opened into two equal parts. In one half was a round indentation, the other had a variety of small buttons that shone with a sort of ultraviolet light.

"Now, I'm going to issue instructions to the portal, for which I'll need your help pressing the buttons in a particular sequence. Just let me move your fingers. Ruth, would you like to do this part?"

"Certainly would," she replied.

As soon as she held box she felt her fingers seemingly moving of their own volition as Euclid entered the various codes he needed. Cornelius watched as the poles they'd placed on the ground began to extend themselves high enough to enable the shuttle to float through between them. The rectangle thus formed began to glow evenly with a pale blue light.

"Well, the equipment seems to be working correctly," said Euclid. "Now we need the crystal."

Ruth, as agreed earlier, took possession of Euclid and left for the British Museum. Less than two minutes later she was back with the crystal in her hand. Cornelius let out a sigh of relief and realised he'd stopped breathing the second Ruth had left.

"Easy-peasy," she said. She placed the crystal into the indentation in the control box. The light changed from blue to a kaleidoscopic pattern of colours.

"Wow!" said Cornelius.

"It's ready," said Euclid. "We can take the crystal back now. The portal will stay up by itself now it's connected. For the return trip it's activated from the far end. We just need to wait now until the connection calibrates. A couple of minutes at most. The light will change to a constant green when it's ready. Once the shuttle goes through it will turn itself off until it's needed again. At least there's still a far end to connect to. I was a little worried there might not be. Even so, if things have gone pear shaped on Farasta there's no guarantee there'll be a friendly welcome at the far end. A chance we'll have to take, I'm afraid."

"Wait!" said Cornelius, "what happens if there are enemies at the far end? The Allas, for instance. Can they get through here?"

Euclid reassured them. "No, not possible. The very fact our connection has been accepted means the protocols haven't changed substantially. Which means the Allas, or any other race for that matter, can't pass through the portal. Only Farastans have the correct brain patterns. Remember?"

They nodded. "Ruth? Are you ready to return the crystal?"

"I am," she said, taking it from its place in the box."

"Do you think I can do the returning? " asked Cornelius. "I feel as though I ought to. Share the risk, I mean."

"If it makes you feel useful, I suppose you can," Ruth teased and smiled the smile which made his heart jump every time he saw it. He smiled back, desperately hoping he was having the same effect on her.

"Young love!" said Euclid, "I shall really miss you two when I'm gone."

"Whoa, that's just about the nicest thing I've heard from you since we met!" said Cornelius.

"I'm just an old softie, really," replied Euclid. "Are you ready?"

"Let's go!"

Cornelius replaced the crystal without a hitch and returned with the smile still on his face, to find that things at the Manor had taken a turn for the worse.

26.

At first, it was too much for Cornelius to take in. How was it possible these two could be here? Standing by the open door of the shuttle was Carfax, with a triumphant grin on his face. A couple of paces to his right on the other side of the door was West, standing behind Ruth, holding her in place with one arm around her shoulders and a gun pointed at her head. Evans stood back in the doorway of the shuttle, out of sight, but watching intently, hoping to surprise one or the other of the intruders.

"I knew it!" shouted Carfax to a stunned West, "I knew he could teleport himself! It was the only possible solution. That's how he escaped from you in the first place and why the surveillance teams couldn't keep track of him."

Cornelius' bewilderment turned rapidly to anger. "You harm one hair on her head," he shouted, looking directly at West, "and I'll -"

"Clichés, clichés!" cut in Carfax. "Is that the best you can come up with? You and your university education? How disappointing. Now where's your other little friend? In here?" Carfax turned to the door of the shuttle. "I can see you. I think it might be wise if you stayed where you are for now, out of harm's way. Don't want anyone accidentally getting shot, do we? Throw your phone out here, there's a good boy. And you, Pye, phone on the ground."

Carfax turned to Ruth and motioned for her to do the same. He picked up all three phones and threw them into the flower bed at the edge of the lawn, then took a gun from his jacket pocket and turned back to Cornelius.

"Now before you do anything stupid, Pye, like teleporting out of here to get help, just be aware that by the time you get back, your girlfriend," he turned to Ruth, "and you really are his girlfriend this time, aren't you?" he said, with a sneer. He returned his gaze to Cornelius. "Your girlfriend will not be here. Do you understand me?"

West smiled horribly at Cornelius. "Not so clever now, are you? You won't get the chance to hypnotise me this time. There's no knowing what might happen to my trigger finger if you so much as try."

"Are you alright, Ruth?" asked Cornelius, his voice shaky.

She nodded and added, "I've been better."

Through Euclid, he sent, "Keep calm, we'll figure this out."

"I know," she responded.

"So, who's your friend in this, this... What *is* this, anyway?" Carfax took a few steps back to get a better view of the shuttle. As he did so, the portal came into view. "And that, what's that?" he asked, pointing.

Cornelius said nothing. Carfax took a small torch out of his jacket pocket and bent down to look under the shuttle, flashing a beam of light back and forth.

"Well normally I would say that's impossible, but we've already seen evidence of teleporting tonight, so nothing can surprise me now. It's alien isn't it? Not of this earth. And that over there, some kind of portal? Oh, this just gets better and better!"

Evans spoke up from his position just inside the shuttle door. "I'd advise you to hand over your guns, especially you, West. You're already in a shit load of trouble."

"Oh, yeah? And who are you to be giving me orders?"

"Detective Inspector Evans. I've been looking for you. I should have known you'd be hiding out here." A worried look passed across West's features but he didn't do as Evans suggested.

"You'll find my associate will be more interested in keeping *me* happy," said Carfax, portentously. "I think, at the moment, we hold all the cards." He turned back to Cornelius. "So, you found a tame policeman to look after you. Well this is a little extra protection in case he tries anything stupid." He waved the gun around and gave Cornelius his own ghastly impression of a smile.

"What are we going to do?" asked Cornelius to Euclid.

"At the moment it's best to keep him talking until we can see an opportunity. Our priority at the moment is keeping Ruth safe."

"You'll get no arguments from me about that. Can we distract them, somehow, and try to get Ruth away? That trick you did at the flat to blind Jez. Can you try that?"

"I'm afraid they're both a little too far away. I need to be up close to get the intensity. It might make things worse. Anyway, DI Evans is still in the shuttle. We wouldn't have time to grab him as well and there's no knowing what they'd do to him if we left him behind. I can only suggest you keep them talking. Let's see what he expects to happen next."

"What is it that you want, Carfax?" shouted Cornelius.

"What do I want? That's a good question. At one point I would have said El Dorado, but I see things have changed. I don't know how you've managed it, but since you came into possession of a book that you told me held no secrets, you've managed to discover how to teleport. If I hadn't seen it with my own eyes I wouldn't have believed it. I know it's not one of your tricks this time because I've been waiting for you to show up. I positioned cameras all around here because I knew you'd be here eventually. And as if teleportation wasn't enough, you're also involved with aliens! I knew you'd have something to do with this spaceship and lo and behold! Just like that, out of thin air, you appeared by the front doors and now I have proof of it on computer. When you've told me how you've managed all of this you're going to make me a very rich man indeed."

"What makes you think I'm going to tell you anything?"

Carfax turned to West. "Take the girl into the house," he said, making sure Cornelius could hear. "Make sure she's securely tied up, then call me for further instructions."

"What are you going to do?" cried Cornelius, his voice cracking. West grabbed Ruth's upper arm and frogmarched her back towards the Manor.

"You and I are going to chat nicely and you're going to tell me what I want to know. He can't do much from here, but back in the house, Mr West has access to all sorts of interesting tools which might help loosen your tongue."

"You're bluffing," shouted Cornelius.

"Am I? Have I been bluffing all this time? Do you take me for an idiot?"

"You'd better not harm her or you'll have me to answer to!" came the voice of DI Evans from inside the shuttle.

"Oh, you think so, do you?" retorted Carfax. "Well, there's nothing that says any one of you three are going to make it through the night. It all depends on whether or not I get what I want and for that Mr Pye here needs to start talking. Come on out of there and go and stand by him, so I can keep an eye on you both."

Evans stepped down from the shuttle and walked warily over to Cornelius.

"I hope you've got some sort of a plan," he muttered under his breath.

"Working on it," murmured Cornelius in return.

"Euclid, what am I going to do? I have to tell him something or he'll hurt Ruth,"

"I imagine, for the moment, you're going to have to tell him what he needs to know, but please warn him not to set foot in the shuttle. Do you understand? That's very important."

"You don't want him to know about Tald?"

"Among other things," replied Euclid. "Give him fair warning, alright?"

Just then, Carfax's phone rang. He answered and put the phone on speaker.

"Are you ready, Mr West? Not giving you any trouble is she?"

"She's all trussed up. She's not going anywhere."

"Up to you now, Mr Pye. Time to start telling your little story."

Cornelius found himself unable to speak. He hardly knew where to start.

"I'm waiting. Do I need to prompt you? Perhaps Mr West can help?"

"No!" shouted Cornelius. "Don't. Don't hurt Ruth. I'm trying to tell you, but I don't think you're going to believe it."

"Don't be shy. Out with it."

"Okay, okay."

Cornelius told as little of the story as he thought he could get away with but with enough detail to keep Carfax from doing anything rash. He didn't tell him about Tald, saying instead that when the shuttle crashed it was close to John Dee's house in Marlow and Euclid was able to take sanctuary in the book. He also didn't mention that Ruth could talk to Euclid and was able to use him to teleport, as Carfax incorrectly had it. After he'd finished, Carfax was silent for a while as he processed what he'd heard. Eventually, he replied.

"That's quite some story. I'm pretty sure you haven't told me everything, but we'll let that pass for now. I'm extremely interested in this shuttle. Think what we could learn from it. And imagine what it would be worth to the highest bidder. The Russians and the Americans would be at each others throats for something like this."

"Is that your only priority? Money!" shouted Cornelius, with what he hoped was a sneer.

"It makes the world go round. Or haven't you grasped that yet?"

"There's more to life than money."

"Ah, the idiocy of youth. Tell me about this alien, Euclid. You say you're the only one who can communicate with him? Very convenient. I assume he's here now?"

"Yes, of course. I told you, he needs to get home. Which is why we're not going to be letting anyone get their hands on him."

Carfax laughed. "How will you stop me? He's not much of a threat for an alien. A few party tricks, which could still have been pulled off by you. What proof can you give me that he's here?"

"Tell him what happened after I made him see the Rupert Bear Annual, Cornelius," said Euclid. "That's something you couldn't possibly know about." Euclid shared the memory, which Cornelius conveyed.

"After Euclid made you see the Rupert Bear Annual, you got up and went to put the book in your wall safe to the right of the desk, next to the bookcase and behind the painting with the elephant. The combination of your safe is 2477914."

"Impressive! Yes, yes, I see. So it's the alien that's responsible for allowing you to teleport at will and by a marvellous stroke of luck you're the only person he can do it for. But no blasters, or death rays, nothing to get the Yanks excited? Pity, they would have liked that. But, then again, nothing to stop me taking the shuttle away from you."

"There's also nothing to stop Euclid from boarding the shuttle and flying it through the portal. Or hadn't you considered that? Euclid's primary objective is to get back home. Ruth and I, we don't matter."

"If that was a card he was going to play, he'd have done it by now. No, Mr Pye, I don't think Euclid will abandon you, although I'm willing to wait here a few minutes to allow him to do so."

"We need to try and force his hand, somehow," said Euclid to Cornelius, "throw him off kilter. It might give us the chance we need to turn the tables."

"What do you suggest?"

"Let's see what happens if he thinks he's underestimated me. Tell him I'm going."

At that moment, bands of blue light started pulsing along the length of the shuttle. It rose another foot in the air and started to move slowly and silently towards the flickering portal.

"What's happening, Cornelius?" cried Evans.

"It's Euclid!" shouted Cornelius to Carfax. "He's had enough. He's going."

To Evans he whispered under his breath, "Watch out to see if Carfax drops his guard. This might be our only chance."

"You'd better not let that shuttle go, Pye. I'm warning you!" Carfax was edging his way along the lawn, keeping pace with the shuttle. Cornelius and Evans moved long with him, keeping their distance.

"Mr West," shouted Carfax, "let the girl have a taste of your special persuaders."

"About time!" they heard West reply, with some enthusiasm.

"NO!" shouted Cornelius. From the phone he heard Ruth scream. A millisecond later he felt a huge blow as something crashed into him, almost knocking him off his feet. Immediately after, startled by the noise and movement, Carfax fired at him. He felt a sudden deep shock in his shoulder and was hurled to the ground. There was a weight on his chest and he couldn't move.

"Fuck you!" shouted Evans, as he started to run towards Carfax but had to stop and drop to his knees as Carfax swung towards him. A second shot rang out, missing his head by inches. He put his hands up.

"I'm a very good shot, detective," said Carfax "That was a warning. Don't try that again."

Cornelius, who had closed his eyes as soon as he was knocked off his feet, was still not sure what had happened, but the weight on his chest was moving around. Oddly enough, he seemed to be beneath someone. He opened his eyes and saw Ruth clinging desperately to him.

"What the -"

"He shot you!" screamed Ruth. "Where did he hit you?"

Evans looked around and saw them both on the floor.

"How the hell did *she* get here?" he shouted at Cornelius

He was about to answer either one or both of them, but his eyes were drawn towards Carfax, now lifting himself onto the still moving shuttle.

"Carfax! No! Do not step inside. Please, for your own safety. Euclid specifically told me not to let you set foot inside the shuttle."

"I don't see how you can stop me. I've told you, this craft is priceless. I'm not letting it get away from me." He was now standing in the doorway, looking back down at Cornelius. "I don't know how you managed to get your girlfriend free, but you'd better tell your alien friend to set me down, otherwise a few well placed bullets in the interior will change his mind."

"Euclid!" said Cornelius, "You need to do as he says. What if he shoots Tald?"

"No risk of that, Cornelius. The shuttle can look after itself. But Carfax needs to get out of there or I can't be held responsible for what happens next."

Cornelius, still struggling to work out how Ruth had suddenly appeared, tried again to talk to Carfax.

"Seriously, you need to leave the shuttle now. It's very dangerous."

"I don't think so, Pye. Your little alien friend would have done something by now if he thought he could overpower me." Carfax turned to face the shuttle's interior. "Now, what would cause the most damage?" he shouted back at them.

He took a step forward and disappeared from their view. As he did so, the shuttle stopped.

"Carfax! Don't" shouted Cornelius and Ruth in unison. They jumped up and ran to the door, then carefully peered inside.

"It's too late," said Euclid.

"What do you mean?" asked Ruth.

"He's gone."

"Gone? Gone where?"

"Remember me telling you about the Allas and how they disappeared when passing through one of our portals? We use the same technology to make sure they can't hijack our ships. It also works on humans."

"But *where* has he gone?" shouted Cornelius.

In their minds there was the suggestion of a shrug.

"Somewhere that agrees with him, hopefully," said Euclid.

Evans came racing over.

"Where's Carfax?" He looked in the shuttle. "I saw him go in. Where is he?"

Ruth explained. "Oh," said Evans, "well, good riddance, I suppose." He turned to Cornelius. "He shot you! Are you okay?"

Cornelius looked at his shoulder but couldn't see any blood.

"He must have missed," said Ruth, looking closely for any damage. She touched his shoulder and Cornelius screamed in pain.

"But I saw him, he shot you," said Evans, "I don't think he meant to. He was taken by surprise when Ruth appeared."

Euclid explained to Cornelius and Ruth and Ruth explained to Evans.

"Apparently, Euclid can create a sort of force field when the need arises. Enough to stop the bullet but not quite enough to take all the sting out of it."

"You're lucky you've got an alien looking after you," replied Evans. Then a new thought came to him. "Damn! West. He'll still be in the house somewhere. I'll be back soon." He ran to edge of the lawn, retrieved his phone, then ran off towards the Manor.

"Thanks for rescuing Ruth," said Cornelius to Euclid.

"I didn't," he replied. "It seems she rescued herself."

"What! But that's impossible, isn't it?"

"Well, I would have said so. Ruth, tell us what happened."

"I'm not sure. The last thing I remember was Carfax telling West to go to work on me. There was a bag on the table and he reached into it and pulled out a pair of pliers. I thought I was going to faint and I was wishing desperately that I could get away Then I just appeared here."

"She jumped alone," said Cornelius.

"Looks like it," replied Euclid. "I didn't think it was possible. However, your brains are wired somewhat differently to the krai. Perhaps the slight changes I made to you two unlocked a latent ability."

"So it's possible we could both do it?" asked Ruth.

"It's possible. I suggest you give it a go, see what happens. But not now. It might be as well to let DI Evans think I rescued Ruth. If it gets out you *can* do it unaided by me, people will never leave you alone."

They looked at each other, smiled, then hugged each other tightly for a second or two until the pain in Cornelius' shoulder was too much for him to bear. He let go, but she held on and they kissed until they were both in tears. They held each other gently for a few minutes before breaking apart, still looking into each others' eyes. Eventually, he broke the silence.

"That was a pretty wild plan, Euclid. It very nearly went wrong."

"Oh, it wasn't so much a plan. I didn't really have one apart from trying to get Carfax on board the shuttle. If that had failed I was just going to dump it on top of him."

"No!" cried Cornelius.

"You wouldn't!" shouted Ruth.

"No. Only joking. Too messy. And, to be honest, I'd much rather we had saved Carfax, but once his mind was set on boarding the shuttle there was nothing you could have said that would have changed his mind. He assumed you were lying when you said it was dangerous."

"But why didn't Phil disappear?"

"Because at the time I was close enough to offer protection. Carfax was just a little too far away. I told you before, my powers, as you call them, have a very limited area of influence."

Evans reappeared.

"I got the drop on West as he was running out through the front door. Almost knocked me over. He must have been watching what was going on through the CCTV and was trying to get away when he saw it was all going pear shaped. I've got him trussed up like a turkey and I'll let the boys in Harlow know where he is when we've finished here."

"Finished?" asked Cornelius. "Oh, yes, the shuttle. Let me find out what's happening."

"Euclid, it's time to go. What do we need to do?"

"Nothing much. Just deliver me to the door. The shuttle is in place, so it's time to be aboard. After we pass through the portal the system will close down until I return."

"You're coming back?" asked Ruth.

"Hopefully. If all goes well, we'll need to move the gateway somewhere where it's not likely to be discovered. It can't remain here. There's a nice little moon circling Neptune which should do the job. A new crew will come through, if there's one ready, and fly the shuttle there. Then we can set up operations once more with a new craft and continue on our way. I'm sure we haven't finished our explorations yet."

"How long before you come back?"

"I'm hoping it will only be a couple of hours. I imagine our appearance on Farasta will be declared a high priority. Will you wait around?"

"Of course!"

Cornelius related the plan to Evans and the three of them walked over to the shuttle. They stood by the open doorway while Euclid transferred himself to the interior.

"Well, goodbye, and good luck," said Cornelius aloud.

"Bye, Euclid," said Ruth, her voice breaking with emotion. "Thanks for everything."

"Say goodbye from me," said Evans. "I just wish I could see or hear him. It's odd to be talking to nothing."

From the shuttle doorway a small diamond hard light popped into being, dazzling them all. It grew a little and formed itself into something like a face, smiled, then faded away. A voice from the interior said, "Goodbye, DI Evans. Thank you for all your help."

"Don't mention it!" replied Evans, waving.

The door closed and the shuttle, bands of colour shimmering along its length, disappeared into the gateway, which then shut down plunging them into darkness.

On the short walk back to the house, Evans phoned the Harlow Police and got them to come and pick up West. While the police were at the house Cornelius and Ruth stayed out of sight to avoid complications. Evans had decided he would say nothing about the events of the night, making no mention of Carfax. His story would be that he had received an anonymous tip that West would be at the Manor and acting alone he'd apprehended his suspect. He advised West to follow the same line, unless he wanted to add further charges to his already lengthy charge sheet. And besides, he added, who would believe him if he started talking about aliens, teleporting humans and flying saucers. He showed West footage of Carfax entering the shuttle and disappearing.

"So he was never here, right?" suggested Evans. "And neither were Cornelius or Ruth. Keep it simple and make life simple for yourself."

After the police had taken West off to Harlow he returned to the house and found Cornelius and Ruth in the room West had been using as his hideaway.

"The SOCO team wanted to come in and have a look around but I managed to put them off until tomorrow. In the meantime I suggest you don't touch anything."

"You didn't want to accompany your prisoner, then?" asked Cornelius.

"What, and miss out on seeing more aliens when Euclid returns? I don't think so." He noticed that they were both holding mugs. "Oh. You touched things. Is that coffee you've got there?"

"Tea, actually, but I think I saw some coffee lying around somewhere."

"For God's sake, make sure you both wipe your prints off everything. After you've made me a coffee, obviously," he added with a resigned sigh.

They discovered that West had made himself comfortable in the Manor. The contents of the room had obviously been here long before the events of the evening so perhaps this was where West and Carfax had held regular meetings. Apart from a fairly comfortable bed in one corner of the room, there were a couple of armchairs, a kitchen table, a fridge stacked with various foodstuffs, a small oven and most importantly, all the things required to make tea or coffee, with various packs of biscuits thrown in for good measure. It wasn't long before Evans had a cup of strong coffee in his hands and a plate of chocolate digestives by his side. Cornelius and Ruth wiped down every surface they thought they'd touched, then the three of them settled down to wait for something to happen.

"It was nice of Carfax to set up this CCTV system," said Ruth, "otherwise, we'd have been sitting outside somewhere. It's gone a bit chilly in the last hour or so."

There were two screens set up to capture images from the grounds, four views on each screen, all of them showing mainly blackness. View number seven was the one they were constantly looking at. It was trained on the location of the portal, in the middle of the lawn. They were desperate not to miss the first inkling of it coming alive.

"How long do you think, now?" asked Ruth.

"At least another eighty minutes, if Euclid is correct," replied Cornelius.

"This is a really boring programme," joked Evans. "Anything on another channel?" They all smiled at each other, but oddly enough, none of them felt much like talking.

The seconds ticked slowly on. Eventually, Cornelius asked Evans about being a policeman. He returned the question to Cornelius and Ruth, about being rocket scientists (jokingly). It was all politeness, more than anything, as they'd never previously conversed on a personal level.

It all went quiet again. Cornelius and Ruth dozed. Suddenly, they were snapped to alertness by Evans shouting, "It's happening!"

They looked at the screen, saw the glow of the portal, then jumped up and ran out of the room, down the stairs and into the night. As they reached the lawn the blue light changed to a swirling rainbow of colours, heralding the reappearance of the shuttle. The light changed to green but it wasn't the shuttle they saw emerging. This was a far sleeker craft, golden in colour, about twice the length and larger all round, looking more like a scaled down version of a modern Japanese bullet train, except there was no obvious windscreen. It glided gracefully to a position on the lawn and hovered silently for a few seconds before dropping to touch the ground. They caught up with it as a doorway in the side slid open. Two tall figures looked out, saw them, then stepped onto the lawn and walked a few paces towards them.

"Cornelius, Ruth, Phil. Greetings." The two aliens unexpectedly held out their right hands, obviously intending to shake.

"This is your custom. Correct?"

"Correct," said Cornelius.

As they were all shaking hands, the first alien continued speaking.

"I am Sarvl, this is Reos, my co-pilot for this journey. As you will have gathered, we are krai from the planet Farasta."

"Pleased to meet you," said Reos."

"And us, you," replied Ruth. Evans found he couldn't say a word, thrilled beyond belief he was meeting actual aliens and seeing another spacecraft. He felt like a small boy visiting Santa's grotto.

"Please, everyone, step aboard the ship. Have a look around. Reos will be busy for a few moments dismantling the portal." They did as he requested, with no hesitation. The new craft was so much bigger

291

than the shuttle, cleaner, brighter and with so many more interesting systems panels and flashing lights.

"How are you able to speak our language?" asked Cornelius.

"The entity you call Euclid accompanies us. We draw on his knowledge," said Sarvl. "He will return to Farasta when we reach the portal's new site, orbiting Neptune. He would like to speak to you, through me." There was a pause of a few seconds before he started talking again.

"Hello, gang," said Euclid, in the voice immediately recognised by Cornelius and Ruth, and to a lesser extent Evans, who had heard him say only a few words. "Well, we made it back, thanks to your efforts."

"How's Tald? Will he be okay?" asked Cornelius.

"I'm told he'll make a full recovery. I haven't yet been able to re-unite myself with him. It will take a few weeks, perhaps, so I made the decision to accompany Sarvl and Reos back here. I only wish Tald could have accompanied us so he could thank you himself for getting us home."

"What about the Allas?"

"At the moment, it's all quiet on the western front. They seem to have entangled themselves with superior forces elsewhere in the galaxy and are having to expend all their energies placating them. We haven't been bothered for a few hundred years, although at one point it was touch and go whether they'd overrun us. Our defences have been tightened up considerably since then, which is why we no longer send single untrained krai on journeys across the stars. Reos is a tactical defence expert, among other things. It's his job to protect this craft as it voyages on from this solar system."

"So your explorations continue?" inquired Ruth.

"Of course! There's still so much to discover. But I think we will return here, perhaps even within your lifetimes. You're such an interesting species! Now, before we go, I have a few private words to say to Cornelius."

"Me, why?"

Euclid stopped talking through Sarvl and addressed Cornelius directly.

"You asked me some questions a while ago, about dark matter and dark energy? In payment of sorts for your help in enabling us to return home, I've been authorised to give you a couple of hints."

"You're joking!"

"Of course I'm not, you idiot! Now listen, you'll still have an awful lot of work to do on the subject, probably quite a few years worth, but this should get you started..."

Euclid finished just as Reos re-entered the ship with the case containing the portal.

"Time to go," said Euclid to everyone through Sarvl once more. " May all your remaining days be happy ones. And remember, let's be careful out there! That last bit was from Hill Street Blues," he added. "Before your time."

They left the ship, saying their goodbyes to Euclid, Sarvl and Reos as they went. The door closed and the ship lifted up into the night sky, becoming invisible almost immediately.

"I'd love to be going with them," said Cornelius.

"What, and leave me all on my lonesome?" said Ruth, smiling. "You heartless monster!" She punched his arm, playfully, which was a mistake, as she'd chosen the side that had been hit by the bullet. Cornelius screamed. "Oh! Sorry! I forgot!"

"It's alright, I deserved it. I wouldn't leave you behind, you know that. It's just..."

"Yeah," replied Ruth, reflectively. "I know. Me too."

"I could've gone," interrupted Evans. They both turned to stare at him.

"Would you have wanted to?" asked Ruth.

"Maybe." He sighed. "I suppose now I'll never know. The worst thing is, I can't even tell anyone, can I?"

They turned back towards the house.

"Do you think we can get a cab to come out here?" asked Cornelius. "I didn't think about us getting home again."

Evans reached into a pocket and pulled out a set of keys, which he waved in the air triumphantly.

"Ta-da! The keys to Carfax's car. He parked it round the back but must have been in such a hurry to get into the house that he left these in the lock. I can drop you off wherever you want to be."

"What will you do with the car, afterwards?"

"I'll return it to Mrs Carfax, along with an explanation as to why she won't be seeing her husband again. God knows what I'm going to say. Whether she'll believe me or not, I have no idea, but I'm willing to bet the news won't be unwelcome. She'll benefit from his estate and she'll be able to join all those church clubs and committees she was missing out on when the miserable sod was around!"

Less than an hour later, Cornelius and Ruth were back at her flat, after promising to keep in touch with Evans as the case against West was built. They would both be needed to make statements. They collapsed in a heap together on the sofa.

"I'm absolutely knackered," croaked Cornelius.

"So am I. I think I could probably sleep for a week.

"Well, tomorrow's Sunday. We don't have to get up for anything in particular."

"A whole day in bed? I like it. There's enough food in the house so we don't need to go out. And no Euclid hustling us to do things. Perfect."

They fell into each other's arms and kissed, lazily.

"Just one thing we need to do before we go to sleep," said Cornelius.

"Is that a little twinkle I see in your eye?"

"No, not that." Cornelius sat up. "Earlier on, you jumped without Euclid. Could you do it again?"

"I don't know. I suppose I should try. What about you? If I can do it, you should be able to."

They could.

Acknowledgements

A huge thank you to my wife, Grace, who read and proofread and believed I could finish this book whenever I didn't have a clue where it was going next. Thank you to Kevin Lally and Charlotte Bruton for reading it critically and giving me copious notes, most of which I took notice of except where I might have had to rewrite huge chunks! Thanks also to various others who read it and told me how good it was! It means a lot. And finally, my thanks to P. G. Wodehouse, the master, without whom I might never have got started.

Printed in Great Britain
by Amazon

26812288R00169